The Farmer's Daughter

MARY NICHOLS

Allison & Busby Limited
12 Fitzroy Mews
London W1T 6DW
allisonandbusby.com

First published in Great Britain by Allison & Busby in 2016.

A CIP catalogue record for this book is available from
the British Library.

First Edition

ISBN 978-0-7490-1979-2

Typeset in 11/16 pt Adobe Garamond Pro by
Allison & Busby Ltd.

The paper used for this Allison & Busby publication
has been produced from trees that have been legally sourced
from well-managed and credibly certified forests.

Printed and bound by
CPI Group (UK) Ltd, Croydon, CR0 4YY

The Farmer's Daughter

Chapter One

6th June, 1944

'This is the BBC Home Service and here is a special bulletin read by John Snagge.' The familiar voice of the newsreader filled the farmhouse kitchen. *'D-Day has come. The first official news came just after half past nine when Supreme Headquarters Allied Expeditionary Force issued Communiqué Number One. This said: "Under the command of General Eisenhower, Allied naval forces, supported by strong air forces began landing on the coast of France . . ."'*

'It's happened at last,' Jean said. It was something the whole country had been speculating on for months. The war had been going in the Allies' favour ever since Rommel had been ousted from Africa at the end of 1942. At that time, Prime Minister Churchill told the nation: *'This is not the end. It is not even the beginning of the end. But it is, perhaps, the end of the beginning.'* Was this, then, the beginning of the end? The signs had all been there: you couldn't hide thousands of troops on the move by rail and lorry, holding up the trains and clogging the roads, and the huge increase of bombers flying overhead; the British at night and the Americans during the day. And no one was allowed to go within ten miles of the coast, all the way round from The Wash to Land's End.

Her mother stopped fussing round her father's wheelchair and sat down to listen while the newsreader went on to give more details: the huge numbers of ships, aircraft and troops and how the attack started at midnight with airborne troops landing behind the lines. There had been some tough fighting, but losses were lighter than expected and everything was going to plan. The king would make a broadcast at nine o'clock.

'Do you think that means the war's nearly over?' Doris queried. 'Will our boys be coming home soon?' Her first thought, as always, was for her son. Gordon had been captured when his Spitfire had been shot down over northern France, while trying to defend the troops on the beaches of Dunkirk, and he had been a prisoner of war ever since.

'Let's hope so.' Jean said, as the newsreader continued with other items: the American Fifth Army had entered Rome unopposed to find the German army gone. Daylight brought thousands of Romans out onto the streets, to greet their liberators with flowers, hugs and kisses. The Russians were advancing in the east, while at sea, the Allied shipping losses were down to 27,000 tonnes, the lowest figure of the war. All seemed set for victory. 'I'll catch it later,' she said, leaving her parents to go back to work.

She had been up since dawn, milking and looking after the livestock, a task which had devolved on her shoulders since her father's stroke. Their farm was a mixed one of pasture for a small dairy herd and a few sheep, with some acres of arable land on the slightly higher ground. Higher ground in the fens meant a bump of land that might, in pre-drainage days when the area was under water much of the time, have been a small island. Pa and Gordon had managed very well with casual labour at busy times, but the war had changed everything. Gordon had not waited to be called up and joined the Royal Air Force as soon as war was declared, much to their father's annoyance. 'How am I to run the farm without you?' he had demanded on being told the news.

'You can get help.'

This had proved impossible; most of the village men had either followed Gordon's example and joined up or they had their own farms or employment on other farms. Jean had given up her job in Wisbech to help out and they had managed with casual labour, but she was nothing like as skilled or as strong as her brother, a lack which her father was not slow to point out. One evening three months before, after a particularly stressful day, Pa had fallen down in a heap, his face distorted and his left arm useless. He had been taken to hospital where they did the best they could for him, but his left arm was useless, he could no longer walk and his speech was slurred. He was only fifty-two – no age at all. It had been left to Jean to take over the running of the farm and dealing with the mounting paperwork, although her father still thought of himself as the boss and he would make the decisions about what needed doing and when. Usually Jean obeyed, but on occasion made up her own mind what to do.

Leaving her mother to the housework, she went out to see to Dobbin and Robin, the two cart horses. Some of the farms had the new tractors imported from America, but on Briar Rose Farm they were still using horses. A tractor was on order, but they had to wait their turn to have one and Pa was in no hurry; he had heard they were nothing but trouble, were devils to start and were always breaking down. Horses were more reliable, even if they were slower.

She let them out to the pasture to graze, then went up the lane to the potato field to hoe between the rows. It was hot, dusty, back-breaking work and she stopped only for a sandwich and a flask of tea in the middle of the day. At five o'clock she left off to fetch the cows into the cowshed to milk them. It was seven when she went back to the house.

Her mother was laying the table for supper in the large flagstoned kitchen. There was a big table in its centre, a coal-fired kitchen range and a dresser along one wall displaying crockery. A rocking chair stood in a corner and a cat snoozed on the hearthrug. 'Give the boys a shout, will you, Jean?' she said.

Jean went to the back door to call her fifteen-year-old brother, Donald, and Terry Jackson, their evacuee, who was a couple of years younger. She had to shout twice before they appeared from the direction of the barn.

'We caught more rats,' Don said. 'Six yesterday and four more today. We put the tails in a bucket.' The tails were docked so that children could not claim their penny-a-tail more than once.

'All right, that's ten pence we owe you,' Doris said. 'Don't you dare sit down, either of you, until you've scrubbed your hands.'

They went to the sink to obey, while Doris wheeled Arthur's chair up to the table and they sat down to eat. There were plenty of vegetables with water or home-made cider to drink and for a while there was silence.

'How was school today?' Doris asked Donald. He attended Wisbech Grammar School, while Terry went to the village school which took pupils from five until they left at fourteen.

'OK, I suppose. We had special prayers in assembly on account of D-Day. They changed our lessons so they could tell us about it. But I knew something was up before that. I heard the bombers going over last night. They woke me up. I tried to count them, but there were too many. Thousands and thousands. They blotted out the sky.'

'We've got Jerry on the run now,' Terry added, with the grin that almost always resulted in him being forgiven for any misdemeanour he had been engaged in. He had arrived in the household in September 1939, a bedraggled, bewildered eight-year-old, who had taken weeks to settle. His behaviour had been erratic and unpredictable and for a time they wondered what they had let themselves in for, but Jean, who had a great capacity for love, had gradually won him over. He had shown his mettle when Arthur had his stroke. Somehow the incapacitated man struck a chord with him and they had become great pals.

'Have you done your homework?'

'I'll do it later.'

'You will go and do it as soon as we've finished dinner. What about you, Don?'

'It's history. I hate history.'

'Nevertheless, you will do it.'

Once the meal was finished, the boys went reluctantly to their homework and Jean helped her mother clear away and wash up. 'We need more help,' she said, voicing what had been in her mind for some time. 'I can't cope on my own. There's hay to cut and the wheat will be ready for harvesting soon. The ditch on the bottom field needs clearing and the hedges are getting untidy. And I've only managed to hoe half the potatoes today.'

'Not in front of Pa,' Doris murmured, nodding towards her husband dozing in his wheelchair. 'You'll only agitate him.'

Jean subsided, but the problem was still on her mind as she left the kitchen to go into the sitting room to deal with the farm accounts and fill in yet more forms. The trouble was that it was almost impossible to get help. All the farms in the neighbourhood were short-staffed. With the men away in the forces, their numbers had been made up with Italian prisoners of war and girls from the Land Army, many of whom were town girls and had no idea about farming. They were learning, it was true, and their help was better than none, but they had to be shown what to do and how to do it and it all took time. 'Fat lot o' good they are,' her father had said when she had first mooted the subject. 'We'll manage without 'em.' But he could not have known he would be incapacitated by a stroke, and even now expected to recover fully and go back to work. She did not think that was likely in the immediate future and something had to be done.

For the next few days everyone was glued to their wireless sets, listening to bulletins as more and more details of the invasion emerged. There was fierce fighting and the first day objectives had not all been taken. The American advance was slower than had been predicted; the terrain was swampy and there were more German troops facing them than had been expected. Caen, an important town for communication and supplies, was still holding out in July. It soon became clear that Hitler was not going to give up and so the slaughter and the taking of prisoners went on.

Going to church was a Sunday ritual for the Coleman family, as it was for most of the older villagers. Here they met to worship, but also to gossip and grumble and share experiences. At the beginning of the war when everyone expected an invasion, the bells had been silenced, only to be rung as a warning that the Germans had landed. The ban had been lifted now and the bells could clearly be heard ringing out over the village.

Terry pushed Arthur in his wheelchair, while the others walked beside them. As they approached the church, the eight bells stopped their carillon and were followed by a single toll which told everyone to hurry. The wheelchair was hoisted over the church step; Don and Terry, who were in the choir, went to the vestry to put on their cassocks, while Jean wheeled her father up to the pew at the front where there was room to park it. Sir Edward and Lady Masterson always occupied the front pew on the other side of the aisle but they had not yet arrived and the service would not begin until they did. Sir Edward owned most of the land in the village including Briar Rose Farm, but he was a benign landlord and, so long as they paid their rent on time, rarely made his presence felt. Their son, Rupert, a captain in the Cambridgeshire Regiment, had been captured when Singapore fell and they did not know if he were alive or dead and, in that respect, he shared the troubles of some of his tenants.

Miss Dawson, the elderly schoolteacher, played the organ while the congregation trooped in and took their places. Besides the villagers, there were some Americans from the nearby base and one or two British airmen who were convalescing at Bushey Hall after being wounded. When the squire and Lady Masterson arrived, the Reverend Archibald Brotherton, with the choir behind him, followed them up the aisle. He conducted the service in the traditional way and everyone could follow it automatically, leaving time to let their thoughts wander. Jean prayed along with everyone else, that the war would soon end, that prisoners would come home, the missing turn up safe and well, and those who had suffered tragic loss would learn to live again. 'And let Pa get better,' she added.

She turned to look at him. He was staring up at the pulpit, where the rector had gone to deliver his sermon. Sometimes he answered back if the parson said something he disagreed with, which embarrassed his wife and drew a smile from the reverend. Today the sermon was about patience and tolerance and loving one's enemies, which didn't go down too well with those who had suffered. She watched her father carefully, ready to lay a restraining hand on his arm.

'The Boy Scouts will bring their collection of paper and metal to the village hall on Saturday afternoon, where a lorry will be waiting to take it away,' the reverend added, after ending the sermon. 'The Women's Institute has arranged a talk about preserving fruit and vegetables which will be held in the church hall on Friday beginning at 7.30 p.m. All are welcome.' He paused to look round as if assessing who was present and who was absent. 'We will conclude with hymn number 217: "*Thy Kingdom Come, O God, Thy rule, O Christ, begin; Break with Thine iron rod, the tyrannies of sin.*"'

With the ending of the hymn, he blessed the congregation, crossed himself and left the pulpit, to be followed down the aisle by the choir, Sir Edward and Lady Masterson and the rest of the congregation. Everyone gathered in the churchyard to comment on the latest news. It was not just the battles abroad, overhead and at sea that filled their minds, but the effects of war at home.

Everyone had been forced to tighten their belts. Everything was either rationed or in short supply. Things like cigarettes, razor blades, safety pins, hair clips and lipstick disappeared under the counter. The 'utility' label was on almost everything manufactured: clothing, furniture, bedding, pots and pans and carpets, which meant they had to be made to strict guidelines. Even those were hard to come by. To save paper, newspapers were confined to four pages and very few books were being published, although there were leaflets in abundance with notice of new regulations, endless recipes for using the bounty of the countryside, and instructions for remaking old clothes into new.

'Have you seen what they've done up at the camp?' Mrs Harris asked Doris.

'No,' Doris said. 'I haven't been that way for some time.'

'Well, I don't usually, but Ted Gould has been working up there and he told me that they have extended it to take thousands more prisoners. We'll be inundated. I don't like it.'

Most German prisoners taken earlier in the conflict had been sent on to Canada and America where it was thought they couldn't cause trouble, but a few, mostly submariners and Luftwaffe, had remained on British soil. Bushey camp housed a few hundred of them but they were confined behind a high wire fence and had caused no trouble.

'I suppose they've got to put them somewhere,' Jean said.

'Not on our doorstep, for goodness' sake.' This from Mr Harris.

'I can't see how you are going to stop it,' Bill Howson said. 'The government can do what it likes.'

Bill owned his own farm on the other side of the village, where he lived with his widowed mother. Jean had known him since he was a grubby five-year-old with wrinkled socks who persisted in treating her as one of the boys. He had grown out of that and was now a strapping six-foot hunk of a man, good-looking in a rugged kind of way and strong as an ox. The land girls who worked on Bridge Farm all sighed after him. Jean had been going out with him ever since they left school and most people assumed they would eventually marry.

'I've finished cutting my wheat,' he told her, as they took their leave of Mr and Mrs Harris and he fell into step beside her. 'I'll lend a hand with yours like I usually do.'

'We're waiting for the reaper,' Jean said. Because the

Colemans only had a very small acreage they did not own a reaper-binder but hired one by the day. Jean had put in a request for it and was waiting to be told when it would be her turn to use it. There was only one field to cut; given good weather, it could be done in a day.

'Let me know when it's coming and I'll alert everyone.' He meant the villagers who traditionally helped each other at harvest time.

'Thank you.'

He let the others go on ahead and took her hand. 'You are looking tired, Jean. Looking after that farm is too much for you.'

'I manage.'

'If you need any help with jobs, just let me know.'

'Thanks, but you've got enough to do on your own farm,' she said. 'And it's not just a few jobs, it's everything. I've advertised for a farm worker but so far I've had no reply.'

'Well, you wouldn't, would you? Try the Land Army.'

'Would they be better than the Italians?' The Italian POWs had been reclassed as collaborators since Italy had changed sides. They were allowed a certain amount of freedom and made full use of it.

'Lord, yes. The men are far more interested in singing and flirting than work and they will down tools at the first excuse. Either it's too hot or too cold or too wet. I wouldn't like to think of one of them annoying you.'

'Do you think I can't look after myself?'

'You're a woman and a very pretty one at that.'

She laughed at the unexpected compliment. 'A woman doing a man's job. There are lots of us doing that, you know.'

'I know. I wish you didn't have to.'

'I don't mind. I just want to find some help from somewhere.

We managed while Pa was well, but now it's all getting on top of me.'

'You would have to apply to the War Ag.' He said, using the popular name for the War Agricultural Executive Committee, an arm of the Ministry of Agriculture. 'They do the allocation of labour.'

'Thanks, I will. In the meantime the boys can help when the school holidays begin.'

'OK, the offer's there if you want it. I must go or Ma will be worrying where I've got to. Fancy the pictures on Saturday?'

On Saturday evenings, Jean usually allowed herself a little leisure. Sometimes they went to the cinema in Wisbech, sometimes to a dance or to listen to a talk in the village hall which might be about any subject the organisers thought might interest the population: natural history, what other people were doing for the war effort, cookery, jam-making, make do and mend.

'Yes, I'd like that.'

'OK, I'll call for you at six-thirty.' He veered off towards the middle of the village and Jean hurried to catch up with her parents.

As they approached the farmhouse from the lane, she was filled with a feeling of pride and love for the place which had been her home all the twenty years of her life. It was a large rambling structure of brick and flint, typical of the area, with small windows and a pantile roof. On one side, across the concrete yard were the farm buildings; stable, cowshed, and barn. The house and outbuildings were unusually extensive, considering the small acreage they farmed. According to her father, there had once been at least twice as much but, in the bad farming years at the end of the last century, her grandfather could not afford to pay the wages of his labourers and had reduced his holding, leaving only as much as the family could manage.

The war, with its emphasis on feeding the population, had made a big difference. There were subsidies and fixed prices to help them and they were now fairly well off. They had to work hard for their money, but everyone had been brought up to that and accepted it as a matter of course. What would happen when hostilities ended she had no idea.

Once home, Donald and Terry went off to change out of their Sunday clothes to go out and let off steam with Laddie, the collie, at their heels. Doris wheeled Arthur into the kitchen to sit by the hearth while she finished cooking Sunday dinner. They had recently slaughtered a pig and the smell of roast pork permeated the kitchen. Since everyone was being encouraged to keep a pig, there were pig clubs springing up in the most unexpected places, even on urban allotments. Slaughtering, which had to have official approval, was done in rotation so that the meat could be distributed among all the members in turn. What was not to be eaten immediately was salted down or smoked to preserve it. Swill buckets were placed everywhere for people to put their scraps in. There was one outside their gate, one outside the village hall and even one in the school playground. It all went towards keeping the pigs and population fed. Those who kept pigs on a larger scale had to keep meticulous records and send all their animals to the pig marketing board. It didn't alter the fact that they sometimes cheated.

'Bill says I have to apply to the War Ag. for help,' Jean told her mother. 'They will send whoever is available.'

'Then you had better do it. I'll square it with your father. He'll have to face facts, he isn't going to go back to work yet awhile.'

Karl had never seen so many ships, thousands and thousands of them, all steaming towards him, bent on destroying him, or so

16

it seemed. The biggest of them were pounding the shore with their heavy guns. The noise was ear-shattering and the heat was so intense it was sending rivulets of sweat running down his back and trickling down his forehead into his eyes. He crouched in the shallow depression in the ground, while shells burst all round him, making more craters and sending up clouds of earth which caught in his lungs and stuck in the two-day stubble on his chin. They had been expecting the invasion for weeks, but all the signs indicated it would be at the Pas-de-Calais, the nearest French coast to Britain. Even now, faced with an army streaming ashore, his superiors were convinced it was a feint to cover the real landing area. If that were really the case, he dreaded to think what that would be like.

He risked a peep over the edge of the depression in which he was sheltering. All round him were wrecked vehicles, guns, bodies and bits of bodies, blood and flies, black swarms of the little devils. Enemy bombers droned overhead, dropping high explosives and causing more craters. One of them hit a tank and it exploded in a wall of flame. He felt exposed and vulnerable.

Beside him in other hollows, his comrades crouched, waiting for the enemy to advance on them through the smoke. Their orders, coming from Hitler himself, were not to give up a metre of ground. How they could hold it without the help of their own tanks he had no idea. Where were they? Everything was in chaos; nobody seemed to be in command and his own captain had been killed. He wriggled over to Otto Herzig who was crouching in a ditch a few yards away. 'What do you reckon we ought to do?'

'I don't know, do I? You're the sergeant.'

'We'd better pull back and try to find our own people.'

'OK. Lead the way.'

There were only about a dozen of them left. He took them through a wood but stopped when it came out onto a road full of troops being dive-bombed. They scattered back into the trees and dived face down in the damp earth. Above the noise of the tanks and the gunfire, he could hear someone shouting.

He woke with a start and sat up still in the midst of his nightmare and, for a moment, didn't know where he was. He looked round him. This was not France, not a road under fire, it was a Nissen hut lined with two-tiered bunks and there was an English sergeant standing in the doorway shouting '*Raus! Raus!*'

Wide awake now and all too aware of his situation, he shook himself and swung his legs over the bed onto the cold concrete floor. Everyone else in the hut was doing the same and shuffling off to the ablutions. The war was over for him and his comrades and he would be a fool not to feel relief. He could not admit it, of course, especially in front of those fanatical Nazis who viewed the invasion as nothing but a minor setback. The enemy would be driven back into the sea, they said, and there would be no rescuing them as had happened at Dunkirk. To them, Hitler was invincible.

The British sent all prisoners to holding camps when they first arrived where they were deloused, fed and interrogated. The Tommies were pretty good at that and when faced with exhausted, hungry, dispirited men, soon found out much of what they wanted to know. He hadn't witnessed any beatings and, as far as he was aware, they stuck to the rules of the Geneva Convention, though rumours were flying that if you were sent to the London Cage, you were in for some rough treatment.

Each prisoner was categorised according to his perceived belief in Hitler's dogma. Those labelled 'black' were the strongest Nazis and likely to cause trouble, the 'whites' were opposed to National Socialism and could, in some measure, be trusted. The majority were 'greys', neither one nor the other; they had fought for their homeland and for their families, not for Hitler and his cohorts. The blacks were sent to special secure camps. Karl had been considered grey, which meant he had been sent to a normal prisoner-of-war camp, here in the fens of East Anglia.

Life in the camp was boring. The men were left to amuse themselves and, under the direction of the *Lagerführer*, Major Schultz, and various other volunteers, organised games and entertainments and educational classes to relieve it and keep them occupied. There was even a newspaper put together by the prisoners themselves. It had a page of events and entertainments being staged, the results of sports and games, snippets of gossip and a letters page. News was culled from hidden wireless sets which were tuned in to *Deutschlandfunk*, and the BBC, translated for those who did not speak English. Being able to read both versions, he was amused by the different slant they put on events.

The attempted assassination of Hitler was a case in point. He had read both accounts, one of which said it proved how unpopular Hitler was with his own people and they would rise up against him and force him to sue for peace, and the other that the crime was down to a handful of traitors and cowards. The editorial comment had said, 'Our beloved Führer is impervious to such traitorous attacks. He has God and Right on his side. The enemy will learn this to his cost, as will the perpetrators of this outrage. Everyone who has had any hand in the conspiracy, however small, will be hunted down and receive the fate they deserve.' It seemed Hitler was decidedly rattled and this latest edition reported that eight very senior officers had been hanged with wire from meat hooks after what Karl guessed was a cursory trial. There had been thousands of arrests and more to come, they were promised, until every traitor had met his just deserts. He wished the plotters had succeeded, but that was a wish he kept to himself. He had no doubt Lieutenant Colonel Williamson, the camp commandant, read every word.

Even so, there were those who considered it their duty to escape and they were busy making plans. Whether they would come to fruition he did not know, but he did not give much for their chances of making it back home, or even off the island. A few, considered trustworthy, were being allowed out to work on farms and building sites. With an English guard, they left the camp in a lorry each morning and returned each evening. He wouldn't mind doing farm work, even if it was for the enemy. It was better than being incarcerated behind barbed wire and listening to his fellow prisoners grumbling and quarrelling.

He returned from the wash house and took his place in the dining hut for breakfast, after which he asked to see the camp commandant.

Lieutenant Colonel Charles Williamson did not relish his job but it was one that had to be done and, as he was too old for front-line duty, he was glad to do his bit. He was a fair man and treated the prisoners kindly so long as they behaved themselves, but he would not tolerate disruption and did not hesitate to put troublemakers in the '*Kühler*' as a punishment.

He smiled at Karl from behind his desk. 'What can I do for you, Sergeant?' he asked in English.

'I should like to go out of the camp to work, *Herr Kolonel*, preferably on a farm.'

'Worked on a farm before, have you?'

'Yes. My folk are farmers, that is if they are still alive. I haven't heard since the Russians bombed my home town over a year ago. We thought the farm was out of range of their bombers, but we were wrong.'

20

'I am sorry to hear that, but war is like that. The good, the bad and the indifferent on both sides, suffer indiscriminately.'

'Yes, *Herr Kolonel.*'

The colonel pulled himself together suddenly and became businesslike. 'Normally we wait until prisoners have settled down before letting them out.'

'I understand.' He knew they had to be sure it was safe to do so and that meant watching him for troublemaking tendencies. A committed 'black' would never be sent on a working party. 'I have been here a month and I need an occupation.'

'Very well, I will bear your request in mind.'

'Thank you, *Herr Kolonel.*'

'You speak excellent English. Where did you learn it?'

'At school and during holidays in England when I was a boy. I came on school exchange visits. My father thought it would be good for me to learn another language and culture.'

'Where did you stay?'

'In Cambridge.'

'Have you kept in touch with your hosts?'

'No. It was frowned upon.'

'Yes, I suppose it would be. Very well. Off you go. I will speak to Major Schultz about your request and let you know in due course.'

Karl saluted him and left. Some of his fellow prisoners had refused to salute and when this had been insisted upon gave the Nazi extended arm salute. This did nothing but alert the British authorities to those who would bear watching. He went back to play chess with Otto, which would last until the midday meal. Food was one of the things they could look forward to; their rations were the same as a British soldier received and infinitely better than any they had had from their own forces.

Their own propaganda had told them the British were starving and near to giving up, but he had seen no evidence of it. He had seen the results of bombing while travelling through the country by train when they first arrived, but the population seemed able to absorb it and carry on. Some were antagonistic and didn't trouble to hide it, but others simply stared at the demoralised prisoners as they shuffled to their trains guarded by British Tommies, most of whom treated them reasonably and shared their cigarettes which made a welcome change from the stinking rubbish called Marhoka they had been issued with.

'Sei nicht so dumm,' Otto said when he told him about his request to work. 'That's aiding and abetting the enemy and you know what happened to Ernst Schumann and Franz Keitel a week or two ago.'

'No, what did happen?'

'They were beaten up.'

'Who by?'

'They said it was the English farmhands, but there was a rumour it was some of our own men out to teach them a lesson. They have refused to go out to work since then.'

'It's only farm work, for goodness' sake, and we can earn camp *Geld* for doing it. It's better than playing chess all day.' Camp *Geld* was token money which they could spend in the camp shop on cigarettes, toiletries and books or a second-hand pair of shoes, things like that, but it was worthless in the outside world.

Otto laughed. 'Which you do very badly, my friend. That's checkmate.'

Karl turned his king over. 'I wasn't paying attention.'

'There's one thing about getting out of camp, you might be able to reconnoitre the lie of the land. It could come in handy.'

'Not you too?'

'What about me?'

'Thinking about escape.'

'Why not? It gives me something to occupy my mind besides chess.'

Karl laughed. 'How do you propose to go about it?'

'I don't know yet. I will tell you when I do. You interested?'

'It depends. It would have to have a good chance of succeeding. I'm not risking my neck on some hare-brained scheme that will cost us our lives.'

'Fair enough. Let's go and eat.'

Karl mused on the idea of escape as they queued up for meat stew, dumplings, mashed swede and potatoes. The thought of making it home was an attractive one, or it would have been if it hadn't been for Hitler and the Nazis. It was true, he had been in the Hitler Youth, but that had not been done out of any ideology on his part, simply because all his pals joined and his life would have been made hell if he had not. After school, all he wanted to do was make an honest living in agriculture. He had gone to work for his father until 1938 when he had been called up. The army had become his home. But here? In England? None of it seemed real. Heidi didn't seem real any more. The last he heard from her was that she was working in a factory in the suburbs of Berlin, but she could be anywhere by now.

When they had arrived in England they had been issued with a printed postcard which said: 'I have fallen into English captivity. I am well.' On the other side, by the stamp, it said: 'Do not write until the POW has notified you of his final address.' Since coming to this camp he had been allowed to write and tell his parents of his address which went through the International Red Cross in Geneva. They could write no more than twenty-five words which were heavily censored. What could you say in that short space except to say you were okay and being well treated? He had, as yet, received no reply.

He took his plateful of food and his cutlery to a table and sat down beside Otto to eat it.

'I'm going for a walk this afternoon,' his friend said.

'Walk!' Karl laughed. 'Where?'

'Round the perimeter to see if there are any weaknesses in the wire.'

'I've no doubt someone has already done that.'

'I want to see for myself. Coming?'

'I might as well, since I've nothing better to do and I need to walk off the effects of this dumpling. It's as heavy as a brick. Nothing like the *Knödel Mutti* used to make.'

As soon as they had finished eating and washed up their used crockery and cutlery, they set off, strolling unhurriedly towards the wire before turning to trace it round the perimeter of the camp. There was nothing to see beyond the wire except flat fields and a distant village whose church spire rose above a stand of trees. Anyone trying to escape that way would find very little cover.

'Talking of going home,' Otto said. 'Where is home for you?'

'Hartsveld. It's a small village halfway between Falkenberg and Eberswalde. My folks are farmers, have been for generations.' Falkenberg was an important railway junction, while Eberswalde was known for its thriving heavy industry. It was why the area had been heavily bombed and why he was so worried about his family. 'How about you?'

'I come from Arnsberg.'

'Isn't that near where English bombers breached the Möhne last year?'

'That's only British propaganda,' Otto said. 'The dams can't be breached, we were promised that when they were built; the

24

concrete is too thick. All they could have done was make a dint in it. I've got a wife who's working in one of the factories in Düsseldorf. Last I heard she and my parents were safe, but I worry about them.'

'I worry about mine too,' Karl said.

'You married?' Otto asked him.

'No, not yet. Engaged though.'

'What's her name?'

'Heidi. I've known her for years.'

'Damn this war.'

'Amen to that.'

Chapter Two

Jean was about to haul a churn of milk onto the platform just outside the farm gate, ready for the lorry from the Milk Marketing Board to pick up, when a camouflaged truck drew up and stopped. She stood up, pushing a stray lock of hair under the scarf she wore as a turban, and watched as an army corporal, gun slung over his shoulder, lowered the tailboard and jumped down. 'Mrs Coleman?'

'That's my mother.' Laddie, who followed her everywhere when the boys were at school, was barking at the man and she grabbed his collar. 'Quiet, Laddie.' He stopped at once.

'I'm Corporal Donnington. I believe you asked for POW help.'

'Yes, we did.'

'How many do you want?'

Jean smiled. 'One is enough, Corporal, so long as he's used to farm work.'

He went to the back of the lorry. 'You,' he said, pointing to one of the men sitting inside. '*Raus.*'

A German POW, in a scruffy field grey uniform with a large

yellow patch on the leg of his trousers and another on the back of his uniform jacket, jumped down onto the road. The corporal climbed back and refastened the tailboard. 'Don't stand for any nonsense, miss,' he said, banging on the side to tell the driver to move off. 'We'll be back to fetch him at six.' The lorry went on its way delivering more workers to other farms and Jean was left facing her new hand.

He was, she decided, a good-looking man, tall and fair with very blue eyes, a typical Aryan in looks, but with none of the arrogance she had expected. On the other hand, he was certainly not cowed. He clicked his heels together and bowed. '*Feldwebel* Karl Muller, *gnädiges Fräulein*,' he said.

She smiled. 'I am Jean Coleman. Do you speak English?'

'Yes, *Fräulein*, I speak English.' He bent to stroke the dog.

'Good,' she said, noting that Laddie appeared pleased to see him, judging by the way he was wagging his tail. 'I don't know a word of German and it might be difficult giving you instructions if you don't understand. Let's go inside and I will introduce you to my parents.'

Without being asked, he picked up the churn and placed it on the platform for her. She thanked him and led him up the drive, across the yard and into the kitchen. Her mother was boiling pig swill on the range. She had the windows open because of the smell.

'Mum, this is *Feldwebel* Karl Muller. He's come to help us.'

Doris turned to face him. 'Know anything about farming?' she asked.

'I was raised on a farm, *gnädige Frau*.'

'I'm Mrs Coleman,' she said. 'I can't be doing with all that German stuff. And what does "*Feldwebel*" mean?'

'Sergeant, Mrs Coleman,' he said with a smile, wondering whether the mess in the pan she was stirring was their dinner.

Perhaps the English were starving, after all. She was far from thin though. 'But Karl will do.'

'That's better.' She lifted the pan off the stove and handed it to him. 'You can take this out to the pigs for a start. Jean will show you where.'

'Where's Pa?' Jean asked her.

'He's having a lie-down in the sitting room. I think he's asleep, better not disturb him.'

Jean led Karl back across the yard to an outbuilding. 'Put it on the bench to cool,' she said. 'Then I'll show you round.'

He did as she asked, then followed her outside and was given a tour of the farm buildings. The cowshed was clean and all milking utensils shone. 'We have six dairy cows and twenty sheep,' she said. 'My father was a shepherd in his early days and he still likes to keep a few for wool and meat but most of this area is arable, known for its strawberries. They aren't growing many of those now; wheat, potatoes and sugar beet are more important. We have a couple of pigs.' She opened the top half of the pigsty door as she spoke. Two fat porkers started to grunt, expecting their swill. 'You'll have to wait,' she told them, opening the door and ushering them out into the orchard where they could feed on fallen apples. It wasn't a proper orchard with evenly spaced rows of fruit trees, but a meadow in which different fruit trees were scattered. It housed the pigsty and the hen coops. Beyond it he could see a large pit.

'Do you and your father work the farm on your own?' he asked as they continued the tour.

'My brother used to work with Pa but, like you, he's a prisoner of war, has been since 1940. Pa has had a stroke and can't do anything very much.'

'Do you mean you manage alone?' he asked in surprise.

'The villagers give a hand at busy times. We all help each other as much as we can, but there is an acute shortage of labour. I expect it is the same where you come from.'

'Yes, it is.'

'There's a cart, a trap, and a pickup truck in here,' she said, opening the door so he could look inside. 'The trap is the best way of getting about, considering petrol is rationed and only allowed for essential business. We have a darling grey pony called Misty to pull it. She spends most of her time in the pasture.'

There was another shed which was a storehouse of strange objects. The walls were hung with garden and farm implements of all kinds – shovels, rakes, sickles, scythes, flails, weed hooks – and iron implements and bits of leather tackle whose original use had been forgotten but which Arthur insisted on keeping. There were bins for chicken feed, bags of seed and trays for storing apples and even an ancient wooden plough. Jars and tins of ointments, powders, scours, linseed oil and turpentine stood on shelves. It had a strange yet familiar smell all of its own. Karl roamed round it smiling and occasionally putting out a hand to touch something.

'Pa can't bear to throw anything away,' she said. 'And some of it comes in handy.'

'My father is like that,' he said. 'This reminds me so much of home.'

'What would you be doing if you were at home now?'

'Much the same as I will do here.'

'What sort of farm do you have?'

'Mixed, like this,' he said. 'But I do not know what has happened to it and my family since the Russian raids. My older brother, Wilhelm, died on the Polish front very early in the war. I have a sister, Elise, and uncles, aunts and cousins, but I don't know what has happened to them either. And I have a fiancée. She is in Berlin.'

'I'm sorry. Perhaps we shouldn't talk about the war.' She remembered the regulations for employing German prisoners: there was to be no fraternisation and all conversation was to be kept to giving instructions about the work they were to do. Already she had broken one of them.

'No, perhaps not.'

She opened the door of the stables. 'This is the home of Dobbin and Robin, our percherons.' The horses snickered with pleasure when Karl patted their necks. 'We are waiting for a tractor, but it hasn't arrived yet.' She looked at the shabby uniform he was wearing. 'Is that all you've got to work in?'

'Yes. When we arrived in England we were issued with a kitbag, a shirt, underwear, socks and toiletries, but no outer clothes.'

'I'll find you some dungarees of Pa's. You'll get filthy otherwise. And you need some rubber boots.'

She led the way back to the house. That was another rule she had broken; the prisoners were not to be allowed into the homes of their employers. He wiped his shoes thoroughly on the mat before he entered the kitchen. Her mother was not there, but her father was sitting by the hearth, reading a newspaper. He let it drop in his lap and turned towards them. 'Who's this?'

'Pa, this is Sergeant Muller. He is here to help us on the farm.'

'I told you I don't want no truck with Jerries. Nasty deceitful people, murderers the lot on 'em.'

'Pa. They are no more murderers than we are. It's the war . . .'

'I will leave,' Karl said.

'You can't,' Jean said. 'Not until you're fetched. We are responsible for you, I signed a paper to say so. Besides, Pa doesn't mean it.'

'Oh, yes I do.'

'Pa,' she said patiently. 'The sergeant is a prisoner, just as

Gordon is. I would like to think the German people are treating him well. Think of that, will you? Sergeant Muller is a farmer, or he was, he could be a great help to me.'

'Then work him hard. Work him damned hard.' He went back to reading his paper.

Jean smiled at Karl. 'Come on. There's work to do.' She found some dungarees and a pair of boots in the hallway and led the way outside again.

'I am sorry to be a trouble to you,' he said.

'You are not. Take no notice of Pa, he's just frustrated and angry that he's so helpless. He still likes to think he's master though.'

'I understand.'

'Your English is very good. Where did you learn it?'

'At school. Some of us came on exchange visits to England during the school holidays. My father was able to afford it and he said it would be a good thing for me to learn. I seem to have a natural aptitude for languages. The officer who interrogated me said I might be useful as an interpreter.' He smiled suddenly. 'In the general confusion they must have forgotten about it because I was sent here, and the only translating I do is for my fellow prisoners.'

Dressed in dungarees over his uniform and wearing a pair of Arthur's rubber boots, he helped her pour the pig swill into the trough to the accompaniment of noisy squealing as the animals pushed each other to get at the food, then she fetched two scythes from the barn. 'Can you use one of these?'

'Yes.'

'Good because I'm hopeless at it. Pa despairs of me.' It did not occur to her that she was handing him a weapon.

She led the way through the orchard to the meadow where he began scything the long grass. His movements were rhythmic and assured. She left him to get on with it, while she concentrated on doing the rough edges along the side of the ditch. They had half of it done when Doris arrived with sandwiches and cider for their lunch. They sat under the hedge to eat and drink.

'This is good,' he said, biting into an egg sandwich. 'In Germany we were told the British were starving and ready to surrender.'

Jean laughed. 'Propaganda. Mind you, rations are pretty tight. We are fortunate in the country, it's not so easy in the towns.' She paused, musing. 'On the other hand townspeople are nearer the shops and can get to them quickly when word gets round there's something new in that's not on ration. By the time we've tidied ourselves up and caught the bus to town, it's all gone.'

'I suppose it is the same for us. Heidi wrote about long lines of people waiting for the shops to open.'

'Heidi is your fiancée, is she?'

'Yes. I proposed when I was called up. We planned to marry when I went on leave the next time, but it was not possible. I have not heard from her in over a year.'

'You are allowed to receive letters in the camp?'

'Yes. They are censored, of course. But I have had no letters since I came here.'

'Does she know you are in England?'

'I do not know. I have written to tell her how to write to me, but . . .' He shrugged.

'She lives in Berlin, you said.'

'Yes, but she comes from Hartsveld, the same as I do. It is a small village, halfway between Berlin and the Polish border. We have known each other all our lives. She was sent to Berlin to work in a factory at the beginning of the war. I am worried about her.'

'Because of the bombing?'

'Yes.'

'I'm sorry. Perhaps you will hear soon. How long have you been here? In England, I mean.'

'Just over a month. I was captured in Normandy.'

'There you are then. No time at all. Letters take a long time, I know. We hear from Gordon, not often but we do hear, though we have no idea exactly where he is, everything is done through the Red Cross. I don't suppose it really matters, a POW camp is a POW camp wherever it is.'

'Yes, on both sides of the North Sea.'

'Mum worries about the air raids.'

'You have not had any near here, have you?'

'A few aimed at the airfields, but I meant our raids on Germany.'

'Oh, I see. But I think perhaps your air force knows where the camps are and do not bomb them. Our aeroplanes do not bomb us because they know where we are.'

'I hadn't thought of that. How do they know?'

'I have no doubt there are ways and means of communicating.'

'Spies, you mean?'

'Perhaps, but there are neutral countries; Switzerland, Sweden and Portugal have access to the news on both sides and pass it on.'

'Can't you find out about your family that way?'

'No.' If he knew any more than that, he was obviously not going to tell her. 'You are very kind to me.'

'Why wouldn't I be? You have done me no harm.'

'Your father does not agree.'

'That was Hitler, not you personally.'

He blinked hard. Harsh treatment he could accept, could shrug his shoulders and endure, but kindness touched the core of him and crumbled his defences. He poured more cider from the heavy jug into his mug and drank deeply to cover his embarrassment, then he rose, picked up his scythe and went back to work.

They finished by the middle of the afternoon. 'A good day's work,' she said. 'I couldn't have done it without you, at least, not in the time.'

They returned to the farm. Leaving Karl to put the scythes away, she fetched the cows into the byre where they knew their own stalls. 'Watch that one,' she told him when he joined her. 'Gertrude's been known to kick.'

He patted the cow's rump and settled himself on the milking stool. '*Sachte, sachte,*' he murmured to the animal as he put his head into her side and washed her udders before taking them into his hands. 'You will soon be more comfortable.'

She watched him finish with Gertrude, measure the milk before pouring it into the churn and begin on the next animal, carefully washing his hands and her teats before starting. There was no doubt he knew what he was doing and the routine must have been familiar to him.

They had finished milking, recorded the yield on the Ministry forms and were settling the cows in for the night, when Doris came to tell them dinner was on the table. 'I have set a place for you, Sergeant Muller,' she said.

'I do not think you are expected to feed me,' he said. 'Your food is rationed.'

'It's a poor do when we can't give a bite to eat to a working man. You have earned it.'

'What about your husband?'

'Oh, pay him no mind. I'll deal with him. Come and eat. Your transport will be here soon.'

They ate at the big table in the kitchen where he met the rest of the family: Mrs Coleman's mother, Mrs Sanderson, who lived in her own cottage but had some of her meals at the farm; two schoolboys, who stared at him with unabashed curiosity, one of whom was Jean's brother, the other an evacuee; and a little girl, called Lily who was the evacuee's sister. She didn't live at the farm but with another family nearby. 'When she's not at school, she spends nearly all her time here,' Jean told him.

'I like being here,' the child said. 'I like the animals. And Mrs Coleman cooks better than Mrs Harris.'

'Shush,' Doris said. 'You mustn't say things like that. Mrs Harris is a very good cook.'

'Not as good as you.'

Arthur laughed. 'She's right there.'

'And you've no call to encourage her, Arthur Coleman. She'll be telling everyone.'

'I'll tell her not to,' Terry said.

'And does she do as she's told?' Jean asked him. She had taken off the unflattering headscarf and brushed out her hair. It was, Karl noticed, a rich brown.

'Ma said I was to look after her and she has to obey me,' Terry said, then turning to Karl. 'Do you have evacuees in your country Mr German Man?'

Karl smiled. 'Yes, we do. Just the same. And my name is Karl.'

'Have you been in many battles, Mr Karl?' Donald asked.

'A few.'

'You're getting good and beat now,' Terry said. 'Monty is a better general than Rommel.'

'Terry, we won't talk about the war,' Jean said.

'Why not?'

'Because in this kitchen, at this table, we are at peace with one another,' she said firmly. 'Find something else to talk about.'

They went on to discuss the farm work and the meal progressed amicably until the sound of a horn alerted them to the arrival of the camp's transport. Jean accompanied Karl to the gate.

'Has he behaved himself?' Corporal Donnington asked, as he let down the tailboard.

'He has been a great help,' Jean told him.

'So you want him back tomorrow?'

'Yes, please. If he wants to come.'

Karl clicked his heels together and bowed. 'I shall come, *Fräulein*.' He scrambled up beside his fellows and was gone.

Jean went back indoors and told Terry to take his sister home, then pushed her father into the sitting room and made him comfortable. 'That wasn't so bad, Pa, was it? He's just a man, obeying orders like everyone else.'

'S'pose so,' he admitted grudgingly. 'What did he mek on the work?'

'He was very good, knew what he was doing. We got the pasture scythed and the milking done in record time. Gertrude didn't kick out once. I think he's going to be quite useful.'

'Still don't like it.'

'Needs must,' she said.

He grunted. 'And the devil's driving this one.'

It was a second or two before she understood his reference. 'Hitler, yes, not Sergeant Muller.'

'If you say so.'

'Pa. It's Hitler and his like who caused all this bother so it's only right the prisoners should help out when our men are away. Call it recompense, if you like.'

'All right, I'll hold me tongue for your sake. Can't have you getting ill on account of me not able to work.'

'You will be able to one day, Pa. It just takes time. Now I must go and help Mum. Is there anything you want before I go?'

'I'll have the *Farmers Weekly* and you can bring me the accounts. I want to check on the cost of feed.'

He liked to keep an eye on their accounts even though he knew she was meticulous in keeping them straight. There would be a new expenditure from now on, because they were expected to pay a labourer's wage for Karl's work. It wasn't given to him directly because he had told her he was paid in tokens which he could only spend in the camp shop. She fetched the magazine and the ledgers and pulled a small table up beside his chair and put them on it.

'All right?' Doris queried, when she returned to the kitchen where her mother was washing up with Donald's help. He didn't like doing it; he maintained it wasn't a man's work and he had to be bullied into it. She took the teacloth from his hands and let him escape.

'Well?' Otto demanded as he wolfed down Karl's supper as well as his own. 'How was it?'

'*Gut. Sehr gut.* I spent the day scything a meadow and milking.'

'What have you discovered?'

'The farm is a small mixed farm and the family, all except the father, were friendly. They are having the same problems that we have at home with rationing and shortages. The cattle are a bit thin and the milk yield is not what it should be, but *Fräulein* Coleman put it down to shortage of feed and not having as much pasture as they once had.'

'*Fräulein* Coleman?' Otto queried with a grin.

'The daughter of the house. She has been trying to run the farm almost single-handed.'

'Good-looking, is she?'

'I suppose so; I never thought about it.'

'I don't believe that. You haven't seen a woman, much less spoken to one, for weeks and all you can say is you "suppose so".'

'I am engaged to be married.'

'What difference does that make?'

'All the difference in the world. Besides, I'd be a fool to try anything on even if I were tempted. I don't fancy a month in the *Kühler*.'

'What else did you see?' His voice was an undertone, not intended to be heard by anyone else.

'I saw trees and lanes and farm buildings, a church and a windmill and a lot of flat fields.'

'No railway lines, no barracks, no airfields, no signposts?'

'No. I think they must have been removed. Since we have been in England I have not seen a single one. I know the village is called Little Bushey and it's in Cambridgeshire – that's a county by the way – but exactly where in Cambridgeshire, I do not know. North, I should think, judging by the terrain.'

'Then try and find out more. I want to know the lie of the land, how far we are from the sea, things like that. I want to add it to my map.'

'You've got a map?' he asked in astonishment.

'Yes.' He patted the breast pocket of his uniform.

'How did you get it?'

'I drew it.' He laughed. 'It was on a poster in the train that brought us here, advertising seaside resorts and places of interest. I copied it.'

'Where did you get the paper?'

'The sandwiches they gave us for the journey were wrapped in brown paper.'

'That was enterprising of you.'

'Wasn't it? The more detail I can add the better.'

'You really are serious about this, aren't you?'

'Yes. It is our duty to escape.'

Karl supposed Otto was right, but he did not want to do

anything to prolong the war. It was hideous and he held no brief for Hitler and his Nazis. Everyone, on both sides, was suffering because of them. On the other hand, he wanted to go home, to find out what had happened to his parents and sister. Most of all to see Heidi again and take her into his arms, to feel her soft compliant body against his own.

'You are silent, my friend,' Otto said.

'I am thinking. I spent some time in England before the war.'

'You never said.'

'No reason to.'

'Where?'

'Cambridge. I learnt to know it quite well. I know where the station is and where the trains go, and some of the countryside around it.'

'How far away from here, is it?'

'I don't know. Probably not far.'

'And how far are we from the coast?'

'Again, probably not far.'

'Which coast, east or west? I know it's not south because that's where we landed and the train was travelling north.' Anyone who had been in the Hitler Youth knew about using the sun and stars to find his way. It was rather like the Boy Scouts in that.

'East.'

Otto put down his spoon and stood up. 'Let's talk about it after roll call.'

Karl followed him to the pan of greasy water in which he washed his plate and cutlery and then they made their way outside for roll call. This inevitably took some time, but they were becoming used to it. Some of their compatriots made it difficult for their guards by dodging about in the lines and shouting insults. As soon as it was done to the commandant's satisfaction, they were herded into their huts and locked in for the night. While the lights were still on, the prisoners amused themselves playing cards or chess, writing or reading magazines and books, a limited supply of which was on a shelf in the corner.

Otto fetched the largest book he could find, an illustrated one of British wild flowers, and he and Karl sat on Karl's bed and appeared to be absorbed in it together. 'I don't want anyone else to see this,' he said, drawing the brown paper from his pocket and spreading it out on the pages of the book. 'The escape committee will take it off me and I'm not having that.'

Karl looked at the somewhat stylised map which was dotted with places of interest, especially seaside towns. 'There's Cambridge,' he said pointing. 'Here would be King's Lynn, here Great Yarmouth and Lowestoft, the most easterly point of the British Isles.'

'A good place to make for, do you think?' Otto gave him a pencil to mark them.

'Possibly. Or we could go to London. It would be easy to conceal ourselves among the crowds. Lots of shipping there, too.'

'None of it going to Germany though?'

'Naturally not.'

'Where then?'

'Middle east, far east. There's Lisbon. Portugal is neutral but how often ships call there, I've no idea.' He paused. 'And Gibraltar, of course. We might be able to make it into Spain from there, assuming we can board a ship going there and leave it undetected. We'd need a good cover story.'

'I'm willing to give it a go. How about you? Just the two of us.'

'I'll think about it. We'd have to get out of here for a start.'

'You go out every day. Suppose I was to volunteer to come with you.'

'*Fräulein* Coleman said they only wanted one man.'

'I could get work nearby. We could meet up and be on our way before anyone missed us.'

Karl knew it would be anything but easy and he would have to deceive *Fräulein* Coleman and her family. Would they be punished for allowing him to escape? They would certainly not be allowed to employ any more prisoners. How would the *Fräulein* manage without help? Why did that matter? It didn't, of course, not against the broader issue of his duty.

'It can't be done in a hurry,' he said. 'We need civilian clothing and identity cards, food and English money.'

'Steal them.' Otto folded the map and put it back in his pocket. They turned a few of the pages in the book and commented on the illustrations to avert the suspicion of their fellows, before returning it to the shelf. Then they began a game of chess which was brought to a sudden end when the lights went out.

Karl undressed in the dark and went to bed, where he lay thinking. The farmhouse kitchen he had been in today was so like the kitchen of his home, he could almost have imagined himself back there. If anything it increased his homesickness. Could he make it back? If he did, would he be sent back to the front line? His guess was that he would. And if he failed, what would the English authorities do to him? He sat up and thumped the lumpy pillow before settling down again and falling asleep.

The tank was rolling ever nearer. There were others continuing an inexorable advance all round him. He could hear the rattle of machine-gun and rifle fire, screams and groans all around him. Staying where he was was not an option. He preferred death from a bullet to being squashed to death. He scrambled out of his foxhole and began to run. There was no way he could outrun the tank. He stumbled and fell. Why the tank commander did not shoot him he did not know. He threw down his rifle and scrambled to his feet, raised his hands above his head and waited.

The tank stopped and an officer in a British uniform climbed out and walked over to him. He had a pistol in his hand. Karl held his breath waiting for the shot that would put an end to his existence. Instead of firing, the officer used it to signal to him to move out of the way and join a crowd of his compatriots being rounded up. He had been spared to become a prisoner. He woke, breathing heavily, to find himself tangled in his blanket and a room full of men snoring about him. In the bunk next to him, Otto Herzig slept soundly. The desperate fear slowly drained away, leaving him limp.

'*Gott sei Dank*,' he murmured and turned over to try and sleep.

Chapter Three

'The reaper is here,' Jean told Karl as soon as he arrived the following Saturday. 'Everyone is up on the top field, ready to begin. Get your overalls on and let's join them.'

A crowd of villagers was on the field, including several children who were on holiday from school, a holiday referred to in the country as the 'harvest holiday' when they were traditionally expected to help bring in the harvest. Bill was there, as promised. Jean introduced Karl.

Bill nodded curtly. Karl bowed his head and said, '*Guten Tag.*'

'Right, let's make a start,' Jean said, aware of the tension between the two men.

The reaper-binder had arrived behind a tractor driven by an employee of the firm who owned it and they set to work along with everyone else to follow behind it as it circled the field. Karl and Jean had already scythed the headland to make room for it.

As the cut corn fell to its blades it passed over conveyor belts which bound it in sheaves and spat them out behind the machine.

It was the job of the helpers to gather them up and stand them upright in stooks at intervals along the field. When all but the last half-dozen rows had been cut, everyone gathered in a circle round what was left with sticks and staves in their hands, as the rabbits, who had been driven further and further into the standing corn for safety, bolted. Then began a wild chase and the sickening thud of weapons being used, at the end of which a goodly number of dead rabbits were destined for the next day's pot.

As soon as the last swathe had been cut, the tractor and its reaper were driven from the field, leaving everyone to return to the farmhouse where Doris had prepared some refreshments. Jean led the way with Karl.

Besides Doris and her mother, there was another woman in the kitchen helping with the refreshments. They had nearly finished and the kitchen table was covered with plates of sandwiches, sausage rolls and home-made buns. 'Will it do?' Doris asked Jean.

'It's a wonderful spread.' Jean turned to Karl. 'The sandwiches are made with our own eggs, and bacon from the pig we slaughtered. Sausages ditto. The butter's churned in our own dairy, so no one will have milk for their tea for a few days. A bit of lard made the pastry.'

'It is a feast,' he said.

'By the way,' she went on. 'This is Mrs Brotherton, the rector's wife.' She indicated a plump lady in her sixties dressed in a tweed skirt and blouse, over which she wore a flowered apron.

He clicked his heels and bowed to her. '*Guten Tag, Gnadige Frau.*'

'How do you do?' The lady gave him a half-hearted smile before returning to her task.

'Help yourselves,' Doris said, addressing everyone who had crowded into the kitchen behind them.

'What's he doing here?' Bill murmured to Jean, indicating Karl with a nod of his head. 'You'd think he was one of us.'

'As far as I am concerned, he is,' she whispered back. 'He has worked hard all morning in spite of your unfriendliness towards him and he has earned his food.'

'Why the hell should I be friendly? He's the enemy. And fraternising is banned by law, as you very well know.'

'What exactly is fraternising? I'm sure it doesn't mean you can't be polite.'

She could see Karl looking at them and went over to him. 'Here, Sergeant, let me fill a plate for you.'

He thanked her and took his plate of sandwiches and a sausage roll out to the scullery to eat it in isolation. She thought it wise not to go after him.

As soon as he had finished he went outside again. Jean joined him just as the lorry drew up. 'I have fetched in the cows,' he told her. 'But I do not have time to help with the milking.'

'It doesn't matter, I can manage.' Jean accompanied him to the gate and then went back to the cowshed.

Gertrude was restive at having to wait and kicked out. Jean just managed to grab the pail of milk before the whole lot went over. 'What was the magic word Karl said to you?' she asked the cow. 'Whatever it was, it worked. I'll have to ask him tomorrow. I know I shouldn't, but I feel sorry for him, so far from home and his fiancée. I don't suppose he wanted this war any more than we did.'

'Who are you talking to?' Bill was standing in the doorway watching her.

'The cow.'

'Oh, and what does she say?'

'Moo.' She laughed. 'You off home?'

'Yes. I'll see you at the dance tonight, shall I?'

'Yes, I'm looking forward to it.'

He left and she finished the milking, then went to shut up the chickens before going back indoors to help her mother finish cooking the evening meal. That was how life was nowadays, unrelenting, going from one job to another, never having time to stop and just do nothing. But on Saturday evenings she could forget about the farm for a little while and what better way to begin it than a long soak in the bath.

She stoked the fire in the range and threw more logs on it to reheat the water and then went up to run five inches of water into the bath, which was all they were supposed to use. It was a big bath in a room converted from a bedroom several years before, and the water hardly covered her legs. Nevertheless she stayed in it until it began to cool. Dressed in a printed cotton skirt and a flowered blouse, and feeling more like a human being and not one of the animals she tended, she set off to walk to the village hall.

Hanging her jacket on a peg in the cloakroom, she made her way into the throng. Mr Harris was in charge of the gramophone and had a pile of records on the table beside it. Already people were dancing to 'A String of Pearls'. There was a noticeable shortage of men, so many of the women were dancing together, laughing at the muddle they were making of it.

Bill beckoned her over to where he had saved seats. 'What are you having to drink?' he asked. 'There's beer while it lasts, or home-made wine. It's some of Mrs Maynard's elderberry, pretty potent, so I'm told. Or there's the cider you sent up.'

'I'll have the cider, please,' Jean said. 'At least I know what's in it.' The Coleman family had been making cider with their apples for generations, for their own use, not for sale, but everyone who

46

came to the farm and sampled it said how good it was.

It was after Bill had brought the drinks and he and Jean were dancing that he asked about the German prisoner of war. 'How did he come to be working for you?'

'I did as you suggested and asked the War Ag. for someone with a farming background and he came.'

'He seems to have made himself at home.'

'Oh, Bill, of course he hasn't. He works hard and I'm glad of his help.'

'You refused my help when it was offered.'

'Bill, I've told you, you've got enough on your plate with your own farm and looking after your mother.'

'I can be the judge of that. I hate to see you struggling.'

'I am not struggling. Lots of women are doing harder jobs than I am and doing them well. I've got nothing to complain of. And I do have some help.'

'The Jerry.'

'Why do you keep on about him, Bill? He works all day and then he goes back to be locked up again until the next day. It's not much of a life, is it?'

'Have you forgotten he's the enemy? He's one of those causing death and destruction and upsetting all our lives.'

'No, I haven't forgotten but he's out of it now and besides, helping us to win the war is his punishment, don't you think?'

'You call it punishment when he's fed and clothed with our taxes.'

'What else are we supposed to do? Now, can we drop the subject? Concentrate on your dancing, you just trod on my foot.'

'Sorry. Will you come for a walk tomorrow afternoon? Just a stroll to blow away the cobwebs.'

She looked up at him and laughed. 'I haven't got any cobwebs,

Bill. I don't have time to stop and let the spiders do their work.'

'All work and no play . . .'

'I'll come for a walk with you, if you promise not to grumble about Sergeant Muller.'

'OK, it's a promise.'

The dance came to an end and they wandered back to their seats. He knew he had annoyed her, but he was annoyed with himself. Why couldn't she see things his way? 'I'll go and ask Rosie to dance,' he said. 'She's looking a bit of a wallflower.'

Rosemary Shelley was Gordon's fiancée. She had declared her intention of waiting for him and refused to go out with anyone else. She was at the dance with her mother who liked dancing as much as anyone and had left her sitting on her own, tapping her foot to the rhythm.

'Come on, Rosie,' he said, taking her hand and pulling her up. 'You're safe with me. I'm spoken for.'

'Everyone knows that,' she said, as the music began for an old time waltz. 'When are you going to make it official?'

'There's plenty of time. Got to get this war over with first.'

'Why?'

'Why? Because life's so uncertain, that's why. You never know what's round the corner.'

'Do you ever? You want to watch out she isn't snapped up by someone else.'

'Like who?'

'I don't know, do I? I wish Gordon and I had tied the knot before he joined up.'

'Would it have made any difference? He'd still be a prisoner.'

'But I would be married, with a gold band on my finger and maybe a baby to look after. Now I'll have to wait for all that until he comes home. God knows when that will be.'

'Oh, you are down, aren't you? Cheer up and enjoy yourself while you can. It will soon be over.'

'Do you really think so?'

'No doubt of it. Jerry's on the run.'

Karl was not taken to the farm on Sundays, much to Arthur's disgust. 'Do they think animals don't eat or need milking on Sundays?' he demanded, when Jean arrived back late for breakfast and everyone was ready for church.

'I, for one, am glad of a day on our own.' Doris told him. 'Are you going to stay at home, Jean?'

'Yes, there isn't time to change and I can find plenty to do. I'll see you later.'

They left and she was alone in the house. She made a fresh pot of tea and some porridge and sat down to eat it with the newspaper propped against a jar containing home-made strawberry jam.

German armed forces were holding up the advance on the Caen-to-Falaise Road and there was heavy fighting. The Russians were approaching Warsaw and the Polish underground army had risen up to try and take the city before they arrived. Did the German POWs hear the news, she wondered, and if they did, what did they make of it? Were they glad to be out of it? Karl was unfailingly polite and worked hard, but she had no idea how he felt. He had reacted calmly to Bill's unfriendliness, but how much self control that had taken, she had no idea. As a man she liked him, as an enemy she ought to keep him at arm's-length.

She cleared her breakfast away and prepared the vegetables for lunch then sat down to make a list of jobs to be done during the week and decide which she would assign to Karl. It was a pity he had to be so closely watched or she would set him to work on his own. Once the sheaves of wheat had dried out, they would have to be loaded onto the cart and taken to the corner of the field where they would be carefully built into a stack with ears facing inwards and thatched with straw to await the arrival of the threshing machine. After that there would be ploughing to do and the ditch alongside one of the fields was becoming choked and needed digging out and there were some hedges that needed trimming. She had almost finished when everyone came back from church and all was noise and bustle again.

'I've been making a list of jobs for Sergeant Muller to do,' she said, as they sat down to eat. 'Do you want to add to it, Pa?' She pushed the list over to him.

'He could mend the window frames in Gran's cottage and give them a lick of paint,' he said, after scanning the list.

Elizabeth, her grandmother, looked up. 'Oh, yes, that would be good,' she said. 'You've no idea how draughty that one in the sitting room is. When it's windy it rattles fit to fall out.'

'I'm not sure I'm allowed to ask him to do jobs like that,' Jean said. 'It's not strictly farm work, is it? I'll see if Mr Gould can do it.'

They had just finished washing-up, when Bill arrived to go for the walk she had promised him. The afternoon was already well advanced and they could not go far before the jobs on their respective farms called them back. He tucked her hand into the crook of his elbow and held it there. Laddie ran along beside them, sniffing here and there along the hedgerows. The sky was overcast and not warm for August.

'The bombers won't be flying tonight,' she said. The Allied bombing of German cities was relentless. She often woke at night to hear the RAF bombers going over and wondered how many of them would not come back. During the day the American Flying Fortresses droned overhead and they suffered badly, too. She thought about the families of those who were lost and her gentle heart felt for them. She was thankful Gordon was out of it.

'Good. With luck we might get a good night's sleep.' His farm was closer to the airfield than Briar Rose.

'Have you tried ear plugs?'

'They don't work. The noise is a constant throb. I swear it shakes my bed. Besides, if I try and block that out I can't hear if Ma calls me.'

'Does she do that often?' She knew he had been born when his mother had been in her late forties, long after she had given up hope of having a child, and the birth had been a difficult one. Consequently his growing up had been a strange mixture of neglect because she was getting on in years and didn't know how to look after him, and overprotection because she was afraid of losing him. Since his father died, she clung to him more than ever.

'Often enough. She seems to lose track of time, sometimes doesn't know night from day.'

'Poor you.'

'I get by, but she is getting worse. God help me, I sometimes stay out of the house just to get some peace and quiet.'

'As you are doing now.'

'Oh, I didn't mean it like that,' he said hastily. 'I want to be with you. I want to be with you all the time, so every minute is precious.' He stopped and turned towards her. 'If it weren't for this war and Ma and . . .'

'And?'

'Oh, you know what.'

'No, I don't.' He took her face in his hands and bent to kiss her. She put her arms round him. 'Is that your answer?' she asked when he drew away.

'For now.'

51

'For now?'

'Yes. There are too many obstacles. One day . . .'

'You are the most infuriating man, do you know that? You are possessive and don't like me even looking at anyone else, but you won't commit yourself. What are you afraid of?'

'I'm not afraid, just being sensible.'

'OK, so we'll be sensible,' she said, turning from him and striding away back towards home.

He dashed after her. 'Don't go. I'm sorry. Don't rush off like that. Let me explain.'

'You don't need to. I understand. You want to wait until the war ends, until your mother no longer needs you, until you can summon up the courage to jump in at the deep end. Let me know when that happens, William Howson. I might still be around. On the other hand, I might not.'

He tugged on her arm. 'Don't be like that, sweetheart. It's not like you.'

'How do you know what I'm like? Have you ever taken the trouble to find out?'

'Course I have. Good God! I've known you since we were in infant school and you've known me. What's got into you?'

'Nothing. I'm tired, that's all.'

'We all are, but I've never known you so disgruntled before.'

'I expect it's the war. I just want it to end.'

'So do I. Isn't that what I've just been saying?'

She did not think so, but she was tired of arguing. She just wanted to go home and have a cup of tea, but there was the milking to do, the other animals to feed and the chickens to shut up before that could happen. 'I'm sorry, Bill,' she said. 'I'm just feeling a bit low today. Let's go home.'

* * *

'Did you enjoy the dance on Saturday?' Karl asked during their midday break the following Monday.

'Yes, it was fun. Do you like dancing?'

'I used to go with Heidi before the war, and when I last had leave, but that was some time ago.'

'Tell me about Heidi. Is she pretty?'

'I think so.' He delved in his tunic pocket and pulled out a battered photograph and handed it across to her. 'This is Heidi.'

'She is beautiful,' she said, studying it before handing it back. 'And such an infectious smile. You must miss her.'

'Yes, I do. It is her birthday next week. She will be twenty-two and I cannot even wish her *fröhlicher Geburtstag*.'

She guessed what that meant. 'I am sure she knows you are thinking it.'

'I hope so. You work very hard,' he said.

'Can't be helped.'

'Have you always wanted to farm?'

'It's the only life I know, but I wasn't expected to run it. I had a job, but I had to give it up when Gordon left.'

'What did you do?'

'I was a shop assistant in a dress shop.' She laughed. 'Surrounded by good clothes. Just look at me now.'

He looked up at her. 'You look beautiful.'

She stared at him, then laughed in embarrassment. 'Flattery, Sergeant, flattery. I am impervious to it.' But she was not. She was inordinately pleased to think he noticed how she looked, though most of the time she was in dungarees, with rubber boots on her feet. In the interests of hygiene her hair was always rolled up and secured under a scarf tied in a turban. How could that be called beautiful?

'Are you engaged to be married?' he asked.

'No, why do you ask?'

'Mr Howson is very . . . How do you say?'

She laughed. 'Jealous?'

'Perhaps. But I do not think he likes me.' He sighed. 'I am not surprised. I am the enemy, a hated Jerry.'

'If the boot were on the other foot and he was a prisoner in Germany working with Heidi, you might feel the same.'

'I expect I would.'

'But you do like working here? I am not such a hard taskmaster, am I?'

'I do,' he said hastily. 'You have treated me with courtesy and given me hope when I was in despair.' He reached out and put a hand on her arm. 'You have shown me that there are good people in the world and one day we will live in peace again. You have made my imprisonment bearable. Given a choice I would still come, that is if nothing happened to prevent me.'

'What, for instance?'

'I don't know. Anything. A disaster.'

She looked sharply at him. 'Are you expecting a disaster?'

'No.' He paused. 'Except the defeat of my country.'

'You have known that for a long time, Karl.'

'Hitler has ordered every kilometre of ground must be defended to the last man.'

'You can keep in touch with what is happening then?'

'We learn it from new prisoners. Some of them are only boys, some are too old to fight and yet they have been in the thick of it.'

'Cheer up. The war will be over soon and you will be able to go home. And my brother and all other prisoners will be repatriated. Life will return to normal.'

'Do you really think that?' he asked. 'I do not think so. Nothing will be the same again, even though we might wish it.'

'But surely Hitler will capitulate when Germany itself is threatened?'

'Germany is threatened all the time by the bombers,' he said. 'It only makes the Führer more defiant.'

'What do your fellow prisoners think about it?'

'Some are depressed but others are convinced the Führer will turn the tide. They talk of a secret weapon that will turn defeat into victory.'

'Do you believe that?'

'I don't know. We don't know what is happening in the homeland, how bad it is, if the air raids are having an effect or if, like the Londoners, they are bearing them and carrying on. We do not know if what we hear or read in the English newspapers is truth or propaganda.'

'Any news from home?'

'No.'

'Poor old Karl.'

'I am not old,' he said, forcing a laugh and getting to his feet. 'And I will prove it. Come on, there is work to be done.'

She packed away their picnic things and went back to work. A few minutes later she heard him singing quietly to himself in German.

'I recognise that tune,' she said, stopping to listen. 'It's one we used to sing in school. We called it "Rosebud, rosebud, rosebud red". It was about a boy who was determined to pick a rose and the rose warned him not to, but he did it anyway and the rose pricked him. I suppose there's a lesson there somewhere.'

'It is the same song.'

'Teach me the German words.'

So they sang together as they worked, their clear voices carrying over the fields. It was not a sensible thing to do she realised later.

Bill, walking along the lane, heard them and tackled her when he called that evening.

'What the devil were you thinking of, singing at the top of your voice with that Jerry, and in German too?' he demanded. 'Do you want to be arrested?'

'What, for singing?'

'No, for singing in German. We are at war with Germany, or didn't you know?'

'He taught me the German words and I taught him the English ones, what's wrong with that?'

'Jean, I do think it was a little indiscreet,' her mother put in. 'You could offend people.'

Jean and Karl established a good working relationship. He knew the way she liked things done and deferred to her as the boss, but sometimes he volunteered suggestions and she was always ready to listen and learn. She did not feel it necessary to follow him about and if it meant they finished all the quicker if they did different tasks, then she did her own and let him get on with his. Bill grumbled, of course.

'You will live to regret it, mark my words,' he told her one day when he came up to the farm and found her milking on her own and Karl in the barn servicing the plough. 'One of these days, you'll find him gone. Not that I care about that,' he admitted. 'He can go to Timbuktu for all I care.'

'If he was going to run, he'd have done it before now,' she said. 'I don't think he's all that keen to go back to fighting for Hitler.'

'Did he tell you that?'

'No, of course not. He's loyal to his roots, but I can tell by the odd things he's said; he's not a Nazi.'

'They all are.'

'No, they are not. Some of the German soldiers hold no brief for Hitler. As for the civilian population, I am convinced they would change things if they could.' She stopped suddenly as Karl appeared in the doorway.

'I have finished that task, *Fräulein*,' he said formally. 'We can begin ploughing as soon as the field is clear.'

'Thank you.'

'What shall I do next, *Fräulein*?'

'Can you finish the milking? I'm going up to the house with Mr Howson.'

'Yes, *Fräulein*, of course.'

She and Bill left him to it.

'"*We* can begin ploughing".' Bill repeated Karl's words. 'Who does he think he is with his "we"?'

'It was just a manner of speaking, Bill. Now, why did you come? You don't usually grace us with your presence in the middle of the day.'

'*Jane Eyre* is on at the pictures. I thought you might like to go tomorrow night.'

'That would be nice. Thank you.'

'I'll call for you at half past six.'

'OK. I'll be ready.'

He left, passing Karl who had finished his work for the day and was waiting at the gate for the lorry to arrive. Karl clicked his heels and came to attention when he saw him. Bill gave him a perfunctory nod and marched past.

Jane Eyre was a dark, sombre production starring Orson Welles and Joan Fontaine, but it was a change from the wartime propaganda films that proliferated. The Pathé news came on between the early and late projections. She didn't suppose it told the whole story, but it did give an idea of what the troops were facing with shots of men dodging through the ruins of Falaise in the face of enemy fire. But they were winning, judging by the long lines of German prisoners being escorted into captivity, fifty thousand, so the commentator said.

'Where on earth are they going to put them all?' she whispered.

'God knows. They can dump them in the sea for all I care.'

There were pictures and commentary about the bitter fighting, not only in France, but in the Far East, as well as Russia. There was some footage of the latest scourge to reach the country from the continent; rockets had replaced the doodlebugs and they had a longer range. The launch sites in France and Belgium had been put out of action by the Allied advance and they were being fired from the Netherlands whence they were capable of reaching East Anglia and the Midlands. They could cause even more destruction than their predecessors, but fortunately were nothing like as reliable and many fell into the North Sea. But they were an ever-present threat and worried the population who had been hoping that Hitler was finished.

'Why can't the Jerries see it's hopeless and give in?' Bill said, as they caught the last bus home.

'They don't think it is hopeless.'

'Is that what your Jerry told you?'

'He's not my Jerry, Bill. His name is Karl. He knows it's all over. He just wants it to end as we do, but he tells me there are people in the camp who still think they can win. They are putting a lot of faith in Hitler's secret weapon.'

'You mean those new rockets?'

'I suppose that's what he meant, he didn't say.'

'The Blitz didn't work and neither will they.'

'Let us hope so. But I don't think Hitler is done yet.'

'Do you talk to the Jerry about it?'

'Sometimes, but what can we say to each other? He is depressed about it and worried about his parents and sister. He thinks the Red Army will soon reach Hartsveld. He is more worried about the Russians than anything.'

'You shouldn't be discussing things like that with him, you know that.'

'I can't work beside him all day and not talk to him, but we do try to keep our conversation to the farm and what needs doing.'

'I'm glad to hear it.'

Karl was passing Mrs Sanderson's cottage two mornings later when he spotted Otto working on her window. 'What are you doing here?'

'You can see what I'm doing. I'm replacing this rotten window frame.'

'You didn't tell me you had a job.'

'I was only told this morning.'

Ted Gould came round the side of the house carrying a pane of glass. 'Haven't you got that frame in yet, Jerry. Come on, chop, chop. We haven't got all day. And who is this?'

'Sergeant Muller,' Karl said. 'I work for Mr Coleman.'

'Then you'd best get on with it and let my man work. I don't pay him to gossip.'

'What's he saying?' Otto asked.

Karl translated, then added, 'I'll see you tonight.'

He passed Mrs Sanderson in the lane as he left. 'No Jean?' she asked.

'She is feeding the hens. I came back for a billhook we left on the field when we were working on the hedge up there.'

'She doesn't usually let you go about on your own.'

'I think she trusts me,' he said. 'I must go back to her.'

He hurried away and she stood looking after him, wondering how trustworthy he really was. She carried on to her cottage to find the window still out. 'Mr Gould, I would have expected it to be done by now,' she said.

'It isn't a standard size, Mrs Sanderson, and the angles are anything but square. That's the trouble with these old properties, nothing's straight. And this great lump . . .' He indicated Otto with a nod of his head. 'Hen't got the first idea about buildin' work, though he said he's done it afore. If he don' soon pull his socks up, I'll send him back and get another.'

Otto, who knew no English, did not understand what they were saying, but he had recognised the tone of contempt in the man's voice and decided that one day, he'd have his revenge.

Karl had abandoned chess in favour of woodwork in a hut set aside for the men to indulge their hobbies and where tools were provided which they had to hand back at the end of each session. The piece of wood he picked up had cried out to be carved. When Otto found him, that evening, it was taking shape as a dog, not unlike Laddie. Not wanting to be questioned on what he was doing, he packed it away. 'How did you get on with the builder?' he asked as he handed in his tools.

'I don't know. Not having the English I can't tell, can I?'

'It might pay you to learn a little of it. There are English classes in the camp. Join one of those.'

'I noticed you did not have a guard when I saw you today. I thought the *Fräulein* went everywhere with you.'

'She usually does, but I think she trusts me now.'

'Good. I asked the escape committee about clothes, but they said our uniforms are too battered for conversion. We will have to steal some. There is nothing suitable at the builder's yard. The man does not live on the premises. You can get enough for both of us, can't you?'

'I don't know. I've never been further in the house than the kitchen. I would need to find out where everything is and I have to do it without arousing suspicion.'

'Are you backing out?'

'No,' he said quickly. 'I am being realistic. If we go before we are properly prepared, we will certainly fail.'

'Then we must make sure we are prepared. We'll tell our employers we're not going to work on that day. We'll say there is going to be a big roll call in the camp and a search of our huts and everyone has to be present. Then we go to work on the transport as usual but we don't report to our employers. I'll meet you at the end of the lane down to your farm. Then we can change into the clothes you've got for us and strike out for London.'

He had still not ventured upstairs in the farmhouse to look for clothes. There was a row of hooks in the passage beside the kitchen on which hung raincoats and caps and where rubber boots were left. Otto would expect him to take those if he could find nothing else. He also knew there was a cashbox in a cupboard beside the kitchen range. It was never locked. But he balked at taking that. 'That won't work. I can't take anything from the farm the night before or it will be missed and reported. I shall have to go to work as usual.'

'That's true.'

They were quietly deciding how to overcome this, or rather Otto was while Karl listened, when the *Lagerführer's* clerk came into the room. 'Major Schultz wants to see you,' he told Otto. 'At once.'

Grumbling, Otto hurried away and Karl was left to muse on

his friend's plans and found himself less than enthusiastic. Was he becoming soft? Was he afraid of what might happen if they were caught? Or was it a reluctance to betray the Colemans and Jean in particular? They had done nothing to deserve that. On the other hand it was his duty to try and escape.

Otto returned, just as he was debating how to tell him that he would go with him but he would not steal from the farm. His friend was in a filthy mood. 'They have rumbled us,' he told Karl. 'Someone heard us talking and informed the commandant and he's been onto the *Lagerführer*.'

'Who informed?'

'You don't suppose the commandant would tell the major that, do you? He has spies everywhere.'

'So what happened? Has he forbidden us to make the attempt?'

'Not exactly. I have been told we must apply to the escape committee and take our turn along with a lot of other hare-brained schemes. We can go when we've been given permission. I was a given a reprimand and told our actions could have ruined everyone else's chances. He said he had had a hard job convincing the commandant that he knew nothing of it and would have condemned it if he had. He's in the colonel's pocket, no doubt of that.'

'Perhaps that's for the best, if it means the colonel trusts him to maintain discipline and leaves us alone.'

'That's all very well, but what about our plan?'

'Postponed, Otto, not scrapped. You must learn a little patience.' He smiled suddenly. 'Along with a little more English.'

Karl wanted to improve his English, to be completely fluent and had asked Jean to borrow books from the library for him. She brought him contemporary English novels. He also wanted to know more about farming in England. He could move about the farm doing whatever work needed doing without constant supervision. He knew Jean trusted him. Even her father was coming round to sharing a glass of cider with him and talking about the relative merits of farming practices in England and Germany. How could he put all that behind him for the sake of a plan to escape that was doomed to fail?

Chapter Four

'I have to go to a meeting in Wisbech,' Jean told Karl one morning. Dressed in a skirt and jumper and not her usual dungarees, she was harnessing Misty to the trap. 'There's a man coming down from the Ministry of Ag. and Fish to give us a lecture. While I'm gone, do you mind giving the new window in my grandmother's cottage a coat of paint? I know it's not strictly farm business . . .'

'I will be happy to do it for her.' She had brushed out her hair and was looking very feminine and attractive.

'I'll drop you off and pick you up on my way back. If it doesn't rain it might be touch dry by this evening.' She handed him a tin of paint and a brush and climbed into the trap. He joined her as she took up the reins.

'Do you expect it to rain?' he asked.

'Pa said it might. He is usually fairly accurate.'

Mrs Sanderson saw them arrive from her kitchen window and opened the door before they reached it. 'Come you in,' she said, ushering them into the kitchen.

'Karl is going to paint your new window frame.'

'Good, but he can have a hot drink before he starts. Cocoa do?'

'I do not want to trouble you, madam,' he said.

'It's no trouble. Sit down. It won't take a jiffy.'

Karl and Jean sat while she busied herself making the drink and fetching out a biscuit tin. 'Home-made oatmeal,' she said. 'I like to keep some in a tin for the children.'

'So that's why they are always so keen to visit you,' Jean said, laughing.

'It might have something to do with it,' the old lady admitted. 'Go on, Sergeant, help yourself.'

He took one from the tin and thanked her. 'Was the window put in to your satisfaction?' he asked her.

'Yes, but it took a lot longer than I expected. Your compatriot was very slow and the more Mr Gould chivvied him, the slower he got. He seemed to be dreaming and looking about him all the time.'

'I expect he was glad to get away from the camp and wanted it to last as long as possible.'

'Very likely.' She pushed a steaming mug of cocoa towards him. 'I haven't noticed you going slow though. You keep up with Jean and she's no slouch.'

'Slouch?' he queried.

'Slow-working,' Jean explained.

'No, you are certainly not that.'

As soon as they had finished their drinks, Jean left him with her grandmother. 'I'll call in on the way back,' she told Karl.

'I'll have some soup ready for you,' Elizabeth told her.

As soon as she had gone, Karl went outside to start on the window. Elizabeth came out to watch him. 'I'm glad you have come to help Jean,' she said, standing with her hands thrust into her apron pockets. 'It was all getting too much for her. I wasn't sure it was a good idea at first, you being a German. We hear such tales . . .' She stopped and shrugged. 'But you have been a blessing.'

'I am glad to be of service.'

'You don't mind doing it?'

'No, it is better than being shut up in camp. It is work I am used to. At home I would be doing the same things as I do here.'

'Jean tells me you have a fiancée.'

'Yes.'

'Tell me about her.'

While he worked he talked of home and Heidi and his parents and what their farm was like, answering when she interrupted with questions.

'You are not really so very different from us, are you?' she said when he paused to stand back and look at his handiwork.

'No, Mrs Sanderson. Hardly different at all.'

'I hope they don't send you away somewhere else . . .'

'If that happened I would have no choice,' he said, thinking of the escape plans. 'Nor any warning.'

'Then I shall speak to Colonel Williamson. I know him well. He will make sure you stay with us.'

'Other men could do the same work.'

'I don't think so, not if they are anything like that friend of yours. He was not a nice man at all.'

'He is sad at being separated from his family, Mrs Sanderson, and he speaks no English so it is doubly difficult for him.'

'I think he is a Nazi.'

'I wouldn't know about that.'

'Are you a Nazi?'

'No. Not all Germans are, you know.'

'I didn't think you were. Proper gentleman, you are.'

66

He chuckled. 'Thank you. I don't think anyone has said that to me before.'

'Unless I go up to the farm, I don't have many people to talk to and, though I can help Doris, I don't always want to be on their doorstep. I lost my husband six years ago, but I still miss him.'

'I am sure you do.'

'Do you have grandparents?'

'My grandmother, that is my father's mother, died of influenza at the end of the last war and it affected my grandfather badly. He didn't seem able to go on without her. He died two years later. I never knew my other grandparents.'

'That flu was terrible, so many people died. Thank goodness we all escaped, but now my son-in-law is struck down with a stroke and the burden of the farm has fallen on Doris and Jean.' She paused. He had almost finished. 'I'm going indoors to put some soup on. Jean will be hungry when she comes back.' With that she left him.

He finished what he was doing, smiling to himself. He had told the old lady more than he had told anyone about his past life; she was easy to talk to, and, he suspected, easy to deceive. On the pretext of going back to the farm, he could explore the village. It was what Otto would expect him to do. He took the paint and brush and knocked on the door. 'I need to clean the brush,' he said.

'I'll find a jam jar of water. You can leave it in that for the moment. Come in. I've made enough soup for you, too.'

He thought about the dog he was carving and stepped inside.

'I believe it is your birthday today,' Karl said, a week later, as they began the afternoon milking. 'August the nineteenth, is that right?'

They had spent the day harvesting the potatoes, with the help of about twenty children from the local school who had arrived in a charabanc, fresh-faced and eager. There had been a great deal of laughter and chattering, but that had gradually subsided as the day wore on. It was back-breaking work bending to pick up the potatoes the digger had turned up and they longed for their elevenses: lemonade and a bun brought to them by Doris. They had returned reluctantly to work afterwards, driven by the thought that it would soon be dinnertime. At four o'clock the charabanc had returned to take them to their various homes, each clutching a pay packet. The bags of potatoes had been taken away by lorry. The rotten and green ones had been heaped at the side of the field to make pig swill.

'Yes, how did you know?'

'Donald told me. Your twenty-first, I believe. It is a special one, no?'

'Yes, key of the door and all that.' She laughed. 'I've had the key of the door for ages, the key to everything really. It's just another birthday.'

'But you are going to celebrate?'

'A small party at home, as it's a Saturday. I wish you could come.'

'And I should like to be there but you know it is not possible.'

'I know.' She sighed. 'I wish you were not a prisoner.'

'I wish it too.'

'Of course you do. You want to be free to go home to your family. And one day it will happen. When it does, I shall miss you.'

'And I you,' he said softly.

'When is your birthday, Karl? I don't even know how old you are.'

'I was twenty-six on the first day of May,' he said. 'I have been in the army for over six years.'

'Since before the war?'

'Yes, every German youth must serve his time and in 1938 it was my turn. Then the war came. We did not expect it to last so long.'

'Neither did we, but we have to carry on as best we can.'

'Yes.'

They heard the lorry arrive just as they finished milking. He washed his hands and delved into his coat pocket to offer her a small parcel. 'I made this for your birthday.'

'Oh, thank you. I never expected . . . May I open it?'

'Of course.'

She unwrapped an exquisite carving of a dog. It was only about six inches long made from a streaky kind of wood whose grain he had used to great effect. It was so detailed she felt she could almost stroke its fur. She did stroke it, overwhelmed by the care that had gone into the making of it. 'Oh, Karl, it's lovely. Thank you so much. It must have taken you ages to make.'

'It was my pleasure.'

They heard the horn again, more impatiently. 'You must go.'

He turned to leave. Impulsively she grabbed his arm and pulled him back to kiss his cheek. It was smooth and cold. 'Thank you again. It's lovely. I shall treasure it.'

She did not go with him to the transport, but stood looking down at the little dog in her hand, wondering what had been going on inside his head while he was carving it. Was he thinking of her or was he thinking of home and Heidi? Had she become a sort of substitute for Heidi? Did his fiancée like dogs? Did she know how clever he was with his hands? She shook herself, wrapped the dog back in its paper, put it in the pocket of her jacket and went into the house.

Instead of going into the kitchen she went up to her bedroom and put the carving beneath the underwear in her dressing table drawer. She had a feeling that her parents, and Bill particularly, would not approve of her accepting it. But she couldn't have refused it, could she? It would have hurt his feelings terribly after he had taken the trouble to make it.

Her mother was laying the table for the evening meal when she returned downstairs. 'I've made sausage rolls and sandwiches for later,' she said. 'I think there will be about fifteen of us.'

'You should have left it to me.'

'You wouldn't have had the time, love.'

'How did you get on today?' her father asked, wheeling himself up to the table. He always wanted to know exactly what she had been doing all day. It wasn't that he didn't trust her, but simply that he liked to think he was still in control.

'Very well. We finished harvesting the potatoes. There was a good crop.'

'Jerry worked, did he?'

'Pa, I've told you over and over, he works very hard and he knows what he's doing. I think we are lucky to have him. Some of the POWs are not keen to work and take as long as they can over a task. Karl's not like that.'

'No, I give you that, but he's a Jerry for all that. So watch it.'

'Pa, he's a just a man.'

'That's what I mean,' he said enigmatically.

'Call the boys, Jean,' Doris said quickly. 'They're supposed to be doing their homework, but somehow I doubt it.'

Always hungry, Donald and Terry did not need calling twice and they all sat down to eat round the kitchen table.

'Are we invited to your do tonight, Jean?' Donald asked, shovelling potato into his mouth.

'Of course you are, you live here, don't you?'

'I've got you a present,' Terry said.

'Oh, what is it?'

'It's . . .'

Don dug him in the ribs. 'You're not supposed to say until tonight. Jean hasn't opened any of her presents yet, have you, Jean?'

Her hesitation lasted only a second. 'I'm saving that pleasure for this evening. By the way, have you managed to collect a few decent records?'

'Mr Harris said he'll bring some.'

'Good. After tea, I want you to help me roll the carpet back in the sitting room.'

Jean, who seemed to spend most of her waking hours in dungarees or trousers, changed into a flowered frock and cardigan for the evening, brushed out her hair and made up her face. It was quite a transformation and for a fleeting moment she wondered what Karl would have thought if he could see her. She took the dog from her drawer and stroked it, then hastened to put it back and go downstairs. It was foolish of her to be so sentimental over it.

The guests began arriving at seven o'clock, led by her grandmother who gave her a tablecloth. It was made of crisp white linen and drawn-thread-work in the same colour. 'I've had it years and years,' she said. 'Now you have it. Put it in your bottom drawer.'

Jean didn't have a bottom drawer, but she thanked her and promised to take great care of it as an heirloom. Gran went to the kitchen to help Doris. Mr and Mrs Harris came with Lily who could not be left at home alone, so she was being allowed to stay up late for the occasion. She was clutching a small package which she put into Jean's hands. It contained two handkerchiefs. 'They cost one shilling and one coupon,' she announced.

Jean gave the child a hug. 'Thank you so much, just what I wanted.'

'Can I give you mine now?' Terry asked.

'Of course you can.'

An untidy parcel wrapped in brown paper and tied with string was thrust into her hands. She unwrapped it and stood turning it over wondering what it was meant to be. Like Karl's gift it was made from wood, but it wasn't carved or polished. Two pieces of wood had been nailed together, one of which had had a V shape cut out of it. 'It's to help you off with your rubber boots,' he said. 'You stand on that bit, put your heel into that bit it and pull. I made it in school.'

'Of course, I can see what it is now. That's going to be very useful. Thank you, Terry.' She went to kiss his cheek but he turned away in embarrassment.

Donald gave her a new bicycle pump because hers had been stolen a few weeks before and she was always borrowing his to pump up her tyres. As more people arrived, she was given more gifts: small handmade things, a needle case, a scarf, a book, even a box of chocolates. The latter were not on ration but very hard to come by and Rosemary must have scoured the shops for it.

She was beginning to wonder where Bill had got to, when he arrived dressed in a grey striped suit in honour of the occasion. 'Sorry I'm a bit late,' he said. 'Ma had one of her bad turns.'

'I'm sorry to hear that,' Jean said. 'I hope she's better now.'

'Yes. Forgive me?'

'Yes, of course.'

He delved into his pocket and produced a parcel. 'Happy birthday, sweetheart.'

It contained a small box. Inside was a silver brooch in the shape of a butterfly, its wings inset with tiny gems.

'It's lovely, Bill. Thank you so much.'

'Mum helped me choose it. Let me pin it on.' He fumbled with the clasp. 'She said to wish you a happy birthday. Here, you had better do it, my fingers are all thumbs.'

She took it and pinned it on the front of her dress. 'Thank you and thank your mother for me.'

'Twenty-one, hey? That's special.'

'So they tell me. I don't feel any different. It seems I've been all grown up for a long time now.'

'Yes, you've had a lot on your plate and you've coped well.'

'You have to, don't you, when things go wrong, I mean. Dad didn't ask to have a stroke and Gordon didn't ask to be shot down. It's the war.'

'Yes, but I reckon we're over the worst. Paris has been liberated and the Russians are at the gates of Warsaw, and what with all the bombing of German industrial cities, I don't see how Jerry can carry on much longer.'

'I'm glad you're so optimistic. But we endured a lot of bombing too: London, Coventry, Portsmouth, Norwich, and we didn't give in, did we? Churchill said "We will never surrender". I've no doubt Hitler is saying the same to his people.'

'My, you are down, aren't you? Come on, let's dance and forget the bloody war for an hour or two.'

She laughed. 'Language!'

'Sorry.'

The room was really too small to dance properly but they circled round almost on the spot with their arms round each other. 'You are looking very beautiful tonight,' he whispered in her ear. 'I want to make love to you.'

'William Howson!' she teased. 'That's a highly improper suggestion.'

'And you are a very proper miss, aren't you?'

'What's that supposed to mean?'

'Nothing. Just remember you are my girl. Don't go running off with anyone else.'

'Who, for instance?'

'I don't know, do I? The Jerry, perhaps.'

'Sergeant Muller? Good Lord, Bill, what's got into you? Where could we run off to, even supposing we wanted to? He's a prisoner of war and though he's not actually tied hand and foot, he can't go anywhere. And he has a fiancée in Germany. He talks about her a lot.'

'OK. 'Nough said.'

'Food on the table in the kitchen,' Doris called out, which was a signal for everyone to stop dancing and gossiping and make their way to the kitchen. Jean and Bill were separated by the crowd for which she was thankful. She was becoming increasingly tired of his obsession with Karl.

'Have you heard from Gordon?' Rosemary asked her.

'No, not recently. I think they are only allowed to write every so often. But last time we heard, he was well.'

'I do so miss him.'

'I'm sure you do. We all do.'

'Alan Hedges wants to take me to the pictures. What do you think? Would I be unfaithful if I went? It's ages since a fellow took me out, not since Gordon.' Alan, who had been turned down for the armed forces because of his asthma, worked for the same agricultural machinery business in Wisbech that she did.

'I'd say go, if you want to. As long as you make it clear where you stand, it can't do any harm, can it?'

The chatter was silenced when Doris clapped her hands. They all turned to look at her. 'Arthur wanted to say a few words,' she

74

said. 'But he has asked me to instead. We just want to say how proud we are of our daughter. Jean has made sacrifices to help us out and worked hard, harder than many men, I might say, and she has kept the old place going for us . . .'

'Mum, don't,' Jean said, thoroughly embarrassed.

'Why not? It needs to be said. We don't tell you enough how much we love and cherish you and we're saying it now. Both of us.' She turned and took Arthur's hand and smiled down at him. 'That's right, Arthur, isn't it?'

'Yes, o' course.'

'It's my home, too,' Jean said. 'And Don's and Gordon's. We all want to keep it going, and we will.'

'I wish you wouldn't keep interrupting,' her mother said. 'I've forgotten what I was going to say now.'

'Good,' Jean said, laughing.

'Then all I can say is happy birthday, love.' Doris stepped forward, gave her an envelope and hugged her, while everyone clapped and echoed her words. 'Open it later.'

Mr and Mrs Harris were the first to leave at nine o'clock, because Lily was so tired she was becoming irritable. Others began drifting away one by one until only Bill remained. 'Walk down to the gate with me,' he said.

It was a clear night. The moon was full and the sky was dotted with pinpoints of light. 'The bombers will be in the air tonight,' he said. 'Mum hates them. Their noise frightens her and she puts her head under the pillow and moans. I worry about her. She's never been the same since Dad died, and I can't seem to do a thing right.'

'I'm sorry,' she said softly.

'I'm sure she doesn't mean to be unkind. It's just her way. If it wasn't for her . . .'

'I know. Pa is sometimes difficult and it's all I can do to keep my temper, but I have to remember he can't help it, it's all because of his stroke. I stop and count to ten, or I walk away until I've calmed down.'

'You did like the brooch, didn't you?'

'Yes, it's lovely. I'll call tomorrow and thank your mother, shall I?'

'That would be great. I'll tell her to expect you for tea.'

They were passing the shed door. He pulled her inside and took her in his arms to kiss her. His hands began to stray where they shouldn't, grabbing her bottom and kneading her buttocks through her clothes. She stiffened, wondering what was coming next but when she made no protest, he reached down and lifted her skirt. She slapped his hand away. 'No, Bill.'

He let the skirt drop. 'You're a tease, do you know that?'

'No, I'm not. You are teasing yourself. You know it's neither the time nor the place . . .'

'Can't I hold you in my arms now? Can't I kiss you and tell you I love you? We are alone, for God's sake.'

'Of course you can, but I've been brought up to know right from wrong and you ought to respect that.'

'Twenty-one years old and still a virgin.'

'What's wrong with that?'

'Nothing, nothing at all. I suppose I'm glad of it, since you won't let me near you.'

'Oh, go home, Bill. You've had too much to drink.' She reached up and kissed his cheek, then added more softly. 'Goodnight, love.'

She watched him from the doorway of the shed as he walked down to the gate, then she walked slowly back to the house. Was she being unreasonable? Should she have allowed him a little licence? Why didn't she want to? Was it because the future was so uncertain, or was she not sure how she felt about him any more? Or was it something else entirely that she didn't want to face? She had almost reached the house when she heard the drone of heavy bombers and looked up to see a squadron of them passing over the house. They hadn't reached their full height and for a moment they blocked out the moon and cast a shadow over the ground. The noise set the chickens squawking.

Doris was gathering up glasses and plates when she went indoors. 'Everything all right?' she asked.

'Yes, why wouldn't it be?' She took the kettle off the range and filled a bowl in the sink to wash the glasses.

'No reason. Bill seemed a little put out. You haven't quarrelled, have you?'

'No, of course not. Why do you ask?'

'I thought you might be disappointed his present wasn't a ring.'

'No, of course I wasn't. He's worried about his mother.'

'She plays him up. It's time he cut the apron strings.'

'It's not as easy as that, Mum. He's got Bridge Farm to run.'

'It's plenty big enough for a family.'

'So it is, but Mrs Howson would still be the boss and I don't think I could cope with that, even if he asked me to, which he hasn't. Besides, I'm needed here.'

'Then you must both be patient.' She paused to look searchingly at her daughter. 'You do know what I mean?'

'Yes, Mum. I know what you mean.'

'Good. Now go up to bed. I'll finish off here. We'll tidy up the sitting room tomorrow.'

'I can't leave it all to you.'

'It won't take me long. You've got to be up early for the milking. It's a pity Sergeant Muller doesn't come earlier, you could have a lie-in.'

Jean laughed. 'So I could. Would you trust him with it?'

'Yes. He's a good man to have around. Now go on, upstairs with you. Have you opened the envelope I gave you?'

'You said open it later.' She dried her hands and took it from her pocket. 'I think it must be a cheque to buy myself a present.' She was right about it being a cheque, but as she slid it out of the envelope she gasped at the amount. 'A hundred pounds! Mum, you shouldn't have.'

'As I said. We love you and appreciate all you do, and the sacrifices you've made.'

'I haven't made any sacrifices, Mum. And I really don't need this.'

'Don't refuse it, love, it would upset your father. And me.'

'Oh, Mum.' She flung herself into her mother's arms. The tears were running down her face. 'I'm not going to refuse it. I'll put it into the bank until I really need something.'

Her mother kissed her cheek. 'Now, don't go all soppy on me, child, or you'll have me in tears too. Off to bed.'

Gathering up the scarf, the handkerchiefs and the box the brooch had come in, she took them up to her room. Putting the handkerchiefs in her drawer, she felt the little dog and took it out to sit on the bed with it in her hands. Of all her presents, this was the nicest. It had been made with such care, especially for her. Already weepy, she wept some more.

Bridge Farm was a large one, the largest in the village. It had several barns, an up-to-date milking shed and all the latest machinery and gadgets. The acreage was several times greater that Briar Rose, as was the dairy herd. The house, set well back from Bridge Lane, was a substantial brick and flint dwelling with a cellar and attic as well as two storeys of spacious rooms, including a vast kitchen.

Mrs Howson answered the door to Jean's knock. 'Come in, Jean. It's lovely to see you. I don't see nearly enough of you and I can't get about like I used to.' She led the way into a well-furnished sitting room as she spoke. It looked out on to a garden where an old man was working.

'I'm sorry, Mrs Howson, but there is always so much to do on the farm.'

'Don't I know it. William never seems to have a spare moment for me, even though we've got old John Taylor and several land girls to help him. They spend more time gossiping than working.' She indicated an armchair. 'Take off your jacket and sit down. Bill will be in with the tea things in a minute.'

'Shall I go and help him?'

'No, he'll manage fine. You stop and talk to me. Did you enjoy your party?'

'Yes, it was a lovely time and everyone was so kind.' She hung her jacket over the back of a chair and sat down. 'I want to thank you for the brooch, Mrs Howson. I expect I shall wear it a lot.'

'William tells me you have a German prisoner working for you.'

'Yes.'

'Aren't you afraid?'

'Good heavens, no. He is quite harmless and he works hard.'

'Who works hard?' Bill came in with a loaded tea tray and set it down on the table at his mother's elbow.

'The German,' his mother answered him, unloading the tray. 'You've brought the Madeira, I told you we'd have the Victoria sponge. I only made it this morning. And what have you put in the sandwiches?'

'Egg and cress.' He picked up the cake plate. 'I'll go and change this.'

'He never listens,' Mrs Howson said with a heavy sigh, as he disappeared again. 'I told him to make ham sandwiches. We smoked a whole hock last time we slaughtered a pig. Sometimes I wonder what he's thinking about when I speak to him.'

'I expect it's work,' Jean suggested.

'Perhaps.' She began pouring the tea from a china teapot into matching cups. 'There was a time, when my husband was alive, when we employed twenty men and now we have to do even more with one old man and a gang of land girls. Sugar?'

'No, thank you. I gave up having sugar in my tea when it was rationed. Now I prefer it that way.' She took the cup and saucer from Mrs Howson's outstretched hand and took a sip. 'Lovely.'

Bill returned with a fresh cake. 'Now you must have a slice of this,' Mrs Howson said cutting into it. 'I'm famous for my sponges and luckily we still have eggs. You can't make a sponge with reconstituted egg. I've tried and it won't rise.'

'No, Mum discovered that. It must be hard for people who don't keep chickens.' Even keeping chickens was fraught with rules and regulations and how many eggs they were allowed to keep back for personal use. They were often flouted.

The conversation was grinding to a halt and Jean did not know what else to say. 'Did you hear the bombers going over last night?' she asked.

'You couldn't fail to hear them,' the old lady said. 'I swear they'll bring the chimney pots down one of these days.' Bridge Farm had tall twisted chimneys on the oldest part of the house.

'I don't think they are as low as they look.'

'Perhaps not. More cake?'

'No, thank you, Mrs Howson. I'll have to go. I need to change before I start milking.'

'I'll walk you home,' Bill said.

Two of the Land Army girls were in the yard as they passed along the side of it to the lane. He stopped to speak to them. 'This is Sadie,' he told Jean, indicating a dark-haired girl in breeches and a khaki shirt. 'And this is Brenda.' Brenda was wearing dungarees and had her blonde hair tied up in a scarf. Jean nodded to them and murmured, 'How do you do?'

'Same to you,' Brenda said, eyeing Jean openly.

'It's nearly milking time,' Bill said. 'Fetch the herd in and make a start. I'll be with you as soon as I've taken Jean home.'

'Poor diddums,' Jean heard Sadie say. 'Not brave enough to take herself home.'

'Or maybe that's not what he has in mind,' Brenda suggested. 'I wouldn't mind some of that.'

Jean looked at Bill, but he gave no indication he had heard. 'Having tea with Ma wasn't so bad, was it?' he queried.

'Of course it wasn't bad, but, you know, you ought to stand up for yourself a little more.'

'It's not worth the aggravation. It only brings on one of her bad turns.'

Jean decided not to say what was in her mind. 'I must hurry. With no Karl on Sundays, I have to manage on my own.'

'Karl, is it? What happened to Sergeant Muller?'

'We can't be formal all the time when we have to work together.'

'It doesn't do to be too familiar either.'

'Oh, Bill, please don't start that again. You have absolutely no cause to be jealous of him.'

'Me, jealous? Don't be daft. Why should I be jealous of him? He's only a Jerry prisoner of war.'

'Isn't that what I've been saying?'

He did not stay when they arrived back at Briar Rose. They both had milking to be done.

Karl arrived the next morning as usual and they set to work cutting the grass in the orchard to make silage. It was not good enough for hay. Dobbin stood by harnessed to a cart to take it to the silage bin.

'Did you enjoy your party?' he asked her when they stopped for a break. She noticed he had a dark bruise on his temple.

'Yes. What happened to your face?'

'I walked into a door.'

'And did this door have two fists?'

'It is nothing. Do not think of it.'

'I bet it's because you come here.'

He jumped up and took her hand to pull her to her feet. 'Come on, we must go back to work if we are to finish by milking time.'

'You are looking tired,' he said, when they finished and returned to the yard.

'Late night on Saturday catching up with me. I'll be all right.'

'I wish I could do more. I would like to see the roses back in your cheeks and the sparkle in your eyes.'

'You can't do any more than you do, Karl,' she said, pretending not to notice the implied compliment. 'I work you hard while you are here. Come on, let's go and get those cows in. The transport will be here before we know it.'

Karl hated going back to the camp. It reminded him that he was a prisoner, something he was almost able to forget when working with Jean. Having to put his hands up, slouch along with all the others, suffer the indignities of being jeered at, poked with rifle barrels, watch his clothes become more and more shabby, beaten and unable to defend himself, all combined to make him feel less than a man.

When he woke each morning, he could not wait to climb in the lorry and be taken away to spend the day doing something he was good at in cheerful company. And when the time came for him to go back, he did so reluctantly and refused to join in the camp life. It was just somewhere to sleep. His compatriots knew that; it was why they baited him, why he had so many 'accidents'. If they were still talking about escape, he was unaware of it; they did not confide in him. They always stopped whatever they were saying when he entered the room. He suspected they thought he was a spy. There was nothing he could do about it except endure. Standing up to them and trying to put over his own point of view resulted in a fist in his face or a bad fall and so he kept his thoughts to himself. But there were odd occasions when he felt he had to speak up. The night before had been because they had made insulting suggestions about his *Fräulein*. It had been foolish of him to rise to the bait. Not for a minute would he have told her about it.

Chapter Five

In September, the steam-driven thresher arrived on the stubble field, along with its itinerant workers. The stack Karl had built in the corner of the field was dismantled and the sheaves taken to the machine which separated the grain from the stalks, flinging out the straw and sending a stream of grain down a chute into a sack. The machine was hot, noisy and smelly and the chaff floating about made everyone cough; they were soon all coated in a fine white dust that stuck to clothes, hair and perspiring skin. By the end of the day they had loaded a lorry with sacks of grain for the miller and there was a new straw stack in the field.

'A good day's work,' Jean told Karl, as they made their way back to the farmyard to do the milking. 'I shall be glad of a hot bath. I itch like mad.'

He laughed. 'So do I, and I'll have a fight to get near the showers.'

'Would you like a bath before you go back? There's plenty of hot water.'

'Oh, I didn't mean . . .'

'I know you didn't. Come on, let's hurry and get the cows in, then we can take it in turns.'

She bathed while he milked and when she came out to him she was wearing a check skirt and an attractive pink jumper. 'Your turn,' she said, tying on a sacking apron. 'I'll finish here.'

It occurred to him that it was the first time he had been upstairs in the house and it would be simplicity itself to search for money and clothes while everyone was busy elsewhere. He had been fighting off Otto's demands to furnish him with information, but how long it could go on before the man realised he was stalling he did not know. His other concern was about the way the war was going. His country was defending every inch of the way, but the Americans were now on German soil and, worse from his point of view, the Red Army had occupied Warsaw and would soon also be on the soil of the Fatherland. He knew he would know no peace until he found out what had happened to his parents. It was almost enough to make him decide to throw in his lot with Otto. Almost, but not quite. If it had been a simple matter of escaping and finding his way home, he might have done it, but it wasn't that simple. Nothing ever was. He had his bath and went downstairs again without venturing anywhere else.

'The Boy Scouts and Girl Guides will gather at the church hall on Saturday afternoon where they will be given baskets to gather rose hips,' the rector told the congregation the following Sunday. 'As you know they are a very important source of vitamin C and will be used to make syrup. Miss Watson will award a rosette to whoever gathers the most.' He looked round the congregation and smiled at Arthur before going on. 'The annual ploughing match will take place on Mr Coleman's ten-acre field on Saturday 21st October, starting at ten o'clock. Volunteers are needed to help mark out the course. Please speak to Mrs Coleman if you would like to do this. She would also like help with refreshments on the day. I know times are hard, but with a little ingenuity we should be able to come up with a few sandwiches and buns. Sir Edward will be on hand to announce the winner and the silver cup will be presented by her ladyship.' He paused to look round as if assessing who was present and who was absent. 'Our last hymn will be number 383: "We plough the fields, and scatter the good seed on the land".'

'Until the rector called for volunteers to help, I had almost forgotten about that ploughing match,' Doris said, as they began to walk home with Terry pushing Arthur. 'I was tempted to say I wouldn't do it this year, it takes so much more organising than it used to and with Pa as he is . . .'

'I'll give a hand marking out the field, Mrs Coleman,' Bill said.

'Thank you, Bill, that will be a great help. I've got some stakes left over from last year and some boards with numbers on. If you can be at the field first thing on the day, we'll soon have it done. I've no idea how many will be taking part. They might all be too busy.'

'I'll ask around,' he said. 'But I don't think the regulars will want to give up the chance to show off.'

Jean laughed. 'You included, I don't doubt.'

'Of course.'

'It won't be the same without Pa.'

Arthur was trying to say something and Jean bent over him. 'What did you say, Pa?'

'No Gordon neither.'

'No, that's true,' Jean said. 'But he'll be back one day to uphold the honour of the Colemans. In the meantime, if you want someone to represent us, I'll do it.'

Her father gave a bark of a laugh. 'You'll make a fool o' yourself.'

'I can plough as well as anyone. I've been doing it ever since Gordon went away, you know I have.'

'Like a dog's hind leg.'

'If you mean that bottom field, then I'll have you know I did that in the dark with only a lantern in the hedge to guide me.'

'I could ha' done better with me eyes shut.'

'Yes, Pa, but I'm not as clever as you.'

Bill touched Arthur's shoulder. 'Give Jean some credit, Mr Coleman. I reckon she'll do OK.'

'Just so long as I don't beat you, you mean,' Jean put in.

'You can always try,' he said, grinning. 'I must be off. Ma will wonder where I've got to.'

'We are going to start ploughing today,' Jean told Karl one day in October. 'I assume you can plough?'

'It is my favourite task. When the harvest is in and the fields are bare, it is soothing to walk behind the plough and think one's thoughts, knowing one is making ready for the year to come. The seasons follow one another, whatever we do. Life goes on.'

'Yes. I'm using the opportunity to practise for the ploughing match next Saturday. Do you have ploughing matches in Germany, Sergeant?'

'Tell me, what is that?'

'The idea is to find out who can plough the best furrow,' she said. 'Straight and deep, but not too deep, and no straw showing. Nice neat turns at each end of the field, too. There have been ploughing matches in the country for generations. Here, in Little Bushey, it has always been held on one of our fields.'

He smiled. 'That is one way to have your field ploughed for nothing. What does the winner receive?'

'A silver cup.' She paused. 'Pa has won it several times.'

The horses were harnessed and attached the plough and they set off up the lane with Laddie at their heels, passed the pit and turned through a gate into the field from which the potatoes had been harvested. Their tops lay on the surface. He bent to set the plough.

'If you guide the horses, I will manage the plough,' he said. 'We will have it done in no time.'

On the day of the ploughing match, Karl went with Jean to the top field in the farm pickup truck loaded with stakes and numbered boards. They were met by Bill who had brought a spade with him.

'Right,' Jean said. 'Let's get started. I've got ten contestants, six using tractors, three using horses and one a Trusty.'

'What is a Trusty?' Karl asked.

'It's a very small tractor,' she told him. 'It's not big enough to ride on, you walk behind and steer it. It's quite powerful and you have to be careful it doesn't run away with you. It's very handy for small out-of-the-way places where you can't get a full-size tractor in.'

'He'll be in a class of his own,' Bill said.

'No. I've spoken to the committee and he's going in with the walk behinds.'

'OK, let's get going then.' He turned to Karl. 'We divide the width of the field into ten and stake and number each section. In England we use yards, not metres.'

'I know that,' Karl said.

'Bring some stakes.' Bill picked up a bundle of stakes and set off across the stubble for the far side of the field, followed by Karl. By midday they had the sections staked out and the farm gate propped open to admit the contestants. They left the pickup and walked back to the farmhouse for something to eat.

As soon as they had finished, they took the horses to the field where the contestants were beginning to arrive. Terry and Don put Arthur into a warm coat, scarf and cap and wheeled him off to join them.

It seemed most of the village was there. The field was full of tractors, horses and ploughs. They stared at Karl for a moment and then ignored him. The boys arrived with Arthur in his wheelchair just as Joe Maynard, who was the chairman of the committee, used a loud hailer to start the proceedings with the tractor-drawn ploughs. He drew numbers out of a hat for the lanes. Bill drew lane 5 which was a good one; the land was fairly level and the ground drier than that on the lower side of the field, nearer the pit.

'Wish me luck,' he called to Jean as he climbed onto his tractor and set off for his starting position. The spectators spread themselves around the field, some at the start which was also the finish, some at the turn at the top of the field which was the trickiest bit. It wasn't a race but the time they took was taken into account.

Arthur asked the boys to take him closer, which they did, bumping him over the rough stubble. 'Have a care,' he cried. 'You'll have me out.'

'Allow me to help,' Karl said, taking the handles of the chair and wheeling him to where he could watch Bill turn at the head of the field. The boys followed.

'Not bad,' Arthur admitted grudgingly as Bill came towards them and turned to set off down the next row.

Karl rejoined Jean and helped her set the plough and harness it to the horses ready for her turn. She was nervous. 'I've drawn lane 3,' she told him. 'It's got that dip in the middle of it.'

'It is no worse than the strip you did with me the other day,' he said. 'You managed that very well. Think of it as a normal day's ploughing. You can do it.'

She picked up the reins to go to her allotted strip, ready for the start.

'Good luck,' he called out as she left him. Then he went to rejoin the watchers.

'Not bad,' Arthur admitted, as Jean came towards them, turned the horses and the plough neatly and set off on the next row. 'That dip in the land might throw her line off though.'

'I think she knows how to manage it,' Karl said. 'I was with her when we ploughed the other field and she knew exactly what to do.'

Jean's furrows looked good, even Arthur had to admit that, but there was some stiff competition. 'I'll leave the plough in the field tonight,' she said, when she returned to them, feeling rather pleased with herself. 'We'll finish off the odd bits on Monday. Let's take the horses back, Karl. Your transport will be here soon. Pa, do you want to come with us?'

'Might as well, I'm getting chilly.'

He was attempting to turn his chair round himself when the elderly John Barry lost control of his Trusty and it careered towards the little group. He tried to hang onto it, but it was too much for him and he let go. Everyone in its path scattered, all except Arthur whose chair was stuck in a rut. Karl grabbed the handles and tried to haul it out of the way. The next moment, Karl, Arthur and the chair were in a heap on the ground.

Bill, who was on his way to join them, managed to catch up with the Trusty and bring it to a stop. Having made sure it was safe, he went to see if he could help Arthur.

Everyone who was not actually ploughing crowded round them. Jean was fussing round her father. 'Pa, are you all right?'

'Get me back in my chair and I'll tell you.'

John Barry was hovering round them. 'I couldn't hold it,' he said, clearly upset. 'I reckon the mix was too strong.' The fuel they used was a mixture of petrol, diesel and kerosene called tractor vaporising oil. 'I thought Arthur were a goner.'

'I'll see he's OK,' Bill said. 'You go home. Have a nip of something, you'll feel better.'

The old man hobbled off, shaking his head.

Karl put his hands under Arthur's arms and hauled him upright. Jean righted the chair and positioned it under him and he was lowered into it. 'The wheel is buckled,' Karl said. He had a bruise on the side of his face which was swelling rapidly.

'How'm I going to get home then?' Arthur demanded.

'In the pickup,' Jean said. 'If I bring it up here, can you lift him into it, Karl?'

'Yes.'

'I'll get him into the pickup,' Bill said. 'No need to bother the sergeant.'

'Very well,' Karl said. 'I will take the horses back.'

'You needn't do that either. There are plenty of people here to help. Take yourself off.'

'He can't,' Jean said. 'He has to be supervised. I'm not allowed to let him go anywhere by himself. You take Pa home and, Don, you go and ask Doctor Norman to come and check Pa over. Karl and I will take the horses.'

Bill looked angrily at the German. 'He's more trouble than he's worth,' he said. 'I told you I'd give you a hand if you needed it.'

'You have enough to do as it is, Bill, and it is more than a hand I need.'

'Will someone get me home?' Arthur said.

Jean fetched the pickup as close as she could, Bill lifted the invalid out of his chair and carried him to the passenger seat. He put the chair into the back and set off to drive back to the farm.

The crowd dispersed, speculating aloud what had happened. 'I reckon the Jerry saved Mr Coleman's life,' one said.

'No, he didn't,' said another. 'It was him that turned the chair over. Tried to kill him, he did.'

'Why?'

'Why? 'Cos he's a Jerry, that's why. I don't know why the Colemans have him working for them. Italians I can just about stomach, but Germans . . . Pah!'

'I'm sorry,' Jean told him when she realised he had overheard. 'Not everyone is like that. I am grateful to you. You did save Pa's life.'

'That is all that matters,' he said. 'I would be unhappy if I thought you believed I would harm you or your father.'

'I don't. What did you think of our ploughing match?'

'It was . . .' He paused. 'Very interesting.'

'You think you could have done better?'

He shrugged. 'We shall never know, shall we?'

'I think you would make a worthy contestant.'

He laughed. 'Thank you. I shall remember that.'

'Now we must get these horses home or your transport will be here before you are ready. You ought to have something done about your face, too.'

He put his hand up to touch it and winced. 'It is not bad. Tomorrow it will be all gone.'

They heard the lorry's horn as they finished settling the horses. 'I do not have time to help with the milking,' he said.

'It doesn't matter.' Jean accompanied him to the gate

'What happened to him?' Donnington demanded when he saw Karl.

'It was an accident,' she told him. 'He saved my father's life.'

'Did he now? Well, that's a turn up for the book. He'll get a medal, no doubt.'

'There is no need to be sarcastic, Corporal,' she said.

'Sorry, miss.'

She turned to Karl. 'Your jaw will probably be stiff tomorrow. If you cannot come to work, I'll understand.'

'I will be here, Miss Coleman.' He scrambled into the back of the lorry followed by the corporal. She could hear his compatriots laughing at him as they drove away.

She was halfway up the drive when the doctor's car passed her. She had been on her way to fetch the cows, who were all gathered at the gate of the field waiting for her, but changed direction and went back to the house.

'No real harm done,' Doctor Norman was telling her mother. 'He'll probably be a bit stiff in the morning.'

'No change there, then,' Arthur said, attempting a joke. 'It's me chair what's broke.'

'I'll get it mended,' Jean said. 'Perhaps Bill will carry you to bed while he's here. I don't think I can manage it.'

'Course I will.' Bill bent and picked Arthur up from the kitchen chair where he had been put. 'Here we go then.'

The small parlour on the other side of the hall from the sitting room had been converted into a bedroom for Arthur. Bill put him on the bed and helped Doris to undress him and put him to bed while Jean went out to see to the milking.

'Are you going to stay for a bite to eat?' Doris asked Bill when they returned to the kitchen.

'No, thanks all the same,' he said. 'Ma will be expecting me.'

'I thought she would come over today. There's nothing wrong, I hope.'

'She is a martyr to her rheumatism, Mrs Coleman, but she is no worse than usual. All the same, I must get back to her.'

'Of course. We mustn't keep you. Thank you for your help.'

He waved a hand dismissively. 'It was nothing. I would do more if only Jean would let me.'

Doris laughed. 'She is too independent for her own good, that one. See you later.'

The village hall was crowded, not only with the inhabitants of Little Bushey but with contestants and their families who had come from further afield. Mr Harris was there with his records for those who wanted to dance. Doris hurried to help with the refreshments and Jean joined Bill. 'How did you get on with your ploughing today?' he asked her, as they danced a waltz. 'In all the bother with your pa's chair, I didn't have a chance to ask.'

'OK, I think.'

'How is he?'

'A bit stiff. Bemoaning the fact he can't get about without his chair. I'll take it in to Wisbech on Monday. The bicycle shop might have a wheel that will fit.'

'I'll take it in for you, if you like.'

'If you can spare the time, that would be a great help.'

'My pleasure. I'll call round first thing on Monday morning and pick it up.'

The dance came to an end and they wandered over to the refreshment table, where Doris was busy with Bill's mother and Mrs Harris serving the hungry dancers and making sure the food was distributed fairly. Jean and Bill were each given a sandwich and a sausage roll on a small plate and took it to a table to eat.

'Ladies and gentleman,' Mr Harris shouted from the stage where he stood by the side of Sir Edward and Lady Masterson. 'We'll take advantage of the break in the music to announce the prize-winners.' This statement was greeted with applause and cheers. When it died down he added, 'I'd like you all to give a big welcome to Sir Edward and his Lady.'

After the applause died down, Sir Edward made a short speech welcoming everyone and the prize-giving began. Jean was startled to learn she had come second, being pipped at the post by Mr Maynard. Poor Mr Barry came nowhere and was not present. The tractor-drawn ploughs came next and, as expected, Bill won that class. He was also the overall winner. Proud of himself, he returned to Jean clutching a large silver cup and a small wooden shield which he put on the table beside Jean's small cup. 'Well done,' she said. 'But I don't reckon you'd have won if Pa had been competing.'

'Oh, you think so, do you? Perhaps next year he'll be back and we'll see, won't we.'

'Amen to that.'

'Anyway, well done you.'

She laughed. 'You didn't think I could do it, did you?'

'Course I did. I have the utmost confidence in you. Your mother told me she thought you were too independent for your own good.'

'What's that supposed to mean?'

'Too proud to accept help when it's offered.'

'Bill, I've told you, you've got enough on your plate with your own farm and looking after your mother. And I *have* accepted your offer to take Pa's chair in for repair.' She stood up. 'I'm going to help with the food and give Mum a break.'

He watched her go, angry with her for what he considered her pride, angry with himself for reacting. Rosemary was sitting with her mother and looking bored. He went to ask her to dance.

'Congratulations on your win,' she said, as they took to the floor.

'Thank you.'

'If Gordon had been here, he'd have beaten you.'

He laughed. 'Not you as well. Jean is convinced her father would have beaten me if he was able.'

'How is Mr Coleman?'

'You were on the field?'

'I came up after work. You'd almost finished by then, but I saw the tractor go off on its own. You did well to stop it.'

'Yes, it was a close shave, but Arthur's OK. It's his chair that's damaged.'

'Who was the man with Jean? I haven't seen him before.'

'He's a German POW sent to help her on the farm.'

'Oh, one of those. I hate the Germans.'

'You and me both. I hope he comes to a sticky end.'

'I hope they all do and then the war will be over and Gordon and Reg can come home.' Reg was her brother, serving abroad somewhere.

'Amen to that.'

'Rosie is missing Gordon,' Jean told her mother, as they walked home.

'I know, so am I. I keep wondering what he's doing, whether he's keeping well and if he is working on a farm like Sergeant Muller is for us.'

'I doubt it, Mum. I don't think officers have to work.'

Gordon sat close to the window of the barrack hut. He had a book in his hands but he was not reading; he was watching someone who was smoking a cigarette, leaning idly on the corner of another hut across the compound. In the middle of the hut behind him, the stove had been removed from its base and three men were grouped around a hole in the floor. Beneath them, twenty feet below ground, a man was tunnelling using nothing more than a home-made trowel, pushing the spoil out behind him to be bagged up and disposed of. It was these full bags they were hauling up from the depths.

'Goon on the prowl,' Gordon said, as the man with the cigarette dropped it and ground it out beneath his foot. Goon was the airmen's name for the German guards.

In seconds, the incriminating bags were dropped back down the hole, the lid was put over the shaft, the stove replaced and the floor swept clean. That done, the men arranged themselves round the table and pretended to be engrossed in a game of whist.

The guard passed by without coming to their hut. 'All clear,' Gordon said, while opening the window and leaning out to throw out a dog-end, a pre-arranged signal to two prisoners apparently deep in conversation with another walking between the huts. They began using their arms to illustrate what they were saying, which was another signal to someone out of Gordon's sight. Behind him, the tunnel was reopened. The man who had been incarcerated down there climbed to the surface, covered in dirt and sweat, and another took his place. The prisoners were digging three tunnels from different huts, not only because if one was discovered they could carry on with the others, but because of the risk of roof falls which might mean it was too dangerous to continue.

The whole project was being organised by the escape committee with military precision. Everyone had his allotted task, from the surveyors, engineers, diggers, tailors making civilian clothes, map-makers and forgers producing essential documents, down to the men disposing of the soil from bags down their trouser legs and lookouts like Gordon. Others tracked every goon and logged his movements the whole time he was in the compound. There was still some way to go before the tunnel reached the trees, fifty or so yards outside the perimeter fence, but already the members of the escape committee were deciding who should make use of it and the order of priority.

Gordon knew he would never escape, not down that tunnel, but he was required to make himself useful to those who could. It made him frustrated and irritable. It wasn't that he begrudged the men who worked so hard and in constant danger to make it possible, but because he was so helpless. He would never be given a place in the tunnel, even supposing he could get down there.

He could see Flying Officer Jeremy Brewster coming across the compound towards the hut. Jeremy's job was to make bags with drawstrings to dispose of the soil. He was always looking for material with which to make them and many a shirt had been sacrificed, as had bed boards for shoring. 'Jeremy's on his way,' he reported.

Jeremy came into the hut and produced two or three bags from inside his greatcoat and handed them over to the men at the top of the shaft. 'Is that all you've got?' Squadron Leader Alexander Jordan tossed them down to the airman waiting below. 'Some of those we're using are all but worn out. If they split and spill the stuff out in a heap, we'll be in real trouble.' The soil they were excavating was a distinct sandy yellow and would easily be spotted if scattered on the compound in any quantity.

'Sorry, I'll try and get more.' Jeremy spotted Gordon sitting by the window. 'I'll have your trouser leg, Coleman.'

'No, you don't.'

'You don't need it, do you? It just flaps about, getting in the way.'

'When I get a new leg, I'll need both trouser legs. And when I do, you won't see me for dust.'

'Oh, come on,' Alex put in. 'You've been waiting for a new leg for three years to my certain knowledge. You don't still think Jerry is going to bother finding one for you, do you? I bet they are in short supply and they've got their own men waiting for them.'

'All the same . . .' Gordon's protest faded. Alex had only put into words what he had known to be true and had been trying hard to ignore. He was not going to be fitted with a coveted new limb, not from his captors, and he was destined to stay in this *Stalag* until the war ended, one way or another; that's if he didn't die of boredom and frustration first.

'It's all for a good cause,' Alex went on. 'Your bit for the war effort.'

'I've done my bit for the war effort.'

'So you have, old chap, no one's denying it, but we really do need more sandbags. Tell you what, when your new leg comes, I'll personally see you get a new pair of trousers. How's that?'

He sighed and gave in. A pair of scissors was fetched and he lost the bottom half of one leg from a decent pair of slacks. They took it from just below the knee so that his stump was not on view. He would have to spend the evening hemming the roughly cut material so that it didn't fray. He held out no more hope of a new pair of trousers than he did of a new leg.

Often, as he sat by the window doing his stint as lookout, he wondered what was going on in Little Bushey. What was Rosemary doing? Was she sitting at home waiting for him or finding someone else? He had had a letter from her, so heavily censored he could hardly make head or tail of it, but she had said she missed him and couldn't wait for him to come home again, which could mean she was waiting impatiently for them to be reunited but could equally mean exactly what it said: she could not wait. It did not make him feel any better about his incarceration.

How was Pa coping? Jean and Don would have to help him. Had they had any air raids? There were a lot of airfields near Little

Bushey and they were prime targets. There were a few illicit wireless sets hidden in the camp which enabled some of the prisoners to listen to the BBC at risk of their lives. They made sure the rest of the camp was kept informed, but the broadcasts never gave much away about specific locations.

He had had a few censored letters from his mother, but she couldn't tell him anything except they were all well and Jean had given up her job to help on the land. He had received a Christmas parcel from his mother months after the event which had been opened and searched by his captors and anything they coveted confiscated. He wrote to thank her and said he had had a good Christmas, all things considered. He had written not a word about losing his leg. He had been hoping to have a tin leg long before now and would be so used to it by the time he returned home it would not even be noticed until he chose to reveal it. He imagined making a joke about it. It was no joke.

He didn't remember much about being shot down, but he did remember seeing the long queues waiting on the beaches at Dunkirk to be taken off by a fleet of little ships and the Stukas bombing them. He had joined in the fight, ferociously angry that the helpless men were being subjected to such horror. He had been watching his petrol gauge and, knowing he could not stay in the air much longer, had gone for a German bomber with his guns blazing. He recalled being hit and the sheer terror of knowing he was going to crash. After that he remembered nothing until he came round in a French hospital taken over by the German army.

It was a miracle he had survived, he was told through an interpreter. He had somehow managed to belly flop his Spitfire in a field before he passed out. 'You were trapped by your left leg,' the doctor told him when a nurse alerted him that their patient was awake. 'It was badly mangled. We had to cut you out of the wreckage. I am afraid we could not save your leg.'

It had taken some seconds for the news to penetrate his befuddled brain. He had simply stared at the doctor, unable or unwilling to comprehend his words. 'The good news is that you still have your knee,' the doctor went on. 'We will try and obtain a false limb for you, but in the meantime you must try and move about on crutches.'

He had been cast so low by this he was unaware of anything going on around him. What sort of future could he expect? He was a strong, active man, he told himself, a farmer, meant to take over from his father when he retired, someone who needed to walk, drive a tractor, follow the plough, to dance with Rosemary. Would she want a man with only one leg? It would have been better if he had died. The doctor and nurses did all they could for him; he had no complaints about his treatment. They could afford to be magnanimous, the war was going their way; Hitler's forces seemed unstoppable. *He* could do nothing to stop them. He had lain in his bed and wallowed in misery and pain. He would never have believed how much pain a missing limb could produce.

'We will have you out of bed today,' the doctor had said one morning a week later. 'You must exercise your good leg and keep that strong. A physiotherapist will bring you some crutches and help you to use them.'

'Then what?'

'You will be sent to a *Durchganglager*. That is a transit camp for prisoners of war. They will decide where you go from there.'

'When?'

'As soon as you are fit to travel. We have many casualties of our own to treat and there is little more we can do for you here.'

He was only given a few days to get used to his crutches. It was not difficult to manage them but they made his arms and shoulders ache. Everything ached: his stump, his good leg and his spine, even the missing limb.

When they deemed he could manage, he was taken by lorry to a *Dulag* near Frankfurt where he found hundreds of other British prisoners, some wounded, but most hale if not hearty. At least he was able to join in the conversation, which he had not been able to do in the hospital, and here he learnt that the expected invasion of Britain had not materialised, but the airfields were being bombed and the air force was taking a pasting but fighting back. 'They won't defeat us while we've got an air force,' someone said.

'They won't defeat us, full stop,' said another.

Gordon did not know whether to be heartened by this or miserable that he was no longer a part of it. He had heard about Douglas Bader who was still flying and fighting in spite of having lost both his legs. Leglessness was not a barrier. The biggest obstacle was the fact that he was a prisoner of war and, as yet, had no artificial limb.

His turn had come to be interrogated. He knew that he was not required to give more than his name, rank and serial number and he stuck to that, though he was asked a whole stream of other questions, much of it about morale at home. He had no idea what morale was like at home; if it was anything like his own, it was pretty low, but he simply repeated the mantra of name, rank and number, and they sent him back to his comrades.

Prisoners came and went all the time, some came by train, others after days of marching, and some had come on barges up the river. Someone said the barges had been intended for the invasion of England but were no longer needed for that. Whether that was true or not he had no way of knowing. Unable to walk very far, he was sent on a train to a more permanent camp, although he had to hobble under guard from the station while others marched. It was somewhere in Poland, he was not sure exactly where, but it had a superb hospital run by the prisoners themselves. Here he was given more treatment for an infected stump and then more physiotherapy, but no new leg. He was there when news filtered through that the Americans had entered the war. The secret wireless sets kept the prisoners informed and this good news was soon followed by bad: Singapore had fallen to the Japanese.

Soon after that he had been sent to another camp. Prisoner-of-war camps were springing up all over Germany and Poland, now firmly under German occupation, and he must have been in a good number of them. It seemed they did not know quite what to do with him and others like him who had lost a limb but were otherwise strong and healthy and no longer needed to be in hospital. At every one he enquired about the artificial leg they had promised him but at all of them he had been fobbed off.

He had arrived at this *Stalag* early in 1943. It was a well-run camp, enclosed as they all were by barbed wire with lookout towers at intervals round the perimeter manned by armed guards. They also operated the searchlights which swept the camp after dark. There was a single strand of wire a few feet from the outer fence over which the prisoners were forbidden, on pain of death, to step.

They lived in huts with bunks two tiers high. Food was scarce and very poor quality, but it was supplemented by Red Cross parcels which were shared out between everyone. They contained canned meat, powdered milk, margarine, perhaps some cheese or coffee, and best of all cigarettes and chocolate. The cigarettes were the accepted camp currency and could be used to barter for anything they needed. A great many had gone towards obtaining documents from the goons to be copied for the escapees.

The men were left to make their own entertainment and ways

of keeping fit, which they did enthusiastically. Gordon, hobbling about on his crutches could not take part in these activities and that added to his frustration.

'If I had a suitable piece of wood and some webbing I could make you a leg,' Flying Officer Stanislaw Fallowski said to him one day when one of his crutches broke and he fell down in the compound coming back from his ablutions. He was trying to get up using the remaining crutch and Stan had run over to help him.

'Could you?'

'Don't see why not. I'm good at whittling. I was a carpenter before the war.'

'I'd be eternally grateful, if you could, but it would have to fit my stump.' Using one crutch was more difficult than two, he decided as he hopped his way slowly back to his hut.

'Of course. I'll ask the commandant if he will authorise some materials and tools for me.'

The result was that Stan was given permission to construct a leg and provided with a block of wood and some hand tools which he was required to return when the job was finished. It was a slow process because the tools were not as sharp as they could have been. Another impediment to its progress was that the tools were often borrowed by other prisoners for jobs they were doing which happened more and more often as the tunnel project progressed. Stan himself was also kept busy because every yard of the tunnel had to be shored up with wooden props made from bed boards and he was one of the carpenters making them. Many a prisoner had fallen through his bed when he had been left with only a couple of boards. Some of them had resorted to making hammock-like contraptions to sleep on.

'It won't be as light as a tin leg,' Stan warned him one day when Gordon sat watching him at work.

'Never mind. I can't have everything.' He was beginning to suspect the job was being deliberately stretched out in order to keep the tools on site for as long as possible.

'And I can't make a foot. I tried, but it just wouldn't work. It'll have to be a peg leg, I'm afraid.'

This was disappointing, but if it enabled him to walk about that, at least, would be an improvement. 'As for moulding the top for the stump that will have to be trial and error, a bit at a time. We'll have to make a harness and adjust it to fit, but that will be relatively simple, once I get my hands on some webbing.'

It was agony on his stump as Stan shaved off a little bit here and a little bit there trying to make the peg leg fit, and when it was deemed he could not improve it any more, it was lined with a pad of cotton and the harness made and fitted.

He soon discovered it was not as easy to get about as he had hoped and sometimes his stump was rubbed raw and he had to leave the leg off to let it heal and go back to the crutch. What drove him on to persevere was the thought that one day, please God, he would return home and if he hadn't been given a proper tin leg by that time, the RAF would make sure he had one and he would be able to adjust to it without the torture he was experiencing now because his stump would already be hardened. Others might laughingly call him 'Peggy' and he might grin ruefully in return, but he had not laughed properly for a long time.

He was at his usual station by the window one day when they noticed unusual activity between the perimeter fence and the trees. Everyone stopped what they were doing and gathered near the fence to see what was going on. 'Do you reckon they've found the tunnel?' he queried.

'Don't think so,' Alex said, as workmen began chopping down the trees.

'There goes our bloody cover,' Jeremy put in furiously. The tunnel was intended to come up in the shelter of the trees. 'What'll we do now?'

While they were talking loads of building materials were brought in and a new perimeter fence put up. It was becoming obvious that their captors were extending the camp and where the tunnel should have ended, would be the middle of a new compound. Alex hurried away to consult the rest of the escape committee.

Even though he would not have been one of those to use the tunnel, Gordon had a proprietorial interest in it. The decision to discontinue it was a bitter blow after all the hard work that had gone into it.

'We are obviously going to concentrate on the other two,' Alex told everyone in the hut that night. 'All is not lost. The goons haven't found it so we can still put it to good use as a storeroom for our escape stuff and a place to dump unwanted soil. It means people will still be coming and going into this hut, so, Peggy, we'll need you as much as ever.'

'It's nice to be wanted,' Gordon said wryly.

They were all in bed when the siren went. 'Not another bloody air raid,' someone said in the darkness.

'Leave off grumbling,' came from somewhere on the other side of the hut. 'They are doing their bit to shorten this war. I don't care if they flatten the place. Wouldn't that be jolly? We could all run out and cause mayhem while Jerry tries to round us all up again.'

Gordon, listening to their banter and their fantasies about escaping, groaned inwardly. If only he had two good legs . . .

Chapter Six

Jean was in the sheep enclosure, clipping the wool away from round the ewe's tails ready for tupping, when Karl found her the next morning. 'How is your father?' he asked.

'A few bruises but otherwise none the worse, thank goodness. What about you?' The huge bruise on the side of his face had turned a nasty shade of purple.

'It's nothing.' He worked his jaw to prove it. 'It will be gone in a day or two. The worst of it was the teasing I had to endure from my compatriots.'

'I suppose they thought you'd been in a fight.'

'Yes. Some thought I had been hit trying to escape.'

'We, in the village, have been assured that's not possible.'

He didn't reply to that. Instead he asked, 'Did you win?'

'No, second in my class.'

'I thought you ought to win.'

'That's kind of you but I am content with second. If I'd won, it would have looked like favouritism. Bill won his class and was the overall winner.'

'Good for him.'

'Can you go back to the farm and fetch the raddle for the rams? It's on the shelf in the shed. I forgot it.'

'Raddle?'

'Red dye.' The rams' bellies were painted so that a splash of colour was left on the ewe after he had serviced her. It was a way of keeping track of pregnancies.

'Oh, I see. Do you want me to apply it?'

'Yes, please.'

He was on his way back with the tin of dye, when he saw Otto, walking down the lane towards him. 'Where are you off to?'

'Home. Arnsberg.'

'Arnsberg! You mean the *Lagerführer* has given permission?'

'No, but I'm not waiting for it. Schultz can go to hell for all I care. It's our duty to escape and he has no right to try and stop us.'

'You didn't say anything before we left this morning.'

'I didn't have a chance. Roll call took so long, your transport came before I could catch you. I reckon something's up.'

'Otto, I'm not coming today. I'm not prepared.'

'I cannot believe you said that, Karl Muller. What's the matter with you? Don't you want to go home?'

'Of course I do. When I'm ready.'

'I think perhaps you will never be ready. I'll go without you.'

Karl shrugged. 'If you must.'

'I must, but I need clothes, money and food.'

'I'm sorry. I can't help you, not today.'

'You are a coward, you know that, don't you? A coward and a traitor and I hope you get what you deserve.' He strode off down the lane, calling over his shoulder. 'And if you raise the alarm, I shall make sure everyone knows who it was that betrayed me.'

Karl had no intention of raising the alarm. Unless the English were incredibly stupid he didn't think Otto would get very far before he was caught. But it left him wondering about his own motives. He could have abandoned the raddle and the sheep and gone with Otto if he had been determined enough. He could have stolen coats and money; even if he were recaptured, he would never be sent back to Briar Rose Farm to face Jean over it. But he could not help picturing her sorrow and disappointment when she realised what he had done. She, who had been kind and generous to him, did not deserve that. Did that make him a traitor?

Otto was furious. He had counted on Karl coming with him and the idiot had let him down, and all because of a handful of sheep, not to mention a woman, and an enemy one at that. Now what was he to do? He had run off from the work the builder had given him and could not go back. In any case, he had no intention of going back. It was notoriously difficult, if not impossible, to get off the island, but he had been sure that with Karl, whose English was almost faultless, they could have done it. He had been relying on his friend to steal clothes, and money too, and now he had to find another way of equipping himself.

He strode off down the lane, kicking at loose stones and muttering curses. Could he break into the farm and steal the things for himself? Karl would be blamed and it would serve him right. Was the house ever left empty? He stopped suddenly. He was outside the old lady's cottage, the one whose window he had repaired. He turned and went up the path to knock on the door.

'Oh, it's you,' she said. 'Why are you back? Where is Mr Gould?'

He pushed past her into the house, ignoring her protests. He had seen a shotgun propped in a corner of the hall when he had been there before. He went straight for it and pointed it at her. 'Clothes,' he said. 'Food.'

'It isn't loaded.' She indicated the gun. 'It's empty.'

He fired at the ceiling but there was nothing but a click. He laughed and turned it round in his hands so that he was holding the barrel and could use the butt as a weapon. 'Food. Clothes,' he repeated.

'I haven't got any.'

He was becoming impatient. He grabbed her by the arm and propelled her ahead of him up the narrow stairs to the bedroom. Here he flung her on the bed. '*Halten Sie still sonst . . .*' He lifted the gun in a threat. Ignoring her cries, he went to the wardrobe and began pulling out clothes flinging them on the floor. They were all female garments, for a small woman at that. He should have known. He turned back to her. 'Clothes for man.'

'I have no man.' She was sitting up on the bed rubbing her arm. 'I am a widow.'

He pulled her roughly to her feet and dragged her downstairs again. There was a big overcoat hanging on a peg in the hall. He put the gun down and shrugged himself into it. She pushed past him and made a dart for the door. He grabbed her back. 'Food. Money.' Picking up the gun again he forced her into the kitchen where he raided her larder for anything edible he could carry away which he put into a canvas bag he found on a hook. She was obviously not going to help him, so he began systematically emptying cupboards and drawers looking for cash.

'If you are looking for money you will be unlucky,' she said.

He marvelled at the old girl's courage, while wishing she would be more cooperative. If she had given him what he wanted, he could have been well on his way by now. There was nothing for it, he would have to rough her up a bit. He grabbed hold of both her arms and shook her violently. '*Geld! Geld!*' he shouted. Still holding her with one hand, he slapped her face hard and watched in satisfaction as tears filled her eyes. 'Money. Where is money?'

'I haven't got any. I'm only a poor widow.'

It was then they heard the dog barking and the door opened. Donald, Terry and Lily, accompanied by Laddie, tumbled into the cottage. 'Gran, we came to . . .' Don stopped suddenly when he saw the man holding his grandmother in front of him, waving his grandfather's old shotgun at them. He was wearing Grandad's old coat which was unfastened and revealed the German prisoner's uniform.

All three children stood and gaped, frozen by fear. But the dog had no such inhibitions, he began to bark and kept on barking. '*Halt deine klapper,*' Otto yelled lifting the gun and bringing it down on the dog's nose. Laddie yelped but instead of cowering, he bounded at the German who overbalanced and fell on top of the old lady. Don grabbed the gun and brought it down on the German's head as hard as he could. It knocked the man out and Elizabeth was able to scramble out from under him.

'I've killed him,' Don said in awe, dropping the gun.

'Don't matter if you have,' Terry said. 'He's only a German.'

Elizabeth sat on the sofa and pulled the tearful Lily onto her lap. 'Sh, sh, it's all right, Lily. Don't be afraid.' To Don, she said, 'You haven't killed him, he's just knocked out, but we had better tie him up before he comes round. There's some rope hanging on a hook in the shed. Terry, run and fetch it quickly.'

Terry sped off, leaving Elizabeth and Don to watch the German for signs of returning consciousness. She knew that if he came round before the boy returned she would have to hit him again. She picked up the discarded gun. The man was just beginning to stir and groan when Terry returned and the boys set about trussing him up. He was fully conscious by the time they finished. He began swearing and shouting in German. Laddie, who hadn't forgotten the biff on his nose, circled menacingly round him as he lay on the floor.

'Now what?' Donald queried.

Elizabeth, ignoring a pain in her shoulder and the bruises coming up on her cheek and upper arms, smiled. 'Good boys. I don't know what I would have done if you hadn't come along, but it's not finished yet. Terry, you run and find Jean. Tell her to bring the pickup. Take Lily with you. Don and I will watch over him while you're gone, but be quick.'

Taking Lily's hand, Terry sped away, leaving Elizabeth and Don staring down at the writhing German. Now the danger had passed, she was feeling decidedly shaky and collapsed into a chair.

'Gran, are you OK?' Don asked, looking at her bruised face.

'Yes, I'll be all right, just a bit shaken up. Make me a cup of tea, will you, son? I'll keep my eye on this fellow here.'

It was some moments before Jean could make head or tail of what the breathless Terry was saying. Lily had run sobbing into Doris's arms as soon as they came in the door and was incoherent. 'A German prisoner of war, you say?' Jean queried.

'Yes. Come quickly before he escapes. Mrs Sanderson said to bring the truck.'

She ran to the open-fronted outhouse that did duty as a garage, just as Karl came out of the shed where he had been putting away the clippers and tin of dye. 'Stay here,' she told him. 'Don't leave the farm whatever you do.'

'Why? What has happened?'

'Can't stop to explain. Go and ask my mother.' With that she climbed into the truck and was off.

The sight of her grandmother drinking tea with a shotgun in her lap and a huge bruise on her face and the man trussed up like a turkey for the oven would have been laughable if it hadn't been so serious. 'Gran, are you all right?' She fell to her knees beside her chair and gently removed the gun. 'What happened?'

'He pushed his way in here demanding food, clothes and money. It's the one who did my window. I didn't like him at the time, for all the excuses Sergeant Muller made for him.'

'Then what?'

Shaky as she was, Elizabeth managed to recount what had happened. 'If it hadn't been for the children, he might have killed me. And just look at the mess.' She gazed round at the contents of drawers and cupboards strewn over the floor. 'He was looking for money. It's the same upstairs.'

'Gran was ever so brave,' Donald put in. 'He hurt her. It made me angry. I hit him as hard as I could when Laddie went for him. I thought I'd killed him.'

'He'll have a headache, I'll be bound,' her grandmother said.

'Serves him right,' Don added.

'I'll have to take him to the police station in the truck,' Jean said. 'I can't carry him. I'm going to have to loosen the bonds on his legs so he can walk.' She handed the gun to Don. 'Watch him while I do it.'

'It's not loaded,' her grandmother said.

'Thank goodness for that.' She began undoing the rope that tied Otto's legs together, while Don stood with the gun poised. 'Get up,' she told the prisoner when she had finished, leaving his hands securely tied behind him.

He did as he was told but not without a string of invective. She took the gun from Don and urged him outside to the truck. 'Don, help Gran to tidy up. I'll be back as soon as I've handed him over to Constable Worth.'

'What if he turns nasty?' Elizabeth said. 'He could have you both in the ditch. Put him in the back and let Don keep an eye on him.'

'I can't leave you here alone. There might be others . . .'

'Then I'll come too. I can tidy up here later. I'm not letting you take that . . . that monster on your own.'

'All right, we'll all go. Make sure the house is locked.'

Elizabeth laughed. 'Locks won't keep out a determined man, if there are more of them roaming the countryside.'

'No, but we'll have to risk it. Come on, I shan't feel easy until he's safely behind bars.'

Otto was made to get in the back of the truck and Don climbed in after him, carrying the gun which was useless except as a club. With Gran in the passenger seat and Jean driving they set off for the village and the police station, which was only a room in the police house where Constable Worth lived.

He did not have anything secure enough to hold a man intent on escape. 'We'd best take him straight back to the camp and let Colonel Williamson deal with him,' he said, looking over the side of the truck at the furious German. 'That's what you get for being friendly with a mad dog. It always turns on you in the end.'

'This man is not the one we have working on our farm,' Jean told him. 'He's at work. My mother is keeping an eye on him, but he's no trouble at all.'

'Well, I hope you're right. Shouldn't be surprised if they don't all get punished for this.'

'That wouldn't be fair. And I need Sergeant Muller.'

'Well, you'll have to talk to Colonel Williamson about it. It's out of my hands.'

He climbed in the back with the German and Jean drove to the camp, where Otto was marched away and she, her grandmother and the constable were shown into the Colonel's office to report on what had happened. Several of the prisoners came up to the wire and stared at Don. Some spat at him, others swore, more just stared with blank expressions.

He was decidedly relieved when Jean and his grandmother returned. 'It was creepy sitting there with all those men watching and shouting at me,' he said. 'Let's go home.'

All three squeezed in the front. 'What's going to happen to him?' he asked.

'He'll be punished,' Jean said. 'Colonel Williamson told me he would be put in what they call "the cooler" on short rations and all privileges withdrawn. They are going to have an extra roll call and a search of the huts to see if anyone else is planning an escape and for any incriminating evidence.'

'Was that why they were so angry?'

'Perhaps. I don't know.'

'What about Sergeant Muller?'

'What about him?'

'Will he be punished, too?'

'I don't know, Don. I'd like to think he didn't know anything about it.'

'What if, when we get home, we discover Sergeant Muller has gone?'

'Then I should have to report it to Colonel Williamson, shouldn't I?' Jean spoke flatly, without emotion, but that wasn't how she felt inside. Her stomach was churning. She had begun to think of Karl as a friend, a helpmate, someone she could trust, but now she was beginning to wonder if her trust had been misplaced. And the feeling was one of enormous disappointment and loss.

'I just hope he hasn't hurt your mum,' Elizabeth said, feeling her bruised cheek.

'I can't believe he would do that. He has never shown the least tendency to violence.'

'Perhaps you should dispense with his services, just to be on the safe side.'

'But I need him.' It was the second time that day she had said that and it set her wondering if it was only help on the farm she needed. The kind of self-questioning led her nowhere and she stopped it at once.

Karl was mucking out when she drove into the yard. Her relief was almost tangible. While Don and her grandmother made their way into the house, she went over to speak to him. And then she didn't know what to say. Her head was full of questions and none of them related to the work on the farm. Had he known what his friend was going to do? Had he intended to go to? Would he have used violence as the other man had done? Could she trust him? Instead, she said, 'You know what happened? Did my mother tell you?'

'Yes. I am sorry, Jean. How is Mrs Sanderson? Terry said he had hit her.'

'He knocked her about a bit but she'll survive. At the moment, she is angry that he made a mess of her house.'

'I am sorry. I would never . . .' He paused, searching her face. 'I would never have condoned that. Please tell Mrs Sanderson I am very sorry. I like the old lady. I like you all. Please believe me.'

'But you knew about it?'

'I knew he was planning to escape, I even thought I might go too, but in the end I could not do it.'

'Why not?'

'I don't know. Perhaps because we would not have gone far before we were caught and I did not like the idea of a spell in the cooler. Perhaps because I like working here . . .' He paused, unwilling to expand on that. 'What happened to Otto?'

'That's his name, is it? I took him to the police station and then back to the camp and left Colonel Williamson dealing with him.'

'There will be repercussions,' he said.

'I imagine so. I'm going indoors to speak to my mother. I'll leave you to get on.'

'Very well. I shall still be here when you come back.'

She laughed suddenly. 'Is that a promise?'

'It is a promise,' he said, but he was not laughing.

He watched her go, then turned back to his task. Mucking out was not the most pleasant of jobs, but it was a peaceful one, a connection with the earth and its rhythms. The horses, quietly chomping on their hay, the occasional snort, the swish of a long tail, reminded him of the timelessness of farming, timeless in the sense that it went on generation after generation, but also timely, geared to the seasons, to the needs of the animals and crops. It ignored the stupidity of man in going to war. Jean understood that. She did not judge him for his race, nor his allegiance and he liked her for that. He liked her very much. He could not tell her that, of course. It would ruin a friendship he had come to cherish and would mean he could never come to Briar Rose Farm again.

The mood in the camp was sombre. Karl felt it as soon as he returned. The men were confined to camp. No one spoke to him, but watched silently as he made his way over to his own bed and sat down. The one next to his was empty.

'Where's Otto Herzig?' he asked, pretending he did not know.

'In the *Kühler*, where else?' *Feldwebel* Joachim Hartmann answered him.

'What's he done?'

'Caught trying to escape. But then you knew about it, didn't you?'

'How could I? I've been at work all day.' He had to remain calm because everyone in the hut was crowding round him and their looks were not friendly.

'Why didn't you go with him? You are his friend, aren't you?'

'I thought I was, but evidently he didn't think so.'

'You know what this means, don't you?'

'I imagine added security.'

'It also means that other plans, proper authorised plans have been ruined. There was a search of the huts, a very thorough one. They all but took the huts apart. They found everything, civilian clothes, forged identity cards, maps, English money, the lot. Major Schultz is furious. He said he expressly forbade *Gemeiner* Herzig to try to escape and he disobeyed. When his time in the *kühler* is done, he'll have to answer to me. I was on the list to go and now I'm stuck here, all because of a stupid scheme that had no hope of success.'

'It has nothing to do with me.'

'You were in it with him. Do you think we are blind and deaf? You were always whispering together, don't think we didn't notice.'

'We were only talking. Herzig did not confide in me.'

The lights went out suddenly and the men returned to their beds, still grumbling. If it was only grumbling he could put up with that, but if they decided grumbling was not enough, he would be in real trouble. He was already looked on with suspicion by his fellows. He did not join in the usual baiting of the guards, nor in the frequent lectures and discussions intended to strengthen their belief in the invincibility of the Führer and the German war machine. His fellow prisoners had not beaten him, as they had others, but he knew one false move and they would. There had already been hints: a leg stuck out to trip him up when he walked past, and on another occasion his plate of food had been 'accidentally' tipped up and spilt into his lap.

The next morning, after a more than usually stringent roll call, he was ordered to report to the commandant's office where he was subjected to the same questions Hartmann had put to him. Again he reiterated he knew nothing of Otto's plans.

'If that is so, why did he come to the farm where you were working? Surely if he meant to go alone he would have set off from his work in Wisbech, not walked all the way to Little Bushey and risked being seen.'

'I don't know, *Herr Kolonel*. Perhaps he thought it would be easy to steal from the old lady. He had worked at her cottage for Mr Gould.'

'He didn't ask you to go with him?'

'If he had I would have refused.'

'Why?'

Karl ventured a smile. 'It would have been attempting the impossible. We know we can't escape.'

'Then why do you try?' Williamson's answering smile was not hostile but he was not going to be fooled.

'It is our duty, *Herr Kolonel*. You know that.'

'But you decided not to go?'

'It was not well-thought-out.'

'I see. Do you know anything about other escape plans?'

'No, *Herr Kolonel*.'

'Are you sure?'

'I am sure.'

'Very well, you may go.'

He left, only to be accosted on the way back to his hut by the *Lagerführer*'s clerk, who ordered him to report to Major Schultz at once. His superior's interrogation was even more searching than the commandant's and certainly no more friendly. At the end of it, he was not sure if he had been convincing enough, but as he had not been the one to disobey the order not to escape, even if Otto had, he was dismissed.

* * *

119

'I hear you had some adventures at Briar Rose yesterday.' Bill fell into step beside Jean on her way back home after morning service. Her mother was not with her, having elected to stay at home with her grandmother, who had been more shaken up by events than she realised at the time.

'You could say that.'

'Tell me about it. There are all sorts of rumours floating about. Some say he killed your gran, but you wouldn't be here now if he had, would you?'

'No, of course not. He hit her and bruised her face and arms but she'll be OK. Mum called the doctor and she stayed with us last night, but she's determined to go home later today. Whether Mum will let her is another matter.'

'So what did happen, exactly?'

'He wanted food and money and Gran wouldn't give them to him, so he hit her. Luckily Don and Terry arrived with Laddie and put a stop to it. Don knocked him out with the butt of Grandad's shotgun. They tied him up and sent for me.'

'That was gutsy of him.'

'Yes. I'm proud of him.'

'Now, perhaps you will believe me.'

'Believe what?'

'Those men are dangerous. They do not hesitate to kill and wound if it suits their purpose.'

'No one was killed and it wasn't Sergeant Muller who hit Gran.'

'They're all the same. You are far too trusting, Jean. How do you know he wouldn't hurt you if he saw an opportunity to escape and you stood in his way? He wouldn't think twice, believe me.'

'I don't think he would hurt me. He told me as much. They are not all bad, you know.'

'He told you as much,' he repeated. 'That's a strange sort of conversation you must have had with him.'

'It was after the accident with Pa's chair. Someone accused him of trying to kill Pa. He told me he would never hurt any of our family.'

'You believe that?'

'Yes, I do. Now will you stop harping on about him? He's a good man, I know it, and I am tired of all this criticism. It's nothing to do with you anyway.'

'Nothing to do with me. OK, so now I know where I stand.' He strode away.

She called after him, but he did not answer. She was sorry he was so touchy, but she was not going to condemn Karl because of something another man had done. If Bill didn't like that, he was going to have to put up with it. She was not prepared to delve too deeply into her own motives lest she uncover something she would not know how to deal with.

Doris was worried, not only about her mother, but about Jean. She seemed to be brushing Bill off and that wasn't fair. 'And there's Sergeant Muller still coming here as if it made no difference what had happened,' she said to Arthur. 'And Jean welcomes him . . .'

'I know, but what else can she do? I'm not a ha'p'orth of good to her, nor to anyone, am I? I have to let my daughter do all the things I should be doing. If the Jerry helps, who am I to argue?'

'Oh, Arthur.' She went over and bent to put her arms about him and lay her cheek against his. 'It's not your fault, any of it. I'm sorry I'm so grumpy. Put it down to the war. I'm fed up with it all.'

'We all are, love. We just have to soldier on, there's naught else for it.'

* * *

When Otto came out of the *kühler*, he was given a dressing down by the *Lagerführer* and sent back to his old hut. Karl did not know who made that decision, but it was ill-thought-out. The rest of the men in the hut, and especially Joachim Hartmann, held him responsible for the discovery of the other escape preparations and gave him a severe beating. When Karl tried to intervene, he was pushed aside.

'I don't need a *Spitzel* to defend me!' Otto shouted. 'I am a loyal patriot which is more than he is. He betrayed me. He is besotted with the English *Fräulein*. He would rather be with her than doing his duty to the Fatherland. She is nothing but a *Nutte*.'

Karl turned and punched him for insulting Jean. Otto staggered back but recovered quickly and was back in the fray with blood pouring from his nose. There ensued a fierce fight. No one else in the room interfered, but the noise of men cheering and the sound of breaking glass alerted the guards and they rushed in to break it up. Both men were escorted to the *Kühler* and locked in separate cells.

The next day Karl, his face and body badly bruised, was again facing the commandant. 'I am very disappointed in you, *Feldwebel* Muller,' Colonel Williamson said. 'I thought you were one of the more peaceful of my charges. What have you to say for yourself?'

Karl remained silent.

'Who struck the first blow?' When Karl gave no answer, he pressed on. 'It is not the first time you have come to blows with your fellows, is it?'

'No, *Kolonel*.'

'Why?'

'I do not know.'

'Oh, I think you do.'

'I am not a *Spitzel, Herr Kolonel*,' he put in quickly.

'I know that. What do you suggest I do with you?'

'Whatever you will, *Herr Kolonel.*'

'It is evident you will be in danger if left in that hut, so I propose to move you to another barrack on the other side of the compound.'

'Thank you, *Herr Kolonel.*'

'Dismissed with a reprimand and four more days in the cooler.'

Karl saluted and was escorted back to his cell. On the way across the compound he saw Jean draw up at the gate in the pony and trap. He hesitated but then continued on his way. He did not think she had seen him, nor did he think he would be allowed to go back to the farm and the thought of that made him doubly miserable.

But on Sunday afternoon, he discovered he was wrong when Colonel Williamson sent for him again; apparently Miss Coleman had asked after him, wanting him back.

He spent the rest of the day wondering what his reception would be like. Could he and Jean return to the easy relationship they had had before, or had Otto spoilt it all? It was, he realised, important to him, though exactly why that was so he would not allow himself to speculate.

Chapter Seven

Jean was gathering eggs, helped by Lily. The child loved to follow her about the farm, chattering away about school and her friends and the games they played. 'Terry got detention today, for talking in class and answering back,' she told her. 'Miss gave him the cane.'

'I don't think you should tell tales, Lily,' Jean said. 'You wouldn't like Terry to tell when you are naughty, would you?'

'I'm not naughty.'

'What? Not ever?'

'Only sometimes. You've missed one.' She pointed to an egg lying in the hedge.

'So I have.' She picked it up and put it in her basket. 'Do you think you can carry this back to Auntie Doris for me?'

'Course I can.' She took the basket and trotted off.

Jean turned and saw Karl watching her. She hadn't heard him arrive and gave him a broad smile. 'You are back. I am so pleased.'

'And I am pleased to be back. You had a little helper, I see.'

'Lily. I shall miss her when she goes home. You get on with children too, don't you?'

'Yes. I like their innocence. They are not corrupted by greed and politics. They say what they think and they don't judge like adults tend to do.'

'I try not to judge.'

'I know, I wasn't thinking of you at all, just people in general.'

They talked as they worked in easy harmony, confiding in each other their hopes and fears. Hers were about the farm and her worry over her father and Gordon; his were about what was happening in Germany.

'Have you heard from your parents or Heidi yet?' she asked him.

'No, nothing. I worry about them. It is dreadful to say, but I have almost forgotten what Heidi looks like.'

'You have her picture.'

'Yes, but when I lie in bed in the dark and try to imagine her face, it comes to me as a blur. I used to be able to see her clearly in my mind but it has gone now.'

'It will come back when you see her again.'

'I hate this war,' he said suddenly. 'I hate everything about it. People on both sides being killed and injured, separated from their families, cities destroyed, the countryside ruined, you and I enemies and for what . . .'

'You are not my enemy, Karl, though your Hitler and those fanatics that do his bidding most certainly are.'

'He is not my Hitler. Please do not class me with him. I hold no brief for him.' He paused. 'I should not have said that. It is disloyal to my country.'

'You can say what you like to me, Karl, I will not betray your confidence. It is a pity more people don't think like you do. They might put a stop to it.'

'They would have to kill the Führer to do it and no one has succeeded yet.'

'But would Hitler's death make any difference? He has men around him who are just as fanatical.'

'But none with his magnetism. There are men in our camp who think he is invincible, more like a god.' He gave a cracked laugh. 'Religion went out of the window when the Nazis came to power.'

'That is dreadful.'

'I should not be talking like this. I could be in serious trouble.'

'I believe you have already been in trouble, haven't you? The week you didn't come to work, you weren't sick, were you?'

'What made you say that?'

'The man who came in your place told me. His English is not as good as yours but I understood the gist of it. Your friend, Otto, accused you of being a coward and a traitor and for that you had to be punished.'

'It was nothing. He should not have told you. I should not have talked as I have. I am German and I love my country, but if the regime could be toppled we might have an armistice and the slaughter would stop.'

'Churchill and Roosevelt have publicly said they would entertain nothing less than total surrender.'

'Then we fight on to the end, until one or other of us is totally annihilated. Such a waste, such a terrible waste of lives.'

He looked so miserable, she put out a hand and laid it over his. 'Perhaps it won't come to that. Try to stay cheerful. Don't give up hope.'

He looked down at her hand as if wondering how it had got there, then picked it up with his other hand and lifted it to his lips. 'I am glad I have you to talk to, but we will speak of it no more, will we?'

'No. I have already forgotten it.'

* * *

The population of Little Bushey watched in mounting apprehension as more and more prisoners were herded off trains and marched through the village to the camp, escorted by a handful of troops. Dirty and unkempt, they were not cowed, but arrogant, singing as they marched and giving anyone they passed a mocking bow.

'The villagers are up in arms,' Jean told Karl. 'They are afraid the prisoners will break out and run amok in the village and we've only got one local bobby.'

'Bobby?'

'Policeman.' It was easy to forget that he was unfamiliar with English slang, though he was learning all the time. She hardly noticed his accent now, but that may have been because she had become used to it. 'Do you think they will try anything like that?'

'I do not know, Jean. I keep to myself and I am here most of the day, but if they did breakout, they would soon be rounded up again.'

'Bill has written to our Member of Parliament about the danger but he has had no reply. He says he's going to write to all the newspapers. There are others in the village who will back him up.'

'What does he want done?'

'He wants the camp shut down. He says it is too near the village.'

'I doubt they will shut it down, Jean. They have to find somewhere to accommodate all the prisoners they are taking. Our camp is a seething mass of men and a lot of them are sleeping in tents. Anyone with building skills is being put to work building more huts but they are not ready, and with so much overcrowding, fights are breaking out over trivial things – who has precedence for the showers, the theft of soap and accusations of favouritism and unequal rations, that sort of thing. The weather doesn't help.

Keeping belongings dry in a tent is not easy, especially when the ground outside it is so wet and muddy.'

'It doesn't help the farmers either.'

'I know.'

'Would you go along with a breakout, Karl?'

'I do not know,' he said slowly. 'If I thought there was a chance of getting home to Germany and finding my parents, I might be tempted to take it, but I do not think that is likely. No one has managed it yet. Talk of escape is all *Latrinenparolen* – latrine talk.'

He returned to the camp one evening to find more prisoners had arrived. It was evident that the careful segregation that had been practiced with earlier prisoners was being performed perfunctorily and sometimes hardly at all. He soon realised that some of the new intake should have been labelled 'black'. Among them was a sergeant calling himself Hans Schmidt who stood out from the rest because of his huge moustache and arrogant posture. Karl recognised him at once as Major Gerhard Richter. He had been in the same cavalry regiment as Karl's brother and Karl had met him at the regimental passing out parade. He had been an enthusiastic member of the National Socialist Party then and Karl had no reason to suppose he had changed.

Schmidt had not been in the camp long before he formed a coterie of men who felt the same way as he did and they would huddle in groups talking quietly. It looked as though he meant to take over the camp and undermine the easy-going Major Schultz. Karl guessed there was more to it than that, otherwise why had he taken a false name and a non-commissioned rank when he could have enjoyed the privileges of an officer POW?

'What's going on?' he asked Otto one evening when they were strolling round the compound before lights out.

'I don't know, do I? No one tells me anything. But Schmidt is talking to everyone who works on the outside.'

'Has he spoken to you?' He and Otto had been through so much together, it seemed childish to remain at loggerheads.

'No, but I expect he will. And you, too.'

'We don't have to go.'

'Are you joking? No one defies *Feldwebel* Schmidt if he wants to keep his balls intact.'

Karl's efforts to avoid Schmidt proved difficult; he seemed to be everywhere and would hold court in the hut he occupied or out in the compound, always surrounded by sycophants, and summon people to his presence. Otto returned from one such meeting to tell Karl, 'He wanted to know everything I had seen while working outside, what Gould's yard was like and what sort of stuff he kept there. He asked particularly if he stored explosives on the premises.'

'Does he?'

'I never saw any.'

'What is he planning to blow up?' Karl mused.

'The guards' quarters, perhaps?'

'Are you prepared to go along with that?'

'Yes, if it gets us out of here and kills a few *Engländern* in the bargain. He wants to see you next.'

'I'm not going.'

Otto shrugged. 'Please yourself.'

Karl left him to go back to his hut where he picked up the camp newspaper and flung himself on his bed. It contained the usual notices about events: the latest offering at the theatre, a schedule of football matches between teams from the huts, foreign language lessons, grumbles about the building work and the food. They were always grumbling about the food, though it was the same as the British troops were given. He let the paper drop and was half dozing when Joachim Hartmann came into the room.

'*Feldwebel* Schmidt wants to see you. He said he'll be waiting by the wire near the ablutions.'

'He will have a long wait then.'

'He wants to discuss something with you. You had better go before he sends his boys to fetch you.'

'Tell him if he wants to talk to me, he knows where to find me.' He picked up his newspaper again and pretended to read a review of a concert performed the week before.

Hartmann left and a few minutes later Hans Schmidt arrived. Karl discarded the newspaper and swung his legs over the edge of the bed. 'Good evening, Major Richter,' he said evenly. 'What can I do for you?'

'You are mistaken, I am *Feldwebel* Schmidt. Whoever this Major Richter is, he is not I. Shall we take a walk outside where we will not be overheard?'

There was no one else in the room but Karl knew he was thinking about hidden microphones. Curiosity led him to obey.

'Did you think I would not recognise you?' he asked, as they strolled across the compound.

'It is unfortunate that we find ourselves in this situation, Muller, but I am sure I can rely on you not to betray me to the commandant or to any of the others.'

'I am equally sure you would not have demoted yourself without a compelling reason.'

'I am obeying orders, as every good soldier does.'

'Oh, and what would they be?'

'To make as much trouble as I can for the enemy. The war is not lost, my friend. Our beloved Führer has more than one trick up his sleeve and we, here in England, have our part to play. We must be ready.'

'Ready for what?'

'I cannot tell you yet. Suffice to say I require your wholehearted co-operation.'

'Why the false identity?'

'Simple, my friend. I needed to get into a camp for other ranks where the men are sent out to work. Officers don't work, they simply sit around in idleness waiting for the war to end. That would never suit me. When surrender seemed inevitable, I took the clothes and identity of my sergeant who had been killed in the battle for Falaise. He was a good man to have at one's side. I mourned his loss, but he is still of use to the Fatherland, even in death. I intend to find out all I can about the British countryside, roads and rivers, where the army camps are, what vehicles and armaments they have, where the airfields are, what aircraft are kept there . . .'

Karl chuckled. 'Are you planning to steal an aeroplane?'

'I might. I transferred from the cavalry to the 6th Parachute Regiment early in the war and part of our training was learning to fly.'

'Good luck to you. I hope you are not shot down, but I do not see how I can help you over that.'

'No, but that is not all. I need information, lots of it. I need to know about the trains and buses and their timetables. Also who in the neighbourhood has a vehicle. I need reliable maps, English money . . .'

'And you think I can help with those?'

'I am sure you can. Your English is very good and I am told you work on a farm where you are made welcome. I am reliably informed there is a young lady who might be sympathetic . . .'

'Your informant is mistaken,' he said, thinking of Otto. 'I am guarded the whole time. There are several members of the family watching me, not just the *Fräulein*.'

'Then you must find a way of slipping your leash.'

A klaxon sounded across the compound warning the prisoners they should retire to their huts, that lights out would be in ten minutes and anyone caught outside after that risked being shot. Karl had never seen anyone shot by the guards, but the threat was ever-present. 'Do not forget I am Hans Schmidt,' the major said, as they bade each other a hasty goodnight. 'I will speak to you again.'

Karl went back to his hut. He could smell trouble and it bothered him.

Jean chuckled as they divested themselves of the thigh-length waders which they had been wearing to clear out a ditch. They were both filthy and smelly.

'Why are you laughing?' he asked.

'You have mud on your nose.' She picked up an old towel hanging on a hook in the barn where they were stripping and reached out to wipe it off. 'And on your cheek.'

'So have you,' he said. 'But you are still beautiful.'

'Oh, Karl, I am not. I am very ordinary.'

'Not to me. To me you are sunshine and smiles and kindness...'

'Oh, Karl, stop.' She was trying to smile through the tears that came unbidden to her eyes, but not quite succeeding.

'Why? Do you not like to hear compliments?'

'Of course I do, but it is not fitting.'

'I do not understand "fitting".'

'Oh, yes you do. You understand everything.'

'I wish I did.'

'What don't you understand?'

'It does not matter. No doubt all will become clear in time.'

'You are being very mysterious.'

He forced a laugh. 'Forget it, Jean. I sometimes feel low. We had better get on with this milking or we will not have it done before my transport arrives.'

They left the waders in the barn and fetched in the cows. She settled herself on a stool at the side of one of them, feeling very unsettled. There had been several enigmatic conversations with Karl lately, as if he were trying to tell her something but was unsure whether he should. Perhaps he was right not to. She was tempted to take the initiative, but maybe the least said the better.

Hans Schmidt somehow infused a new enthusiasm for escape among the prisoners. When told that no one had yet got off the island, he cited instances of how some had almost succeeded and would have done if they hadn't had bad luck. There was a tale of a group of escapees who had stowed away on an Allied landing craft on the south coast and taken it over after setting sail, only to be sunk by the German shore batteries on the French coast. And another stole a motor boat but was caught while he was trying to start it. 'One of our airmen stole a Spitfire and would have made it if he hadn't been shot down by our own anti-aircraft guns over the Dutch coast,' he told them. They were talking in what was supposed to be a lecture on the threat posed by Russia which had done nothing to cheer Karl up; he didn't know why he had bothered to attend. They had abandoned it when Hans had interrupted the lecturer to deliver his own homily.

'Myths,' Karl said. 'Fairy stories.'

'No, they are not. With care and proper preparation, it is possible.' He turned to the rows of men who had come to hear a lecture on communism and were instead being harangued about escape. 'Even if we do not succeed we can cause the *Engländern* a lot of trouble while we are loose.' He smiled at those around him, some very young, others old soldiers who knew all the dodges and had survived. Some were like himself, strong, fit, patriotic young men. 'Do you know there are a quarter of a million of us in camps all over the British Isles and we're being guarded by middle-aged Tommies too old to fight. Every able-bodied soldier has been sent to France where the generals are scraping the bottom of the barrel to find replacements for the men they have lost. Arnhem was a great victory for us, it has set the enemy back months, years, perhaps for ever.

'The Allies are not winning this war, my friends, not by a long way. Our beloved Führer has more tricks up his sleeve and we must play our part. We are not here to sit on our backsides wiling away our time while others do the work.' He paused to let his words sink in, then added, 'I want ten volunteers.'

There was a rush to take him up on that and he chose ten men to meet him in the latrines afterwards to discuss what needed to be done, among them was Otto Herzig.

'Why didn't you volunteer?' Otto asked Karl when they met up again later.

Karl shrugged. 'Didn't fancy it. What did he want you to do?'

'Escape, of course.'

'Is that all?'

'No. We have been given special tasks and after we have done those we have to allow ourselves to be recaptured, so we can bring the information back.'

'And get yourselves thrown into the *Kühler* for your trouble, not to mention loss of privileges. You tried it once before, remember?'

'I'm not likely to forget it, but I have a duty to the Fatherland, as have you, my friend. *Feldwebel* Schmidt is very disappointed in you.'

'I want to end this war in one piece and the sooner the better.'

'I called you a coward once before, don't make me denounce you again.'

Karl shrugged, pretending it was of no consequence, but he did not fancy another beating. 'You know I am not a coward, Otto. We simply see things differently.'

'You know,' Otto said, searching his face. 'I think the *Fräulein* has got you in her claws. If you do not struggle to free yourself, she will eat you.'

'Don't be ridiculous. And why did you tell Schmidt about her?'

'I thought he ought to know. She might be useful if you play your cards right.'

'I can't see how. After your botched attempt last time, everyone is being doubly cautious about revealing anything, or leaving valuables about.' This was not strictly true.

Otto shrugged. 'We'll see.'

Later Hans came himself to talk to Karl and what he told him worried him more than ever. 'I am glad you were not one of the volunteers,' he said. 'I need you at that farm, trusted by your hosts. When the time comes, you will be told what to do.'

'When will that be?'

'I don't know yet. Not long. In the meantime, keep your eyes and ears open.'

It was happening again, this thirst for information which had put him in jeopardy once before. Otto had put an end to it the last time by being caught, but he had a feeling that Gerhard Richter was cleverer than that. It crossed his mind to warn the commandant that something was afoot, but he was not a traitor and he could not do it, so he went about his work and said nothing.

Roll call the next morning revealed ten men missing. While the remaining men were still gathered in the compound, a huge search was conducted for the missing prisoners. All the huts were turned inside out but revealed nothing. Guards searching the perimeter reported the wire had been cut. The lorry that usually took the men on work parties came and went away empty. Karl was glad they had finished the threshing; Jean would not have been able to load the sacks of grain without his help.

He stood about with the other men discussing this latest development. Few realised its significance beyond a wish to be free; to them it was something to cheer about and they baited the guards with catcalls as they tried to keep them in order. Karl stood a little apart until Gerhard Richter came and stood beside him.

'Now we shall see how good the English are at rounding up prisoners,' he said, 'and how good their security is on the army and air force bases.'

'Then what?'

Hans tapped his nose. 'I will tell you when you need to know. You will be given a chance to avenge your brother's death.'

'You knew he had died?'

'I was with him. He was a brave man. We should have walked across Poland without any trouble but it was harder than we thought it would be; the Poles put up a spirited resistance once they had got over the shock. Wilhelm fought like a lion. A sniper got him from the roof of a building in Warsaw.'

'Warsaw has fallen to the Russians.'

'I know. It is of no consequence. They will get no further.'

'I hope you are right. My home is not far from the border.'

Hans slapped him on the back. 'You will go back there in triumph, my friend. Have faith.'

* * *

Colonel Williamson lost no time in putting the escape procedure into practice. He telephoned the commanding officer of the nearest army base, then Constable Worth, who alerted his superiors in Wisbech, then Sir Edward Masterson, who had commanded the local Home Guard. They had been disbanded, but Sir Edward called them out anyway, pulling many of them off the farms and leaving the women to lock themselves in their homes. The men in the army camp set off in trucks and jeeps armed with rifles and grenades, set up roadblocks and checked everyone's identity card. Guards were stationed at the nearest ports – King's Lynn, Great Yarmouth and Lowestoft – though few thought the escapees would get that far.

The inhabitants of Little Bushey were agog and apprehensive at the same time as Constable Worth pedalled round on his bicycle warning everyone to be on their guard.

'I said this would happen,' Bill told his mother, after the constable had left. 'Stay indoors and lock the door after me.'

'You're never going to leave me here alone?' She was trembling, convinced she was about to be murdered. She, along with everyone else, knew the ordeal Elizabeth Sanderson had gone through when one of the prisoners had tried to escape before.

'I'll take you over to the Colemans', if you like. I'm sure they'll let you stay with them until it's all over.'

They heard the sound of gunfire as he spoke, making her cringe. 'Is it safe to go?'

'Course it is. They aren't firing at us. Put on a warm coat, it's cold out and bring your knitting. It will help take your mind off it.'

He drove her to Briar Rose Farm in the Austin, for which, as a farmer, he had a petrol ration. Doris made her welcome. 'It's a bad do,' she said, addressing Bill. 'Do you know how many got out?'

'No, but best stay inside and keep the windows and doors locked until we know it's safe.'

'Don't be silly; I've got work to do,' Jean said. 'And without Karl . . .'

'What about your precious Karl? Is he on the loose? Will he come here and try to force you to help him?'

'No, of course he won't.'

'You've got more faith in him than I have. If I see him, he'll know about it.' He lifted his shotgun. 'Then perhaps you will come to your senses and not be so gullible. I'm off to see what's going on.'

'Oh, do take care,' his mother cried as he made for the door.

On the way to the village, he saw soldiers from the barracks, rifles at the ready, combing the woods and ditches and walking in line across the ploughed fields. He found Sir Edward patrolling the village with his men, some of whom had been sent to the railway station to make sure none of the prisoners boarded a train. 'How many are out?' he asked.

'Don't know. A lot, I should think by all the fuss.'

'Any sign of them?'

'Not yet, but we'll get them, never fear.'

One by one the escaped prisoners were recaptured. Hartmann was caught on the airfield snooping round the aircraft; two more were arrested wandering round the perimeter of the army camp, others were arrested at the bus station in Wisbech and the rest scattered about the countryside. Otto, who knew his way around the area more than the others and had more information to add to the map he already had, walked back to the camp and gave himself up, much to the astonishment of Colonel Williamson.

It was not the only thing that puzzled the commandant.

None of the prisoners had made any real attempt to leave the area. He sent all the recaptured men to the cooler and decided to work on Otto Herzig. It was a waste of time, the man simply said he felt like a day out and he had done nothing but wander round and enjoy his freedom. He had never intended to stay out all night. 'It's too cold at this time of the year,' he said. 'And I was hungry.'

The colonel discovered it was the same in other camps, all over the country, particularly in the south-west and the Midlands; groups of prisoners were breaking out and then allowing themselves to be recaptured, offering only a token resistance or none at all. Something was definitely afoot, but what it was he could only guess at. He thought he ought to keep all the men confined to camp but that would be hard on the 'whites', whose only ambition was to wait out the war and earn a little to buy a few necessities in the camp shop. Besides, it would alert the troublemakers that they were being watched. He managed to implant a few more microphones in the huts and let the camp routine go on as normal. A week after the breakout, Karl went back to work at the farm.

He staggered out to the transport, carrying a wooden sled on which was balanced a small doll's house and a wooden box. 'What's all that in aid of?' Corporal Donnington asked him as he put it on the tailboard and pushed it further into the lorry.

He did not answer; sometimes it paid to pretend not to understand English. But that didn't stop his compatriots asking the same question. 'Making a little money on the side,' he told them, unwilling to admit he was giving the enemy gifts.

Jean was equally curious when he climbed down and reached inside to extract his handiwork. 'I made them for the children for Christmas,' he told her. 'Where shall I put them?'

'That is kind of you. Let's put them in the barn for now.' She led the way and took them from him to stack in the corner and cover them with a couple of sacks. 'They are beautifully made,' she said. 'How clever you are, but it's a little early for Christmas.'

'Yes, but I had nowhere to store them and they might have been damaged.'

'What happened up at the camp? Did those men really think they could escape all the way back to Germany?'

'I don't know,' he said guardedly. 'It was unrealistic if they did. They were all retaken inside twenty-four hours.'

'It frightened everyone in the village. Bill brought Mrs Howson to stay with us while he joined the hunt. You didn't come to work and I was afraid you might be one of them and you'd be hurt. There were soldiers with guns all over the place.'

'The rest of us were confined to camp. I could not let you know.'

'I'm glad you did not take part, Karl. I know you are anxious to go home and I can understand that, but the war is nearly over and you will soon be going home a free man. There is no need to escape.'

He gave a twisted smile. 'Would it were that easy.'

'Why do you say that?'

He paused, debating what to tell her. 'There will be chaos. And I do not know if my home is there any more. The Russians are getting closer all the time. I know my father, he will not give up his farm without a fight and *Mutti* will never leave him. Besides, where would they flee to? The Tommies and the Amis are already on German soil. As for Heidi . . .' He stopped in mid-sentence.

'What is it, Karl? What's the matter?'

'I have had a letter at last . . .'

'From Heidi?'

'No, from my mother. She tells me they are well, but much of her letter was blacked out by the censor, so I could not read it.'

'But at least it's news. They are OK and they know where you are.'

'Yes, but there was more. Heidi is married.' He spoke flatly. 'She has married a Gestapo officer in Berlin.'

'Oh, Karl, I am so sorry.' She reached over to put a hand on his arm. 'I don't know what to say.'

'Don't say anything. I have been half expecting something like it.'

'Even so, it must be a dreadful shock. All that waiting and hoping . . .'

'And now the hope is gone.' He reached in his breast pocket and took out the well-thumbed snapshot of Heidi. He looked at it for a moment, then tore it into tiny shreds, letting the pieces drift from his hand.

She watched the wind take them across the field until they faded from sight. 'Oh, Karl, I am so sorry.'

'Please, let us not speak of it again.'

'Very well, but if you want to talk, I'll listen.'

'There is nothing else to say.'

She thought he was more hurt than he liked to admit, but there was nothing she could do about it, except sympathise and try to take his mind off it.

Karl at last learnt from Major Richter what all the preparations were about and they filled him with foreboding. 'The time has come,' he had told him that evening while they made their way across the compound to the latrines. No one said anything important in the buildings; they knew they were bugged. 'We are going to take over the camp.'

'Who is "we"?'

'The company of volunteers I have selected. On Friday, we will rush the guards after morning roll call and seize their weapons. They will be held in the guardroom, while the weapons store is raided. With these we will break out of the camp.'

'Armed?' That worried him.

'Of course.'

'How many?'

'All but the most weak-hearted, the cowards and the English-lovers.'

'How many do you expect to reach home and safety?'

'Every single one.' Hans had grinned at him. 'But not yet. We have other work to do before that. Every camp up and down the country has plans to break out. It is being timed with a counteroffensive in the Ardennes. We must gather more weapons, transport, tanks if we can find them, machines guns, artillery with carriers . . .

'After we have broken out we will meet up with others, coming down from the north and west, and march on to London. So many Allied troops have been sent to the front line, the city is largely undefended. The Führer has promised a mass parachute drop to support us. The swastika will fly over Buckingham Palace and the Houses of Parliament. Without a government the enemy will collapse.'

'*Gott in Himmel!* How do you know all this?'

'It has been planned for some time.'

'Before you were captured?'

'Before I allowed myself to be captured.'

'You are mad.'

'Not mad, my friend – inspired. It can be done. Are you with us?'

Karl had thought it expedient to agree, if only to find out more. 'What do you want of me?'

'When your transport reaches your place of work on Friday – what is it called – Briar Rose Farm?' Karl nodded. 'You will disarm and dispatch the escort. You will then enter the farmhouse and find money, civilian clothes and food. If anyone offers resistance, you know what to do. When you've got that, take their vehicle and pick me up at the crossroads where the village road meets the main road from Wisbech.'

'What about the other men in the transport?'

'They will not be your usual companions, except Otto Herzig who has reconnoitred the way, but hand-picked men, ready to do their duty. We will drive to Cambridge and join up with others from camps round there. Together we march south, collecting more men on the way. By the time we reach London we will be a formidable army, more than a match for those decrepit troops, left behind to take care of their country.' The man was so pleased with himself he was laughing. 'Oh, what a panic we will cause. The enemy will not know which way to turn.'

'You will meet resistance.'

'Bah, nothing to speak of and we will be able to deal with it.' He laughed. 'They will be wishing they had not disbanded the Home Guard.'

Karl, hosing down the yard the next day, could think of nothing else. Jean was looking at him in puzzlement, but he could not respond to her questioning expression. He had too much on his mind. One half of him applauded the daring of the plan and wished it would succeed, the other knew it was madness borne of desperation. His own orders – and he had been left in no doubt they were orders to be obeyed – worried him more than a little. Dispatch the escort and driver meant shoot them. On a battlefield he would have had no compunction about doing that, but in England, as a prisoner of war with every man's hand against them? He had been right to call it madness.

Worst of all were his instructions regarding Jean and the Coleman family. How could he repay her kindness with treachery like that? His refusal to do so when Otto had tried to escape and the punishment he received for it, paled into insignificance. He might well lose his life over it.

Jean turned off the tap and the jet of water dribbled to a halt. 'Karl, what's the matter?'

'Nothing.'

'I know there is. I can tell by the grim look on your face. They are not moving you away, are they?'

He was tempted to say yes, that was it, but if he refused to board the lorry tomorrow Richter would only send someone else. He took a deep breath. 'Tomorrow I may not come to work. I think there will be an extra roll call and a search of the huts.'

'Oh, no, not another escape attempt.'

'I cannot say. But please, when the transport comes in the morning, do not come out to meet it. Stay inside and lock all the doors and windows. If I am there and ask to come in, do not admit me.'

'I don't understand you. What is going to happen?'

'I cannot tell you.'

'Karl, you are scaring me.'

'I am sorry. I do not wish to frighten you, but please do as I ask, for everyone's sake. Perhaps you will see me again and perhaps you will not.' He dropped the hose and took both her hands in his and searched her face. 'Try not to think badly of me.'

'It sounds as if you are saying goodbye.'

'Perhaps I am. I do not know. It is out of my hands.' He turned his head as a lorry drew up at the end of the drive. 'There is my

144

transport.' He raised her hands one by one to his lips and left her.

Afraid and miserable, she coiled the hose and hung it over the tap, then went back indoors, deep in thought. Something was going to happen with the POWs, something big enough for Karl to try and warn her. She knew the ways of the prisoners well enough to know that if his fellows learnt he had warned her he would be punished as he had been before. But he *had* warned her, so what was she to do?

Her mother was preparing the evening meal. Her father sat in his chair by the kitchen fire, simply staring at the flames. He hardly read the newspapers nowadays and only glanced at his *Farmers Weekly*. Poor Pa, he was so helpless and not improving and though she had done her best to keep the farm running smoothly, she knew she fell far short of his high standards. He would be glad to hand over to Gordon. After more than five years of war, her mother, too, was feeling the strain. Everyone, all over the world, wanted peace.

'Sit down, Mum,' she said, taking the paring knife from her mother to finish peeling the potatoes. 'I'll do this.' She put the potatoes on the stove and sat down at the table, drawing her mother down beside her. 'Mum, Karl just told me something very worrying. He warned me to keep all the doors and windows locked and not to answer the door if he arrives tomorrow. But he might not come.'

'What did he mean?'

'I don't know. I think perhaps some of the prisoners are going to try and escape.'

'What, again? They'll be caught like they were last time.'

'Yes, but why would he tell me not to let him in? I think he's being forced to go along with them.'

'Forced?'

145

'Yes, I am sure of it. He seemed agitated and upset . . .'

'Jean, you had better ring Colonel Williamson. Do it now.'

Colonel Williamson had gone to London for a meeting, she was told by the sergeant who answered her call, but he would tell him the minute he returned. In the meantime he would keep a sharp lookout for trouble brewing. He thanked her and she rang off and went to the cottage to fetch her grandmother. 'I don't know what it's about,' she told her, 'but you'll be safer with us if anything does happen.'

Chapter Eight

'Secret information has come from a reliable source,' Colonel Alexander Scotland told the camp commandants who were gathered at the house in Kensington Palace Gardens, referred to by everyone as the 'London Cage'. It was said he knew more about the German army than its own generals. 'The German POWs are planning something big. We can't be sure exactly what they have in mind, but intelligence suggests a mass breakout. We think it is connected with what is happening on the Continent. Hitler has asked for volunteers for a special mission. They are required to speak perfect English.'

One of his listeners laughed. 'Is he thinking of invading Britain?'

'Perhaps not as far-fetched as that,' the colonel said, smiling. 'But there are a quarter of a million prisoners on UK soil and they could cause a helluva lot of trouble one way or another. The German high command might think we would have to pull troops from the fighting in France to deal with them.'

'So, that's what that earlier breakout was in aid of,' Colonel

Williamson said. 'I couldn't make out why they didn't venture far from the camp and allowed themselves to be recaptured so easily. One of them even strolled back to the camp the same evening and gave himself up.'

'That happened to us, too,' another put in and it soon became apparent that they were not the only ones.

'How the hell do they communicate with each other?' Colonel Upton asked.

'They may have found a way, but I think it more likely they communicate with Berlin by radio and Berlin issues the orders the same way,' Colonel Scotland told him. 'No doubt some of the more recent prisoners have come ready primed.'

'What has that to do with speaking English?' someone else had asked.

'We are not sure, but there have been a lot of instances of Germans dressed as American officers, driving American jeeps, countermanding orders and issuing new ones. It's causing havoc in the American lines and they are arresting perfectly innocent officers even when they know the passwords. It is all a prelude to something.'

'Trust Jerry to come up with something diabolical like that.'

'Naturally, we do not want the general public to know anything about this, so keep it under wraps, but keep on your toes, increase your surveillance. Let us know of any unusual activity in your camps, anything at all. Talk to your moles, find out what they know.'

A general discussion followed, as everyone exchanged news about their own situation and made suggestions for dealing with an outbreak. It was very late by the time the meeting broke up and Colonel Williamson was able to go for his train. He was tempted to stay in town overnight, but what he had learnt made him decide to catch the last train back to Wisbech. If there was trouble brewing he ought to be at the camp.

Halfway to Cambridge, the train was shunted into a siding while a series of armament trains went through bound for Southampton, and the passengers were left shivering for hours. He could not find a taxi when he finally arrived at Wisbech and, cursing, he found a telephone box and rang the camp for someone to fetch him.

It was three in the morning when he finally arrived. All was quiet. The guard on the gate told him everything was normal, roll call had gone through without any disruption and the men were all locked in their huts, safe and sound. Thoroughly relieved and very tired, he did not go into his office but went home to bed.

Roll call took longer than usual the next morning. There was an air of suppressed excitement as people dodged about making counting difficult. No attempt was made to tackle the guards and Karl wondered if the idea of everyone breaking out was just a pipe dream on Hans Schmidt's part. They were still milling about in the compound when the lorry arrived for the outworkers and drew up at the gate. Karl walked over to it and climbed in.

'Roll call's late today,' Corporal Donnington commented. He was not carrying his rifle; it was propped in a corner.

'Yes. Don't know why.'

Karl sat down on the bench near the tailboard as others joined him. Major Richter had been right; they were not the usual workers. One of them was Hartmann. Last to board was Otto. He grinned at Karl but did not speak.

As they drove off, they could hear gun shots behind them, but their driver did not stop and no one spoke. The corporal, suddenly realising they had missed a turning, banged on the back of the cab. 'Ted, where d'you think you're off to? We're supposed to drop some of these men off at Emneth first.'

The man turned his head and the corporal gasped as he realised the driver was not Ted. He turned to the men, who were all laughing. 'What's going on?'

The laughing stopped as Hartmann picked up the corporal's rifle and pointed it at him. Otto let down the tailboard. 'Out,' Hartmann said, prodding him towards the back of the vehicle. Donnington shuffled forward. He was teetering on the edge when Hartmann shot him in the back. He toppled into the road.

'*Verdammt*, Hartmann, did you have to kill him?' Karl asked.

'Why not? A dead Englishman is the best kind and there will be plenty more before we're done. If you don't like it, you can join him.'

Karl said no more. It was not the time to protest. He wanted to be alive when they reached the farm which they soon did, directed by Otto, the only one, apart from himself, who knew where it was.

'You know your orders, Muller?' Hartmann asked him, as they drew to a stop.

'Yes, but these people have been kind to me. I don't want to hurt them.' Even in his own eyes this excuse sounded feeble. 'Can't you get what you want from somewhere else?'

'No doubt we will,' Hartmann said. 'Everywhere we can, but you have to play your part too.'

'Karl, it's a test of your loyalty,' Otto put in.

Every one of the dozen men was looking at him, waiting for him to respond, all bloodthirsty men who did not like being incarcerated and did not seem to care that the object of the menace was one of their own. They wanted action.

Reluctantly he jumped down and walked up to the house, aware that Hartmann was behind him with the rifle. He knocked on the door, desperately hoping Jean had heeded his warning.

'Don't open it, *mein Liebling*,' he prayed silently.

The window above their heads opened and Jean leant out. She could hardly miss seeing Hartmann with the rifle pointed at his back. 'Sergeant Muller, you are late for work,' she said.

'I know.' A prod in the back from the rifle, urged him to go on. 'If you let me in, *Fräulein*, I will explain.'

'Certainly not. Go and get on with your work.'

He turned to Hartmann and spread his hands in a gesture of helplessness. Hartmann rattled the door but it was locked.

'Tell her that if she does not obey I am going to shoot you.' He heard the click of the safety catch behind him and held his breath.

Jean disappeared and he thought she meant to obey, but she was soon back at the window with a shotgun. 'Tell that man to leave,' she told Karl. 'Or I will shoot him.'

The rifle which had been aimed at his back was suddenly lifted towards the window where Jean stood defiantly with her finger on the trigger. Karl couldn't let it happen. He lifted his arm, trying to knock the rifle out of Hartmann's hands. A pain shot through his side and he crumpled to the ground. He did not hear the lorry turn and drive away at speed, nor the shot that felled Hartmann. He knew nothing until he regained consciousness on the settee in the farm living room. Jean was kneeling at his side.

'The doctor's on his way.'

He smiled and shut his eyes again.

'What are we going to do about the man on the doorstep?' Doris asked after they had half-carried, half-dragged Karl into the sitting room and laid him on the settee. She had tried to dissuade Jean from confronting the men but Jean could be obstinate when she needed to be. 'Is he dead?'

'I doubt it.' Karl's warning had become clear as soon as she saw the man with the gun, who was evidently prepared to use it. Something had to be done.

'I rang the camp. The colonel was too busy to talk to me,' Doris said. 'The man I spoke to seemed to be in a bit of a flap, so I rang Constable Worth. His wife said he was out chasing escaped prisoners, but she would tell him when he came in. I don't like the idea of a body on our doorstep. Pa is really agitated and the children will be home from school soon.'

They realised the German was far from dead when they heard someone start their truck and drive away, but she had no time to worry about that as Doctor Norman arrived to examine the patient.

'All hell's let loose,' he said, as he worked. 'Half the POWs at the camp have legged it.'

'I shot one of them,' Jean said. 'He got away in our farm truck.'

'I doubt he'll get far. There's a major alert on.' He nodded towards Karl. 'What about him?'

'He's my farm worker,' she said. 'Not one of them.'

'He's got a bullet in his side. Luckily it's gone in at an angle and is not very deep, but it needs to come out. I should turn him over to the camp doctor, but I reckon he's got his hands full. I'll order an ambulance to take him to Wisbech hospital.'

'Can't you get it out?'

'Of course I can. I didn't serve as a medic in the last war without learning how to do that. The question is, should I?'

'Yes, you should. It will be half an hour at least before an ambulance can get him to hospital, that's if it isn't busy elsewhere. In the meantime, he could die. Do it, please. I'll help you.'

He hesitated before answering. 'Very well, on your head be it. I'll have to go home and fetch my instruments and some ether. Keep him calm while I'm gone. Don't let him thrash about.'

After he had gone, Jean sat on the side of the bed holding Karl's hand, watching his laboured breathing and praying for him not to die.

Doris came into the room. 'What's happening?'

'Doctor Norman has gone to get his instruments and anaesthetic. He's going to take the bullet out of Karl's side.'

'He's going to do it here?'

'Yes. It will be safer.'

'Safer? Who for?'

'Karl.'

'Sergeant Muller was one of them.'

'No, Mum, he wasn't. He tried to warn us what would happen and because of that he was shot. That man was intent on getting into the house and he would have shot me if Karl hadn't stopped him. We owe him.'

Doris had no time to reply because Constable Worth arrived. Jean explained what had happened. 'The ones in the lorry drove off but one of them took our pickup. It doesn't have much petrol in it, so maybe he won't get far.'

'Right. I'll report that. We found a body in the lane. A British corporal by the look of it.'

'Oh no! How dreadful. It must be Corporal Donnington. He was the guard on the transport. Poor, poor man, he didn't deserve that. I wonder if he has any family.'

'It's a real bad do.' He nodded towards Karl, still deeply unconscious. 'What do you want me to do about that one?'

'Nothing. Doctor Norman is going to take the bullet out of him and then we'll put him to bed. Don't worry about him. He won't harm us.'

'I'm not sure if I should allow it.'

'Well, I *am* sure.'

'Then I'd better get back to helping round up the others.' He settled his helmet back on his head and left them.

'Where are we going to put him to bed?' Doris asked, after he had gone.

'In Gordon's room. Terry can move in with Don.'

'I'm not sure that's a good idea. It's all very well to be friendly with the man, but this is taking it too far. We could all be in trouble.'

'Mum, it will be all right. I'm not letting Karl go back to that camp until he's fully fit.' To herself, she added, 'And not then if I can help it.'

'Jean, you are not becoming too fond of him, are you?'

She felt the colour rush into her face. Her mother knew, of course she did. 'Oh, Mum, don't be silly. I like him and feel sorry for him, that's all. It would be cruel to send him back in his condition.'

'You might not have any choice if Colonel Williamson sends for him.'

But Colonel Williamson was too busy to do anything like that. He had a major incident on his hands and it required all his attention.

What Colonel Scotland had feared had come about. He had learnt most of the plot through listening devices, interrogation and other means he was not prepared to divulge, but what he had not known was when it would take place. He had been left in no doubt when, on Friday 15th December, prisoners began breaking out from camps up and down the country, spreading themselves about the countryside and causing fear among those who lived near enough to see the efforts being made to round them up. Although the majority of the population knew nothing of it, some news leaked out that a few prisoners had escaped, but were being rapidly recaptured. People were warned to be vigilant, but that was all.

'It's all under control,' he told Colonel Williamson over the telephone. 'Have you contained your lot?'

'Yes. They are all back in camp bar three. Two stole a farm truck and made off in it. I am confident they will be caught before long. The other was shot by one of his fellows and is recuperating at the farm where he's been working.'

'That's a bit irregular, isn't it?'

'I suppose it is, but I do not think he poses a threat.'

'You can never tell, Charles. Get him back under lock and key until everything calms down.'

'Very well, Colonel.'

Karl slept most of the next two days, during which time Jean sat on a chair close to his bed, leaving him only for a couple of hours' sleep. Doris and Donald milked the cows, fed the animals and collected the eggs, which had to be done; the rest of the work was neglected, she had no time for it. In vain did her mother protest that the patient did not need such constant care, that she could safely leave him for an hour or two.

When he woke on the third morning, he was looking a great deal better. His colour had returned and he was anxious to be up and working again, even though he had a thick bandage round his chest and was wearing a pair of Arthur's pyjamas, which Jean had helped Doris put on him. He was also worried about what had happened at the camp.

'They caught them all, except the one who shot you,' Jean told him. 'He made off in the farm truck. I peppered him with shots, so I don't think he'll be feeling too good.'

'He shot Corporal Donnington. I could not stop him.'

'Yes, poor man. They found his body in the lane. That man has a lot to answer for when they catch him.' She paused. 'You could have gone with them. You needn't have warned me. You certainly needn't have risked being shot.'

'But he was going to shoot you. I could not have allowed that. My life is nothing compared to yours. Without you, my existence would be a black hole of misery. You have brought me contentment and a kind of peace.'

'Oh, Karl, what a lovely thing to say.' She picked his hand off the bed cover and put the palm to her cheek. 'I thought you might die. I knew if that happened, I would want to die too.'

'You love me?'

'Yes. Don't sound so surprised.'

'And I love you.'

'Really? What about Heidi? You were in love with her once.'

He smiled. 'No, I do not think I was. We were both very young when the war separated us. I think I clung onto the idea of loving her simply to keep me sane during the bad times. Now I have you and that, I promise you, is infinitely better.' He paused, searching her face. 'We cannot know what the future holds for us, but if God is willing, perhaps we can live it together.'

'I should like that, I should like it very much.' She bent over to kiss him. He put his arm up and round her neck and drew her down beside him to kiss her and stroke her face. His tenderness sent tingling shivers of longing right through her body.

'What will your parents say?' he murmured when, at last, he let her go.

She sat up and ran her hands through her tousled hair. 'I think Mum has already guessed how I feel about you.'

'And?'

'And nothing. She is worried about what others will think, but I couldn't care less.'

'But you should care, *Liebling*. These are your people and they are at war with mine. And you have been forbidden to fraternise with us . . .'

'Rubbish. How can we work together under those conditions?'

'All the same, I think we must not say anything to anyone yet. Wait until the war is over.'

'You will have to go back to Germany.'

'Yes, but Germany will be ruined. I will want to see my parents, but after that . . .' He smiled. 'I don't have to stay there, do I?'

She brightened. 'You will come back?'

'If you want me to, I will come back.'

'Then I will wait.'

They were stroking and kissing each other with growing fervour which only his injury prevented from escalating, when they heard a thunderous knocking on the front door and loud voices as her mother answered it, followed by heavy footsteps on the stairs. The bedroom door was flung open and Doris rushed in, followed by two uniformed soldiers, one a sergeant, one a private. 'Jean, these men have come for Sergeant Muller.'

'Well, they can't have him,' she said. 'He's been wounded and is recovering from surgery. He can't be moved.'

'We have our orders, miss. He's an escaped prisoner and you are harbouring him. That is a serious offence. If you don't hand him over, you will undoubtedly be prosecuted.'

'That's nonsense. He works on this farm. He was never part of the escape.'

'So you say.' It was the sergeant who did the talking. The private was silently watchful, holding his rifle at the ready, as if he expected Karl to make a run for it.

'It's the truth. How do you think he was wounded? Not trying to escape, I can tell you. He was shot saving me.'

'Makes no difference. I'm here to arrest him and arrest him I will.'

'No.' She stood up, putting herself between the sergeant and the bed. 'He'll go back to camp when he is well enough.'

'It comes to something when an Englishwoman protects a Jerry,' the sergeant went on. 'That's treason in my book.'

'Oh, don't be ridiculous.' She was angry and aware as she spoke that Karl was getting out of bed.

'If you pass me my clothes, I will come with you,' he said to the sergeant.

The sergeant looked about him, saw the uniform garments on a chair and flung them at him. 'Make haste. We haven't got all day.'

'No,' Jean said, watching Karl struggle to dress himself. 'You are not well enough.'

'I shall be all right, *Fräulein*,' he said. 'It is best.'

Doris helped him finish dressing. 'I'm sorry,' she said.

'You have no reason to be sorry, Mrs Coleman. It is I who am sorry for putting you to all this trouble.'

'I'll give you trouble if you don't come quietly,' the sergeant put in. 'We've had our fill of chasing filthy Jerries all over the countryside. I'd shoot the lot if I had my way.' The sergeant grabbed Karl's arm and hustled him downstairs and out to a waiting truck, followed by the private still pointing his rifle.

Jean followed and watched them go. She was crying when she went indoors. 'It's not fair,' she told her mother. 'He is no danger to anyone. Colonel Williamson knows that. I'm going up there to give him a piece of my mind.'

'I shouldn't do that, Jean,' her mother said. 'Let things calm down a bit. Everyone has had a pretty bad scare and you flying of the handle isn't going to help, especially if you want him back.'

'Of course I want him back.'

'I am right, aren't I? You have fallen for him.'

'Is that so very bad?'

'We are at war with Germany.'

'Not for much longer.'

'Then what?'

'I don't know, Mum, really I don't.'

'Have you talked to him about it?'

'A little, but what is there to say? There is nothing we can do about it.'

'No. Best left. Least said, soonest mended.'

'Mum, there's nothing to mend. I've got to get back to work. Let's not talk about it any more.'

She went to the field gate where the cows, heavy with milk, were waiting. She opened the gate and drove them towards the yard. Her conversation with her mother played on her mind. Mum had guessed the truth and thought it ought to be nipped in the bud, but the trouble was she didn't want to do that. The prospect of saying goodbye to Karl and never seeing him again was something she didn't like to contemplate.

'I would have come sooner,' Bill said. 'But I was busy helping to round up the Jerries. They were everywhere, hiding in sheds and ditches, one had buried himself in a haystack. Some went to the station and others were caught trudging down the road towards Littleport.'

'How many got out?'

'Half the camp, I should think. They overcame the guards and stole their weapons and raided the ammunition stores. It was nasty while it lasted. Most gave themselves up without much trouble, one or two were a bit braver and boasted that Hitler would beat us yet and all the prisoners all over the country were out and marching on London, which they would take with the help of paratroopers. Did you ever hear anything so bizarre?'

'It doesn't bear thinking about,' Doris said.

'One of them killed poor Corporal Donnington,' Jean said. 'He shot Karl, too.'

'Is he dead?'

'No, he isn't dead.'

'Pity.'

'How can you say that? He saved my life. That man was going to shoot me. If he had got into the house, he would have killed everyone . . .'

'Jean helped Doctor Norman to take the bullet out of him,' Donald added. 'Then the soldiers came and arrested him and took him away.'

'Good thing too,' Bill said. 'He won't be let out again.'

'I had to do all the farm work while Jean looked after him,' the boy grumbled.

'All the work?' his mother queried. 'You don't know what real work is, young man.'

'Yes, I do. I hate farm work.'

'Nevertheless, we will all work together and get things done,' Doris said. 'That right, Pa?'

He grunted an assent.

'I can give you a hand, if you need one,' Bill said.

'Thanks, but we can manage,' Jean said. 'And perhaps Sergeant Muller will come back when he recovers.' She had refused his help before when it had been her pride and independence governing her; there was no question of accepting it now. It would have been hypocritical.

Frustrated and angry, he took his leave. He wished that Jerry to kingdom come. If he'd caught him out in the open when the prisoners were all running loose, he'd have given him both barrels. Someone else had done it for him but he had made sure Colonel Williamson knew where the man was hiding.

Colonel Williamson came to see Karl in the sick bay. 'Are you being looked after, Sergeant?'

'Yes, thank you.'

'Tell me how it happened?'

'I got in the way of a stray bullet. It was an accident.'

'Accident?'

'Yes.'

'But you were taking part in the escape?'

'No. I was going to work as usual.'

'Even if that is true, you knew what was being planned. You warned Miss Coleman and she alerted me.'

'Oh.' He hadn't known Jean had done that, but he should have guessed she would.

'It is thanks to her timely warning that we were able to contain the breakout to the immediate area,' the colonel went on. 'I imagine you would not want your fellow prisoners to know that. They are all back in the camp.'

'All of them? Even *Feldwebel* Hartmann?'

'He was picked up this morning. He is in the surgery at the moment having some shotgun pellets extracted. After that, he will be sent to a civilian prison and tried for the murder of Corporal Donnington.'

'I am sorry about the corporal.'

'So am I. He had a wife and two small children. It is in your best interests to tell me all you know, Sergeant. It is the only way that I can protect you.'

'*Herr Kolonel*, you know as much as I do. And if everyone is safely back in camp, I cannot see how I can help you.'

'That is a pity. As soon as the doctor says you are fit, you will be sent back to join your fellow prisoners.' They both knew what his fate would be. The other prisoners might guess someone had tipped off the commandant and it would not be long before they came to the conclusion that he was to blame for their failure. His actions would be seen as cowardice at best, treason at worst. If the colonel had hoped that might make Karl more amenable, he was disappointed.

'When can I go back to work?'

'That I don't know. For the moment everyone is confined to camp with loss of privileges.'

Gerhard Richter, otherwise known as *Feldwebel* Hans Schmidt, had managed to reach the outskirts of Ely with the help of Hartmann and the farm truck. When the truck ran out of fuel, they had split up, running across the fields to avoid a roadblock. The inhabitants of that town had been warned and, seeing a man running over sodden winter fields, had given chase. He had been caught when he fell into one of the many dykes that criss-crossed the fens. Brought back to Little Bushey, wet and freezing, he was sullen and angry. It was impossible to confine all the men in the cells, so all but the known ringleaders were sent back to their quarters. Colonel Williamson was fairly sure Schmidt was one of them, but no one would betray him, least of all Sergeant Muller. Consequently he was free to roam about the compound and inevitably encountered Karl after roll call three mornings later. He was surrounded by his cohorts.

'Ah, here we have the teller of tales,' he said. 'I think a trial is called for. We will convene in the latrines in half an hour.'

The latrines were chosen because it was easier to find hidden microphones there than in the huts. In less than the stipulated thirty minutes they were so crowded no one could have used them for their proper purpose. Gerhard presided, but he was far from an unbiased judge, he was also the main accuser. 'I took you for a friend,' he said, addressing Karl, who had been dragged there by Schumann and Keitel with his hands tied behind his back. 'I told you things I would never have done if I had known your true colours, and you betrayed me. Because of you, we were not able to carry out our orders. The whole course of the war has altered because of our failure.'

'That's rubbish.' Karl knew from the newspapers he had seen at the farm that there had been no parachute drop on London and the counteroffensive in the Ardennes had been halted.

'Silence! You will speak when I give you leave.' He looked round at the crowd of men, everyone angry that he had been recaptured so easily and they were looking for a scapegoat. 'I have *Feldwebel* Hartmann's sworn testimony that you tried to prevent the escape and all for *eine Englishe Flittchen*.'

Calling Jean filthy names was the last straw for Karl. He roared with anger and struggled against his bonds. He was rewarded with a punch from Schumann. It caught him on the still-healing wound in his side, making him grunt with pain. He would have remained upright if Keitel, on his other side, had not punched him in the kidney. He dropped to his knees.

'That's better,' Gerhard said. 'Do you confess to being a *Spitzel* and an informer?'

'No.' This time it was more convenient to kick him than punch him, and both men used their boots to great effect.

'What say you,' his accuser addressed the men. 'Guilty or not guilty?'

A resounding 'Guilty!' answered this, and those nearest

stepped forward to add their kicks. Someone trod on his face.

A rope was put round his neck and the end was being flung over a rafter when the door burst open and two guards rushed in, followed by others, all armed. Karl, more dead than alive, was carried out and taken back to the infirmary. In the general melee, the men scattered.

Colonel Williamson held an enquiry and questioned everyone but they all clammed up and refused to speak, even *Feldwebel* Muller when he was well enough to answer questions. He didn't need the *Feldwebel* to tell him the truth, he knew it. He had men in the camp who kept him informed, as well as radio listening points hidden in the huts. He didn't learn everything, of course, the prisoners guessed where some of the bugging devices were and destroyed them. But he knew exactly what had happened when *Gefreiter* Herzig had been sent back to his hut after his attempted escape. Two half dead men could not be disguised as an accident, even though he was told they had been fighting each other. He had thought it was a single incident, but this latest injury had made him realise the *Feldwebel* could be in serious danger. He asked the German doctor to keep him in hospital until he could arrange the transfer of Schmidt, Keitel and Schumann.

Chapter Nine

It was only two days until Christmas and the wooden toys were still hidden in the barn. Jean had hoped that Karl would be back at work and able to give them to the children himself as he had planned, but she had heard nothing of him. Other prisoners, those considered 'white' who had not attempted to escape, were back at work, so what had happened to Karl? She was worried sick. He had been beaten before for no good reason and she did not doubt his fellows would punish him if they knew what he had done to thwart them. Would Colonel Williamson be able to protect him? Would he even want to? She found it hard to work with that on her mind.

Outwardly she was her usual self, albeit a little subdued. The schools had broken up for the holiday so Donald and Terry were able to help her, though reluctantly, and the work was done. But she missed Karl. Oh, how she missed him! She remembered his kindness and gentleness, his lack of arrogance and his willingness to work. She recalled the laughter they had shared, the singing which had made the work easier, the snatched kisses which could have been so much more, and the little carved dog he had made for her. One morning, feeling more than usually miserable, she took it from her drawer and sat on her bed with it in her hands and wept. One way or another she had to find out what had happened to him. She put the dog back in her drawer and went downstairs and out of the house without speaking to anyone.

Colonel Williamson received her in his office. 'He is in the infirmary,' he told her. 'Unfortunately he has sustained some injuries. If you need a farm worker, I can supply someone else.'

'I don't want anyone else. I have become used to him. And I would have expected him to have recovered from that gunshot wound by now. It wasn't all that serious.'

'It was not the gunshot that did the damage, Miss Coleman.'

'You mean his fellow prisoners beat him. I half expected that and so did he.'

'I'm afraid so.'

'You sent him back among them, knowing what would happen. It wasn't the first time, was it, Colonel Williamson? Surely it is part of your duty to keep the prisoners safe, even from each other? You could have left him with me. You knew where he was and you knew he would not try to escape. Instead you sent two armed soldiers to drag him out of bed.'

'I had to account for all the prisoners, Miss Coleman. I had to have him back in a secure environment until the extent of what had happened and who was involved could be resolved. I needed to question him.'

'That's no excuse for deliberately allowing him to be put in danger.'

'As soon as I was alerted to what was happening we pulled him out.'

'How is he?'

'He is recovering, but the camp doctor is keeping him under observation.'

'And then, I suppose, he'll be sent back to suffer it all again.'

'No, the ringleaders have been punished and sent to other camps.'

'I sincerely hope you are right. Will he be allowed to come back to work?'

'I cannot say. I am sorry I cannot be of more help, Miss Coleman.' He picked up a bell on his desk and rang it. 'Now, if you don't mind, I have work to do . . .'

She stood up. 'May I write to him?'

'I wouldn't, Miss Coleman. It would be construed as fraternisation. I could already report you for allowing him into your house.'

'Was I supposed to leave him lying on the doorstep?'

'No, but . . .'

Afraid of where her anger might lead her, she left, picked up her bicycle from the railing where she had propped it and cycled home. Her visit had gained her nothing and she was more worried than ever. Her imagination painted horrible pictures of the extent of his injuries. And it was all because he tried to save her. Not being able to speak to him or even write to him tortured her. She did not feel a bit like celebrating Christmas, but she would have to put on a cheerful face if only for the rest of the family.

Doris was determined to make Christmas as festive as possible. She had already made the cake with dried fruit she and her mother had been hoarding, bulked out with apples and carrots as she had done every year since rationing began. She had been unsuccessful queuing up for a turkey but they had been fattening up one of the chickens.

'I can't believe this is the sixth year of the war,' she said, mixing flour paste in a jam jar so the children could make paper chains.

'I'm sure this is the last,' Jean said. 'It just can't go on much longer. With all the bombing there can't be much left of Germany.' She couldn't help thinking of Karl, knowing he must be worried about his parents and sister.

'When are you going to dig up the Christmas tree?'

'I'll do it later this morning and I'll gather some holly from the hedgerows and mistletoe from the apple trees in the orchard.'

As soon as Jean had left, Doris spread newspaper on the dining room table and gave the children paste brushes and some old coloured magazines to cut up to make the paper chains. As they worked, they talked about the presents they hoped to receive. 'I want a new bike,' Donald said. 'Then you can have my old one, Terry.'

'Why can't I have a new one if you do?'

'Because you're an evacuee and you don't have any money. Your mum don't even send what she's supposed to. That's why you have to have my old clothes . . .'

Terry flung down his brush, spattering paste everywhere, and fled to the sanctuary of his bedroom so that no one could see his tears. Doris, working in the kitchen, heard the door bang upstairs and went into the dining room to see what had happened. 'Donald, have you been quarrelling with Terry again?'

'No. I said if I had a new bike for Christmas he could have my old one. He just ran out.'

'Don said we didn't have any money 'cause our mum don't send any,' Lily piped up.

'Where did you get that idea, Don?'

'I heard you tell Jean.'

'You should not have been listening and especially you should

168

not have repeated it. Now you have hurt Terry's feelings. How would you feel if someone said that about me?'

'But they wouldn't, would they?'

'That's not the point. Poor Terry, it's bad enough having to live with strangers a long way from home, without you making it worse. Now go upstairs and apologise. Tell Terry you must have misunderstood. Be kind to him.' She smiled suddenly. 'And what makes you think you will get a new bicycle for Christmas?'

'I only said that's what I want.'

'You can't always have what you want, especially with the war and everything. Now go on.'

He disappeared. Doris picked up the string of paper chains they had made and piled them on the sideboard, then gathered up the paste brushes, the pot and the sticky newspaper. 'It's time you went home,' she told Lily. 'Mrs Harris will have your dinner ready.'

Lily followed her into the kitchen. 'Can't I stay here?'

'I'm sorry, Lily, but you are billeted with Mrs Harris, not me. Run along, there's a good girl. You can come back this afternoon.'

The tree had grown during the year and it was a struggle to dig up, but Jean had the help of the boys and together they hauled it back to the house that afternoon, with Lily dancing along behind them, bubbling over with excitement. They planted it in a bucket of sand and stood it in the corner of the sitting room, where Arthur, who had been snoozing by the fire, woke up to watch them. The box of decorations, which Doris fetched from the attic, had been used every year since the one before the war began and were looking a little bedraggled. 'We could do with new ones,' she said. 'These are past their best.'

Nevertheless they did what they could. Terry had cut out some stars from coloured cardboard which he had painted with some abstract design in bright colours. He tied them on the branches with coloured thread. There were some glass baubles, small tinplate toys, last year's candles almost burnt down to stubs and a few strands of tinsel. When Elizabeth arrived with the gingerbread men she had been making and they were added, they deemed they had done a good job given the circumstances. The paper chains were tacked up across the room from each corner to the electric light fitting in the centre of the ceiling, and the holly and ivy placed along the mantelpiece and over the pictures.

'Happy Christmas, son,' Doris murmured, laying a frond of greenery over the picture of Gordon that stood on the mantelpiece. 'Let's pray you are home before the next one.'

'Amen to that,' Jean said. Would Karl have gone home by then? She didn't want to think about it. But it reminded her of the toys in the barn. Had he known when he brought them he would not be here on Christmas Eve?

She fetched them and put them down in the middle of the floor. 'Did you know in Germany they always give presents out on Christmas Eve?' she said to the children who were looking mystified and expectant. 'Sergeant Muller made these for you and, as he isn't here, I'm doing it in his place.' She handed the carved box to Don and the sled to Terry and beckoned Lily to her. 'This is for you.'

The child screamed with delight and flung herself into Jean's arms. It should've been Karl she was hugging, Jean thought as she gently pulled away. 'Look inside.'

Lily knelt down and opened the front to find the doll's house fully furnished and, in no time, was engrossed in rearranging it. 'You have made one little girl very happy,' Jean murmured to the absent Karl.

Doris went into the kitchen and came back with a plate of mince pies. She had queued up for an hour to get one jar of mincemeat on points. 'One each now,' she said. 'The rest tomorrow.'

A bottle of cider was opened and the adults drank a glass each, wishing each other, 'Happy Christmas.'

'Back to work now,' Jean said afterwards. 'I can hear the cows from here.'

She had finished and was back in the house when Bill arrived. Jean was upstairs changing and Doris let him in. 'I thought I'd bring these today,' he said, indicating the parcels he was carrying. 'I'll be spending the day with Ma tomorrow.'

'Thank you, Bill, that's very kind of you. Come and say hallo to everyone. You can put them under the tree.'

He followed her into the sitting room. 'You've got a sizeable tree there.'

'Yes. It's last year's. Jean and the boys dug it up from the orchard. It has grown more than we realised but I don't think it looks too bad, do you?'

'It looks fine to me.' He added his parcels to the heap beneath the tree.

'Jean's changing. She'll be down in a jiffy. I must get on.' She went back to the kitchen where she had been stuffing the chicken with sage and onion. If you didn't grow your own onions they were almost impossible to come by.

'Do you think it will snow soon?' Terry was squatting on the floor beside the tree. 'I've got a new toboggan. Mr Karl made it for me.'

'Did he now? Aren't you the lucky one?'

'He made Don a box with a lid and his name carved on it. And he made Lily a doll's house. It's got furniture in it and everything.'

He digested that piece of information with a sinking heart. The man was locked up in Bushey camp and yet he still managed to be a presence in the house. 'And what did he bring Jean?'

'Nothing,' Jean said, coming into the room and catching the last of the exchange. 'Why would he? The prisoners are encouraged to work at their hobbies and Karl likes working with wood. He is very good at it. What better use could he make of the things he's made than give them to the children?'

'He's not working here again, is he? I thought he was safely locked up in Bushey camp.'

'As far as I know that's where he is, but he could have been moved. There were a lot of moves after that breakout.'

'You are managing?'

'Course she's managing,' Arthur put in. 'Don's on holiday and there's not much to do at this time of year.'

'Good.'

'I've got a present for you,' Jean said. Fetching the parcel from under the tree, she put it into his hands. 'Happy Christmas, Bill.'

'May I open it now?'

'If you like.'

It was a pullover in slate grey with an intricate cable pattern which had had her puzzling over it for several evenings. 'I hope it fits.'

'I'm sure it will.' He wrapped it again. 'I'd better be getting back. You know where I am if you need me.'

'Yes.' She accompanied him to the door. 'You'll be at church tomorrow?'

'All being well.'

Doris and Jean took time off from the preparations for Christmas dinner the following morning to join everyone as they opened their presents. The sixth Christmas of the war was no less austere than those that had gone before. There was still rationing and shortages and the gifts were simple things: handkerchiefs, a few sweets, needle cases, knitting patterns, home-made toys. Donald had his wish and there was a bicycle for him. It wasn't new, of course. Jean had had a hard job finding even that. It hadn't been in working order but the man in the bicycle shop had repaired it and given it a lick of paint. It was certainly better than his old one which was now too small for him. He passed that on to Terry and nothing more was said about Terry's mother not paying. Bill's gift to Jean was a blouse. Made of white cotton with long buttoned sleeves and a neat collar, it was the sort of blouse she had worn to her job in Wisbech, useful rather than pretty.

While the chicken was left to cook, everyone went to church. Singing the familiar carols and hearing once again the story of the nativity was soothing and induced a feeling of optimism. Things could only get better, but Christmas was spoilt for Jean because of her worry about Karl. He was constantly in her thoughts and having to pretend there was nothing wrong was wearing her down.

They streamed out of the church at the end of the service to find there had been a light dusting of snow. 'A white Christmas,' Jean said as they congregated in the churchyard and the children began scraping it up in their gloved hands. There was hardly enough to make a snowball. Jean went over to Bill and Mrs Howson. 'Thank you for the blouse,' she said, after wishing them a happy Christmas. 'I shall probably wear it a lot.'

'I told William that you would be a thirty-four and I was right, wasn't I?' Mrs Howson said.

'Yes, it fits beautifully.'

'I'll pick you up for the New Year's Eve dance, shall I?' Bill queried.

He had been taking her to the dance in the village hall every year since her parents decided she was old enough to go out with boys. She could think of no valid reason for refusing to go this year. To have done so would have invited an interrogation and she didn't want that. 'Yes, I'm looking forward to it.'

Arthur complained of being cold, although he was wearing a thick scarf over his coat and had a warm rug wrapped round his legs. 'Let's get home in the warm.'

Doris wished everyone a happy Christmas and turned to the boys and Lily. 'Come along, you three, we're going home for our dinner.'

Lily was coming back with them for the rest of the day, so that she could be with Terry. She slipped her hand into Jean's and skipped happily along beside her. 'Father Christmas came in the night and put presents in my sock.'

'What did he bring you?'

'A colouring book and coloured crayons and some mittens. See.' She held up her hands to show off a pair of bright red mittens. 'There was an apple and a bag of jelly babies. I bit the heads off them.'

In spite of the rationing and the shortages, Christmas dinner was a feast and afterwards Don and Terry went off on their bicycles. Jean and Doris decided to take Lily for a walk, leaving Arthur snoozing by the fire.

Their road took them through the village, where they stopped to chat to other people they met, and on to the road past the POW camp. There were one or two prisoners walking about the compound, but most were inside. They could hear singing coming from one of the huts. The tune was familiar to them but the words were not. *Stille Nacht, heilige Nacht.*

'It's "Silent Night",' Jean said as they stood and listened. 'How lovely it sounds. You see, they are not a Godless nation.' The end of the first verse, '*Schlaf in himmlischer Ruh!*' faded into silence. 'They sing of peace, just as we do.'

'It's a lovely carol,' Doris said. 'But the rector wouldn't have it in the service when we were discussing the carols. He said it might offend some people.'

'How narrow-minded. Those men in there,' she nodded towards the high wire, 'want peace as much as we do. They have homes and loved ones and they are worried about them, just as we are about ours.' If she had hoped for a glimpse of Karl, she was disappointed. Did it mean he was still in hospital? 'We'd better turn back. I've got the cows to milk and all the rest of the animals to feed before tea.'

Bill, dressed in a lounge suit and striped tie and with his hair slicked down, came at seven o'clock on New Year's Eve to take Jean to the dance. She had taken trouble with her appearance, dressing up, setting her hair nicely and making-up her face, wearing her one and only pair of silk stockings.

'Will I do?' she asked, twirling and making the skirt of her blue silk dress swirl about her.

He looked her up and down. 'You look smashing.'

'I'll get my coat and hat.'

The blackout had been lifted except for attic windows, and lights shone from every window of the village hall. They could hear the music long before they reached it. 'More like old times,' Bill said.

'Yes, isn't it?' They shed their coats and in no time at all they were dancing. He was determined not to quarrel with her and was particularly attentive, helped by some of Mrs Maynard's elderberry wine. The big clock over the door reached midnight and everyone stopped dancing to wish each other a happy new year. The last waltz was danced very slowly, with their arms round each other, at the end of which they sang 'Auld Lang Syne' and stood to attention for the national anthem. Mr Harris packed up his records and everyone drifted out into the cold January air. They walked back to the farm at peace with each other.

'Mustn't wake everyone up,' she whispered, leading the way into the kitchen. 'I'll make some cocoa.'

'Never mind the cocoa,' he said, trying to take her into his arms. She wriggled away. 'Now what's the matter?'

'Nothing.' The euphoria of the dance had worn off and she was acutely aware that she should have been honest with him and told him how she felt about Karl. The deception was wearing her out. 'Bill . . .' she began but stopped when she heard someone come out of a bedroom upstairs.

'Is that you, Jean?' Doris called down from the landing.

'Yes, Mum. I'm just coming up.'

Bill grinned ruefully. 'I'd better go. I don't want your Ma coming down, accusing me of leading you astray.' He grinned. 'Not that I wouldn't like to . . .'

She gave him a gentle push towards the door.

The new year began very coldly with several inches of snow. Donald and Terry helped Jean clear the yard, shovelling snow up on one side where they made a huge snowman, with two coal eyes and a carrot nose. When Jean considered they had done their bit, they were allowed to go off and try out the toboggan on the nearest hill. With Lily screaming in front of him, Terry sent it flying down towards the pit, careful to steer away before they tumbled in. Donald took his turn. They did it again and again until, rosy-cheeked, they put Lily on the sled and pulled it to Mrs Harris's house, where she ran indoors. The boys continued on their way.

'Where'd you get the sledge?' Eddie Slater asked. He was with a crowd of other boys.

'Sergeant Muller made it for me.' Terry said. 'It's a beaut, ain't it?'

'The Jerry, you mean? You aren't supposed to talk to them, let alone take presents off them. I'll tell on yer.'

'And I'll tell on you, getting sausages and chops for your ma,' Terry retorted.

'She don't hev more than her ration.'

'Oh, yeh, pull the other one.'

The result was a brawl. Others who had been standing by awaiting developments joined in and the result was several bloody noses.

Doris was appalled when the boys finally arrived home. 'What on earth have you two been up to?' she demanded. 'Have you been fighting? Really boys, why can't you get on together without quarrelling?'

'We haven't quarrelled,' Terry said. 'At least not with each other. It was Eddie Slater. He said my toboggan had to be confiscated on account I wasn't supposed to take presents from a Jerry. Is that true?'

'Well, in a way, I suppose it is,' Jean said. 'Not about it being confiscated, but about accepting gifts. Perhaps you should not have said who gave it to you.'

'I wouldn't have, if I'd known. Now he's got it.'

'He took it off you?'

'Him and about six others,' Donald said. 'If he'd been alone he never would have.'

Jean reached for her coat and hat. 'I'm going to sort this out right now.'

She found Eddie at home having a black eye bathed by his

mother. 'What do you want?' Mrs Slater demanded before Jean could speak.

'I've come for Terry's toboggan. Your son stole it from him.'

'He shouldn't have had it in the first place. It's ag'in the law to take things off Jerries.'

'And who are you to say what's law and what isn't? I know enough to know that taking something that doesn't belong to you is theft.'

'You going to report it then? What do you think Constable Worth will say? You're the one in trouble, not my Eddie. Look what your boys did to him.'

Jean kept her temper with an effort. 'We shall see, shall we? Do you want your son up before Sir Edward like all the other criminals he has to deal with? He will be if I go to the constable, and he'll have a criminal record against him. Where Terry got the toboggan from makes no difference to that.' She sincerely hoped she was right because Mrs Slater was wavering.

'Eddie hasn't got it. I don't know where it is.'

Jean turned to the boy; he looked as though he had come off worse than Don or Terry in the skirmish. 'We were playing on it and it went in the pit.'

'Which pit?'

'Yours. That's the only place where there's a bit of a hill.'

'He nearly went in himself,' Mrs Slater said. 'As it is his trousers and socks were soaked.'

'Are you telling the truth, Eddie?' Jean demanded.

'Yes, honest to God. We only wanted to have a go on it.'

'I'll soon find out.'

As she turned and left she heard Mrs Slater say, 'Jerry-lover.'

She ignored it but the shaft went home. Was that what she could expect, simply because she befriended a lonely prisoner of war? Or had everyone guessed the truth? How much did she care? She cared for Karl's sake, not her own, and was glad he had not heard it. It was already dark, too late to try and retrieve the toboggan even if it was retrievable. It would have to be left until the next day.

The pit was frozen, but there was a hole in the ice near the edge where the toboggan had gone through. Knowing how deep it was, Jean was afraid there was nothing they could do to get it out.

'Couldn't we dangle a hook in and try to grab it?' Terry suggested. He was really down over its loss, especially as Don and Lily still had their gifts.

'You'd have to go on the ice to do that and it isn't thick enough to bear your weight,' Jean said. 'You are not to attempt it, do you hear? I don't want to have to tell your mum you drowned in our pit.'

'Could we try from the bank with a fishing rod?'

'I doubt it would work, but if you promise not to go on the ice, you can try if you like. I've got work to do.'

She left them. They fetched a fishing rod and some string and tied one of the meat hooks used for hanging bacon on the end and cast it into the hole. It took several tries even to get into the hole and then they hooked up nothing but weeds. They tried all morning before giving up and going back to the farm. 'Mr Karl made that 'specially for me, what's he going to say?' Terry said. He was both angry and tearful, though the tears he tried to keep hidden.

'He'll know it wasn't your fault,' Jean said, while wondering if he would ever hear of it. She had no idea how he was or even if he was still at Bushey camp. Not knowing was tearing her to pieces.

On the last day of January, the Russians crossed the German border and Jean's heart went out to Karl, knowing he was bound to hear of it. And in the Netherlands the Allies reached the Rhine. It could not be long now before Hitler sued for peace. He would surely not allow his people to be put in jeopardy by fighting on German soil? They had already suffered enough through the relentless bombing. Her mother talked about it all the time, always with reference to Gordon.

'It must be over soon,' she said more than once. 'Oh, it will be so good to have him home and working on the farm like he used to.'

The men in the *Stalag* could hear the Russian guns clearly and bets were being taken on how long it would be before they reached it. After nearly six years of war, all they wanted was to be free. The Germans were defending every inch but the camp security was not relaxed one jot. There was still roll call twice a day and rations were even smaller than they had been, nothing but barley soup and coarse bread. If it had not been for the Red Cross parcels they would surely have starved. Or frozen. It was bitterly cold and the snow was several inches deep. Keeping warm was another struggle. They had resorted to burning their bunks and sleeping on the floor. Some of the prisoners were set to work clearing the snow from around the huts. It was a way of keeping warm, Gordon supposed, but he could not do it without slipping and falling over. His request for a proper false limb had gone unanswered and he knew he would not be given one now until he reached home.

They were not digging tunnels now. A good number had escaped through the last one the year before, although all but three had been caught. While on the run they had caused widespread disruption and had hundreds of German military looking for them, a fact which pleased those left in the camp. There had been other failed attempts but now it looked as though it would be the Red Army who freed them and that worried some, particularly the Poles, who knew what the Russian regime was like.

'I'm off as soon as I see them on the road,' Stanislaw told Gordon. 'No way am I going to land in their hands. I'd rather die first.'

'They are our allies.'

'So long as it suits them. You wait. You'll find out how much they care about that, if you let them take you.'

The guns were closer now. The German guards were jittery, everyone could see that, and the *Kommandant* had ordered a huge bonfire outside his office where they were burning papers. Smoke and black smuts drifted across the compound. Stan was making his preparations, gathering what food and warm clothing he could. Gordon would have liked to go with him, but he would have been a liability and would not ask it of his friend.

In the end Stanislaw did not need to set off alone because they were all told to be ready to leave the following morning. Speculating on where they were going and how they were going to get there, they gathered up their belongings, mostly spare socks and underwear, a tin used to eat out of, a spoon and whatever food they had hoarded which was little enough, tying it up in blankets. It was quite weighty for men weakened by hunger.

'If we have far to walk we'll never manage it,' Gordon said, wondering what to discard.

The next day, they stood about after roll call, dressed in every vestige of clothing they had, carrying their pathetic bundles. They were each issued with a Red Cross parcel. 'Where the hell have these come from?' Gordon demanded. 'The devils have been holding back on us.' There was no sign of transport. Nor would there be. They were expected to march in batches of a hundred. Gordon, Alex, Jeremy and Stanislaw stuck close together and were counted off to go with the second batch.

A farm wagon pulled by a skinny carthorse arrived suddenly and those too disabled to walk were loaded onto it. Anyone too ill, even for that, was left behind in the sick bay. Gordon started off walking, hobbling along on his peg leg, helped by his single crutch. They were going west, away from the oncoming Russians, a fact that pleased Stanislaw.

'Where are we going?' Gordon asked one of the guards who walked beside them. The man's boots were full of holes, Gordon noticed, and he did not have a greatcoat. No wonder he was looking miserable.

The German shrugged but did not reply. In fact he did not seem at all interested in his charges and kept looking behind him and up at the sky. The boom of cannon was certainly coming nearer.

They were watched by the population of the villages through which they passed. Some spat, some threw stones, but some came out and offered a drink of water or a cup of thin soup to those in the wagon. At midday, they stopped beside the road for something to eat, but not knowing how long the Red Cross parcels were expected to last, they did not consume everything. When they were ready to start again, those on the cart who could manage to walk a little way were exchanged with others who were flagging. Gordon, whose stump was giving him hell, enjoyed a few miles' respite.

No one had much inclination to chat, but when they did it was speculation about what the Germans intended to do with them. 'They are going to march us until we all fall dead from starvation and exhaustion,' Jeremy said.

'More likely we're all going to be shot,' Stan said. 'In revenge for the bombing.'

'We are fighter pilots, not bombers,' Gordon said.

'Makes no difference. To them we are all *Terrorfliegers*.'

'I don't think they'd dare do that,' Alex put in. 'Think of the repercussions when the Allies find out.'

'What do you suggest they are going to do, meekly hand us over to the British or Americans? There's the whole of Germany between us and them. We'd never make it like this.'

That was patently obvious. They had not covered many miles when the weakest began to drop out. Some were left where they were, others were loaded onto the already overloaded wagon. At dusk, cold, exhausted and hungry, they were herded into a barn for the night.

'I'm going to try and find out what's what,' Alex said, and went off to speak to the sergeant, the most senior of their guards, who were sharing the same conditions as the prisoners. Except for the colour of the uniform and the fact the guards carried rifles, it was hard to tell one from the other. The commandant and his officers had passed them long before in a staff car.

Gordon collapsed into a corner and took off the peg leg to give his stump some relief. He took his shoe off and wrung the water out of his sock, then tucked it between his overcoat and tunic in the hope what little heat he had in his body might dry it, or at least warm it. Because he had only one leg, he had spare socks in his bundle and he put one of these on. It was bliss.

'He doesn't know any more than we do,' Alex said, returning to the little group. 'All I could get out of him was Moosburg.'

'Where the hell's that?' Jeremy asked, but no one seemed to know.

'Better eat what we can and get our heads down,' Alex said. They huddled close to each other in order to keep warm and were soon sound asleep in spite of the bitter cold.

Gordon was roused at dawn to the sound of banging and wondered, for a moment, if the Red Army had caught up with them, but then he realised it was Stanislaw. His friend had ripped a shutter from the barn and was busy working on it with some strips of wood and some bent nails which he was endeavouring to straighten with a hammer he had found in the back of the barn. 'What are you doing?'

'Making a sledge to pull our stuff on. Anyone got any rope?'

No one had, but Alex had a leather belt, Jeremy had a tie and Gordon had a scarf his mother had knitted for him and they were handed over and joined together so they had something with which to pull the sled.

When the guard came in to hand out the ration of bread and barley soup that served for breakfast, they had already forced their frozen feet back into their footwear and tied their belongings on the sled. Half an hour later they set off again.

When the horse, which had not been fed, stumbled and could not rise, the guards unhitched it and one of them put a bullet in its head. There was talk of butchering it and eating it, but as none had the means nor the strength to do it, this source of sustenance was left to the local population. From then on the prisoners formed gangs who took it in turns to pull the wagon. Gordon was back to walking. He could only take his mind off the pain in his stump by dreaming of home.

It was warm in the farmhouse kitchen. His mother was baking cakes, his father was in his rocking chair, smoking his pipe and reading *Farmers Weekly*. He was in his stockinged feet;

his boots stood on the mat by the kitchen door where he had left them, Donald was playing with the cat, teasing it with a feather on the end of a piece of string. Jean was looking very pretty in a flowered skirt and blue blouse. She was off to a dance with Bill. Goodness, she must be twenty-one now. Had they married? And Don was fifteen. They had grown up while he had been away. Rosie was there, too. Fair-haired, blue-eyed, funny little Rosie. What would they all make of the man he had become, a man with only one leg? Would this long march ever be done? Would he ever see them again?

Chapter Ten

The noose was closing in on Nazi Germany but still Hitler made his troops fight on; he was still sending rockets to terrify Londoners, but all the talk was of peace and rebuilding and jobs and houses for the demobilised servicemen. Terry, who had turned fourteen, left school at Easter and Mrs Jackson had come down to take both her children home. Lily didn't want to go, which upset her mother, but Terry was looking forward to following in his father's footsteps and becoming a warehouseman on the docks.

He was not the only one looking forward to the end of his schooldays; Donald was due to leave school in July after he had sat his school certificate exams, and there was much discussion about what he should do. 'He'll work on the farm with Gordon,' his father said. 'Stands to reason.' Arthur had been talking of retiring and handing the farm over, lock, stock and barrel, to Gordon when he came home and moving into a smaller home with Doris, if they could find one. The housing shortage was acute.

'I don't want to work for Gordon,' Donald said. 'Farming is boring and you never get any time off and, besides, it doesn't pay enough.'

'What do you want to do then?'

'I don't know yet.'

'You could go to agricultural college,' Doris said. 'I think we could find the money for that. You'd learn new ways of farming, specialise in something, machinery or something that interests you.'

'I'll think about it.'

'In the meantime you will work on the farm in the school holidays,' his father said. 'There's plenty for you to do.'

With everyone talking about what they would do when the war ended, Jean felt cut off, in a kind of limbo, unable to make plans, unable even to think straight. She could not brush aside her feelings for Karl as if they were a temporary aberration she would get over. He was the love of her life. Without him, her life would be barren. Surely he would not go back to Germany at the end of the war without ever seeing her again? The thought was tormenting her.

'What's on your mind, Jean?' Gran asked her one day when she was at the farm, helping to clean the eggs ready to be sent to the packing station. The snow had gone, the pit was once again a sheet of water and there were snowdrops in flower in the woods surrounding Sir Edward's estate.

'Nothing.'

'I know there is. I suppose it's Karl.' Her grandmother always sensed her moods quicker than anyone.

'I keep wondering how he is.'

'Have you written to him?'

'No, I can't. Colonel Williamson warned me it would be construed as fraternising.'

'And you are eating your heart out for him.'

Startled, she turned towards her grandmother. 'What makes you say that?'

'I've got eyes, child. And ears. I can see your expression when you look at him and hear the softness in your voice when you speak of him.'

'Oh.' Did she really wear her heart on her sleeve? 'Have you discussed this with Mum?'

'Certainly not.'

'What am I to do, Gran? Everything is going round and round in my head until I'm dizzy with it.'

'There is nothing you can do. You can't help who you fall in love with. Have you talked to Sergeant Muller about it?'

'He feels the same as I do, but he will go back to his family. He talked about coming back, but . . .' she shrugged.

'Are you afraid he will go and forget you?'

'I don't know. I hope not.'

'I'd say it depends how strong your feelings are for each other. Have patience. Love will find a way, no matter what.'

'You don't condemn me?'

'Lord no, but others might. It is a rocky road you have chosen to travel, my child.'

She sighed. 'And I can't see the end of it.'

'How are you managing the farm without him?' her grandmother asked, changing tack suddenly.

'All right, I suppose. This time of the year I can get by doing just the essential jobs, but I suppose it will all catch up with me in the end. Don does what he's asked to do when he has time but he's studying for his school certificate and I don't want to jeopardise that.'

'Couldn't you ask Colonel Williamson to let Karl come back to work?'

'Perhaps he doesn't want to.'

'You won't know unless you ask, will you?'

A week later, Jean was feeding the noisy, hungry pigs when she heard a vehicle draw up at the gate, but assuming it was the milk lorry come to collect the churn, carried on with what she was doing and took the empty swill buckets back to the shed. Karl was waiting by the door. She dropped the buckets and flung herself into his arms. He held her tight and pulled her into the building out of sight of the house and kissed her over and over again.

'Oh, Karl, I've missed you so much.'

'And I you.'

'What's been happening?' She leant back to look into his face. He was a lot thinner and his cheeks had a grey tinge. His nose was crooked and there was a long scar down one side of his face. She traced it with her finger. 'You were beaten again, weren't you?'

'It was nothing. They blamed me for the failure of the escape plot.'

'My fault.'

'Of course not. It was doomed to fail from the start.'

It had taken a long time to recover from the beating inflicted by his compatriots. He had sustained a broken arm which he had raised to protect his head, and several broken ribs from the boots of his attackers. As for his face, that had been a mess with black eyes, broken cheeks and jaw, not to mention bruising around his neck from the noose. Even when he recovered, Colonel Williamson asked the doctor to keep him in the infirmary longer than he needed until all his attackers had been dealt with and sent to more secure prisons. Hartmann had been tried in a civilian court for the murder of Corporal Donnington and hanged at Pentonville with ringleaders from other camps. February was well-advanced before he returned to his hut.

'Karl, what are we going to do?'

'What about?'

'Us. Do we tell them or not? I do so hate the deceit.'

'You must decide that, *Liebling*, but remember that fraternisation is forbidden. Your parents might tell the colonel and I will not be allowed to come here again . . .'

'Mum would not do that. I know she wouldn't, and neither would Pa.'

'But others might learn of it, a thoughtless word from your mother or brother to a friend, the way we look at each other, anything. People are naturally suspicious. Some are revengeful.'

'I couldn't bear that.'

'Our secret, then. We can live with it, can't we?'

'Yes, if you think it best.'

'Then we carry on as we always have done. I am your prisoner.' He chuckled. 'In more ways than one. You hold my heart fast.' He picked up her hand and put it over his heart. 'Feel it?'

'Yes. And you have mine. Always. The war will soon be over and then we can tell the world.'

'I will have to go home first.'

'Have you had news?'

'No. The Russians are advancing rapidly. If they reach Hartsveld it will not be good there.'

'Perhaps your family will leave before that.'

'I don't know. There is the farm, you see. They won't want to leave it . . .'

'I understand. I am sure my parents would feel the same if it happened here.'

'But it never will. I wish the Führer would sue for peace, then the Russians will stop their advance.'

'Perhaps he will.'

He gave a grunt of a laugh. 'Not he. And there are still people in the camp who are convinced he will come up with some grand plan to turn the tide. They talk of it all the time and what they will do when it happens.'

'What can they do? They tried before and failed.'

'I know. It's – what do you say? – all hot air.'

'I hope, for your sake, you hear soon.' She reached up to kiss his cheek. 'Now we must do some work before Mum wonders what we are up to.'

'What would you like me to do?'

'I was planning to give the stables a good going over. I've got some whitewash for the walls and creosote for the door. We'll soon have it spick and span.'

They took the horses out to the pasture before raking out the old bedding, loading it on a wheelbarrow and taking it to the muck heap across the yard. Then they hosed the floor down, before beginning on the whitewashing. Arthur insisted on being wheeled out to watch progress, but when Doris brought tea and sandwiches out to them, he complained of being cold and she took him back indoors.

'He never used to feel cold,' Jean told Karl. 'He'd be out in all weathers working all day and he wouldn't come in until it was too dark to see.'

'I expect it is the inactivity that makes him notice it more.'

'Yes. I feel so sorry for him, brought so low. He's only fifty-three. It isn't fair.'

'Nothing is fair in the world today.'

'No, or we would not have to pretend to be indifferent to each other. It's ludicrous.'

'It is,' he agreed. 'Instead, I would be taking you to the cinema or dancing, or for a long walk holding your hand. I might even sing you a love song.' He began to sing very softly.

Du, du liegst mir im Herzen,
du, du liegst mir im Sinn.
Du, du machst mir viel Schmerzen,
weißt nicht wie gut ich dir bin.

'What does it mean?'

'"You, you are in my heart. You, you are in my mind. You, you cause me much pain, you do not know how good I am for you".'

'It sounds better in German.'

'It goes on: "So as I love you so, so love me too. The most tender desires I alone feel only for you . . ."'

'Oh, Karl, please stop or you will make me cry.'

'Make you cry? I would rather make you laugh.'

'You do, often. You make me happy.'

They went back to work and finished as the last of the light faded.

'Better get the cows in and milked,' she said. They cleared away the buckets of whitewash and cleaned their brushes, brought the horses back and then went to fetch the cows who were already bunched up at the field gate waiting for them.

They herded the animals into the cowshed and set to work. Apart from the occasional swish of a cow's tail and a soft lowing, it was peaceful and quiet. They did not need to talk.

'Oh, I forgot, I've got something for you,' she said as they finished. 'Wait here.'

She dashed back into the house and came back with his Christmas parcel. 'I was going to give this to you on Christmas

Eve when you gave the children their toys. Better late than never.'

She watched as he undid it to reveal a pullover in dark green wool. It had long sleeves and a V-neck. 'You made this for me?'

'Yes. It's only pulled out wool, I'm afraid, but it's thick and warm. I hope it fits.'

'I am sure it does.' He took off his jacket and pulled it on over his shirt. 'Perfect,' he said, reaching across to kiss her. 'Did the children like their presents?'

'They were over the moon. Lily hugged me. She should have been hugging you.' She paused, wondering whether to tell him but he would find out anyway. 'Terry took his toboggan out when it snowed and some boys pinched it. They let it go into the pit. It's lost, I'm afraid. He was really down about it.'

'I'll make him another.'

'He's gone home, Karl. So has Lily.'

'Do you miss them?'

'Yes. After five years, the house seems strangely quiet without them. Did you know you would not be coming on Christmas Eve?'

'I had an idea I might not.'

'That was a terrible time, really terrible. I was so worried about you and angry with Colonel Williamson for not protecting you. He knew what would happen when they took you back. And he told me not to write to you because that would be fraternising.'

'He was right. I worried about you, too. I thought you would be in trouble . . .'

'Only mild threats. I took no notice.'

'Did you get your pickup truck back?'

'Yes. Bill took me to fetch it. It had no petrol in it but was otherwise undamaged.'

'You still see Mr Howson, then?'

'Occasionally. I can't tell him, can I? About us, I mean.'

'No.'

'We don't have a lot to say to each other and I don't encourage him. Still, the war is all but over . . .'

'Not quite, my love. There has been no surrender, no armistice. Some of my fellow prisoners are simply waiting for that to happen, but others are convinced the Führer will turn things around. A few are even talking of escape, but as the ringleader of the December breakout, a man I had known in Germany, has been moved to another camp, few are enthusiastic enough to do anything about it.'

'You are not in any danger from them now, are you?'

'No, I do not think so.'

'You will take care, though, won't you? Don't do anything to rile them.'

'Rile?'

'Annoy.'

'I will try not to.'

'I wish you didn't have to go back every night.'

'I wish it, too. Please God, one day I will not have to. Remember that when you are feeling low.' They heard the lorry stop at the gate. 'I must go.' He kissed her and strode away. She noticed there was a spring in his step that had not been there when he arrived. And she felt a hundred times more cheerful. He was right; they were good for each other.

After a cold January and wet February, March was unusually mild. There were cowslips in the meadow and celandines in the hedgerows, daffodils and wallflowers in the garden and new lambs in the field and others being born. Jean had her hands full looking after them.

'There's a dead one over there,' she told Karl when he arrived to join her. She nodded in its direction; the ewe was standing over it as if expecting it to get to its feet. 'It happened before I got here. I've been too busy to see to it.'

He knelt to help her. The ewe's twins were born, cleaned up with straw and put to the mother. She was prepared to accept one, but not the other, nudging it roughly out of the way whenever it came near.

'I'll have to hand-rear it.' She laughed. 'Goodbye restful nights.'

'We could put it to the ewe that lost her lamb.'

'She won't accept one that's not her own.'

'We can deceive her into thinking it is.' He fetched the dead lamb and rubbed it all over the live one. 'I have known shepherds skin a dead lamb and dress the live one in the skin to trick the ewe,' he said. 'But perhaps this will work.'

He carried the hungry little animal to the ewe and set it down close to her udder. 'Go on,' he murmured. 'Have your breakfast.' He watched carefully in case the ewe tried to kick the little one, but she stood unmoving. He held the lamb close to the nipple and squeezed it. Milk squirted over its nose. With Karl's help it began to suck. He left the pair and went round the flock to see if there were any more ewes ready to give birth, but though some were not far off, they did not appear uncomfortable. He returned to Jean. 'I think that's all for now. Tomorrow there will be more.'

'Right.' She stood up and flexed her aching back. 'Do you think you could fetch a spade from the shed and bury that one?' She indicated the dead lamb which had enabled another to live. 'I'll go and feed the pigs and chickens. The poor things are left so much to their own devices nowadays.'

He fetched a spade and dug a grave under a hedge for the little lamb. It made him sad. He didn't know whether his sorrow was due to the loss of the lamb or the situation in which he found himself.

The men were grouped around the illicit radio when he returned that evening, listening to the German account of the latest news on *Deutschlandfunk*. The Red Army under Marshal Zhukov had been halted at the Oder river and the American advance had been held up when the Schwammenauel Dam was opened, making it impossible to cross the Ruhr. The bulletin went on. 'The Führer has appointed General Wenck to command the new offensive to the east of Berlin and the Soviet army will be sent back to where they came from in disarray. There have been heavy air raids on many German cities, but it cost the Allies dearly in men and machines. Factories and industrial plants have not been affected and are in full production.'

'What did I tell you?' Otto said. 'We're not done for yet, not by a long way. The English exaggerate as they always do.'

'Guard approaching,' the lookout warned them.

There was a wild scramble to hide the wireless and any other incriminating evidence and by the time the corporal entered the hut, they were all engaged in innocent pursuits.

'*Feldwebel* Muller, Colonel Williamson wants to see you,' the guard said without coming in any further than the doorway. 'Now.'

Mystified, Karl followed him out, aware of the muttering going on behind him. If, on his return, he could not give a good account of why he had been sent for, he would be in more trouble.

Lieutenant Colonel Williamson could see part of the compound from his office window. There were men strolling about, others playing games, some working on the little gardens round the huts. The camp was like a small town, except there were no women, no children. It housed the good and the bad, the meek and the brash, the strong and the weak, the hopeful and those with no hope. Since the December breakout and the departure of the troublemakers it had been relatively peaceful.

There had been much discussion at government level about what to do with the prisoners when the war ended. They would have to be repatriated, but that would not happen overnight. Transport would have to be found for them which would take some organising. The Home Office and Ministry of Agriculture were in favour of keeping the prisoners as long as possible; the Home Office wanted builders and the Ministry of Agriculture needed farm workers. 'Their labour is crucial,' someone from the agricultural ministry said at one of the interminable meetings he had attended. 'Until our own men are demobbed and we know how many are going back into agriculture, there will be an acute shortage of manpower. The Italians, many of whom already live on the farms where they work, will be sent home first. Perhaps the farmers would be prepared to board German prisoners in their place.'

'What about non-fraternisation? How would that work?'

'It wouldn't, would it? But would it be necessary when hostilities cease?'

Charles had smiled; in his experience the ban was honoured more in the breach than the observance, certainly in Little Bushey. 'Perhaps we could try it on a small scale and see how it works,' he had suggested.

No date for this trial was set, though it was assumed it would not happen until the war ended, but he intended to jump the gun. Miss Coleman's accusations had bothered his conscience. He had known what would happen putting Muller in among his fellows after the shooting, what he hadn't realised was just how severe his punishment would be. If he had not been alerted by the *Lagerführer*, the man would have died. An external enquiry would not have looked good on his record.

He turned from the window as *Feldwebel* Muller was shown into the room. He sent the guard away with a nod of his head. 'Sit down, Sergeant.' He indicated a chair on the other side of his desk.

Karl sat and waited.

'How was work today, Sergeant?'

'It was work,' he answered warily. 'Something to keep me busy.'

'And away from your fellow prisoners.'

'I do not understand.'

'Oh, I think you do. I know you are not popular among your compatriots.' He held up his hand to stop Karl speaking. 'Don't worry, I am not about to ask you to tell me. I doubt you would anyway.'

'No, *Herr Kolonel*.'

'The reason I sent for you is to tell you that some German prisoners of war who have been found to be cooperative and not a danger to the civilian population are to be allowed to live on the farms where they work, with the farmer's agreement, of course, because they will be responsible for the men living with them.' He paused to let the man digest this. 'Would you like to live on Briar Rose Farm, *Feldwebel* Muller?'

'Has Mr Coleman agreed?'

'I haven't asked him yet, but I will do so, if that's what you want.'

'I should like that. I never arrive in time to do the morning milking and I don't go on a Sunday. I think it would help them.'

'Then I'll see what Mr Coleman says.'

Karl left him, wondering what Jean would make of the request. But it lifted his spirits more than he could say.

* * *

'We've had a letter from Colonel Williamson,' Doris told Jean a couple of mornings later. 'Apparently some of the better behaved prisoners are going to be allowed to stay on the farms where they work. He's suggesting Sergeant Muller should live on the premises.'

'Live-in?'

'Yes, read it for yourself.'

Jean scanned it quickly and then read it again more slowly. 'What do you think?' she said, careful not to sound too eager.

'I don't know. It needs thinking about.'

'He's a Jerry,' her father said.

'So what? He's not dangerous. You know that. He was shot saving us, don't forget. If anything like that happened again . . .' Her voice tailed off.

'Don't be daft. The war's all but over. Even Jerry must know that.'

'Some of them don't. Some are still convinced Hitler will turn things around.'

'Did Sergeant Muller tell you that?'

'Yes, he told me there are still men in the Bushey camp talking about escape. A man about the place might be useful.'

'All right, no need to rub it in.'

'I didn't mean it like that, Pa, you know I didn't. I meant he would be on the premises for the morning milking and anything else that needs doing early. He'd be here Sundays, too. But it's your decision.'

'So it is, and don't you forget it, girl.'

'I don't know,' her mother said. 'If he came, where would he sleep?'

'In the barn.' This from her father.

'Pa, you can't expect a man to live like an animal and do a day's work as well. He can have Gordon's room.' The room, until recently, had been occupied by Terry.

'But what if Gordon comes home?' her mother queried.

'Mum, you have to face it, that's not going to happen before the war ends and then Sergeant Muller will go back to his own home. We really could do with the extra help.'

'All right, we'll give it a try,' her father said. 'If it doesn't work we can always send him back.'

Jean knew that sending him back would mean more beatings. The other prisoners hated him because he was against Hitler. She suspected Colonel Williamson knew it. Perhaps he wanted to protect him. 'Then write and agree, Mum. I'll sort the room out.' She tapped the letter. 'It says here *Feldwebel* Muller has indicated his willingness to come. I wonder why he never said.'

'I did not dare hope,' he told her when she taxed him with keeping it from her later that day. He had found her in the barn, sorting seed potatoes and they had greeted each other with more than one kiss. 'I didn't think your parents would agree.'

'Well they have. We get more help and you don't bump into so many doors.'

He let that pass. 'Are you sure?'

'Karl, why would I not be sure? Not so long ago you said the time might come when you would not have to go back every night. And now it has. I couldn't be more pleased.'

'Where will I sleep and eat?'

'With us, of course, one of the family.'

'Sweetheart, I think that is not wise. We have a secret to keep and that will be very difficult if we are living under the same roof.'

'Don't you want to come?'

'Of course I do. The prospect excites me, but we shall have to be very careful not to give ourselves away.'

She laughed. 'Oh, I shall work you harder than ever, never

fear. I shall be the hardest taskmaster you could ever imagine.'

'I doubt that.' He grinned ruefully. 'Hard taskmasters do not usually kiss their slaves.'

'You are not my slave.'

'Oh, but I am, so let us get to work before you fetch out the whip.'

They spent the day planting potatoes. He sang softly as he worked.

'When will you move in?' she asked while they were doing the afternoon milking. 'I'll have your room ready for you.'

'As soon as the paperwork is done. I think in a few days.'

The transport brought him one morning less than a week later, together with all his belongings, a pitifully small bundle in Jean's eyes. But he was more than pleased, she could tell by the spring in his step and a grin he took no trouble to hide.

'Whose room is this?' he asked when she took him upstairs. 'It is not yours, is it?'

'No, it's Gordon's. He doesn't need it at the moment, does he? I'll leave you to settle in. Come down when you are ready.' A snatched kiss and she was gone.

He sat on the bed and looked about him. It was obviously a boy's room. There were sporting trophies on the shelves and books about football and flying. Hanging on the wall were photographs of a young man in cricket flannels, another of the same young man standing beside a Spitfire. He stood up to look at it more closely.

Gordon must be three or four years older than Jean, he guessed, if he had been old enough to join the RAF in 1939. He was tall and confident, proud of himself. He could not have known his flying career would be so short. 'I hope that my countrymen are being as kind to you as yours have been to me,' he murmured.

* * *

201

Gordon had lost all track of time. Days, weeks, even months had passed in an endless shuffle. He had lost count of the number of barns, deserted schools, warehouses and bombed-out houses they had sheltered in. The column of one hundred was down to less than fifty. The roads behind them were littered with corpses and belongings they no longer had the strength to carry. With the warmer weather, the sled had been abandoned and many who had started out with greatcoats had discarded them. The wagon had long since fallen to pieces. For a time those still on their feet had made stretchers from poles and blankets and carried the invalids, but that didn't last; no one had the strength. Sometimes the guards had carried the stretchers. There was no one on stretchers now, they had all succumbed to the diseases that plagued them: pneumonia, diphtheria, but mostly dysentery due to their strange diet and lack of anything like hygienic conditions.

He had wondered if the German authorities knew where they were, but now and again they were issued with more Red Cross parcels, so they must be keeping track of them. What they apparently were not sure of was how many men had fallen by the wayside because the same number of parcels arrived for the survivors to share. He suspected the guards had not reported the deaths.

He had kept going on willpower, though his stump was torn to shreds. Alex, Jeremy and Stanislaw had refused to leave him behind though he begged them to. They took it in turns to haul him along, until one evening, Stanislaw had disappeared and come back with an ancient bath chair. 'I talked an old lady into giving it to me in exchange for a rabbit,' he told them. 'It was her late husband's.' Thereafter he no longer had to hobble along beside them, though pushing the chair could not have been easy for the others and he would sometimes walk for a bit, pushing the chair himself with their belongings heaped on it.

Stanislaw was a great scavenger. Whenever they stopped for the night he would disappear and come back with food, vegetables or half a loaf, quite often a dead animal he had killed, skinned and jointed. How Stan had managed to conceal the knife through so many searches, was a mystery. If they asked him what it was, he would say 'Rabbit.' Gordon suspected the joints might be cat or rat, but it was meat and they would light a fire and cook it.

They rarely went into the towns, but passed close to Nuremberg and Dresden. The latter had recently been devastated by bombing. They often had to fling themselves into the nearest ditch when Allied bombers went over. Apart from the bombers, they had no idea how the war was progressing. Nor did they seem any nearer their destination. They had been travelling in a westerly direction but recently had turned south. 'You were right,' he said to Stan one evening. He had been walking to give the chair pushers a rest and had taken off his peg leg to ease his stump as soon as they stopped. 'They are going to keep marching us until we all drop dead. There is no such place as Moosburg.'

'Do you think we should drop out and try and find our own way?' Jeremy asked.

'Where to?' Alex asked. 'And how would we survive? We need those Red Cross parcels. Let's get some sleep. There's another day tomorrow.'

But for Stanislaw there was no tomorrow.

Gordon was the first to notice he was not moving when everyone stirred their cramped limbs the next morning. He touched him and realised he had died. Stanislaw, the energetic scavenger, the man who kept them all cheerful with his jokes and songs, who could charm the birds from the trees when he chose, who had made his peg leg and found ointment for his stump, who bartered for a bath chair for him, was gone. He stared at him, unable to believe it until Alex and Jeremy noticed his silence and came over to him. 'He's dead,' he said and burst into tears.

They would not abandon him to the wild animals, as they had abandoned many others. The whole column was kept waiting while they held a funeral service and managed to dig a shallow grave. 'Rest in peace, my friend,' Gordon murmured, sticking a crude cross into the earth. He had used Stan's knife to inscribe it: 'Flying Officer Stanislaw Fallowski. 1921–1945 RIP.' Even the guards, who knew about the knife and his nightly forays and had done nothing to stop him, were affected.

The column continued its relentless march, only it was not a march, simply a short column of men, getting shorter, putting one foot in front of the other, doomed, they were beginning to think, to shuffle along until not a single one of them was left.

Bill came to the farm one day to see for himself if the rumour he had heard was true and found Jean in the barn inspecting the new tractor which had just been delivered.

'I hear Jerry's living-in now.'

'Yes, he is.'

'My God, Jean, whatever were you thinking of to agree to it? I'm surprised at Colonel Williamson allowing it, considering the ban on fraternisation . . .'

'It was his idea. Karl was badly beaten by his fellow prisoners for thwarting the escape. He is safer here.'

'Where is he?'

'Looking after the new calf from that heifer I bought. She's a little beauty. She was born last night. We were up most of the night . . .'

'You are changing the subject.'

'No, I'm not. I would not have had his help if he had still been living in the camp.'

'I give up,' he said in exasperation.

'Is that all you came over for, just to grumble about Karl?'

'No, I thought you might like to come to the pictures with me one evening. *Henry V* is on. You'd like to see it, wouldn't you?'

She didn't want Bill to know about her relationship with Karl; they had both agreed to carry on as if it did not exist and that meant allowing Bill to take her out. 'Yes, I'd like that.'

'Saturday then. I'll call for you.'

The film was exciting and the audience was in tune with its mood of patriotism and the stirring speeches delivered by Laurence Olivier, who was at his majestic best. It was the newsreel that shocked everyone and caused a mass exodus from the cinema. Women were crying and some even being sick and the men were grim. What they were seeing were scenes from hell. But this hell was on earth, in the heart of Germany, at Belsen and Dachau. There were naked men and women, no more than living skeletons wandering about among thousands of dead bodies lying in heaps. There had been rumours of death camps for some time, but nothing had prepared them for this. Jean could not bear to watch and rushed from the cinema followed by Bill, who put his arm about her shoulders and made her slow down.

'They've shown themselves in their true colours now, haven't they?' he said when she was calmer and they were making their way to the bus stop. 'They are worse than beasts. Even animals don't treat each other in that sickening way.'

'No, you're right, they don't.'

'Not defending them, then?'

'Good Lord! What makes you think I would do that?'

'You're pretty thick with that Jerry. I think it clouds your judgement.'

'That's rubbish. I am sure he would be as sickened by it as we are.'

'Forget him, Jean. Let's start again. Go out like we used to. It was good, wasn't it?'

'Yes, but I don't think you can ever go back; time passes, we all change.'

'I haven't changed.'

'No, but perhaps I have.'

The bus arrived and they boarded it in silence. In silence they sat side by side and in silence they walked from the bus stop in Little Bushey to her gate.

'Goodnight, Bill,' she said. 'Thank you for the pictures. I'm sorry I can't think about the future at the moment.'

'Forget it,' he said and strode off up the lane. Sighing, she went indoors.

Karl was summoned back to the camp to watch the film, compulsory viewing for all German prisoners of war. When it finished, there was a stunned silence, as they digested the awful images they had seen. The silence was broken by angry comments. 'Allied propaganda,' many said. Others blamed the Russians. 'It's one of their camps, not ours, and they're using it to hoodwink us.'

Karl felt sick. He did not subscribe to the propaganda theory, but he found it hard to believe that human beings could treat other human beings in that horrendous way. Jean must know about it, perhaps she had even seen the film herself. She would certainly have read about it in the newspapers. How would that affect the way she thought about him? Was this dreadful crime against humanity going to ruin his only chance of lasting happiness? Mrs Coleman must be deeply affected if she thought that was the way all prisoners were treated in Germany. He was inclined to agree with some of the other men who refused to leave the camp to go to work for fear of reprisals.

He left the hut where the film had been shown and wandered into the compound in a numb daze, his thoughts whirring. Jean was sitting in the pony and trap outside the main gate, waiting to take him back to the farm. She smiled and waved to him. He showed his pass to the guard on the gate and joined her.

'I am not sure I should come back to the farm,' he said, standing beside the trap and looking up at her. His heart ached.

'Why not?'

'You must be sickened by all Germans. I am ashamed, so very ashamed . . . And your poor mother . . .'

'My mother hasn't seen the film, only the newspaper pictures and they have not shown the worst. She doesn't realise how bad it was.'

'All the same . . .'

'You didn't do it, did you? Nor would you.'

'No, of course not.'

'Karl, I feel nothing but pity and compassion for those poor people, but they are not servicemen, are they, not ordinary prisoners of war? Gordon would not be among them. His letters have said he is being well-treated. Mum clings to that. Come home, Karl, it's where you belong. I can't manage without you.'

Behind him some of the prisoners had assembled near the gate and were shouting at him. '*Engländerin* lover! Collaborator! Traitor!' He was glad she would not understand some of the adjectives they were using.

'Is that what you have to put up with?' she asked.

'Sometimes. They are upset by the film . . .'

'Get in, Karl. I can't leave you here.'

He clambered up beside her.

His reception at the farm was constrained. How much of that was due to the revelations about the death camps, he did not know, but decided his best course was to do the work required of him and stay in the background as much as possible. He ate at the kitchen table with the family, but afterwards retired to his room where he started to read one of the books on Gordon's shelf; *Biggles Goes to War*, it was called, and listened to the wireless Jean had given him. It was an old one that used accumulators and had been discarded when the house had been wired for electricity.

Jean heard him switch it on and twiddle the knobs to find some music. 'He's lonely up there,' she said to her mother as they tackled the washing-up.

'Best let him be,' Doris said.

'You don't blame him, Mum, do you?'

'For what? For making you fall in love with him?'

'He didn't make me. It happened.'

'You are on a hiding to nothing, Jean. The war will end soon and he will go back, back to those monstrous people and you will be left without a friend in the world, because you have cut them all off . . .'

'I haven't cut them off; it's more likely the opposite is true.'

'And there's poor Bill, eating his heart out for you . . .'

'He's not eating his heart out. He's taking one of his land girls out.'

'That's only because you snubbed him.'

'Mum, please. I've known Bill all my life and everyone seems to have decided we'd make a good match, but I didn't. I was never

208

sure. I didn't know what love was until I met Karl. You don't blame me, do you?'

Her mother sighed. 'You are my daughter and your happiness is my only concern, Pa's too, but I don't know how it's all going to end, I really don't.'

Jean dropped the teacloth and reached over to kiss her mother's cheek. 'Thank you, Mum. I knew you would understand.'

'You aren't planning to go to Germany, are you?'

'No, nothing like that. Karl wants to find his parents to make sure they are safe, then he plans to come back. Back to a country at peace.'

'You may have a long wait.'

'So what? I'll wait.'

'I hope Gordon is home by then. I worry about him more than ever now the fighting is in Germany itself. What if . . . ?'

'Mum, stop it, stop torturing yourself. He'll be OK.'

Chapter Eleven

Moosburg did exist. It was a town just a few miles north of Munich, situated on a plain surrounded by hills. It had a huge prisoner-of-war camp. Built in 1939 to house 10,000 Polish prisoners of war, by the time Gordon hobbled through its gates in April 1945, it was occupied by every nationality that had ever opposed the Nazis, over 100,000 Poles, British, French, Belgian, Dutch, Greek, Yugoslavian, American and Russian. Many had been there a long time, but even more had arrived recently, coming from all over Germany and its satellite states. Most had walked, though the luckier ones had been transported by train.

As soon as they arrived, they were registered, interrogated and deloused. Getting rid of lice was an ongoing task and a thankless one; the little pests always came back. The situation was not helped by the filthy state they were in, with long beards, matted hair and clothing in rags. Gordon could not remember the last time he had had a proper wash. 'My mother would never recognise me,' he said, as they made their way to join 500 others in one of the barracks intended for 200. There was hardly room to move and certainly no room to lie down properly. Outside the compound was filled with tents.

'The Americans are not far away,' they were told by one inmate. 'You can hear the guns.'

'Do they know this place is here?' Gordon asked. The boom of guns reminded him of their flight from the Russians. It seemed a lifetime ago.

The man shrugged. 'I doubt it. They've already bombed us. Some of us have taken to sleeping in air-raid trenches.'

'Then shouldn't someone let them know before they blow us to smithereens?'

'How? We are surrounded by barbed wire and lookout towers and the guards are still patrolling to prevent escapes. They must be deaf if they can't hear their own doom.'

They had been there a week when a white car displaying a Red Cross flag arrived and the two occupants hurried into the commandant's office. The prisoners waited, speculating on what would happen next. Five minutes later, two senior officers among the prisoners were asked to join them.

'Do you think they are going to hand the camp over to us?' Gordon asked Alex.

'"Us" being who? Who among all this lot can be said to be representative of the whole and maintain discipline? I wouldn't like to try it.'

'Those guns are getting nearer,' Jeremy put in. 'We're sitting ducks.'

A senior SS officer arrived and joined the conference. By this time the prisoners were all gathering in the various compounds, eager to know what was going on. Later, the grapevine – always a sure method of communication – told them that *Oberst* Otto

Burger, the commandant, had asked that there should be no fighting in the vicinity of the camp, something the SS officer would not agree to. However, he was reminded of the rules of the Geneva Convention and the result was a proposal to request the American commander that the area round the camp be declared a neutral zone. Gordon and the other prisoners watched the delegation drive off in the Red Cross car to put it to him.

They returned several hours later, looking grim. The US General had turned down the proposal. The river bridge was inside the area they were talking about and he wanted the bridge intact or his troops could not cross the river.

The battle began almost immediately. The prisoners had nowhere to hide and waited for the end. 'The final irony,' Alex said as a shell landed on one of the barracks occupied by the guards. 'Killed by our Allies. What a way to die.'

'I reckon it will be over quickly one way or another,' Gordon said. 'The Germans have no heavy artillery.'

'How do you know that?'

'They'd be using it if they had. Besides one of the goons told me. He also said the Yanks – he called them *Amis* – had agreed not to use their heavy artillery because of us.'

'Then what was that?' Jeremy asked as a loud bang made them jump.

'Mortar fire.'

There were no more shells, but they could hear gunfire all round them. After two and a half hours living on tenterhooks, there was silence. They looked at each other in disbelief that they had survived. 'My God! That was a close call.' Gordon echoed the feeling of all of them.

The arrival of a party of Americans at the camp entrance a

little while later was greeted with subdued cheers. It didn't mean they were not overjoyed, they most certainly were, which they told their liberators as they handed out chocolate and cigarettes, but they had been through so much and were so exhausted, many of them too ill to care, it was hardly surprising that exuberance was lacking.

'We're free,' Gordon said. 'Free at last.' But his relief was tinged with sadness that some of those with whom he had shared his imprisonment had not survived, particularly Stanislaw. If anyone had deserved to come out of it alive, it was Stan.

'Yes, but the war's not over yet,' Alex reminded him.

If Gordon and his friends thought they would be on their way home immediately, they were disappointed. *Oberst* Burger and his staff continued to administer the camp. The guards had been taken prisoner but that didn't mean the prisoners could come and go as they pleased. Nothing had changed except they were now well fed. That in itself caused problems; stomachs unused to good food rebelled, and they were advised to take it easy. They were also provided with writing materials and could write home to their loved ones, to tell them they were safe and well. Gordon had started several letters, but when it came to explaining that he was now a cripple, he could not find the words. 'By the way, I've lost my leg. But not to worry, I've got a peg leg and my friends call me Peggy.' How would they take something like that, however he dressed it in fancy words? He gave up.

The Russians were in the outskirts of Berlin and still the Germans fought on, though they must have realised it was hopeless. On the last day of April, after eight days of hand-to-hand fighting, the Reichstag, the centre of the German administration fell to the Red Army, Hitler and his new wife committed suicide, and it was all but over. The war in Europe officially came to an end one minute past midnight on 8th May which was declared a public holiday.

In London and the big cities, huge crowds thronged the streets. People leant over balconies, climbed lamp posts and statues. Flags and bunting were brought out of attics and cupboards and draped everywhere. Strangers kissed each other, musical instruments appeared and there was singing and dancing that went on all night and well into the next day. Outside Buckingham Palace a great crowd gathered, calling for the king and queen. They eventually appeared on the balcony with the two princesses and Winston Churchill. Princess Elizabeth was in ATS uniform.

Street parties with tables loaded with food appeared as if by magic in every town. In Little Bushey the celebrations echoed those going on all round the country. Flags were brought out of storage and strung from poles and windows, a huge bonfire was lit on the common and everyone gathered round to sing and dance and roast potatoes. The wireless was put on to hear Churchill's speech in which he outlined how the surrender had been signed. After praising the allies, including the Russians, he added: 'We may allow ourselves a brief period of rejoicing; but let us not forget for a moment the toil and efforts that lie ahead. Japan, with all her treachery and greed, remains unsubdued. The injury she has inflicted on Great Britain, the United States, and other countries, and her detestable cruelties, call for justice and retribution. We must now devote all our strength and resources to the completion of our task, both at home and abroad. Advance, Britannia! Long live the cause of freedom! God save the king!'

It reminded everyone that the war was not over quite yet;

there was still bitter fighting in the Far East, a theatre of war less often mentioned. It seemed to many in England it was too far away to worry about. Those who had husbands, sons and brothers in Japanese prisons, many of them belonging to the Norfolk and Cambridgeshire regiments, tried to follow what was happening, praying that now Hitler had been defeated, the Japanese would give up too. They felt their loved ones had been forgotten.

'What did your compatriots think when they heard the war was over?' Jean asked Karl. Every so often he returned to the camp to report to the colonel's office to see if there were any letters for him and to buy a new tube of toothpaste, some razor blades or soap with the *Lagergeld* he earned. Jean had taken him in the pony and trap and waited for him outside.

'Sighs of relief, but no rejoicing, no celebration. Most of them simply want to go home.'

'As you do.'

'Not wanting to leave you, I am torn, but if I am honest I must say, yes, in a way I do; it is huge logistical problem. Those in prison in Germany have to be brought home and the German prisoners in Allied camps have to be repatriated. It will not happen in a hurry.'

'I will have you for a little longer, then?'

'Yes. It looks like it.'

Now there was peace, some prisoners were treated in a more friendly fashion by the local population, while for others they remained enemies and always would. One concession was that they were allowed to take the patches off their uniforms. You could still see where they had been though; the material was darker.

'Have you any news of your brother?' he asked.

'No. Mum is getting very worried. Now the war is over, she expected to hear straightaway. It said on the news that Allied prisoners of war were being flown home as a matter of urgency.'

'There will be many thousands of them. If anything bad had happened to him since you last heard, your parents would have been told. Tell her not to worry.'

'I have, but it would be nice to know.'

It was a very bumpy ride sitting on the floor of a Lancaster bomber, especially as they had no cushions and their backsides had very little flesh on them. Gordon was more than relieved when they touched down on the soil of England, exactly five years after he had left it. Asked if he needed help, he declined and managed to clamber down the ladder onto the runway. Jeremy, following him down, knelt and kissed the ground. 'Get up, you fool,' Alex said, but he was laughing.

There was a welcoming committee who sprayed their clothing for lice before ushering them into the social club where refreshments were set out for them.

'How long before we can go home?' Alex asked the squadron leader who appeared to be in charge.

'It depends. There's some red tape to be got through first, medical, haircut, new uniform and suchlike. If you're found fit enough, you'll go on leave. If not, it's hospital until you are. You can send a free telegram to your folks, if you like. I think it says something like: 'Arrived safely. See you soon.' He looked at Gordon. 'You look as though you could do with a spell in the sick bay, Flight Lieutenant.'

'It's this damned stump. Get that right and I'll be OK.'

* * *

Doris was reluctant to open the yellow envelope the telegraph boy delivered. Yellow envelopes handed over by telegraph boys had brought bad news throughout the war. 'The War Office regrets to inform you . . .' they always began. Surely to God, he hadn't been killed? The war was over, wasn't it? Had he died a long time ago and they had only now found out?'

'For God's sake, open it,' Arthur said impatiently. 'Let's hear the worst.'

'You do it.' Her hand shook as she handed it over.

He slit it open and began to read, then he laughed. 'It says: "Arrived safely. See you soon. Gordon."'

'Arrived safely?' her face lit up. 'That means he's back in England, doesn't it? Oh, Arthur, our boy is back.'

'Seems like it.'

She snatched the telegram from his hand and rushed out of the house, across the orchard to the field where Jean and Karl were cutting the hay. He was driving the tractor and she was spreading the grass out behind it. Jean called her, waving the piece of paper, too out of breath to speak. Jean walked over and took it from her.

'Gordon's back in England. Oh, Mum.' She flung her arms about her mother and hugged her, while Karl quietly continued with the job in hand. 'But it doesn't say where he is or when he is coming home.'

'No, but it says "see you soon". I can't wait. I must go back to Pa. There's so much to do.' Still breathless, she hurried away.

'I am pleased for you,' Karl said, when he had brought the tractor to a stop and she had told him the news.

'I wonder why the telegram said so little. Why couldn't he say where he was and give us an address?'

He smiled, all too aware that he was occupying the young

man's bed and would have to give it up. 'Perhaps they did not want thousands of eager relatives invading the place. And there would be procedures to go through, paperwork, questions, medicals, things like that. I am sure he will contact you as soon as he can.'

'You are right, of course. We must have patience. But what about us? You and me.'

'I shall have to go back to living at the camp, I know that, and perhaps you will not need me any more.'

'I will always need you. Always and for ever.'

'And I you. It doesn't change that, nothing can.'

A week later a second telegram arrived. 'Arriving by train 4 p.m. Thursday 21st June. Gordon.' He had obviously counted the cost of each word and kept them to a minimum. But it had been enough to start a flurry of excited preparations.

Doris and Jean stood on the platform waiting for the train. In a few more minutes the long, long wait would be over and Gordon would be back home with his family. 'The train's late,' Doris said, looking at her watch for the umpteenth time.

'Only ten minutes, Mum. He'll be here soon.'

A minute later they heard the train and then it came into view, drew up at the platform in a cloud of steam and stopped. Doors opened and people stepped down, others climbed in. 'Where is he?' Doris asked, seizing Jean's hand so tightly it hurt.

'There.' Jean pointed.

A head and an arm had come out of the window to open a door. And then a kitbag was thrown out, followed by a pair of crutches and then Gordon. His awkwardness should have alerted Doris, but she was too impatient to notice and rushed down the platform just as he managed to alight and stood uncertainly, waiting. She had almost reached him when she stopped suddenly. 'Gordon.' Her voice was a whisper.

'Well, here I am, Mum,' he said, cheerfully.

She pulled herself together to go forward and kiss him. She would have hugged him tightly but she was afraid he might fall over if she did. Instead, she wept.

'Hey,' he said. 'It's nothing to cry about.'

'Mum's crying because she's happy,' Jean said, moving forward to plant a kiss on his cheek. 'Let's get you home and then you can tell us all about it. Can you make it to the truck?'

'Course I can.' He set off down the platform, his gait ungainly as he went from his good leg to the wooden peg, visible beneath a new pair of uniform trousers. They could certainly hear it: *tap, tap, tap*. Jean picked up his crutches and kitbag and followed; he seemed to have forgotten them.

'Jean, what are we going to do?' Doris whispered, watching his back. 'He's crippled.'

'Don't say that in front of him, Mum.'

'I won't. Of course I won't. And he's so terribly thin. I don't think there's an ounce of fat on him.'

'No, but we can feed him up.'

'What do you think your father will say?'

'We'll soon find out.'

Gordon had negotiated the steep slope down to the road, passed through the passenger gate and was stomping towards the truck. There was just room to squeeze three in the front. 'Mum, you go in the middle,' Jean said. 'I'll help Gordon in.'

'I don't need any help, thank you very much,' he said sharply. 'I can manage. In fact, I think I'll drive.'

'You will not,' Doris said, while Jean put the crutches and kitbag in the back. 'You will get in and behave yourself.'

He laughed as he climbed in beside his mother. 'Now I know I'm home. No one has said that to me since I left.'

'How long . . . ?' Doris began as Jean drove through the village.

'How long have I had this contraption?' He tapped it with his knuckle. 'One of the chaps in the camp made it for me. Very useful it is, too.'

Jean realised, even if her mother did not, that his cheerfulness was all on the surface, put on for their benefit. Later, perhaps, she would try and talk to him on his own; it was important to know how he really felt.

As they turned in at the gate of the farm, he noticed the big banner across the front of the house. 'Welcome home, Gordon', it said.

'God, no!' he shouted. 'Bloody hell! I could do without that. Whose great idea was that?'

'Don's,' his mother said, as they drew up and stopped. 'He's excited at having you home.'

'Well, I don't want any of that nonsense. I'm not a conquering hero. I've done nothing but sit on my backside for five years. It's got to come down.'

'Oh,' Doris said and fell silent.

'We are all glad to have you home, Gordon,' Jean said. 'Don't spoil it.'

He climbed out and stumped into the house, leaving the women to follow. There was an appetising smell of roast pork coming from the kitchen. Don was sitting at the table, stringing bunting for the party in the village hall they had arranged for the following evening.

'Hallo, young 'un,' Gordon said.

'Gordon, you're back.' He jumped up and then stopped. 'What's that?' he asked, pointing.

'Donald!' Doris remonstrated. 'Don't be rude.'

'You can see what it is,' Gordon said. 'It's a wooden leg.' He lifted it with his hands and put it on the seat of a chair, balancing himself on his good leg. 'Take a good look, if you like.'

'I don't want to look at it.'

'No, I don't suppose you do. I don't want to either, but I've no choice.' He put it down again.

'You won't be able to dance.'

'Dance?'

'Yes, at the party tomorrow. We're putting it on in the village hall, 'specially to welcome you home. Everyone is coming.'

'Then they can have it without me.'

'But you can't not go.'

'Don, that's enough,' Doris said. 'Let Gordon get in the door before you start arguing with him. I'm sure he's tired after his journey.' She turned to Gordon. 'Can you make it up the stairs?'

'Yes.' He looked about him. 'Where's Pa? Milking, is he?'

'No. He's in the front room with Gran. Go and say hallo, then go up and have a rest before dinner.'

He left the room. The two women looked at each other and Doris burst into tears. 'I never imagined . . . I thought he might be thin and perhaps not well and we could make him better . . .'

'I'm afraid we can't cure the loss of a leg, Mum. We have to accept that's how he is now. He seems to be managing very well.'

'Why didn't he tell us? He wrote, he could have said . . .'

'Dry your eyes and go and see what they are talking about. I must go out and see how Karl is managing with the milking.'

It was Karl's last day. He could not stay at the farm now Gordon was back, she had told him. 'I expect he will want to take over running the farm,' she had said, with a half-laugh meant to disguise the fact that she was not looking forward to the prospect. 'I will become a simple farmhand.'

'And he will not need me.'

She noted that he had said 'he' and not 'you'. She needed him as much, if not more, than ever. 'I'm sorry, Karl. If I had my way you'd stay, you know that, but Pa says it won't be necessary.' But that was before they knew about his amputation.

Karl was finishing the last of the milking when she entered the cowshed. 'He's home then?' he queried without looking up.

'Yes, but it's not quite what we imagined . . .' She paused, watching him rise from the stool, a tall, well-muscled, handsome man whom she could not help but love. 'He's lost half his leg and is getting around on a wooden peg leg. Poor Mum has taken it hard.'

He went to a bowl of water to wash his hands. 'I am sorry, *Liebling.*'

'I don't know how much he will be able to do on the farm. He could work about the yard, if that's what he wants, but as for going over the fields . . . I think perhaps I shall still need you.'

He flung down the towel and strode over to take both her hands in his own and search her face. 'Jean, my dearest love, if you need me, then I will move heaven and earth to come. Unless something occurs over which I have no control, I will always come.' He spoke quietly, still holding her hands. 'Wherever I am.'

'I'll see what Pa and Gordon say about it,' she said, trying to be practical but he was making it very difficult with his tender concern. 'I'll send up to the camp for you if they agree. I'll take you back in the trap now. Have you got your bag?' He had packed it earlier so she could prepare Gordon's room.

He let go of her hands. 'It's in the barn.'

'Fetch it and harness Misty up, while I go and tell Mum we're going.'

Gordon was sitting by the kitchen range in her father's old rocking chair. Pa hadn't used it since his stroke. Moving him from one chair to another was not easy and he hadn't felt safe in it. 'Everything all right?' she asked.

He looked up. 'Why didn't you tell me Pa was like that? You could have put it in a letter.'

'For the same reason you didn't tell us you'd had half your leg amputated, I expect,' she said tartly. 'We didn't want to worry you.'

'I could hardly understand a word he was saying.'

'You'll get used to it. We have.'

'Can't he walk at all?'

'No.'

'Then I'm better off than he is, I suppose. I never in my wildest dreams . . . How on earth have you managed?'

'I had a little help.'

'Is it true you've got a Jerry POW working here?'

'Until today, yes. I didn't think we would need him once you were home.'

'A ruddy Jerry . . .'

'Yes, Gordon. If it hadn't been for him, I wouldn't have been able to keep the farm going and you would have had nothing to come home to, so we'll have no insults, if you please.'

'He's gone now?'

'I'm just going to take him back to the camp in the trap. I won't be long. We can talk when I come back. Your room's all ready. I've taken your bag up. Do you want help getting upstairs?'

'No, I can manage.'

'Then go and have a rest. We'll talk later.'

* * *

He managed the stairs, one step at a time, hauling on the handrail, and went into his bedroom. It was just as he had left it. His cricket bat was still propped in a corner by the window. The same pictures decorated the walls; the same books occupied the bookcase. His model aeroplanes were still suspended from the ceiling. He opened his wardrobe door. It was full of his civilian clothes and shoes. It was as if he had never left, or had simply gone out for the day and was expected to return by nightfall. He bent to pick up his football boots and then it hit him. Nothing had changed and yet everything had.

He threw the boots back and sank onto the bed. God, he was tired and his stump ached like hell. He let down his trousers, unbuckled the harness and dropped the leg on the floor beside the bed. Then he fell back and slept.

'*Raus! Raus!*' He woke with a start, picked up the nearest thing to hand – a small bedside clock – and flung it at the intruder. It hit the wall and smashed.

'Hey, you didn't need to do that.' Donald was aggrieved. 'I only came to tell you dinner's ready. Now you've broken it.'

'And you didn't have to shout like that. I've had five years of it. I don't want to hear it ever again. I won't be responsible for my actions if I do.'

'Sorry.' He noticed the peg leg on the floor. 'Is that it? You can take it on and off, can you?' He was more curious than repelled.

'You didn't suppose I slept in it, did you?'

'I didn't suppose anything. I didn't know anything about it, did I? Mum's pretty cut up.'

'Not half as cut up as I was,' he said, attempting a joke.

'Are you coming down to dinner? You'll have to strap it on again, won't you?'

'That's the reason I'll give dinner a miss. My stump is sore. And you don't need to tell Mum that. Just say I'm tired. I'll see you all tomorrow.'

Donald left him, but now he was awake he could not go back to sleep. He lay there staring at the ceiling, thinking of his childhood, running about the farm on two good legs, playing cricket and football, helping to look after the animals, walking behind the plough, courting Rosemary. Rosie. That was another ordeal he would have to face. If ever anyone was useless, he was.

He heard a soft tap at the door and looked towards it as Jean put her head round it. 'May I come in?'

'Yes, of course.' He scrambled into a sitting position and pulled up his trousers.

'Don said you threw the clock at him.'

'Yes, sorry about that, but he shouldn't have shouted like that. I've heard nothing but *"Raus! Raus!"* for five years and I just reacted. Where did he learn it?'

'I've no idea.' She crossed the room to sit on the side of his bed. 'From that German worker, I suppose.'

'Karl? I doubt it. He speaks very good English. It may have been the escaped prisoner who pushed his way into Gran's cottage. He didn't speak English. Don and Terry walked in on him when he was terrifying the life out of her. They knocked him out and tied him up.'

'Good Lord! Bully for them.'

'Yes, they were very brave. It made the newspapers.' She looked at the contraption lying on the floor at her feet. 'Don said your stump was sore.'

'I told him not to tell Mum.'

'He didn't, he told me. Is there anything I can do? Have you got some cream or something?'

'Yes, it's in my bag.'

225

She rose and went to his bag, fetched the tube of cream and handed it to him. 'I'll unpack for you, shall I?'

'Yes, please. There's not much.' He began creaming his stump while she busied herself putting his things away. 'I didn't have anything much in the camp and I left most of it behind when we were liberated. The Red Cross gave us some things and we were kitted out with new uniforms at Cosford.'

'You aren't going to need the uniform any more, are you?'

'Why not?'

'I imagined you'd been discharged.'

'No, I'm on leave. I have to report back to Cosford in six weeks' time. If they won't let me fly again, I'll get my discharge after that.'

'Is that what you want to do, go on flying?'

'Yes, if they'll let me.'

'And if they don't?'

'I don't know. I'm hoping they'll give me a false leg, one with a foot on it. I'll be able to walk properly then, instead of stomping around like Long John Silver.'

'How did it happen? When did it happen?'

'When I was shot down. They had to cut me out of my kite and left part of my leg behind. I didn't know anything about it until I woke up in hospital. I'll say that for Jerry, his doctors are first class. They said I'd be given a new leg, but it never happened. Still, I should get one now.'

'Will you be able to work on the farm?'

'I don't know until I try. Not immediately. Don't feel up to it.'

'No, I understand. There will be adjustments to make. I was thinking of Karl . . .'

'The Jerry.'

'He is a good man, Gordon. He had no time for Hitler or the Nazis and he's an excellent worker . . .'

'So Pa said.'

'I think it would be best if he still came to work. I need him. He won't be able to live-in, there isn't room, but he could come from the camp every day like he used to. You could perhaps help with the morning milking before he arrives.'

'Don't try organising me, Jean. I've had quite enough of that.'

'I'm sure you have, but the farm work has to be organised or we'd never get anything done. You should know that.'

'OK, don't rub it in.'

She finished what she was doing and went to stand beside the bed. 'That looks very red. Is it often like that?'

'Only when I've been on it a long time. The journey down from Cosford took ages and I had to change trains. It will be fine tomorrow.' He couldn't tell her about the long march, not yet anyway, perhaps not at all. The memory of it was still too raw.

'Do you need any help washing and bathing?'

'Bath?' He gave a hollow laugh. 'I got into one at the hospital where they sent me to have my stump seen to. It was an interesting experience. I ended up on the floor. But don't worry, I'll manage. I've no intention of calling for help every five minutes.'

'Good for you, but don't be too proud to ask for it if you need it.'

There was a tap at the door and Doris came in with a loaded tray. She almost stumbled when she saw Gordon's exposed stump, but quickly recovered herself. 'I've brought your dinner, since you don't feel up to joining us.'

'No, Mum. It would mean strapping that thing on again, and I don't really want to. It'll be OK in the morning.'

She put the tray on the bedside table. 'Can you undress yourself?'

'Of course I can. I'm not a child.'

'No, but you're still *my* child,' she said softly.

227

'Oh, Mum, I'm sorry.' He reached up and took her hand. 'I didn't mean to snap. I've been in that camp too long and forgotten my manners. If I seem grumpy, forgive me. I can't quite believe I'm home.'

'That's all right, son. We'll leave you to it. Bang on the floor if you want anything.'

He laughed and picked up the peg leg. 'And I've got a handy implement to do it with.' He used it to rap on the floor. 'You'll hear that all right, won't you?'

He waited until they had left and then tackled a dinner the like of which he had not had for five long years.

'Do you think he's all right?' Doris asked Jean as they returned to the kitchen. 'He didn't used to be so snappy.'

'He's been through a lot, Mum, we have to make allowances.'

'I know that, silly. Oh dear, there's me snapping now. I'm sorry. I just didn't think he'd be like he is. If only he'd told us, I would have been prepared.'

'At least he's home, and he tells me the RAF will provide him with a proper false leg with a foot on it. That will make all the difference. It's marvellous what they can do nowadays.' She paused as they entered the kitchen. Donald had helped himself and his father to plum duff and custard. 'Did he tell you he had to report back in six weeks?'

'Yes. But then he'll be home again.'

'I think we'll still need Karl,' Jean said, sitting down and helping herself to pudding. 'He could come on a daily basis like he used to. What do you think, Pa?'

'Ask Gordon,' he said. 'He's in charge now.'

It was like a blow to the stomach. Gordon was home and all her hard work counted for nothing. Like many other women who had been working throughout the war, doing work usually done by men, she was expected to slide back into anonymity, do the jobs women traditionally did – marry, raise a family. Marriage for her was a distant dream, but one she clung to. If Gordon refused to allow Karl to come back, how was she to go on seeing him?

'Will you persuade him to come to the party tomorrow?' Donald asked her. 'We can't cancel it, can we? And it will be a washout if he's not there.'

'I'll try.' It made her think of Rosemary. What would she make of it all?

Chapter Twelve

Rosemary could not understand why Gordon had not rushed to see her the minute he arrived home. She had dressed in her best frock, put on her only pair of nylons and washed and set her blonde hair, put on make-up and waited.

'Doesn't he care for me any more?' she asked her mother. She had taken the afternoon off from work and had been watching on tenterhooks all afternoon to see him come up the garden path. 'I'm going up there to see what's going on.'

'I shouldn't. He'll be with his family and maybe he's not well.'

'But I'm going to be his family, the most important person in his life, that's what he told me.' She rose from the table where they had just finished a meal of fishcakes, made with a tiny piece of cod her mother had queued up for in Wisbech and were more potato that fish. Still, fish was a rare luxury.

'Can't you leave it until tomorrow?'

'You know I've got to go to work tomorrow and I don't want our reunion to be witnessed by dozens of people at a party.'

She put on her coat and hat and left the house for the ten minute walk to Briar Rose Farm.

She was nervous. It was over five years since she had waved him goodbye. Eighteen years old she had been, much too young to be committing herself, her mother had told her, but she had ignored that advice and had said she would wait for him. He had gone cheerfully, telling her it would all be over by Christmas and then he would be home again and they would be married. Far from being over, it had barely started when he was taken prisoner. In five years how much had he changed? How much had she? War altered the way you viewed life. The leisurely pace of rural life vanished in the need to work long hours, to make every second count towards winning the war. You worked hard but you also played hard, and it had been difficult keeping that promise to be true to him; the longer it went on the harder it had become. Was going out with Alan Hedges breaking it?

She had told Alan that now Gordon was coming home, she would not go out with him again. He had taken it badly. 'You haven't seen him for five years,' he had said bitterly. 'You don't know what he's like. He's probably moved on . . .'

'He couldn't move far in a prison camp, could he? And I told you at the beginning . . .'

'I know what you said. I didn't think you meant it.' He had seized her in his arms and kissed her soundly. 'When you discover everything is not so rosy in the garden, then you'll change your mind.' Was it his words making her so nervous?

Jean answered her knock. 'Oh, Rosie, it's you. Come in.'

'Is he back? Is Gordon home?'

'Yes, but he's very tired. He's gone to bed.' She led the way into the sitting room, where she and her parents had been listening to a concert on the wireless. Doris switched it off when she saw their visitor.

'Rosemary, how nice to see you. Come in and sit down. Would you like a cup of cocoa? I was going to make one for us.' She hardly waited for the girl to say 'Yes, please', before she scuttled away, leaving Jean to deal with Rosemary.

Rosemary looked round her. 'I hoped I would see him.'

'I am sure he'll want to see you as soon as he's rested, but it was a long journey, Rosie, he's tired and not himself.'

'Not himself? What do you mean?'

'I don't know how to tell you this . . .'

'Then don't,' Gordon said from the doorway. He was in pyjamas and a dressing gown.

'Gordon!' they both said together.

Rosemary ran forward but then stopped. There was something strange about the way he was standing. Then he pushed the door open further and she saw the reason for it. 'Oh.'

He stomped further into the room. 'I'm not quite myself,' he said, proving he had overheard, 'because I left part of me back in France.'

'You said you were going to stay in bed,' Jean said.

'I couldn't sleep and I was sitting looking out of the window when I saw Rosie coming up the drive. I wanted her to see for herself the half man who had come back to her.' He paused. 'Rosie, you are quiet. Cat got your tongue?'

'I don't think I'll stay for cocoa,' she said and fled.

'Well, that went well,' Gordon said in the silence that followed.

Jean tackled Gordon about the party at breakfast the next morning. While she had been doing the milking alone, he had managed to wash, shave and dress himself and come down to the kitchen. Doris was cooking him bacon and eggs.

'Did you sleep well?' she asked, scraping marmalade on a piece of toast.

'Apart from wondering what the hell to do about Rosie, you mean?'

'It was shock. She'll come round. You'll see her at the party tonight. It will be different then.'

'Yes, because I won't be there. If everyone runs off at the sight of me, the hall will empty in no time. You can enjoy yourselves without me.'

'Gordon, I think you should come. A lot of people have made sacrifices to make it a good do, donating food and drink they can ill spare because they are pleased you are home safe and sound.'

'Safe but not sound.'

'Of course you are. You can walk, you can talk, and you seem to have a hearty appetite. You've just eaten everyone's bacon ration for a week.'

'Oh.' He looked up at his mother, busy making a fresh pot of tea. 'Is that right?'

'Don't think of it, son. Jean should not have said anything. You are too thin and we must build you up.'

'The food over there was pretty lousy. Watery soup and dry black bread. Thank God for the Red Cross.'

'Our rations aren't all that good, but we can do better than that.'

'Do *you* think I ought to go to this party, Mum?'

'Not if you really hate the idea, but I wouldn't like to think of you hiding yourself away. I thought you had more guts than that. You're still a Coleman, still our son. I'm proud of you and I want to tell the world I am, and the fact that you've lost part of your leg in the service of your country is not something to hide, but something to be proud of. Besides, it doesn't look nearly as bad as you think.'

'Is Pa going?'

'Wouldn't miss it,' his father said.

'All right, I'll go.'

And so they all went to the party. Donald wheeled Arthur there, but Doris and Jean drove Gordon in the truck. Jean was becoming a little worried about the amount of petrol they would have to use ferrying her brother about. It was only supposed to be used for essential farm work.

Forewarned by Elizabeth, everyone greeted Gordon enthusiastically and he was soon sitting in the middle of a crowd, regaling them with highly exaggerated stories of life in a prisoner-of-war camp. Jean found herself standing next to Bill.

'He's on good form,' he said, as a gale of laughter came from those surrounding her brother. 'I didn't know he'd lost his leg.'

'We didn't either until we saw him. It was quite a shock.'

'He won't be much use on a farm like that.'

'He is going to be fitted with a proper false leg and then he'll be able to do most things.'

'I bet he wasn't pleased to see Sergeant Muller.'

'He hasn't seen him. Karl has gone back to the camp.'

'Good. That's where he belongs.'

'He'll be back. At least until Gordon can take over.'

'We haven't been out together for ages.'

'Last time it was mentioned, you said you'd rather take Brenda.'

'Did I? I didn't mean it.'

'Oh, I believe you did.'

'You're not jealous of her, are you?' He laughed as he spoke, making her cross.

'No more than you are jealous of Karl. Now, I had better go and help Mum with the refreshments.'

* * *

234

Gordon hadn't expected Rosemary to turn up, but Jean had persuaded her and she arrived, if a little late. The crowd around Gordon melted away so that they could sit together. Mrs Harris put on some dance music and several couples began to move about the floor.

'Gordon, I'm sorry,' she said. 'I shouldn't have run away. I was shocked, that's all. I'd been dreaming of your homecoming ever since your mother told me about it and . . .'

'It was a let-down.'

'Well, you didn't exactly behave like the returning lover, did you?'

'No, s'pose not. But you've no idea what it's been like.'

'No, but you are going to tell me, aren't you?'

'Probably not.'

'Why not? You were telling everyone else when I arrived.'

'That was different, that was joking . . .' He stopped when he saw Alan Hedges approaching them.

'You don't mind if I take Rosie off for a dance, do you, Gordon?' He didn't wait for a reply before holding out his hand to Rosemary. She looked briefly at Gordon who nodded, then took Alan's hand and he was left to watch them.

'Who asked him to come?' he asked Jean when she brought him a plate of sandwiches and sat down beside him.

'We issued an open invitation. Why, don't you like him?'

'I don't like the way he's mauling Rosie. Look at them, giggling like a pair of lovers.'

'She's only dancing with him, Gordon. There's nothing in it.' She hoped that was true.

'I haven't seen her for five years and she's hardly given me the time of day.'

'She will. You need to get used to each other again, that's all.'

'Take me home.'

'You've hardly got here.'

'All the same, I'm tired.'

'Very well. I'll go and tell Mum. I'll come back for her later.'

Doris went round telling everyone that Gordon was tired and all the excitement was too much for him and they prepared to leave. Jean tapped Rosemary on the shoulder. 'I'm taking Gordon home. He's had enough. Go and say goodnight to him.'

Rosemary obeyed, but what they said to each other she did not know. Gordon was silent all the way home.

It was a strange, upsetting time. Gordon hardly ventured from his room and when he did, he was morose and uncommunicative. Jean knew it was difficult for him, but it was hard for the rest of the family too, especially their mother, who did everything she could to make him comfortable and cheer him up. Jean lost patience with him.

'There are a lot of people worse off than you,' she said when she found him sitting in the kitchen stirring a cold cup of tea, stirring it round and round, on and on. 'You are making everyone miserable. Poor Mum is trying so hard and you are not making it easy. She's got enough on her plate with looking after Pa.'

'You don't understand. I'm useless, no good to anyone . . .'

'You won't be, if you don't try. Come out and help me with the milking. You can still do that, can't you?'

Reluctantly he followed her out to the cowshed and settled on a stool by Gertrude's udder. For a moment, he seemed content as the milk gushed into the pail, but then he tipped the pail over while trying to stand up. The whole yield from one cow ran across the floor. Angrily, he stomped back into the house, leaving her to hose the milk down the drain and record the mishap in the yield book.

Karl had to come back. She tackled Gordon about it that evening, but he refused point-blank. 'If you think I'm going to work alongside a Jerry, you'll have to think again,' he told her. 'We'll manage. Don can help.'

'Don is revising for his school cert. I don't want to spoil his chances.'

'Does he need a certificate to work on the farm?'

'Gordon, he doesn't want to work on the farm. He's planning to go to college.'

'Find an English labourer then.'

'Do you think I didn't try? When Pa had his stroke . . .'

'Leave off, Jean. I'll soon have my new leg. We'll manage.'

Gordon was in the orchard filling the pig troughs the next morning when Elizabeth passed on her way up to have Sunday lunch at the farm. She stopped to speak to him. 'How are you getting along, son?'

'OK. More than enough to do.'

'Is it what you want to do, Gordon? Farming, I mean.'

'It's what I was born to do.'

'That's not what I asked.'

'Then the answer is yes and no. Farming is changing. It has to if it is to survive and we have to change with it. More specialisation, more mechanisation, that's what's needed. We're still farming the way we did when Grandpa was a nipper. I've been talking to Pa about it, but he won't see it. He says he's happy to go on hiring the machinery he needs from the Ministry of Ag. depot, but that won't go on for ever.'

'What does Jean think?'

'Don't know. I haven't asked her.'

'Why not? Surely she deserves to be consulted. She ran this place almost single-handed while you were away. It wasn't easy.'

'I know that.'

'Jean is exhausted, Gordon. You have no idea what it's been like for her. Sergeant Muller turned out to be a godsend.'

'What are you getting at? I'm not the equal of a Jerry, is that it?'

'Not at all, but we're coming up to the busiest time of the year. Don't you think it would help to ask Colonel Williamson if Sergeant Muller could come back? Just for a little while.'

He looked closely at her. 'What's between Jean and the Jerry, Gran? There's more to it than just work, isn't there?'

'I wouldn't know.'

'Oh, come on, Gran, you know everything.'

'It's their business, not mine.'

'She must be mad. I don't like it, I really don't. Has she thought about the consequences? It's against the law for a start. And she'll lose all her friends.'

'Then they're not real friends. Besides, I don't know that it's got that far. All I want to do is get him back here to work to give Jean a break. Let the future take care of itself. You must admit you could do with a strong man about the place. There are still jobs you must find difficult. I can't see you working on top of a haystack, for instance. And if Don takes himself off to college . . .'

'OK, I'll talk to Pa about it.'

Elizabeth deplored the way that Jean was now being excluded from decisions about the farm, but decided she had said enough for the time being.

Two days later, Gordon clambered down into a ditch to clear a bramble that had become so overgrown it was obstructing the flow of water and in so doing his peg leg became stuck in several inches of mud. After struggling for several minutes and shouting for someone to give him a hand, he realised there was nothing for it but to unstrap the leg and haul himself out without it. He was lying exhausted on the bank when Jean found him.

She fetched his crutches, so that he could make his way back to the house. 'Whatever made you do it?' she said, walking slowly beside him.

'It needed doing.'

'I know, but I can't be everywhere at once. Now I've got to put waders on and retrieve that leg. I could have done without that, Gordon.'

'OK. Get the Jerry back. Just until I get my new leg.'

It was hell being a prisoner again after the relative freedom of Briar Rose Farm, made worse by the snide remarks of his fellows. 'Here comes the *Engländer*' one of them taunted as he entered the hut and dropped his kitbag onto one of the beds. '*Fräulein* turn you out, did she?'

'No. The son of the house has been repatriated.'

'The British are being repatriated, but what about us? They are never going to send us home. Slave labour, that's all we are to them. It's time we repatriated ourselves.'

'The war is over, surely you are not still talking about escape?'

'Yes, we are.'

'You can count me out.'

'Don't you want to go home?'

'Naturally, I do, but I am prepared to wait. The Geneva Convention says the opposing sides have to repatriate their prisoners as soon as possible after an armistice.'

'Studied it, have you?'

'I've read it.'

'But what if there is no armistice, no government to negotiate with, no country even? They can do what they like with us.'

He could see the reasoning behind their argument and it cast a doubt in his mind. Then he shook it from him. There were plans to repatriate them, there must be. The population of Great Britain would not stand for thousands of aliens in the country once their own men were all home again.

He existed from day-to-day, doing woodwork, playing chess with Otto and teaching English to some of his fellow prisoners. It was a boring existence; he would much rather have been working at the farm. He thought constantly of Jean, remembering their conversations, her laughter, the touch of her hand, the sweetness of her lips on his. Would he ever feel that again? She had told him they would still need him, but that seemed not to be the case. He would simply have to wait to be sent home. Repatriation was going to take time, it stood to reason, but he would not join in with the crazy idea to escape. It would only result in the escapees' repatriation being delayed. He knew the 'whites' were due to be sent home first, followed by the 'greys', according to how long they had been prisoners. Perhaps he ought to concentrate on that.

He was wondering whether he dare risk trying to sneak out of camp to see Jean, when he was sent for and told he was being sent back to the farm. Mr Coleman had asked for him.

The arrival of Karl lifted a great burden from Jean's shoulders. 'Oh, Karl, I'm so pleased to see you.'

'And I you. I did not think your family wanted me again.'

'Can't do without you,' she said cheerfully.

'You are looking tired. It's not been easy, has it?'

He seemed to understand her moods better than she did herself. 'You could say that. I lost my patience with Gordon and

240

now I feel really guilty. I should try harder to understand. He didn't want to go to that damned party and I persuaded him. It must have been terrible for him watching everyone dancing and not being able to do it himself. Even his fiancée left him to dance with someone else.'

'That was perhaps insensitive of her.'

'Yes and so I told her and now we are not speaking to each other and Gordon's in a filthy mood. It's all such a mess.' She paused. 'I shouldn't be talking to you like this.'

'Why not? You can tell me whatever you like, I shall not repeat it. But I can understand how your brother feels. We long for freedom, but when it comes . . .' He shrugged. 'We are not sure how to deal with it.'

She looked at him sharply. 'You've had news about your repatriation?'

'No, nor is there likely to be. Europe is full of people in the wrong place, wandering about, trying to find their way home. The Red Cross are doing their best and the military authorities have to sort out priorities but it all takes time.' Germany had been divided into four zones for administration purposes: British, American, Russian and French. Berlin was firmly in the Russian zone but that, too, had been divided into four with a long corridor giving the other Allies access. How that would work in practice, he had no idea. Germany as a state no longer existed.

'Have you heard from your parents?'

'No. I've been allowed to write postcards, but nothing so far. I'll have to go when my time comes. You do understand, don't you?'

'Yes, of course.'

'But if you want me, I will come back.'

'I want you, you know I do.'

241

'Then I will move heaven and earth to be here.' He paused to search her face. 'It will not be easy for you, you know that, don't you? There will be animosity and prejudice. I do not want you to be under any illusions about that.'

'I'm not. As long as we have each other, we'll manage.'

He paused as if wanting to add to that, but then changed his mind. 'What would you like me to do this morning?'

'Let's feed the pigs for a start, then we'll make a start on the hay.'

They fetched the buckets of pig swill from the shed, picked them up and crossed the yard to the orchard. He smiled. 'You were doing this when I first came to work for you, do you remember? It is almost exactly a year.'

'Yes, it must be. A lot has happened, some good and some bad, but the best has been meeting you.'

'And I you. *Ich liebe dich, mein Liebling.*'

'One of these days you must teach me German.'

She turned to see Gordon limping towards them. The ground in the orchard was rough and his progress was slow, but neither went to help him. Jean knew he would shrug them off if they did. Karl stood with an empty bucket in his hand and waited.

'Gordon, this is Sergeant Muller,' she said when he reached them. 'Karl, my brother, Gordon.'

Karl came to attention and bowed his head. Gordon did not offer his hand but looked him up and down. 'What did you have your heads together about?'

'We were talking about cutting the hay. Are you going to help us with it?'

'I don't think so. I'm off to the pub. I'll see you later.' He turned and made his way back to the yard.

They took the swill buckets back, then made their way to the meadow as they had done the year before, except now they used cutters attached to the tractor and not scythes. That was not the only difference; they were no longer strangers, no longer guard and prisoner. In all but the consummate act, they were lovers. They had been tempted, had kissed, petted and stroked, but had always drawn back, not because of lack of commitment but because the future was so uncertain and pregnancy a risk they were not prepared to take. But it was oh-so hard, and becoming harder.

June gave way to July. Jean and Karl were kept busy shearing sheep, raking up the hay and building a stack, and preparing for the harvest, not helped by Gordon who didn't seem to want to do anything. Jean's gentle chivvying only produced an angry retort to leave him alone.

He would spend hours in the Plough and Harrow, sometimes alone, sometimes with the elderly John Barry who always occupied the chair by the hearth, summer and winter, and sometimes with Bill Howson when he had finished his day's work. What they found to talk about, Jean had no idea. Sometimes he came home half-drunk, his spirits high and he would laugh and joke and tease. At other times he would be morose and uncommunicative and snap at everyone.

'I do think he might make a bit of effort,' Jean said to her mother one lunchtime after a particularly trying morning.

'I don't suppose he feels up to it yet,' Doris said. Gordon had not come home for the midday meal and she was putting his plate of food on a saucepan of boiling water to keep it hot.

'He wasn't put to work in the camp and he's got out of the habit of it,' Jean said. 'It's a pity they didn't make the officers work as well as the men.'

'He wouldn't have been able to do it, would he? Not with his leg. Be patient, Jean. Give him time. He deserves a bit of a holiday. Besides, when he goes back to Cosford, they'll give him a proper leg and that will make all the difference.'

Jean, who was almost crying with fatigue, left the house before she could say what she really thought of her idle brother. She admitted there were some jobs he could not do, but he could feed the chickens and pigs and help with the milking, but he said that was women's work. 'Besides,' he had said, when she remonstrated with him. 'You've got all the help you need. You don't need me.'

Telling Karl not to come was not the answer; Gordon could not do everything Karl did. Besides, she didn't want to lose him. It was seeing his cheerful countenance and hearing him singing as he worked that kept her going.

Gordon returned to Cosford at the end of his leave and was gone a week. When he came back he was still wearing his peg leg. It was raining hard and blowing a gale and he had a job to keep his balance as he walked down the slope of the railway platform to the lane where Jean had parked the truck. He was determined not to use the crutches which Jean was carrying for him.

'How was it?' she asked when he was settled in the passenger seat and they set off for home.

'I've been measured up for a new leg. I have to go back when they send for me to have it fitted.'

'Are you disappointed you didn't get it straight away?'

'Course I am. German surgeons don't do things quite the same way as the English ones and Stanislaw, the man who made the peg leg, was a carpenter not a medical man, and he didn't understand about muscles and tendons, things like that, so they are going to have to take a bit more off my stump.'

'Oh, dear. Will you lose your knee?'

'They said not. I just have to be patient for a little longer, but after waiting five years, it's a bit of a blow.'

'Yes, but it's best to get it right, isn't it? Then you will be ready for anything.'

'Even Rosie. If she can get over bursting into tears the minute she sees me.'

'She will. Give her time.'

'We had a long talk the last time I saw her. She promised to try, but she wouldn't promise not to go dancing.'

'Gordon, you can't expect her to. She hasn't lost her leg and she loves dancing. As long as she loves you and wants to be with you, you'll get on. And who knows, when you get the hang of your new leg, you might be able to dance too.'

He laughed. 'Oh, Sis, you sound just like Mum, talking to me as if I were a child. She has some excuse, but not you.'

'Sorry, didn't mean to preach. Rosie still loves you, you know.'

He laughed. 'Put your own love life in order before you meddle in mine, Sis.'

'I don't have a love life.'

'What about Bill?'

'That died a death, if it ever was.'

'Are you sure about that? I don't think Bill thinks so.'

'Have you been talking to him about me?'

'No, only he said you were a bit cool with him these days and he blamed the Jerry.'

'His name's Karl, not Jerry,' she said. 'Why can't you say his name? And it has nothing to do with him.'

'OK, keep your shirt on. But I should warn you people are talking.'

'It's a pity they haven't got something better to talk about. Let's go home. Mum will be on tenterhooks to know how you got on.'

A general election in July resulted in a landslide victory for Clement Attlee and his Labour Party based on a promise to the returning troops that there would be jobs and houses for all. It was a promise impossible to keep. There was austerity and hardship; rationing was as strict as ever and there was a chronic shortage of housing. Women who had worked throughout the war were being dismissed in favour of returning soldiers which caused a certain amount of resentment among them. In Little Bushey, the men found it difficult to settle down to being farm labourers again and, on some farms, mechanisation had taken the place of men and they became redundant.

Knowing he could not manage the farm, even with Jean's help, Gordon settled for a wary working relationship with Karl. Every morning Karl went to Gordon and politely asked for instructions. Gordon, who stuck strictly to the no fraternisation rules, would answer curtly and Karl would go to find Jean.

'He said to plough in the potato tops,' he told her one morning.

'OK. I think we'd better use the horses. That tractor drinks petrol.' She sighed. 'Gordon thinks we should sell them. He says they don't pay for their keep now we have the tractor. Pa is against it, but I suppose it will have to happen one day.'

'Will you have the ploughing match again this year?' he asked, as they brought Dobbin and Robin out of the stable.

'I expect so, but I don't think I'll enter. It might upset Gordon. He was once very good at it himself. Pa taught him when he was only a nipper. He won't want to watch me doing something he would like to do.'

'Perhaps he can try this year.' He paused, looking up to see

Gordon limping towards them. He was still having trouble with his stump. 'He is coming across to us.'

Karl carried on working but Jean paused to wait for her brother. 'Were you talking about me?' he said. 'I thought I heard my name.'

'We were talking about the ploughing match,' Jean said quickly. 'And how good you used to be. I was wondering if you might like to try this year. You wouldn't need to walk behind now we've the tractor.'

'I'll think about it. Mum wants some eggs. She says the egg girl is due and she's short of a few.'

'Can't you get them?'

'No, I've other things to do. Poultry is women's work.' He turned and left them.

'I'd better go,' she told Karl. 'You make a start on that field. I'll join you when I've taken the eggs to the house.'

Karl finished putting the harness on the horses and went to the cart shed to fetch out the plough. Gordon was standing by the tractor. Ignoring Karl, he picked up the starting handle. 'What are you going to do?' Karl asked.

'I'm going to plough in the potato tops.'

'We were going to use the horses.'

'Well, I'm going to use this.'

The Fordson was a brute to start and needed a strong arm and a lot of patience. Gordon had neither. After several attempts, Karl offered to do it for him. 'No, I'll do it. Just get out of my way. Find something else to do.'

Karl went off to find Jean. 'Your brother says he is going to do the ploughing.'

'Then we had better let him.'

'He is struggling to start the tractor and will not let me help him.'

'Oh dear. Let's go and see if he's managed it.'

As she placed the eggs she found in the hedge into a basket, Jean led the way back to the cart shed. Gordon was sitting on the floor beside the tractor, nursing his wrist. 'I think I've broken it and now I can't get up. I can't put my weight on my arms.'

They both ran to him. Jean put down the basket of eggs and knelt beside him. 'Let me see.'

His wrist was a strange shape and beginning to swell. 'I think you may be right. I'll have to get you to hospital. Karl, can you get him up?'

Karl went behind him and put his arms round him to haul him up. He held him while he found his balance. Still holding his wrist, Gordon shrugged him off and limped towards the garage where the truck was housed, with Jean on one side of him and Karl on the other. They were not touching him but ready to catch him if he fell.

'Karl, go and tell my mother what has happened,' Jean said. 'Ask her to give you a scarf to use as a sling.'

He sped away. By the time they reached the truck, Karl was back with her mother who had her father's scarf in her hand. 'What happened? Sergeant Muller said Gordon was trying to start the tractor.'

'That damned handle few out of my hand and knocked me sideways,' Gordon told her. He winced with pain as Jean gingerly lifted his arm to attach the sling.

'What on earth were you doing playing with it in the first place?'

'I wasn't *playing* with it. I was going to do some ploughing. You all keep telling me to get on and do something, so I thought I would.'

'Jean should have stopped you.'

248

'Jean was busy elsewhere, and anyway it was her idea.'

Doris looked at Jean, who was knotting the scarf behind Gordon's neck. 'I'll tell you later, Mum. Let's get him to hospital. Gordon, can you get in the truck?' She held the door for him.

'Yes, stop fussing.' He sat on the seat and swivelled himself round. Jean lifted his peg leg in after him. 'Karl, make a start on the ploughing will you, please? I won't be any longer than I can help.' She climbed in the driver's seat. 'Mum, I've left a basket of eggs on the floor of the cart shed.'

'I'll fetch them, don't worry.'

'You're going to let Jerry get on with it alone?' Gordon asked as they set off. 'Isn't he supposed to be supervised?'

'His name is Karl, not Jerry, Gordon, and I don't need to supervise him. I can trust him to do a good job.'

'How do you know that? He's a German. I wouldn't trust one as far as I could throw him. And believe me, I've had plenty of time to study the race.'

'I know him.'

'Know him? You mean, in the biblical sense?'

'Don't be so crude.'

'That's not an answer.'

'I don't have to answer to you.'

'No, but indulge me.'

'Of course I don't know him in the biblical sense. Satisfied?'

'Thank goodness for that.'

'What do you mean by that?' she asked sharply.

'I wouldn't like to think of a handful of little Nazis running about the place.'

'Do you know, Gordon, you've become coarse and bigoted. You're not in that prison camp now, so try to be civilised, will you?'

'Sorry, Sis.'

'Karl is not a Nazi, he abhors them. He is an ordinary man trying to do his best in a difficult situation. Mum and Pa have accepted him and so should you. Until you are fully fit, we need him. And now you've hurt yourself, we will probably need him even more.'

'OK, point taken. But I don't have to be bosom pals with him, do I?'

She laughed. 'No, I think that might be asking too much.' She was drawing into the car park at the hospital as she spoke. 'Let's get you in and seen to. I need to get back.'

Chapter Thirteen

Karl was at the far end of the field when he spotted Jean walking towards him. She had her head down watching where she was putting her feet, but he could tell she was despondent by the roundness of her shoulders. She had far too much to do for one woman. She ought to be able to have fun, but with her brother the way he was, the hoped-for break was not going to come. It was a pity he could no longer live-in on the premises; he could help her a great deal more. He pulled the horses to a stop and waited for her to come to him.

'I'm sorry it took so long,' she said. 'We had to wait.'

'How is he?'

'His arm's in plaster and he's more grumpy than ever.'

'I'm sorry.' His sympathy was directed at her, not her brother.

'It's my fault for talking about that ploughing match. I should have realised he'd have trouble starting the tractor. I goaded him into it, just as I goaded him into going to that party. I could kick myself.'

'Not your fault, Jean. You mustn't blame yourself for everything that goes wrong.'

She looked about her. 'You've done well. Do you think we'll have it done tomorrow?'

'I don't see why not.'

'We'd better get back for the evening milking. We don't have so much time now you have to go back to camp every night.'

'No, that is true.'

They unhitched the plough and left it by the hedge near the gate and walked the horses back to the farm. 'Is it very bad at the camp?' she asked.

'No worse than usual. Don't worry about me. I am content.'

'Really?' She was surprised.

'As content as it is possible to be considering everything. I am doing a job I love with the woman I love. Nothing else matters.'

'Jean, are you all right?' her mother asked. She was laying the table for the evening meal. 'You're looking peaky. You're not sickening for anything, are you?'

'No, of course not. I expect it's worrying about Gordon. He seems to invite trouble.'

'Maybe,' Doris said doubtfully. 'It's bad enough having him with only one good leg, but now he can't use his arm either. I don't know what we're going to do, I really don't.' Tears welled in her eyes and Jean hurried over to hug her.

'Don't upset yourself, Mum. We'll manage somehow. Shall I see if I can hire a nurse to come in and help him get dressed and undressed?'

'Can we afford it?'

'Yes, I think so. Where is he?'

'In his bedroom. I heard him stomping about up there.'

'I'll go and talk to him.'

Gordon was sitting in a chair by the window, looking out

across the yard and the rolling fields in the distance. He did not turn towards her as she entered.

'How's it going?' she asked cheerfully. 'Are you going to be able to manage?'

'What do you think?'

'I think it might be a bit of a problem to wash and dress yourself until your wrist heals. You mustn't get that plaster wet. You will need some help.'

'So?' He gave a grunt of a laugh. 'You volunteering?'

'I will if I need to.'

'Good old Jean, always ready and willing. Don't you ever want to shout "To hell with it all!" from the rooftop?'

'It wouldn't do any good.'

'I do,' he went on as if she had not spoken. 'For two pins I'd throw myself off it, then you'd be rid of me.'

'Gordon, for God's sake, don't talk like that. No one wants to be rid of you. Your wrist will get better and you'll get a proper false leg, and then you'll be able to do all the things you used to . . . most of them anyway.'

'You think so, do you?'

'Yes. In the meantime, I'm thinking of hiring a nurse to help you wash and dress in the morning and help you to bed in the evening. Would you agree to that? It would make Mum feel a lot better. I found her shedding tears just now and that's not like her.'

'Poor Mum. I can't help being grouchy, Jean, really I can't. Things look so bleak sometimes. It's like a huge black shadow hanging over me and blotting out the light. I just want to hit out at everyone and everything.'

'It will pass.'

'I've even managed to alienate Rosie.'

'Make it up with her. I'm sure she would listen if you explained how you felt.'

'I don't know how to.'

'Yes, you do. Tell her what you've just told me.' She paused. 'Sitting up here doing nothing is not going to help, Gordon. Come down and have dinner with us. For Mum's sake. And Pa's. It hasn't been easy for him either.'

He stood up and turned towards her. His face was streaked with tears. Her heart went out to him. 'Oh, Gordon, we all love you. Remember that, please.'

He followed her downstairs and went into the kitchen where everyone was assembling for the evening meal. He hobbled over and kissed his mother's cheek as she stood dishing food onto plates.

'What's that for?' she asked, smiling.

'Just to say I'm glad to be home.' He sat down and attacked the meal with apparent relish, talking all the time, making jokes, making plans, telling them what he intended to do when he was given his new leg. He was so voluble it was almost as frightening as his long silences.

Jean made a point of going to see Rosemary the following evening. She and her widowed mother lived in a cottage next door to the Dog and Duck in the middle of the village. 'Mum's gone to a Women's Institute meeting,' Rosie said, leading the way into the sitting room and indicating a chair on the other side of the empty hearth.

'Yes, my mother's gone too. I came to see you.'

'Oh, what about? Or shall I guess? Gordon asked you to come.'

'No, he didn't. He doesn't know I'm here. Rosie, did you know he has had a bad fall and broken his wrist?'

'No, I didn't. How could I? I haven't seen him since the party.'

'What happened then?'

'He was angry that I'd danced with Alan. He said if dancing was all I thought about, then he would be no good to me and we'd better break it off.'

'He didn't mean it. He's frustrated and angry and very, very unhappy. He needs you, Rosie, he needs you to stand by him.'

'I never thought he'd come back like that.'

'None of us did, but we have to make the best of it and make allowances.'

'Don't lecture me, Jean Coleman, I haven't done anything wrong. If he can't stand me talking to another man, then we're best apart.'

'I thought you loved him.'

'I did. I suppose I still do, but . . .'

'You can't stop loving him just because he's been wounded, surely? I know he still loves you.' She hoped that was true. 'Rosie, come and talk to him, see him through this, at least until he's been given a proper new leg. He'll be his old self then.'

'He'll never be his old self.'

'I meant cheerful and ready to tackle anything. Please, please, don't abandon him. He needs help, we all do.'

'He's playing you up as well, is he?'

'You could say that. He was talking earlier about throwing himself off the roof.'

'Why on earth would he do that?'

'I told you, he is very unhappy. He thinks he's worthless and we would all rather be rid of him. Mum is at her wits' end. Please come and talk to him, but don't tell him I asked you to come and don't say anything about jumping off the roof.'

'All right, I'll come tomorrow, after work, but if he's nasty to me, I'm not staying. I don't have to put up with it.'

'Thank you.'

'It's the damnable war. It's ruined everyone and everything. We thought when it ended that would be it, but it isn't the end, is it? We're still suffering.'

'Yes, but we can only go on doing our best. I'd better be off.'

'Aren't you going to stay for a cuppa? I can soon make one.'

'No, thanks all the same. Pa and Gordon are alone in the house. Two helpless men. I dread to think what they might get up to. Don't get up, I'll see myself out.'

Gordon went up to his room immediately after the evening meal the next day. 'I'm going to lie on my bed and read a good book,' he said.

Jean could not tell him Rosemary was coming because he would want to know when she had seen her and if she had asked her to come; she didn't want to admit it, nor lie about it. She went behind him as he slowly climbed the stairs hanging onto the handrail with his good hand. She watched him go into his room and returned downstairs to help her mother with the washing-up. She heard him turn on the old wireless to listen to *It's That Man Again*. Perhaps the silly jokes would cheer him up.

'He seems a little more cheerful today,' Doris said.

'Yes, let's hope it lasts.'

They had just finished putting the crockery back on the sideboard when Rosemary arrived. She had taken trouble with her appearance. Her printed cotton skirt was topped by a pink blouse on which was pinned the RAF brooch Gordon had given her before he left on operations. She had set her hair and added make-up, including a cherry-red lipstick.

'Gordon has gone to his room,' Doris said. 'But he won't have undressed, so I suppose it's all right for you to go up.'

Jean gave Rosemary an encouraging smile and followed her to the foot of the stairs. 'It's the first door on the left. Try and cheer him up if you can.'

She had hardly returned to the kitchen when she heard footsteps flying down the stairs and the back door slam. They looked at each other. 'Was that Rosemary or Don?'

Jean looked out of the kitchen window which had a clear view of the garden path. The flying figure was certainly not her younger brother. 'Rosemary running as if the demons of hell were after her. I'd better go and find out what happened.'

'Nothing happened,' Gordon told her. 'I was lying here, reading. She took one look at me and burst into tears. Am I that ugly, Sis?'

'No, but you are lying there without your trousers and that leg on the floor. Whatever were you thinking of?'

'I told her, if we are to have any future together, she would have to get used to the sight of it. God, it's only a stump. It's perfectly clean, not pouring blood or anything. What was I supposed to do, hide it? If she can't stand the sight of it, there's no hope.'

Jean could see his point, but she thought he might have been a little more subtle. 'Gordon, you've had five years to get used to it. It was a shock for Rosie to see it like that.'

'It was a shock to me when I first saw it too, but no one pussyfooted round me. I had to put up with it.'

'Oh, I give up!' She turned on her heel and went downstairs to tell her parents what had happened.

'The boy's right,' her father said. 'She'll be no good to him if she can't come to terms with it. If they were married, she'd have to get into bed with him.'

'Pa!' Doris exclaimed.

'Well, I'm right, aren't I? Look at me. I'm no beauty, but you didn't run screaming from me when I had my stroke, did you?'

'No, but . . .'

'Same thing.'

'I'm going up to help him undress for bed,' Doris said, putting down the newspaper she had just picked up. 'He'll be miserable over it, poor boy.' She left them looking at each other. A minute later they heard him sobbing and then Doris closed the bedroom door, shutting out the sound.

Bill was in the Plough and Harrow nursing half a glass of beer when Gordon arrived the next day. He ordered and paid for a pint and went to join him. 'Phew, it's hot today.'

'It's all right for you, Gordon, you don't have to work. I've been harvesting all morning and I'm sweating like a pig. The tractor was red hot, you could fry an egg on it. I've left the others to have their dockey and come here to cool down.'

'Do you think you'll be finished today?'

'Might be. Why?'

'Jean tells me it's our turn for the reaper next. Have you had a good turnout?'

'Yes, plenty of volunteers, though with that Jerry there, you'll be lucky if they come to you.'

Gordon took a gulp of beer and wiped the back of his hand over his mouth. 'I can't help about him. Not my fault. Blame Jean.'

'Oh, I do. I don't know what he's got that I haven't, but if I could do him a bad turn, I would.'

'You and me too, my friend, but how would that help?'

'It would make me feel a whole lot better.'

Gordon laughed and raised his glass. 'Confusion to our enemies.'

Bill chinked his against it. 'Confusion to our enemies. The sooner they go home the better, and we can get back to normal.'

'There's no getting back to normal for me, Bill. I'll always be a man with only one leg.'

'Sorry, I didn't think. But you are getting on all right, aren't you? You seem to be walking much better.'

'Oh, I am, but there are still things I find difficult and always will, even when I get my new leg. And I still have to convince Rosie I'm not a monster.'

'Is that still on between you two?'

'Supposed to be. What about you? Still on with Jean?'

'Goodness knows. I can't make her out these days.'

'She's had a lot to cope with, Bill. Pa's no help and I'm not much better. You know when I was a kid, all I wanted to do was follow in Pa's footsteps and farm. Now I don't know what I want. Watching Jean struggle just irritates me.'

'I offered to help but she refused. Seems she'd rather employ that Jerry.'

'You've got your own farm to look after, Bill.' He chuckled suddenly. 'And if you did help out, who would be governor? She can boss Muller about and he does exactly as he's told. That wouldn't suit you, would it?'

Bill laughed. 'No, course not. But I'm blowed if I'm going to grovel. There's plenty more fish in the sea.' He drank the last of his beer and put his glass down. 'I'm off back to work or we'll never be done.'

Gordon sat on, sipping his beer now and again, and when it was finished called for another.

'Sorry, Gordon, I don't have any more until the brewer delivers,' John Heacham, the landlord, told him. 'You can have a whisky, if you like. I keep it under the counter for regulars.'

'Make it a double.'

* * *

Gordon had warned Jean the villagers would not turn up to help with the harvest but Jean hadn't believed him. They had always helped each other when the time came, had been doing it for generations and she didn't see why they would refuse this year. Whatever the reason, it seemed Gordon was right. The reaper and the man and land girl who came with it turned up on time, but the villagers did not, not even the children. Jean looked for them in vain. 'Looks as though we are on our own,' she told Karl. 'They must have more important things to do.'

'All of them?' he queried.

'Seems so. You carry on. I'm going back to the house to round up some help.'

The rest of the family were having breakfast when she arrived. 'Don, I need you,' she said. 'The reaper is in the field and there's no one to do the stooking.'

'I told you so,' Gordon said.

'Yes, you did. Now I wonder why they haven't come?'

'I don't know, do I?' Gordon said. He was dressed and shaved so the nurse had been and gone.

'I think you do. It's to do with Karl, isn't it? He was here last year and no one batted an eyelid, so why would they decide not to turn up this year if someone hadn't got at them? What did you tell them? That he was dangerous or something equally silly?'

'Me? Why should I do that?'

'Because you are mean and uncharitable and you've got a chip on your shoulder as big as a tree.'

'Jean!' their mother protested.

'It's true, Mum, and you know it. Now I'm short of workers and if the villagers won't come, then I need to call on the family.'

'Well, it's no good calling on me,' Gordon said.

'No, I know that,' she retorted. 'Don, hurry and finish your breakfast and get up to the top field. We've only got the reaper for today.'

'I hate working on the farm.'

'Nevertheless you will do it,' Doris told him quietly. She turned to Jean. 'I'll settle your father and come up myself later. I've no doubt Gran will give a hand too. I'll call in on my way.'

Jean hugged her mother. 'Thanks, Mum, you're a brick.' As she left Jean heard her mother gently chiding Gordon and her father grunting angrily, but she doubted it would make any difference.

The reaper did its job and the wheat was cut. Her little band of workers, the land girl, Karl, Don, her mother and grandmother, helped her pick up the sheaves of cut corn the binder had tied and set them in stooks in neat rows across the field. The last few yards of standing corn had sent the rabbits scurrying for safety and most of these had been dispatched. Everyone went back to the house, very hot, very tired and very grubby, but satisfied with their day's work.

'It was because of me, wasn't it?' Karl said to Jean as they walked back to the farm. 'The people will not work with me.'

'We don't know that. After all, you were with us last year; no one objected to your presence or refused to work then. Anyway, it doesn't matter. We got the job done without them.' She smiled wryly. 'When the chips are down, you find out who your real friends are.'

'Chips are down?' he queried. 'What does that mean?'

She laughed. 'It's just a saying. It means when you are in trouble, it is your true friends who come to your aid.'

'Your family, yes?'

'And you. I would rather have you than a dozen villagers.'

'Jean, that is a foolish thing to say. They are your people, you have known them all your life. You have to live with them . . .'

'When you are gone, is that what you mean?'

'I suppose I do.'

'Let's not think of that. You are here now.'

'I am going to dive into the pit to cool off,' he said, nodding towards the expanse of water at the end of the orchard. On a hot day like this it reflected the blue of the sky and looked inviting.

'Have you got a costume?'

He laughed. 'Do I need one?'

'Just make sure you're not seen, that's all. And be careful, that pit is deep and full of weeds. I'll see you later.' Nowadays it did not cross her mind that she ought to supervise him. In any case, she could hardly stand over him while he took his dip.

Gordon was in the yard. 'Where's Jerry?'

'Gone swimming to cool off.'

'Good. I hope he drowns.'

'Gordon, why do you hate him so much?'

'He's a Jerry, an enemy of all we stand for, that's why.'

'But the Bible teaches us to love our enemies.'

'Good God, Jean, you don't love the man, do you?'

'I do not hate him.' To her relief he let that pass. 'You know, Gordon, you are becoming a bore. Talk about the Nazis being fanatical, you are just as bad.'

'With good reason. I've witnessed what they can do first-hand and it is far from pleasant. I could tell you tales that would make your hair stand on end . . .' He stopped suddenly.

'Not Karl's fault.'

'They're all the same. I'm off where the company's more congenial.'

He turned his back on her and stomped away. He was limping badly and she wondered if he was in pain, which might account for some of his bad temper. She had little idea what he had been through while a prisoner, he always stopped short of talking about it. She ought to be more sympathetic.

She went back to the house. All the doors and windows were open but the air outside was as hot as that inside. Her father was reading the newspaper in the sitting room which was cooler than the kitchen. Her mother was cleaning eggs in the dairy. The stone floor and marble worktops kept the temperature down a little. Jean went up to her room, changed into her swimming costume, put her shirt and slacks over the top, grabbed a towel and went out again.

Karl was floating on his back in the middle of the pit. He was not completely naked; she could see he was still wearing his army issue underpants. She stripped off her trousers and shirt and waded in where the cows had trodden a path down to the water. Usually it was muddy, but now the sun had baked it into hard ridges. As soon as she was up to her waist, she started to swim towards him.

He turned himself over and reached out for her hands. They trod water. She found herself looking into his face, shining with droplets of water; there was one in his eyelashes, she noticed, and his wet hair curled in his neck and over his ears. Like that he was even more desirable. She put her arms about his neck. '*Ich liebe dich*,' she murmured.

'You are learning,' he said, kissing her. She tilted her face upwards. The sky was an unbroken blue, the sun a brilliant orb.

'It's so peaceful here,' she murmured. 'There is no hate, no one is killing anyone else. I wish it could be like this everywhere.'

'Amen to that.'

Suddenly she laughed, broke away and began slapping her hands on the surface to shower him with water. He dived. She had no idea where he was. She looked about her but he didn't come up again. 'Karl!' she shouted, swimming round in a circle and growing more and more panic-stricken. 'Where are you? Don't play the fool.'

He surfaced right in front of her, shaking the water from his hair and laughing. 'God, you frightened me,' she said, her panic subsiding a little. 'Don't ever do that to me again, Karl Muller. I thought you'd got tangled in the weeds. It happened once, years ago, a young lad drowned. It was awful.'

His laughter died and he reached for her hands again. 'I was only teasing, *Liebling*. I did not mean to distress you. I am sorry.'

'So you should be. We'd better get out. It's time to fetch the cows in.'

They swam together to the side and clambered out, dripping water. His clothes were in a neat pile on the grass; hers were where she had flung them. She picked up the towel and began drying herself while he watched. 'Are you going to put your trousers on over those wet pants?' she asked.

He laughed. 'If you turn your back a moment, I will take them off.'

She was tempted to refuse, but then did as he asked. 'Here, use my towel,' she said, trying to hand it to him without looking round. He stepped forward to take it from her and she saw a length of bare leg and a well-honed thigh. Tempted, she turned to face him.

'Cheat!' he said, laughing. He had a beautiful body, well-rounded and muscular, which was hardly surprising considering the work he did. Given the slightest encouragement she would have flung herself at him, to feel it next to her own, but he was busy towelling himself.

'It is not the first time I have seen you without clothes,' she said. 'You were unconscious the last time. Mum and I put you into Pa's pyjamas.'

'What are you going to do?' he asked, putting on his trousers. 'Am I to have the privilege of seeing you struggling to be modest?'

It was on days like this she regretted the pact they had made not to indulge in sex. It would be so easy to lie together on the grass and give their passion full rein. 'I am going to put my shirt and slacks over my costume and go back to the house to dress properly while you fetch in the cows,' she said.

'Yes, perhaps you are right,' he said, suddenly serious.

He put on his socks and shoes, picked up his wet pants, wrung the water out of them and carried them as they made their way back to the yard. They did not touch each other in case someone saw them. 'I'll wash and mangle those,' she said, taking the underwear from him. 'They'll be dry in no time.'

She crept up to her room without her mother seeing her. It reminded her of how it was when she had been mischievous as a child and didn't want to be found out. Would it always be like that? Would she never be able to express her feelings, let the world know that she loved Karl, no matter what his nationality? Loving without a future was hard to bear.

Gordon knew he had been a fool, more than that, downright mean. It all came about because of the conversation he had had with Bill, together with his hatred of anything German. Jean couldn't understand that, but then she had not spent five years incarcerated in an overcrowded camp on starvation rations, guarded by jackbooted devils who would kick you and beat you as soon as look at you. She hadn't been hobbling around on a peg leg watching other people plan to escape. She hadn't shuffled for hundreds of miles, nor seen people die and abandoned by the roadside to be eaten by wild animals. She had not found a good friend dead of exhaustion because he always put other people before himself. He could never tell her about that.

And there were those awful death camps. He wouldn't believe the German population had known nothing about them. He knew what Jerry was capable of. He had told Bill so and everyone in the pub had heard him. He hadn't actually incited them to refuse to work. He could hardly do that when it was the family livelihood at stake, but perhaps Bill had. Bill was jealous of Muller.

Chapter Fourteen

Karl was still in England working on the farm in August when the atomic bombs brought the Japanese war to an end. Most Allied prisoners of war in Germany had been repatriated and those in Japanese hands were being brought back as a matter of priority. They were all half-starved, some no more than living skeletons who would take years to recover, if they ever did. There were happy reunions and not-so-happy ones, as returning servicemen discovered wives and sweethearts had found other loves, or life was not quite as they imagined it would be. Sir Edward and Lady Masterson were bowed down when they learnt their only son had died in captivity. A memorial service was held in the church for him and all the others from the area who would not be coming home.

In September Donald went off to college and Gordon, his wrist healed and out of plaster, received the summons to present himself at the RAF hospital in Ely to have the operation to tidy up his stump and have his new leg fitted. He came back six weeks later, sporting a tin leg with a foot in a sock and shoe on the end of it.

'How was it?' Jean asked when he was settled in the passenger seat of the pickup and they set off for home.

'OK, but it's going to get some getting used to. It feels strange, like an alien thing on the end of my leg and there's no articulation in the ankle. I'm told they are trying to develop something that will work. In the meantime, I have to learn to walk again. I thought because I was used to the peg leg, going from one to the other would be easy, but it wasn't. As soon as the new stump had healed, they had me out of bed on a contraption like another peg leg, just to get my muscles moving again. They fitted my tin leg a couple of weeks ago. I'm using a different set of muscles and ached all over to start with. And I can't tell you how many times I fell down when they first put it on. I had to learn to do it without hurting myself and getting up again without help. Mind you, I did plenty of that in Germany.'

'You'll master it, I'm sure.'

'The physio said it would take several months before I'm really sure-footed.'

'Then you will be ready for anything.'

'Even Rosie. If she can get over bursting into tears the minute she sees me.'

'She will. Give her time.'

After greeting the family, showing off his new foot and eating a huge meal to celebrate his return, he said he was going to see Rosie.

'If you wait a minute while I speak to Karl, I'll run you there in the truck,' Jean said.

'No, thanks, Sis. I'm going to walk.'

'I don't think that's a good idea,' his mother said. 'It must be nearly a mile each way.'

'I've got to get the hang of this thing sooner or later, and the sooner the better.'

He knew it was going to be an ordeal, but he had made up his mind. He wanted Rosie to see him walking up the garden path, just as he used to. He had hardly covered half the distance when he realised his mother had been right. His ungainly gait used up a lot of energy and he was exhausted. And his back ached. Doggedly, he kept going. It was an effort to smile when he finally opened her garden gate and she ran down the path to meet him.

'Gordon, you're back! And just look at you. Back to how you were.'

'Not quite. Can we go indoors? I need to sit down.'

'You never walked here?'

'Yes, I did. I mean to walk everywhere now.'

He followed her into the house and sank gratefully into an easy chair while she bustled about making tea. 'Mum's gone into Wisbech on the bus,' she called through from the kitchen. 'We can have a cosy chat.'

She brought in two mugs of tea, put them on a small table beside his chair, then squatted on the floor at his side. He bent over and kissed her.

'You know what kept me going?' he murmured when the long kiss came to an end. 'Thinking of you and how proud you would be of me.'

'Oh, I am.'

'But there's one hurdle you still have to get over, Rosie.' He tapped his false leg. 'This might look good when I'm dressed, but when I go to bed, it has to come off.'

'I know. Are you suggesting we go to bed, Gordon?'

He laughed. 'It's an idea.'

'I've never done it before . . .'

'I should hope not! But we are supposed to be engaged.'

'All the same, it's not right. . . .' She paused. 'Besides, Mum will be home soon. What if she came in?'

'You want to wait until our wedding night? What happens if you can't stand the sight of me and my stump? It will be too late to change your mind then.'

'Drink your tea.'

'Damn the tea. I've had to get used to it and I'm the one who has to wear it. If you can't face looking at it . . .'

'I never expected it to be like this. I thought the war would end and you would come back and everything would be as it was.'

'Did you never wonder if I might be killed or injured?'

'I tried not to. And when you were taken prisoner I thought at least you were safe. I had no idea . . . You could have let me know.'

'Would it have made any difference?'

'I don't know, do I?'

He pulled up his trouser leg to reveal his false leg with a foot wearing a sock and shoe. 'Look at it, Rosie.'

She picked up her mug of tea and drank, using it as an excuse to keep her eyes averted.

'If you don't, I'll leave and that will be that, all over between us.'

She forced herself to look at the contraption. His stump, encased in a soft stocking, was hidden by the strapping.

'Good,' he said. 'I'd take it off, but that means letting my trousers down. Shall I do that?'

'No, for goodness' sake, Mum might be back any minute.'

He gave a hollow laugh and pulled the trouser leg down again. 'I suppose we have made some progress, but it's not enough, Rosie. We've got to find some time to be properly alone.'

'Another time.'

They heard the back door open and shut and Mrs Shelley

came into the room. 'Oh, you're back, Gordon. How are you?'

'Fine, Mrs Shelley. I came to say hallo to Rosie. I'm just off.' He pulled himself up. 'I'll see you soon, Rosie.' And with that he hobbled out.

'At least he looks a bit more presentable,' her mother said, lifting the teapot to see if there was another cup of tea in it, and pouring one for herself.

'Yes, he does. But he's different. It's not only his leg, it's everything . . .'

'Are you sure you want to go on with this engagement, Rosie? He won't be a lot of good as a husband. I can't see him being able to do the heavy work on the farm and what else can he do to support a wife and family? Think on that, child.'

Rosemary sighed. 'I don't know what I want, Mum, I really don't. But he's been through a lot. It wouldn't be fair to break it off now.'

'I just hope you know what you're letting yourself in for, that's all.'

The day Karl did not come to work worried Jean. Was he being sent home? Had he already gone? Surely to God he would have found some way to let her know? She was in two minds whether to go up to the camp and ask, when Gordon came back from the village with the news that a dozen prisoners had left the camp without permission and the army and the police were out looking for them. 'I said they couldn't be trusted, didn't I?' he told Jean. 'I bet your precious Karl is among them.'

'That's silly, the war is over. They will all be sent home soon. That is, those who want to go home. Some don't.'

'And does *Feldwebel* Muller want to go home?'

'Of course he does. He has family . . .'

'Well, it seems they cannot wait to be sent and have decided to make their own way back to Germany. The police and army are out looking for them.'

'Oh, not again,' Doris said. 'I thought they had done with all that. Go and fetch Gran, Gordon. If she hears about this she'll be terrified. Did Jean tell you what happened before?'

'Yes. I'll go now.' He stopped on the way out to pick up his shotgun and some cartridges, calling over his shoulder, 'Stay close to the house.'

Elizabeth was coming up the lane towards the farm. He turned and took her back to the house, leaving her at the door. 'Tell Mum I'm going to see if Rosie's OK.'

He found Mrs Shelley alone, convinced she was about to be murdered. She, along with everyone else, knew the ordeal Elizabeth Sanderson had gone through when one of the prisoners had tried to escape before and then there was the time when half the camp had got out. 'They never should have built that camp so close to the village,' she said. 'Nor let them out to work. And since the end of the war, they've been strolling about as if they own the place.'

'If I catch any of them, they'll get both barrels,' he said, lifting his gun. 'I'll take you home with me. You can stay with Ma and Pa, until Rosie comes home.'

'She'll be late. She said she was going to the pictures after work.'

'It doesn't matter. We can leave a note for her.'

The Way to the Stars was a film about life on a British bomber base. It starred Michael Redgrave, John Mills, Trevor Howard, Jean Simmons and a host of other popular actors. But it was more than just another war film; it was also a poignant love story of how men and women learn to cope when war tears their lives apart.

Rosemary could not stop the flood of tears when she heard the poem: 'Do not despair for . . . Johnny-head-in-air'. It made her think of Gordon and what he must have gone through after he was shot down.

Finding it impossible to cope with his moodiness, up one minute, down the next, and still unable to bring herself to look at his stump which he insisted had to be done if they were ever to have a life together, she had given in to Alan and agreed to go out with him again.

In her heart she knew Gordon was right, but it didn't help. It was looking as if it was the end of the road for them. It was a great shame because she still loved him, or at least loved the man he was. If he had been whole, they would have been planning a wedding by now, instead of bickering over her inability to 'face facts', as he put it, and her refusal to let him make love to her. She had tried to imagine what it would be like and it sickened her. Alan had been a cheerful alternative.

When the film and the newsreel finished, they stood together for the national anthem before making their way out into the street. 'You don't need to see me home,' she said. 'I'll get the bus.'

'Of course I'll see you home. What do you take me for?'

'But you'll have to walk back.'

'So what?'

She was glad he had insisted when they realised there were a lot of soldiers about and they were all carrying rifles. There was one standing near the bus stop.

'What's happening?' Alan asked him.

'Some Jerries have escaped from the Bushey camp. I'd get your girl safely home as soon as you can, if I were you.'

The bus drew up and they climbed aboard where everyone was talking about the breakout. According to the gossip, dozens of prisoners were loose in the countryside and terrorising everyone. 'They caught one of them on Little Bushey Common,' one of the passengers said. 'My son's a copper and he told me. The whole constabulary is on the alert and the army is out in force.'

As soon as they left the bus at the Bushey post office, Rosemary began to run. Alan pulled her back. 'What's the rush?'

'I'm worried about Mum.'

It became apparent as soon as they entered the house, there was no one there. She shut the door and switched on the light. 'Where is she?' The sitting room was deserted and the fire had gone out. 'What's happened? Oh, I should never have gone out with you!'

'What difference would that have made?' He went and pulled the curtains across the window.

'I would have been here to look after her.'

'There's a note propped against the clock.' He nodded towards the mantelpiece.

She grabbed it. 'Gordon came and fetched her back to his place,' she said after scanning it. 'If I'm late, she'll stay there tonight.'

'Good.'

'What do you mean, "good"?'

'What do you think?' He grabbed her, pulled her into his arms and kissed her. 'We've got the place to ourselves. Let's make the most of it.'

'Oh, Alan, I don't know.'

'It'll be all right, I promise.'

He pulled her down onto the settee, pushed her back and began undoing the buttons on her blouse. She grabbed his hand and pulled it away. 'No, Alan.'

'Oh, come on, sweetheart, don't be a tease.' He kissed her again, forcing her mouth open and sticking his tongue inside, at the same time as he put his hand up her skirt, feeling up her thigh for her suspender. She felt sick and afraid. Nothing and no one had prepared her for this. She tried pushing him away. It made him lift his head. She gulped for air. 'Get off me, Alan, please. I don't like it.'

'I don't believe you. You've been leading me on long enough. It's time I had my reward.' He flung himself across her and tried to kiss her again, but she turned her head away. 'Get off me. I'll scream.'

'Scream away. Who's going to hear you?'

She opened her mouth and let out the loudest yell she could.

'Does that make you feel better?' he asked. 'Now, settle down and enjoy it. It'll be better than you'd get from that one-legged excuse for a man.'

'He's ten times the man you are, Alan Hedges.'

'Then where is he? Not looking after you, is he?'

'Oh, yes he is.'

Startled, they both looked round at the sound of the voice. Gordon was standing in the doorway and he was carrying a shotgun.

'Gordon!' she cried, pushing on Alan's chest. 'Get him off me.'

'OK, I'm going,' Alan said. He got to his feet and made for the door. He had to pass Gordon. As soon as he was within striking distance, Gordon punched him hard. He staggered back, grabbing the muzzle of the gun, more to save himself than take possession of it. Gordon hoisted it upwards and at the same time lifted his false leg and kicked Alan with it. He laughed suddenly. 'That hurt you more than it did me, my friend.' He wrenched the gun from the other's grasp. 'Now get out before I give you both barrels where it will be very inconvenient for your love life.'

Alan, who had taken the full force of the leg on his shin, hobbled out and slammed the door behind him.

'I knew that leg would come in handy some day,' Gordon said, sitting down beside Rosemary on the settee. She stared at him. 'Gordon, I didn't mean it to happen. I didn't . . .' She burst into tears. He put his arm about her and hugged her.

'It's OK, love. I know you didn't. I was coming up the garden path when I heard you scream. I came in by the kitchen door and overheard the rest.'

'Thank goodness you came. I was terrified. I was sure he was going to rape me.'

'It's over now and perhaps you will learn not to be so trusting in future.'

'But what about you? Can I trust you? After all, we are alone . . .'

'Rosie, I would never do anything you did not want me to, surely you know that? I love you. But you hurt me, hurt me badly because you couldn't accept the man I am now.'

'I'm sorry, I never meant to hurt you.'

He grinned suddenly. 'I've never used that leg as a weapon before and I think I've twisted it. It's damned uncomfortable.'

'I'm sorry.'

'So am I because I'm going to have to take it off and sort it out. Shut your eyes if you don't want to look.' He stood up, let down his trousers and sat down again. Then he undid the harness and removed the leg, putting it on the floor at his side. He glanced sideways and realised she was watching him. Deciding not to comment on that, he rubbed the stump. 'I could do with a bit of cream on this.'

'I'll find some.' She disappeared and he wondered if it was an excuse to flee from something she found repulsive. But he had misjudged her; she returned and handed him a tube of ointment.

He cocked one eye at her. 'Do you want to do it for me?'

'No, I might hurt you.'

'You wouldn't, no more than you already have but no matter, we are making progress.'

'Does it hurt?' She was looking at it properly now.

He laughed. 'Only when I do something stupid like kicking someone.'

She took the tube of cream from him, knelt down and smoothed some into his stump. He grinned with pleasure. 'Oh, that feels so good.'

She finished and sat back on her heels. 'I won't go out with Alan again.'

'I should hope not.' He picked up the leg and began strapping it on again. 'I might not be around to rescue you next time.'

'I hope you'll always be around.'

'You mean that?'

'Yes. I've been silly, haven't I?'

'I forgive you.' He paused. 'You know, I don't sleep in the damned thing.'

'I didn't think you did.'

'It wouldn't make any difference to you-know-what. I've lost a bit of me, but the rest is all there, all functional.' He stood up to pull his trousers up.

She laughed. 'Just what are you doing here, Gordon Coleman?'

'Your mother was worried about you being here all alone with escaped prisoners on the loose. I came to fetch you back to the farm. You can both stay the night with us.' He paused and sat down again. 'But first there is something I want to do.'

'What's that?'

'Kiss you.' And suiting action to words, he did just that. 'When are we going to get married, Rosie?' he asked when, breathless, they drew apart.

'Whenever you like.'

'You mean that?'

'Yes.'

'Then let it be soon.'

'All right. But where will we live?'

'Ah, that's a point. We'll have to give it some thought. Not tonight though. Our respective parents will be wondering what we've been up to.' He stood up and pulled her to her feet. 'I wouldn't mind if we had . . .'

'You won't tell them about Alan?'

'Why not?'

'I'm too ashamed.'

'It's not you who should be ashamed, but OK, if that's the way you want it.' He kissed her again. 'Let's go and tell everyone the good news.'

Most of the prisoners were recaptured, but with no telltale patches on their uniforms and the fact that they were allowed to walk to their work and stroll about the countryside, even if they could not go into public houses and cinemas, one or two managed to stay free, including Otto. Karl wished him well. Those left behind spent the week confined to camp but, in the face of demands from the farmers and builders to have their workers back, Colonel Williamson lifted the ban. Karl returned to Briar Rose Farm.

He found them all in high spirits. There was to be a wedding and everyone was excited about it. 'It has taken them long enough to make up their minds,' Jean told him. 'Funny, but it was the prisoners escaping that triggered it off.'

He smiled wryly. 'I'm glad it had a positive effect somewhere.'

'Why did they do it?'

'I think they were angry at the slowness of the repatriation and decided to take matters into their own hands.'

'Did they really think they could get all the way back to Germany?'

'I don't know,' he said guardedly. 'It was unrealistic if they did. Mind you, there are still one or two on the loose, but I expect they are far away by now.'

'You once said that if there were a chance of success, you would be tempted to go too. Do you remember?'

'Yes, but that was before I fell in love with you. I do not want to jeopardise my turn to go. The sooner I do, the sooner I will come back.'

'There is that, I suppose.'

'How did the ploughing match go?'

'Oh, I forgot you weren't there. It went very well. There were the usual entries.'

'Did you enter?'

'No, but Gordon did. It was so good to see him joining in as if he'd never been away. I do believe he is learning to cope with that leg. And Rosie agreeing to marry him has lifted his spirits enormously.'

'I am glad. When is the wedding to be?'

'In December. There isn't so much to do on the farm then and they will be able to have a honeymoon. The first banns were called last Sunday. Mum is in a fair old lather about it. It should be the bride's parents who arrange it, but Rosie's only got her mother and she's not the world's best organiser, so Mum has offered to have the reception here at the farm. I've no doubt the whole village will be invited, and some of Gordon's air force friends and people from Rosie's workplace. Austerity or not, it's going to be quite a do.'

'You will be busy, too.'

'I'll give a hand with the catering and I'll have to find something to wear that won't look too dowdy.'

'Whatever you wear, you will look lovely,' he said. 'And don't worry about the farm work, I can see to it.'

Gordon came home from visiting air force friends one day carrying a huge bundle of white silk. 'Is that a parachute?' Doris asked him.

'Yes.' He dumped it on the kitchen table. 'A mate of mine works in the packing shed and this one was rejected. Its seams are not strong enough. Can you make use of it?'

'Can we make use of it?' Jean repeated. 'My, can we! There's enough here for everyone's dresses. But won't your friend get into trouble?'

'Shouldn't think so. If 'chutes are damaged or not up to standard, they'd only be thrown away. That's what he said, anyway.'

'Have you shown it to Rosie?' Doris asked.

'No, she'll be at work. I'll see her later.'

'Fetch her over. We'll have to have a conference. Some of it will need dyeing. Rosie must decide on the colours she wants.'

'That's the dresses sorted,' Jean said. 'What about the cake?'

'I've been saving fruit for our Christmas cake,' Doris said. 'Rosie's mum said she'd give me her ration as well, so we should have enough. I'll use that. I'll make a couple of Victoria sponges as well and some sausage rolls. As for sandwiches, we'll find some fillings for those.'

'What'll we do for Christmas then?' Gordon asked.

'We'll manage something. Weddings are more important.'

'Mum, you're a wonder.' He stepped forward and hugged her. 'I'm more than grateful and Rosie will be too.'

'Oh, go on with you. Now go and talk to Pa. I've got work to do.'

Doris turned to Jean after he left, a broad smile on her face. 'It's so good to see him happy. I was beginning to wonder if he would ever come out of the doldrums. I don't know what happened when he went to fetch Rosie that night, but whatever it was, it did the trick. He was like the cat that got the cream.'

'So I saw. I just hope it spreads to doing some work on the farm.'

'He will, give him time. Then we won't need Sergeant Muller any more.'

'Are you so anxious to be rid of Karl, Mum?'

'I think it would be for the best. The war is over, we should be getting back to normal.'

'What is "normal", Mum? I don't know any more. I don't think anyone does. Do you think all the women who have been working in the factories, on the land, in the forces, will be content to go back to being housewives? I don't. Am I supposed to hand over the farm to Gordon and become a shop assistant again?'

'You wouldn't need to if you married Bill.'

'Mum, I am not going to marry Bill. Please put that out of your head.'

'Not even when Sergeant Muller goes back to Germany?'

'Not even then.'

Jean was not sure if Bill himself had given up the idea; she saw very little of him. He had been at the ploughing match where he and Gordon had enjoyed a friendly rivalry and gone off to the Plough and Harrow together afterwards. He had asked her to dance at the prize-giving that evening but they had had little to say to each other and he went on to flirt with Brenda. If that was a ploy to make her jealous, it failed. Her heart had been irrevocably given elsewhere.

* * *

The wedding, attended by half the village, went off as planned. The bride looked radiant in her white silk gown and the groom handsome and smart in his RAF uniform. The dyeing had resulted in blue dresses for Jean and Doreen, one of Rosie's friends, and a beige blouse for Doris which she wore with a new skirt. The beige was accomplished with a large bottle of camp coffee. Doris and Elizabeth had spent days and days sewing. Afraid the wearers would be cold, they combed the second-hand shops in Wisbech and King's Lynn and as far afield as Norwich and managed to find a white fur cape for Rosemary and coloured shawls for Jean and Doreen. Everyone else had coats.

Bride and groom gave their responses in firm clear voices and afterwards left the church between a guard of honour made up of friends from Gordon's old squadron and two airmen who had been in the prison camp with him. He introduced them as Squadron Leader Alexander Jordan and Flying Officer Jeremy Brewster. Jean became aware of Karl standing behind one of the larger tombstones, with his chin buried in his upturned coat collar. It was an old coat of Pa's she had given him, not his uniform, but she hoped fervently that no one would see and recognise him. He had gone by the time everyone began to disperse and make their way to the farmhouse for the reception.

It was a noisy, happy affair. Alex, the best man, stood up to toast the bride and groom. His speech was full of jokes about life in the camp, which he referred to as their long holiday, but no one was under any misapprehension about that, especially Jean and her parents, who had seen the darker side of Gordon when he first came home. There were still things he could not talk about, perhaps never would. Gordon's reply was short, his jokes the ones most bridegrooms make, but he ended on a more serious note. 'My good friend Alex has spoken of the lighter side of camp life, but there were, of course, many who did not make it back, and we must not forget them.' He raised his glass. 'On this happy day, the happiest of my life, I raise a glass to absent friends. We will remember them.' The guests echoed that and Gordon sat down. Alex patted him on the back and whispered something Jean could not hear.

The cake, without icing, was cut and distributed and everyone was soon laughing and joking again. Jean sat back, happy to see her brother happy, but there was, deep inside her, a pool of misery. The man she loved was excluded from the occasion. Would he ever become accepted? Would she ever sit at this table in a wedding dress with him at her side?

After Gordon and Rosie had left to catch a train to the Lake District for their honeymoon, Jean changed out of her dress in order to help Karl with the milking. She took a piece of wedding cake out to him and asked him why he had gone to the church.

'I wanted to see you in your dress,' he said. 'All that sewing was certainly worthwhile. You looked beautiful.'

'So did Rosie.'

'Of course. Brides are always radiant. One day it will be you.'

'Only if you come back to me.'

'God willing.'

His way of saying that put a tiny doubt in her mind. As if he was doubtful himself. He had told her that he did not trust the Russians and that many of his compatriots, whose homes were in the Russian zone, had asked to stay in England. He would not do that, she knew; his bond with his parents was too strong. Stronger than his with her perhaps.

'How silly of me,' Doris said, looking down at the cutlery in her hand. 'There's only three of us now, but I've got knives and forks out for six.'

'Gordon will be back from his honeymoon soon and Don will come home for Christmas and we'll be six again,' Jean said. Gordon and Rosemary were going to live at the farm and Doris had been decorating his room and replacing his single bed with a double one. Good furniture was never given away and they thought the little bed might come in handy, so it was consigned to a box room along with a baby's cot and a lot of other clutter which Doris could not bear to throw away. How mother and daughter-in-law would get on under one roof, Jean did not know, but it made her feel even more isolated.

'Just like old times.'

'Yes and no.'

'You are thinking about Karl?'

'Yes.'

'Has he heard from home?'

'No, I don't think so. He's very worried. He says the Russians are bent on revenge for what they suffered and are brutal to those they conquer.'

'You can hardly blame them.'

'He says they take everything and what they don't take they destroy, not to mention raping the women. He has a young sister . . .'

'And you are worried he'll go home and not come back.'

'He might not be able to, that's the trouble.'

'There's nothing you can do about it, Jean. And maybe it's for the best.'

'Mum, how can you say that?'

'I'm sorry, love, I'm just trying to be practical.'

'I don't want to think about it. He says he is unlikely to go for some time.'

'Then we shall have to wait and see.'

'He tells me he's coming to work on Christmas Day.'

'Can't you manage without him?'

'Of course I can.' She meant the farm work, not anything else. 'He knows we don't do much except feed and water the animals and do the milking, and Gordon and Donald can help with that, but he is adamant. He says he wants me to have a good time and not have to worry about the livestock.'

'That is kind of him. I would ask him to have Christmas dinner with us, but I don't think Gordon would approve and I don't want to upset him now he seems more cheerful.'

That was indicative of how it was going to be, she supposed.

Chapter Fifteen

Gordon and Rosie came back from their honeymoon, full of the beauties of the Lake District and the walking they had done.

'I must go over and see Mum,' Rosemary said, after they had unpacked and eaten the meal Doris had cooked for them. 'She'll want to know we're back.'

Gordon elected to go with her and afterwards they called in at the Plough and Harrow. Bill was there, along with the usual regulars.

'How is married life?' Bill greeted them. 'You look well on it.'

'We are,' Gordon said. 'I can recommend it.'

'All well at home?'

'Yes, apart from having to put up with the Jerry. You don't know of any labourers looking for work, do you?'

'I'll ask around, but men who've travelled and seen a bit of life, aren't so keen to settle down. I'm having to pay top wages for my men.'

'I've yet to get to grips with the accounts. Pa still likes to do those, but I wonder how many mistakes he's made. Jean says he doesn't, but what does she know?'

'How is your father? Is he any better?'

'No. I doubt he will improve now. Do you know, they never even let me know he'd had a stroke? I couldn't believe what he was like when I saw him, so weak and shrivelled, petulant too, like a big child. He's nothing like the man he was.'

'Are any of us?'

'He and Mum are talking about retiring and moving to a cottage, leaving me to take over the farm. It's Mum's idea really, but he seems to go along with it.'

'That will be better for you, won't it? Two women in one kitchen is not a good idea.'

'Three, if you count Jean.' Gordon smiled wryly. 'It's about time you took her in hand, Bill.'

Jean had knitted Karl another jumper to replace the one he'd had stolen and decided to give it to him on Christmas Eve, after they had finished the milking and were waiting for his transport. 'It's to make up for the other one,' she said, putting the parcel into his hands.

He took it from her and stood looking down at the thick jumper without speaking for a moment. Then he said, 'You didn't have to do this, Jean. I shouldn't have told you I lost the other one.'

'I would have noticed you weren't wearing it. And I loved doing it. Every stitch was made with love.'

'Thank you and bless you.' He leant forward and kissed her. It was a gentle, undemanding kiss, a feather-light brushing of his lips against hers, but it started such a tumult inside her she felt she would explode if he didn't kiss her properly. She took his face in her hands and kissed him back. It was getting harder and harder to exercise the restraint they had promised each other. He was the first to draw away.

'I must go before I do something we will both regret.'

'I won't regret it, Karl.'

He smiled. 'I think you might. I will be here tomorrow.' He wrapped the paper round the pullover again and put it on the bench next to the dungarees he had taken off. 'I will leave this here, it will be safer.'

She watched his back as he walked down the drive to the waiting transport, then turned and went indoors to the bright light and warmth of the house where the jollity had already begun. Don and Rosie were decorating the tree, Gordon was sitting by the kitchen fire opposite their father; they had a glass of cider each. Doris and Elizabeth were preparing the evening meal. She stood looking at them all. Here was home, family and love and she ought to be grateful for it.

Karl did not need telling what needed doing and it was after breakfast when she went out to him the next day, taking a mug of tea and a mince pie on a paper napkin with her. He was wearing his new pullover with dungarees over his trousers, filling the water troughs outside the stables from the hosepipe. 'Happy Christmas,' she said cheerfully.

He turned off the water and smiled at her. 'Happy Christmas to you too, but you need not have come out. I have fed the chickens and the pigs.'

'I know, I heard them.' She handed him the tea and mince pie. 'These will warm you up a bit.'

'Thank you.' He bit into the hot pie and waved his hand about his open mouth to cool it.

She laughed. 'I should have told you it was hot.'

'It is delicious. Did you bake it?'

'No, Mum did.'

'Thank her for me.'

'I will.'

'I have something for you.' He went to the pocket of his coat which he had hung on a hook in the stable and brought out a small package. 'It is for your dressing table,' he said, as she unwrapped a small wooden bowl with a lid which had a point on it. 'It is for a powder puff and the spike is for your rings.'

'It's beautiful.' She wrapped her arms about him. 'Hold me, Karl. Hold me tight. Never let me go.'

He hugged her, then gently put her from him. 'It's Christmas Day, my love. Go back to your family. I can keep myself busy.'

'I ought to help.'

'No need. You will make that lovely skirt and jumper dirty. It suits you, brings out the lovely green of your eyes.'

She gave a tremulous laugh. 'Thank you, kind sir. We are just off to church. Would you like to come too?'

He smiled. 'It is a nice thought, but I think not. I would not want to start a riot, today of all days.'

She sighed, recognising the wisdom of that. 'Aren't you lonely?'

'Sometimes, but I have my thoughts to keep me company.'

'They are not always happy ones, are they?'

'No, but then I tell myself I am luckier than some and I think of all the good things in my life: a childhood I can treasure, family, good friends and you. What more can a man ask . . . ?' Instead of elaborating on that, he added, 'Please go back to your folks.'

There was a full congregation in church, all anxious to give thanks for the first Christmas in peace. Afterwards they loitered in the churchyard gossiping and wishing each other a happy Christmas and talking about the men who had come home, and those who never would. Happiness mixed with sadness.

'How are things?' Bill dropped into step beside Jean. Gordon was wheeling her father ahead of them, her mother and Rosie walked alongside.

'OK.'

'It can't be easy with Rosie living with you.'

'We get along.'

'I'm sure Gordon would rather have the house to himself when your parents retire.'

She turned sharply to look at him. 'What makes you say that? Have you been talking to him about it?'

'No, of course not, but it stands to reason.'

'The farm is my home. Where else would I go?' It was a question that had been bothering her and she supposed that, sooner or later, she would have to find a job and somewhere to live, but it was not a decision she was in a hurry to make. It really all depended on Karl.

'Marry me. You'll have a good home with me.'

He didn't understand why she burst out laughing. 'What's so funny about that?' he asked.

'Oh, Bill, that is about the least romantic proposal anyone could possibly have.'

'Well, you know me. I tell it as it is. Do you want me to get down on one knee with a red rose in my teeth?'

'No.' She stopped laughing. 'Hadn't it occurred to you that if I married you, I'd be sharing a home with your mother, so what's the difference?'

'It wouldn't be the same. You would be a married woman, my wife. Ma would understand that.'

Knowing his mother, she doubted it. 'Perhaps I don't want to marry. Not every woman does, you know.'

'I can't believe that. Why, I seem to remember you grumbling not so long ago that I would not commit myself, and now I have, you laugh.'

290

'That was ages ago and things have moved on. I'm sorry I laughed. That was unkind of me.'

'OK, point taken. Forget I spoke.'

Not a word about being in love, she noticed, as he left her and she hurried to catch up with her parents.

They were all trooping across the yard to the house when Doris spotted Karl through the open door of the stable, grooming one of the horses. 'We can't leave him out here in the cold with no dinner while we stuff ourselves,' she said. 'Gordon, you wouldn't mind if I ask him in, would you? After all, he used to have his meals with us before you came home.'

Jean held her breath because it looked as though her brother was going to refuse, but he was in a benevolent mood and said, 'OK, but talk of the war is banned.'

'It would be anyway.' Doris went over to Karl to issue the invitation. Jean resisted the temptation to go too and continued with the others to the house. A little while later, minus the dungarees, Karl came into the kitchen with Doris and was given a glass of cider while the women finished cooking and serving the dinner. Gordon was inclined to be terse and unfriendly, but everyone else accepted Karl as they had done for over a year and a second glass of cider mellowed her brother. Jean allowed herself to relax.

Karl did not stay long after the meal was finished but went back to work. Jean covered her good clothes with an overall and joined him at milking time. 'Thank you for today,' he said.

'It wasn't my doing. You came to work and Mum invited you for dinner, nothing out of the ordinary in that, is there?'

'On Christmas Day, there is. You have made me feel almost one of the family.'

'Good. Your transport is here.' They went to the gate together.

The sound of men's voices singing '*O Tannenbaum*' rang out from the canvas-covered lorry. 'The men are in good spirits by the sound of it.'

He bade her goodnight, climbed in with them and was borne away. She turned and went back indoors.

The new year came and went. The Nazi leaders who had survived and those running the death camps were put on trial and the country listened to the reports on the BBC in horror and disgust. It didn't help the popularity of the German prisoners of war. Jean knew some were being treated very badly, while others were accepted. And relations between Western Europe and Russia were worsening.

Churchill, no longer Prime Minister, travelled to America in March 1946 where he made a speech outlining his fears about Russian dominance in Eastern Europe where the alliance of wartime was rapidly turning into hostility. Having praised the Russian people as staunch allies, he went on to say: 'From Stettin in the Baltic to Trieste in the Adriatic, an iron curtain has descended across the Continent.'

Karl, listening to a report of it in the kitchen of Briar Rose Farm during a tea break, was cast into gloom. Churchill was only saying what he had told Jean months before. Poland, under Russian dominance, had shifted its borders westwards and he was afraid Hartsveld might soon be swallowed up. Even if it were not, it was now deep inside the Russian zone. If he were sent back there, would he ever be able to leave again? And could he get his parents out, even supposing they consented?

Occasionally, resting under a hedge during a lunch break, he and Jean might touch upon the future and speak about what they would like to happen, how and where they would live, but they could not make any real plans. And peace was bringing its own problems. There was austerity and hardship and bread was rationed for the first time, something that had never happened during the war. There was a chronic shortage of housing, too. Her parents had had no luck finding a cottage to suit them. They wanted one in the village which made the search more difficult. Jean suspected they were not trying very hard.

After protests were made in Parliament, a start was made on sending some German POWs home, beginning with the 'whites', but it was a slow process. Karl was not a 'white', though in hindsight he supposed he could have been, nor was he a builder or a miner, who were desperately needed to rebuild his shattered country and were being given priority. Added to that, his spells in the cooler had been set against his record, so he was not among the early leavers. Those left behind in the camps were subjected to a programme of re-education, destined to teach them about democracy and fit them for life when they went home. They were told about the hardships facing them; everything in the garden would not be lovely. Of a population of seventy million in Europe as a whole, they were told, thirty million were searching for someone. A missing persons' bureau in Hamburg was receiving thousands of enquiries every day. It depressed Karl, who had had no news of home.

'The trouble is that the names of towns and streets in the Russian zone have been changed to sound more Russian,' their lecturer told him when he spoke to him after one session. 'If you sent letters to the old name, they would not have been delivered.'

'How can I find out what the new name is?'

The man shrugged. 'It's difficult. The Russians are not very forthcoming. Are you planning to go to the Russian Zone?'

'Yes, that's where my parents are, if they are still alive.'

'They might have left. Thousands have fled from east to west, hoping to find shelter somewhere. Have you any relations in the west, they might go to?'

'Cousins, I suppose, but I do not think my parents would leave their farm.'

'If you want my advice, you'll try them first. Don't venture into the Russian zone unless you are very sure that's what you want. Have you been given any idea when you will go?'

'No.'

'Then you must be patient.'

Karl talked to Jean about it. 'Some of us have already been sent home,' he told her one day while they did the evening milking. 'I don't know when my turn will come, and I cannot even guess what I will find when I get there, or how easy it will be to move about. I might be gone some time.'

'I will wait. Forever if I have to.' She rose from her milking stool, measured the cow's yield and poured the milk into the churn.

'I hope and pray it will not come to that.' He joined her at the sink to wash his hands.

'How much warning will you get?'

'I don't know, probably not more than a few hours.'

'Then each goodbye we say could be the last.'

'Yes.'

'Oh, Karl.' She turned towards him and he wrapped his arms around her. 'It's bad enough that you have to go back to camp every night, but wondering if you will ever return will be a torment.'

He smiled and kissed her. 'You will survive, my love. As I will. As I must.' They clung to each other a moment longer. 'I must go, I don't want to be posted missing, that would not help.' He was

294

no longer brought to work in a lorry but allowed to make his own way. It was near enough to walk.

She didn't go to the gate with him, but stayed to record the milk yield and shut up the hens for the night. By the time she had finished, she had regained control of her seething emotions, at least on the surface.

This unhappy time was balanced by a christening. Rosemary had a son in early September, whom they called Stanley Arthur Winston. Stanley, so Gordon told them, after the man who had made his peg leg. He was a Pole and his real name had been Stanislaw but Rosie would not agree to that, so Stanley it was, soon to be shortened to Stan. Rosemary was a doting mother and the whole house seemed to revolve around the baby's needs: his feed times; his sleep times, when everyone had to creep around for fear of waking him; the washing line was always full of his little garments and the sitting room was scattered with his toys. Jean was often called in to babysit so that Gordon and Rosemary could go out. Plodding along as usual, she knew the time was not far off when she would have to leave the only home she had ever known or become an unpaid nanny and labourer.

The ban on fraternisation was lifted in time for Christmas 1946, and it was now possible to show friendship to former enemies. Some people invited them into their homes for the festivities, others, who had lost loved ones in the war, still hated them. It didn't make it any easier for Jean and Karl. They were either ignored or scorned by people Jean had once called her friends. 'Isn't Bill good enough for you now?' one of the women shouted when she and Karl were walking in the village one day. 'Traitor! Nazi whore!' It bothered Karl more than it did her. She was determined not to hide away, too scared to go out.

Gordon just managed to tolerate him. He was, in no sense, free. The one occasion he and Jean had popped into the Plough and Harrow for a drink had been a disaster. John Heacham had refused to serve him and Jean had been angry, with the result they were both now barred. He was sorry for that, he told her, he ought to have known better than to risk it.

'I warned you that would happen, didn't I?' her mother said when she learnt of it from Gordon, who had been told about it by John.

'Yes, but I don't care. Besides, we are not the only ones. As soon as the ban was lifted, there they were, had probably been like us all the time, couples trying to hide their feelings for each other.'

'There is still a ban on marriage. You can't marry him, Jean.'

'Not yet,' she said enigmatically.

'I give up.'

'Good.'

January arrived bitterly cold with an icy east wind. Jean and Karl did their best to keep the animals warm and fed. When it started to snow, they brought them all inside and were glad they did. The snow was the heaviest they'd had for years. Karl really did not need to come to work, there was little they could do, but he never failed. It would have been easier for him to stay on the farm, but she knew Gordon would be against it and Karl himself did not want to. She wondered if he was reluctant to leave the camp in case he missed his turn to go home.

'The winters are harder where I come from,' he told her, as they cleared a path to the pigsties, chicken coops and silage bins. Jean was glad they had made as much silage as they could; it was keeping the animals alive. 'For weeks on end we have snow. As children, my brother and I would go about on skis. Can you ski?'

'I've never tried.'

'If this goes on, I think I will make some to come to work.'

'The snow might be gone by the time you finish them,' she said. 'There's a pair of snow shoes in the shed. I don't know how old they are, but I remember Pa using them to go across the fields when we had heavy snowfalls like we did the first winter of the war. I imagine his father did before him. I'll dig them out for you.'

They were needed. The snow continued on and off throughout January. It piled itself into huge drifts, blocked roads and railway lines and caused chaos with the housebuilding programme. Some remote villages were cut off from the outside world and arrangements were made to supply them from the air. Livestock left in the open died under heaps of snow. Coal supplies to the power stations were so low the government was forced to put restrictions on the use of electricity. Supplies to industry were stopped altogether, while households were only allowed to use it for nineteen hours a day. Rosemary wailed about the unfairness of it. 'I've got a baby to feed and keep warm,' she said. 'And it's so dark . . .'

Jean and Doris fetched out the old oil lamps from the shelf in the shed where they had been abandoned, though paraffin was also in short supply, and they lit the fire under the copper in the wash house so that Rosie could boil Stanley's nappies. There was very little coal. They were glad of the woodpile Karl and Jean had made with some of the elm tree that had fallen the previous March. As if that were not bad enough, dockers and transport workers went on strike and there was a threat of food shortages. It had to be delivered by the army. Never had Jean been more glad that the farm was almost self-sufficient.

They could not even keep up with the news properly; radio broadcasts were limited and television, a new form of entertainment that was becoming popular with people who could afford it, was suspended. 'It's worse than the war,' Doris complained.

On the morning the snow stopped and a weak sun broke through the clouds, Jean stood at the orchard gate looking across at the snow-covered pit, pristine and sparkling. The more adventurous of the villagers would be along soon with their skates, flying over the ice, taking a break from the miseries of a winter the like of which no one could remember. She turned as Karl joined her. As usual he had come over the fields on the snow shoes.

'The ice must be feet thick on there,' she said, nodding towards the pit. 'Thick enough for skating.'

'I'm sure it is. Do you have skates?'

'Yes, most fen people have them.' She laughed suddenly. 'Let's go and look for them.'

She took his hand and led the way to the shed where she rummaged in a cupboard and pulled out several strange objects before her hands fastened on a pair of skates. They were not attached to boots but had straps for fastening them to ordinary boots. 'These are Gordon's,' she said, and reached inside again to pull out another pair. 'Come on, let's go and see if the ice will hold.' She handed Gordon's skates to him.

'Do you think we ought?'

'Why not? "All work and no play makes Jack a dull boy".'

'I have never heard that before.'

'It's an old saying. I'll teach you some more if you like.' She picked up the yard broom, intending to use it to clear the snow from the ice. 'I take it you can skate?'

'Of course.' He looked at the skates in his hands. 'These are very long.'

'They are fen-runners, meant for speed skating. Before the war,

298

the farmers used to flood their fields to make huge ice rinks. Men used to come from far and wide to race. It was a kind of knockout competition. The contestants were paired off to race against each other the length of the rink, round a barrel and back again. The winner went on to the next round. Some reached prodigious speeds. Mind you, most of the time it was fen villagers organising their own small competitions. Sir Edward used to give a pig to the winner of the Great and Little Bushey races. Pa was very good at it, and Gordon was, too. I was never much good, though I enjoyed skating round the edges. I wonder if they'll start up again.'

Instead of trying to flounder across the orchard to the pit, they went down the lane which had been partially cleared by a snow plough fixed to the front of a tractor, leaving huge piles of snow each side. He would not let her go on the ice until he made sure it was safe. He took the broom and pushed it ahead of him clearing a path through the snow. 'It is good,' he said, coming back to her.

She strapped on her skates and tentatively ventured onto the ice. He put on the other pair and followed her. He soon cleared an expanse of ice so that they could skate. He was much better at it than she was and she watched enviously as he sped over the ice, doing twists and turns, going faster and faster. She had not gone far before she overbalanced and found herself sitting on the ice, her legs out in front of her. They both laughed as he skated up and helped her back on her feet.

He started to hum 'The Blue Danube' waltz. 'Come, let us dance,' he said, turning her to face him and putting one hand about her waist. With the other he took her hand. She was nervous at first, but he held her firmly and they were soon skimming over the ice, both humming the tune. Her eyes were alight and the cold air had made her cheeks rosy. For a few short minutes, she was carefree, hardship and work forgotten, as he whirled her round. It could not last, it was, after all, only a moment's respite from the daily grind and they had to return to that.

'I won't say anything to Gordon,' she said, as they put the skates back where they found them. 'It would make him sad to think he can't do it any more.'

February brought no relief from the bitter cold. Everyone went about muffled in layer upon layer of clothes to keep warm. It was March before the thaw set in and the snow melted. And that was when their troubles really began.

The snow melted off the orchard and top fields and ran into the pit which, unable to hold so much, overflowed onto ground still frozen. The orchard flooded, the lane flooded and the sheep pasture was inundated. The farmhouse was on slightly higher ground and they watched as water began to rise all about them. Gordon drove the pickup truck very slowly down the lane to fetch Elizabeth to safety, while Jean milked the cows and fed them and looked after the sheep. Some of them were due to lamb before long. Karl did not come. It may have been because he could not get through the floods, but it might equally have been that he was on his way home to Germany. She tried not to think about that. She could not ring Colonel Williamson because gales had brought the telephone lines down.

The same thing was happening all over the fens. Small areas of floodwater became wide expanses, whipped up into waves by the gale-force winds. In some areas of the fens, caused by the shrinking of the peat, the rivers were higher than the surrounding land and only kept in check by high banks. The army, prisoners of war and anyone else who could lend a hand were called in to repair breaches with clay brought up in barges from Ely. Gordon insisted on going to help, driving himself along roads awash with melted snow, but he was soon back to Rosie's intense relief.

'I couldn't stand up against the wind,' he said, sinking into the rocking chair by the kitchen fire. 'Nobody could. They say it's up to a hundred miles an hour and I can believe it. I've never experienced anything like it. The water's so high the barges can't get under the bridges. They've had to abandon the work until the wind dies down. I saw acres and acres of floods, cows stuck on little islands, houses up to their first floor in water, people sitting on the roofs of bungalows. They've got boats out to rescue them.' He paused. 'I saw Karl.'

'Karl?' Jean could not keep the eagerness from her voice. 'Where?'

'On the banks with a crowd of other POWs. Give them their due, they were working like Trojans.'

Karl would not go back to the camp while there were people in trouble. He manned one of the rowing boats the army had collected and set off to row across the flooded fen to a row of cottages he could see a little way off. He supposed they lined a road, but there was no sign of one. The boat was tossing on waves whipped up by the wind and it was taking all his strength to make headway. As he came closer, an upstairs window was flung open and a young woman put her head out. She screamed for help.

He rowed alongside. He was four or five feet below her. 'Can you jump down?'

'I've got a baby.'

'Drop it down gently. I'll catch it.'

'Are you sure?'

'Yes.'

She left the window and came back with a tightly wrapped bundle, leant over the windowsill and let it go. Karl, who was standing in the boat trying to keep it steady, caught it and laid it gently in the bottom of the boat. 'Now you. Get out on the windowsill with your back to me and let your feet down first. I'll grab you.'

By this time windows were being opened all along the row and people were leaning out, not wanting him to miss them. He did not think he could take them all in one go. He loaded the boat with the children and older women, who were nervous about letting themselves out of the windows and had to be helped. 'I'll come back for the rest of you,' he told those left behind.

With a loaded boat, it was even harder work going back; he felt as if his arms were being wrenched out of their sockets and his chest ached. It was bitterly cold, his passengers were shivering, but he was sweating. The baby was crying, a thin wail of distress, which set the other children crying too. One of the women took an oar from him. He let her have it with a weary smile. Together they made it back to dry land but he was on the point of exhaustion.

'There's more people stranded,' he told the British captain who was organising everything in their section. 'I have to go back.'

'I'll send someone else, you're done for.'

'What shall I do?'

'Go back to camp. There's transport to take you. You've done a good job. Couldn't have managed without you.'

'Jerry or not, he's a hero,' said the woman with the baby. 'I'll never forget him.'

He walked wearily back to the lorry, hauled himself up and collapsed in a corner. There were other men there but they were all nearly as exhausted as he was and no one spoke.

When he arrived back at the camp he found Otto, sitting on one of the beds, reading a German newspaper. '*Mein Gott*, Otto, where have you sprung from?' he demanded. 'Where have you been?'

'Home.'

'You got home?' He was astonished.

'Yes, and now I'm back.'

'What happened?'

'I made it to London, sneaked aboard a freighter and pretended to be a Dutch member of the crew. It was going to Hamburg. It was a city in ruins. I managed to get on a train . . .'

'What did you use for money?'

'They took English money. Half the railways were out of action and I saw a lot of the country while I going from one train to another, catching buses and walking. Everywhere was in ruins, Karl, nothing but rubble. People were scavenging for food and begging and when the snow came they died . . .'

'But your folks?'

'Dead, Karl, dead. They died in the floods when the Möhne was breached. The letter I had from them was written before the raid.' He gave a hollow laugh. 'So I came back and gave myself up. Here I am and here I stay.'

It was strange that Otto, who was so keen go home, was going to stay in England while he, who wanted more than anything to make his home here, was down to go back to Germany.

'I shouldn't go,' Otto said, reading his thoughts. 'In the Russian zone it's worse. I heard that anyone who has been in Allied hands is sent straight to Siberia.'

The efforts of the German prisoners during the floods, particularly Karl's, were praised by everyone and some of the animosity towards them eased. Gradually the land dried out and the farmers tried to catch up with the sowing and planting, but the ground was still sticky and they had no idea how much would germinate. Lost livestock had to be replaced. The Colemans were lucky in

303

that respect; they had lost no animals, though the milk yield was down. The sheep had lambed indoors but as soon as there was grass enough for them, they were put outside to graze. Karl's labour was needed more than ever. Gordon went from animosity to toleration, which Jean supposed was a step in the right direction.

The ban on British women marrying Germans was lifted in July, which was followed by a flurry of weddings. 'It's for you to decide, sweetheart,' Karl told Jean, when they debated whether to follow suit.

'I want to more than anything,' she said. 'But I think we should wait until you have been home. See your parents first.'

'You are probably right,' he said, thinking of what Otto had told him. If he was prevented from coming back he would be leaving her in an untenable position. Married, perhaps pregnant, but unable to marry again until she could go through the courts for a divorce; messy, expensive and time-consuming. She obviously realised that herself and he was glad of it, even if it did mean more self-restraint than ever.

Chapter Sixteen

Colonel Williamson was smiling broadly as he addressed the group of men he had summoned. 'You are next for repatriation. Transport will take you to the holding camp in Leicestershire tomorrow morning immediately after breakfast. I suggest you collect your belongings together. Please bear in mind the restrictions on what you may take.' He handed them each a sheet of paper. 'Mr Muller, stay behind please.' It was the first time Karl had been addressed as mister since the use of military titles had been abolished and it sounded strange. On the other hand that was how he wanted to be addressed when he came back. If he came back.

He waited until everyone else had left the room. 'Can't we even warn our employers?' he asked.

'I don't see how you can.' Colonel Williamson said. 'I am aware of your relationship with Miss Coleman, Mr Muller, I would have to be blind not to be. I could have reported it . . .'

'We appreciate that you did not, Colonel.'

'I am surprised you haven't asked to stay. The Russians will not make you welcome.'

'I know that, Colonel, but I must find out what has happened to my family.'

'You know that if your home is with the Russians, you may choose the zone you want to be repatriated to?'

'So I have been told.' He knew the British and Americans had combined their zones for administrative purposes. 'I will ask to go to the Bizone. I have cousins who live in Osnabrück. They might be able to tell me more.'

'Do you want to come back to England?'

'Yes, Colonel, eventually.'

'Then I think I can help you. If you buy a return ticket, you will have four weeks to decide whether to stay in Germany or come back. If you stay, you will forfeit the cost of the ticket, if you come back it will be refunded. How does that sound?'

'It sounds very good, sir.'

'Then it will be arranged. Go and pack your belongings.'

He left to obey, cramming as much food and as many cigarettes into his luggage as he had managed to hoard, even though rationed food was on the list of banned items – along with government property, uncensored mail and English currency. He had his issue clothes but also garments that Jean had given him: an overcoat, flannelette shirts and pyjamas, warm socks, jumpers and dungarees. It made a hefty kitbag full, just below the weight restriction.

Then he sat on his bed and contemplated not being able to say goodbye to Jean. 'I'm off,' he told Otto, standing up suddenly and reaching for his cap. 'If anyone wants to know where I've gone, I am in the latrines. Stomach upset. Too much excitement. I'll be back.'

Jean was sitting close to the lamp, darning a ladder in a lisle stocking, picking up the stitch with a crochet hook and carefully working up to the hole where it started before darning it in, when she heard someone knocking on the back door. Everyone else had gone to bed. She had only stayed up because the last conversation with Karl had made her feel uneasy and she knew she would not sleep. The knock came again, not loud, but insistent. She rose to answer it.

'Karl!' She pulled him into the kitchen. 'What's happened? Why are you here?'

'I'm leaving tomorrow, first thing. My turn has come.'

'Oh, Karl.'

They wrapped their arms around each other.

'I don't know how I am going to manage without you,' she said.

'The colonel will send someone else to replace me.'

She gave a watery giggle. 'I didn't mean that and you know it.'

'I know. I was only trying to cheer you up.'

'Nothing can. I shall be miserable until I see you again.'

'No, please, my love, do not be miserable. Be happy. It is not the end of the world. The future is ours and, if God so pleases, it will be a future together. Hold onto that thought.'

'I'll try.' She clung to him, unwilling to let him go. 'Oh, Karl, I have so been dreading this moment.'

'So have I, but it has to be. We have always known that. I must go back before I am missed.' He kissed her, moving his mouth all over her face and neck, tasting her sweetness, smelling the lavender scent she wore, trying to store it in his memory for the days and weeks to come.

They pulled apart as the door opened behind them and Doris stood there in her dressing gown and slippers. 'I heard voices. Karl, what are you doing here?'

'He's come to say goodbye, Mum. He's being sent home tomorrow.'

'Oh, I see.' She looked at Karl, who was still holding Jean's hand. 'Are you going for good?'

'I hope not, Mrs Coleman. I should very much like to come back, if I can and if you will have me . . .'

'It's not up to me, is it? It's up to Jean.' She looked from one to the other. 'I'll leave you to see him to the door, Jean.' It was most certainly a dismissal and made Jean smile.

She accompanied Karl to the back door. Outside, a full moon lit up the garden and the outline of the outbuildings in a grey-scape of sharp angles. Beyond the orchard, the water in the pit shimmered in a light breeze. He took her in his arms and held her close against him. She put her head on his shoulder. 'Come back to me, Karl, please come back.'

'I will do my utmost. Remember, my love, *auf Wiedersehen* is not goodbye.' He took her face in both hands and tipped it up so that he could kiss her, then pulled away and strode off down the drive. She watched him go, then went back into the kitchen and fell sobbing into her mother's arms.

The next morning he was taken by lorry to the transit camp. If he thought interrogations were at an end, he was wrong. There were more questions, many of which he had already answered. Had he belonged to the Hitler Youth? What had been his job in civilian life? How long had he been in the army? Which branch of the army? Had he ever made political speeches? What had he learnt from the re-education programme? His answers satisfied his interrogators and three days later he was on his way to Hull which was teeming with others on their way home, all cheerful and joking and loaded with baggage. The ship that was to take them was an old German freighter captured early on in the war. Streaks of rust and drab grey paint proclaimed its age. They laughed when they saw it. They didn't care; they were going home. Karl, taking his place in the long column going up the gangplank, was torn between elation and despondency.

The accommodation was spartan and crowded, but they had all known worse. Karl left his kitbag on his bunk and went on deck to watch the coastline of Britain fading into the distance. It was all very well to tell Jean *auf Wiedersehen* was not goodbye, but as the distance between them increased, it certainly felt like it. He had his return ticket safely in his wallet, but would he ever be able to use it?

Twenty-four hours later, the ship docked at Cuxhaven and Karl found himself back on the soil of his homeland, being greeted by members of the German Red Cross with hot coffee and sandwiches. They did not linger long on the quayside but were shepherded to a waiting train. Now he was here, he began to feel a little different, a little more eager, a little more anxious. The countryside beside the rails was ravaged. There was evidence of bomb damage everywhere and the people looked so drab, shuffling about in shabby clothing.

His next stop was Munsterlager, which had once been an army camp and later a camp for British prisoners of war. They had all gone home, of course, and now it was a demobilisation centre for returning German prisoners. Before that could happen there were more questions, even more searching than the previous ones, designed to weed out any Nazis who had slipped through the net. He was provided with civilian clothes, given forty *Reichsmark* in lieu of back pay and handed in his *Soldbuch* which he had kept in his possession all through his captivity. It contained his military registration and identity disc numbers, his medical history and a record of his rise through the ranks, pay and awards. In exchange he was handed his *Wehrpass*, which was given to every serviceman on his release and held a record of his military service. He tucked it safely in his wallet with the money, his new identity card, new ration book and return ticket, and made his way to the train station to find a train going to Osnabrück. At last, at long last, he was a free man.

Otto had not been exaggerating. Karl had been prepared for devastation but not on the scale he saw it. Two years after the end of hostilities, the country was still in ruins. Train services were unreliable and his journey to Osnabrück was delayed more than once by a need to leave the train and make his way to the next stretch of line that was working. Every town through which he passed seemed to be a heap of rubble. A start had been made on clearing it. He saw women with shovels or just their hands, piling trucks with broken bricks, twisted metal and shards of glass. They were thin and ill-clothed.

Osnabrück, when he finally reached it, was particularly bad. It took him some time to find the address he wanted because of the destruction. The house was still standing but badly damaged; he did not think it was habitable. If that were the case, where would he go next? He rapped on the door. There was no response. He rapped again.

The door opened a chink and he saw the side of a woman's face and one eye. 'Who are you? What do you want?'

'I am Karl. Karl Muller. I am looking for *Frau* Gabrielle Braun or Maria.'

The door opened wider to reveal a mousey-haired, unkempt woman dressed in a thick black skirt, a yellowing blouse which had once been white, and a grey cardigan. She appeared to be old, but on looking closer he realised she was not much older than he was. 'Muller?' She sounded doubtful.

'Yes. Are you Maria?'

'Karl Muller?'

He smiled. 'Yes. If you are Maria, then I am your cousin. Are you going to let me in? I have come a long way.'

She stood aside to allow him to enter. Instead of finding himself in a home, he was faced with ruin. He could see right through to the back garden. 'This way.' She led him down to the cellar. There was a semblance of normality in that it was sparsely furnished and there was a fire in the grate. An older woman was stirring something in a pot over the flames.

'*Mutti*, here is Cousin Karl,' Maria said.

The old lady turned to face him. He had not seen her since he was a child but he could clearly see the likeness to his mother, though when he had last seen her, *Mutti* had not been so ravaged. 'Hello, *Tante* Gabi,' he said.

She screamed and dropped the spoon. He put his kitbag down and ran to help her to a chair. 'I'm sorry if I have given you a shock.'

'My goodness you have. Where have you come from?'

'England.'

'Oh, yes, Elise said you were a prisoner.'

'Lisa?' he queried. 'You have spoken to her?'

'Of course. She will be back from work soon. She is lucky, she works at the barracks in the office of the military governor.'

'You mean she is here, in Osnabrück?'

'Yes. She came in '44,' Maria added.

'*Vati und Mutti?*'

'As far as we know, they are still in Hartsveld. Your father would not leave the farm and your mother would not leave him, but they both insisted that Elise escape while she could.'

'I was afraid of that. Do you know how they are?'

311

'You had better ask Elise. Here she is.'

He twisted round to see his sister coming through the door. She was carrying a shopping bag. 'Lisa,' he said.

'*Mein Gott!* Karl.' She dropped the shopping and stared at him. 'Are you a ghost?'

'No, I am real enough.' He held his arms wide and she ran into them. He could feel her boniness through her clothes.

'Let me look at you,' she said, leaning back to scan his face. Her eyes were bright with tears. 'You have not changed. A little older looking perhaps, but you are still my beloved big brother.'

'You have not changed either,' he lied. She was desperately thin and in spite of being three years younger than he was, looked much older. Her hair was pale and wispy, not the gold of ripened corn that he remembered. Her eyes, blue as cornflowers, had not changed.

Maria had picked up the shopping bag and was emptying its contents onto the table: a dozen small potatoes, a turnip, a tiny jar of ersatz coffee, a tin of dried milk and a canvas bag containing a few lumps of coal. 'We do quite well,' she told Karl. 'Because Elise works at the camp, she can sometimes get stuff for us.'

'It is because I speak English,' Elise explained. 'I translate. Now tell me all about you. Have you been discharged?'

'Yes.' He delved into his kitbag and produced the food he had brought with him: tea and sugar, both of which had been on the forbidden list, a tin of milk, a tin of spam and another of peaches, several packets of razor blades, three bars of chocolate and the cigarettes, which he piled on the table beside Elise's shopping. 'I couldn't carry any more,' he said.

They stared at it for several seconds before falling on it and handling every item as if to ascertain it was real. Maria gathered up the cigarettes. 'Better than money,' she told him. 'They will buy us many things.'

'I have money,' he said, taking his wallet from his pocket.

Elise put a hand over his. 'No, you keep that. You will need it. I am paid wages.'

It was apparent that it was Elise who was the breadwinner but she did not seem to mind. They were grateful they were not as badly off as some of the other citizens, crammed into the habitable buildings, existing on what they could barter, beg or pilfer. 'Maria is the scavenger,' Elise told him. 'Finding food, wood and coal is a full-time job.'

The more they told him, the more horrified he became. He had never thought of his life in England as luxurious, but it was, compared with what they had suffered and were still suffering.

'Do you know about Heidi Beauman?' Elise asked him, as Gabrielle set about making a better meal than the one she had envisaged.

'I know she married a Gestapo officer.'

'Yes, I could have slapped her for it, but she suffered for it in the end. Both she and her husband died in Berlin. The Russians killed them.'

'Oh.' He sat down and was about to light a cigarette from the packet he took from his pocket, but stopped himself. If cigarettes were currency, he should not burn them. He put it back in the packet and laid it on the table, together with a lighter he had bought with *Lagergeld* in Bushey. Maria scooped them up in triumph.

'I'm sorry, but I had to tell you.'

'It is of no consequence. I got over her a long time ago.'

'Good.' She paused. 'Are you staying, Karl? Rebuilding has started, but with so few men . . .'

313

'I want to see *Vater* and *Mutter*,' he said.

'Don't.'

'But I must. They are all right, aren't they?'

'As far as I know. The border between east and west was closed last year and now you need an interzone travel passport. If you apply for one of those, they will interrogate you before issuing one and then you have to wait nine weeks while it is processed. Unless you have a plausible story, the Russians will know you were in England and that will be enough to condemn you. You will be followed and arrested as a spy as soon as you arrive.'

'Is it that bad?'

'Yes. The Russians and the German border police are everywhere, patrolling the border between the zones, shooting anyone they don't like the look of. It is worse since the British and Americans combined their zones at the beginning of this year. At one time it was easy to go to the east and visit relatives, but now the Soviets are more intransigent than ever.'

'Perhaps I can smuggle my way across.'

'What then? You will still have many miles of Soviet-occupied country to cover before you reach Hartsveld. You could do better staying here and finding a job. Men are needed.'

So many men had died or been wounded, manpower was scarce in Osnabrück; there were thousands more women than men, and women were doing most of the work clearing the rubble so that reconstruction could begin. There were very few fully habitable houses and some of those had been requisitioned for the occupying forces, something the inhabitants resented. The town was surrounded by farmland and workers were wanted there too. Wages were barely above subsistence level, even if there had been goods to buy. Karl's cigarettes and chocolate would be put to good use but he knew they would soon run out of those. He was a burden on their limited supplies. Overriding that was his determination to go to Hartsveld. He had no coherent plan of what he would do after that. It all depended on what he found when he arrived.

'I'll think about it,' he said, thinking of Jean waiting for him to return. But how could he leave these people, his kith and kin, and his homeland in such a mess? He was torn between two loves, between his duty and a promise.

Chapter Seventeen

Gordon had managed to find a labourer to do the work Karl had been doing. Joe Bunford worked well enough, but he did not have Karl's enthusiasm, nor his cheerfulness. He did not sing as he worked. Jean was prepared to tolerate him only until Karl came back. She had not heard from him. Telling herself that letters could take a long time to arrive did not make her feel any better.

She stayed out of doors as long as she could because there were tensions in the house between her mother and Rosemary. Rosie wanted to do things her way and they rarely coincided with the way Doris had been doing them all her life, especially when it came to looking after babies. Jean knew her mother was unhappy. She wasn't sure about her father; he seemed to have shrunk even more inside himself. Now Gordon had taken over, Pa did not even have the farm to occupy his mind, or if it did, he did not speak of it. She worried about them both.

'Gran, we really must do something to help Mum and Pa,' she said to her grandmother one day when she visited her, as she often did. 'Rosie is becoming a bore and Gordon always sides with her. Have you heard of any property going that might suit them?'

'No, love, or I would have told you.'

'I'm going into Wisbech tomorrow. I'll go to the estate agents to see what's on the market.'

'Very little, I think.' She paused and scanned Jean's face. 'What about you?'

'What about me?'

'Do you get on with Rosie?'

'We rub along. I'm outside most of the day, so I hardly come into conflict with her.'

'You will want your own home one day.'

'I can't think about that now.' The war had disrupted so many lives; country people were moving to the towns, townspeople deciding they wanted to settle down in the country, especially if their homes had been bombed. Finding somewhere to live was an unending obsession. Jobs that had been secure before the war were no longer there. Mechanisation had come to the farms and did the work of an army of men. Gordon had embraced it as far as funds would allow. Robin and Dobbin were sold, far too cheaply in Jean's opinion. She missed them and she knew parting with them had distressed Pa. Misty was kept because, with petrol in short supply, they still needed her. Donald lived in digs in Peterborough. He came home occasionally when he and Gordon would have their heads together over some new piece of machinery.

It was all so unsettling. She was lost, bewildered. She did not seem to fit in anywhere. Most of her friends were married or courting, even Bill. He and Brenda were going out together and it looked as though there might be a wedding soon. She wished him well. If her mother thought she had made the wrong choice, she refrained from saying so. Gordon needed her and so did her parents, so she had no choice but to stay where she was and hope things would improve.

They did not. The country was on the verge of bankruptcy and needed a huge loan from America to keep afloat. Rations were cut yet again. They had never starved during the war, but some people were wondering if they might starve now. The Colemans, being farmers, fared better than most but, apart from a little pork, they relied on bought meat and there was now only a shilling's worth per person per week. As usual Rosie grumbled, though Doris was adept at making a little go a long way. Gordon shot rabbits and pigeons and these supplemented the meat. In spite of keeping the worst from him, Arthur grew more and more restless with bouts of angry frustration alternating with morose predictions of disaster. He wanted to be up doing something about it.

Jean was woken one day in August by a white-faced, trembling mother who was having trouble hanging onto her self control. 'Jean, ring Doctor Norman. It's your father. He's . . .' She stopped, choking on a sob she was valiantly trying to hold back.

Jean scrambled out of bed. 'Where is he?'

'In bed. He must have . . .' She blinked hard. 'Gone in his sleep.'

'Oh, Mum.'

She flung her dressing gown on and rushed downstairs to her father's room, banging on Gordon's door as she passed it.

She dashed into the downstairs room that had become her father's bedroom. He lay as if asleep, but she knew it was a sleep from which he would not wake. She fell on her knees beside his bed and took his hand, already growing cold. 'Pa. Oh, Pa.'

Doris, followed by Gordon, still half asleep, came into the room and stood behind her. Jean rose from her knees and put her arms around her. 'He is at peace, Mum.'

Gordon made a choking sound and hurried from the room.

'He was a good man,' Doris said. She spoke quietly but there was a calmness about her that spoke of courage, not insensitivity. 'He loved us all.'

'I know, Mum, and we all loved him.'

'He worked hard all his life and kept us fed and clothed, even through the depression and the war, until he had that stroke. Even then . . .' Her voice trailed away.

'Yes.' Now the shock had passed, Jean could feel the tears gathering in her eyes but she blinked them back. If her mother could keep them at bay, so must she. 'Sit down, Mum, stay with him for a bit. I'm going to see where Gordon's got to and ring the doctor and Don.' She helped her mother to sit in the chair by the bed, where she had sat so often to read the newspaper or the *Farmers Weekly* to him, and left the room. Only then did she weep.

The shock of Arthur's passing united the whole village in grief. He had been born and lived in the same house all his life, as his father had before him and his father before him. He had been part of the fabric of the village: reliable, opinionated, with a wry sense of humour, respected for his knowledge of the countryside. A steady stream of people came to the house to pay their respects and offer words of comfort. Some brought flowers, many offered help. They filed past his coffin which stood on trestles in the middle of the room where he had died. Bill came, genuinely distressed, bringing apologies from his mother. Jean thought

319

Mrs Howson had not forgiven her for turning Bill down. Mr and Mrs Harris and Mr and Mrs Maynard came, so too did the butcher, the baker and the blacksmith, old John Barry and even Ted Gould. Doris bore it all with a calmness that Jean envied. She wanted to scream, to shout at them to go away and leave them alone. Instead she followed her mother's example, thanked them for coming and quietly went on with the funeral arrangements, helped by her grandmother.

Gordon stomped about the farm, silently grieving. Jean did not try to comfort him, knowing he would push her away. Rosemary was quiet and bewildered, although Stanley kept her busy. Between them they coped, too busy in those early days to brood or have time to wonder what the future would be without the man of the house.

The Reverend Brotherton, who had been the first of their callers, apart from the undertaker, was to take the funeral service and afterwards there would be refreshments at the farmhouse. Jean wanted to employ a caterer, but her mother insisted on doing it herself. 'It's the least I can do for him,' she said, as though he would know if she failed him. In a way, Jean understood that; Pa's presence was everywhere. Whatever she was doing, he was there beside her, instructing her, finding fault sometimes, sometimes praising. It was foolish, she knew, but she thought even the animals missed him.

The church was full for the funeral service. Almost every villager had taken time off to attend. Mrs Jackson came down with Terry and Lily and followed the family into the church behind the coffin. Terry was quite the young man, but Lily was the same lovable child she had always been.

The rector spoke of Arthur's stalwart loyalty to the community, his love of animals, particularly the horses, and his devotion to his family. Gordon spoke a eulogy in a voice husky with emotion, though he tried to lighten it with a joke or two. Most of the congregation went back for refreshments at the farm which soon became noisy. An occasional laugh meant someone had told an amusing story. It was after they had all gone and only the family were left to sit looking at the crumb-laden plates, the dregs left in the wine glasses, the slowly stewing tea, that the truth really hit them and the tears flowed. Jean hugged her mother, Gordon hugged Rosie, Elizabeth hugged Donald, who was trying very hard to be brave.

Donald pulled away and went up to his room; no one tried to stop him. Rosie went to feed Stanley and Elizabeth set about clearing away the debris and washing-up. Jean and Doris went to help her. 'We've got to settle things,' Doris said.

'What do you mean?' Jean asked, though she had a very good idea. Arthur's only legacy had been the farm which was rented, his life insurance and a few hundred pounds in the bank. The farm would go to Gordon, Sir Edward had already told him that changing the name on the tenancy agreement was only a formality. Doris would have the insurance money to supplement her pension and the money, what little there was of it, was to be divided between his offspring. 'You'll stay here now, won't you?'

'It depends on Gordon. The farm is his now, but his family will grow.'

'If anyone leaves, it will be me,' Jean said. She had been thinking of doing that for some time, but had been putting off doing anything about it until Karl came back. If he came back. She was beginning to doubt it. He had gone from her life almost as if he had never been part of it, but he had left his mark, just as Pa had done, and neither could be erased from her thoughts or her heart.

* * *

Karl straightened his aching back and looked about him. He was in the middle of a field of mangel-wurzels, rows and rows of them. They were used for animal feed, not human consumption, though it didn't stop people from raiding the field at night. He worked in a gang, some of them freed prisoners of war, as he was. They toiled for long hours, pulling the crop out of the ground, chopping off the heads and throwing the roots into a cart pulled by a thin horse. On the far side of the field he could see barges and a few sailing craft, making their way slowly along the Mittelland Canal.

'Where are they bound?' he asked Herman Buchmann, the man who owned the field and had been working beside him.

Buchmann shrugged. 'Anywhere between the Rheine and Berlin.'

'They are allowed to cross the border, then?'

'If they have the right papers, yes. Are you contemplating a voyage?'

'I might be.' He had thought of taking a train but he knew there would be a lengthy stop at the border for papers to be examined and the only ones he had were those given to him in Munsterlager and, if Elise was right, they would hinder rather than help him. Going by road needed a vehicle and he did not have one.

'Risky.'

'I know. Do you know anyone who might take me?'

'I might. Meet me tomorrow evening at the Café Lotte.'

Café Lotte was a meeting place where it was possible to sit over a cup of coffee or a tankard of beer all evening, smoke a cigarette if you had one, and set the world to rights. Karl went there sometimes in the evening to relieve the boredom of life with three women with whom he had nothing in common. The main topic of conversation was the shortage of everything. In rural Lower Saxony they had not witnessed the Allies' destruction of the factories and industries that had supplied the war effort, but the economic result of their disappearance was felt all over the country. The gloomiest said Germany would never recover; those of a more optimistic frame of mind said that once they rid themselves of the occupying forces, they could please themselves with what they manufactured. He listened to the debate but did not take part.

The next evening he found Herman there with another man whom he introduced as Johannes Brand, a Dutchman from Enschede just over the border with the Netherlands. Johannes had a barge on which he transported some of the produce of Holland to the Soviet zone and brought back watches and cameras and artwork. Karl explained his mission. 'Can you take me?'

'I do not suppose you have papers allowing you to travel?' He spoke *Plattdeutsch*, a local dialect close to Dutch, but he easily understood standard German.

'No, only those given to me on my discharge.'

'It will cost you.'

'I expected that.'

'I will be passing by Herman's field at ten o'clock tomorrow morning. If I see you on the bank, I will stop for you, but I shall not wait for you. You will need to bring food and money, as much of both as you can. My vessel is called the *Wilhelmina*.' He drained his glass and stood up. '*Bis Morgen*.' And he was gone.

Elise was not pleased when he told her of his plans. They had come to rely on his wages along with hers and now he was going to abandon them. Not only that, he proposed taking some of their precious food. He placated them with the gift of his pyjamas, spare shirts, his razor and all but one spare pair of socks, which Maria could barter. The rest of his belongings made a very small bundle.

'If you must, you must,' she said. 'But if you are arrested, do not say I did not warn you.'

The next morning she made up a parcel of all the food they could spare and kissed him. 'God keep you safe, brother. Give our parents my love. Tell them I am well and happy. And come back safely.'

He hugged her, shouldered his kit bag and set off to go to work as usual. At half past nine he nodded to Herman, picked up his bundle and crossed the field to the canal bank. The barge was not yet in sight. He watched the river traffic, scanning the names of the barges and wondering if he was being led on a wild goose chase when he spotted what he was looking for. He found a place where it was easy to get to the water's edge and waited there until the barge drew up alongside. He jumped aboard before it stopped and they were on their way.

Johannes shook his hand. 'You have brought the money?'

'Thirty *Reichsmark* and ten English pound notes.' He knew he would have to pay in advance and had the money ready.

'Good. I like pound notes. The exchange rate is better.' He took the money, crammed it into his trouser pocket and returned to the wheel. 'I doubt we will be stopped before we reach the crossing at Buchhorst, so sit back and enjoy the ride.'

Karl threw his bundle down and perched on the roof of the cabin at the rear of the barge. It was unusually warm for September. He was glad to leave the heat of the wurzel field and feel the cool breeze as they chugged over the water. Going this way was slower than train or road, but it was infinitely more enjoyable.

'What are you carrying?' he asked.

'Tomatoes, apples and clothing.' He grinned at Karl. 'And a stowaway.'

'Stowaway?'

'Of course. If you are discovered hiding among my boxes of fruit, I shall deny all knowledge of you.'

Karl suddenly realised that he had been unwise to trust the man. After all, he knew nothing about him. He could take his money and still betray him. There was nothing he could do about it but take his chances.

'Have you taken many people across the border?'

'Some, but most going in the opposite direction, coming out, not going in.'

'More than one at a time perhaps?'

'Oh, I see. You are going to fetch someone out.'

'If they are prepared to come.'

'I cannot hide more than one. Others will have to have false papers and that costs much more than you have given me today. The risks are far greater, you understand.'

Karl was left to muse on this and they were silent for some time.

'Would you like to take over the wheel while I prepare something to eat?' Johannes asked when the sun was at its highest in the sky and the heat bounced off the roof of the cabin.

'OK.' He slid down beside his host. 'There's food in my pack: bread, a little butter, some home-made jam – I have no idea what it's made of – a handful of potatoes and some cooked chicken. My sister could not spare any more.'

'We'll leave that for later.'

A few minutes later, he pulled into the bank and switched off the engine while they ate bread and cheese and apples, washed down with weak tea.

'What are rations like in the Netherlands?' Karl asked.

'Not good but better than in Germany.' He grinned. 'We were on the winning side, after all. We are not plagued by reparations.' He speared a piece of cheese on the point of his knife. 'When did you last eat cheese?'

'In England, over a month ago.'

'You were a prisoner?'

'Yes.'

'Tell me what England is like. I have often thought I should like to go there.'

They wiled away the rest of that day's voyage talking about England and Holland; the two countries had much in common and both had been inundated with floods in the spring. Karl avoided the subject of the occupation and forced labour or anything that might inflame the Dutchman. It wasn't a subject he wanted to talk about anyway. They moored up for the night. He could have slept in one of the two bunks in the cabin but elected to sleep outside where it was cooler and where he could see the stars, the same stars shining over his parents at Hartsveld, on his sister in Osnabrück and Jean in England. Jean. He had not told his aunt or sister about her. He did not know why, except that, for all she worked for the military governor, Elise was no lover of the British. What they had suffered as the result of bombing raids and invasion, could not easily be forgiven. Any idea of bringing Jean to Germany had soon been abandoned. Besides, he knew she would not come, not even for him.

He lay on his back staring upwards as the barge rocked

gently on its moorings, and remembered their last goodbye. Had it really been the last? He ached to be with her, to hold her in his arms, to see again the sparkle in her eyes when he amused her, to hear her singing *Rosslein* in atrocious German, to work beside her on the little farm. His return ticket ran out at the end of the following week. It did not look as though he was going to make it.

Chapter Eighteen

'This is your home,' Gordon said, when his mother broached the subject of moving. 'It will always be your home, especially now with Pa gone. Rosie agrees with that, don't you, darling?'

'Yes, of course you must stay with us,' Rosie said. They were sitting in the kitchen after having a little party to celebrate Stan's first birthday. He was hauling himself up on his feet now and would soon be walking. Surrounded by women who doted on him, he was a little spoilt. Nothing was too good for him. Rosie was always buying him clothes and toys, using her own clothing coupons as well as his, and often begged some from Doris. All the small children in the village had been invited. It had been noisy with laughter, tears and more than a few tantrums. It had taken Jean all her time to keep the little imps in order, but she loved them all. The children had gone home and Stan, worn out by the excitement, was fast asleep in his cot.

'How will I manage without you?' Rosie went on. 'I don't know anything about being a farmer's wife.' This was perfectly true. She was prepared to gather eggs but drew the line at wringing the neck of a chicken, plucking and cleaning it ready for cooking. And she hated the noisy, smelly pigs and their disgusting pigswill. When she should have been outside helping with the farm work, looking after the animals, learning to milk, she would be indoors playing with Stanley or painting her nails. Jean had no idea where she had managed to find the bright red polish.

'I don't think Rosie will ever be able to take over my jobs,' Jean said to her grandmother one day. She was spending more and more of what little leisure time she had down at the cottage where she was at ease and could unburden herself. 'Gordon can't do everything. I do miss Karl.'

'Have you heard from him?'

'I had a letter, nearly a fortnight ago now, saying he had arrived at his cousin's safely and found his sister there. He said conditions are pretty bad, but not a word about when he was coming back. I keep wondering where he is and if he has managed to find his parents . . .'

'Jean, you have to consider that his love of his parents and his home is as great as yours for your mother and the farm. His parents may need him as much as your father needed you.'

'I know. I just don't want to believe he would abandon me.'

'Is that what you've been thinking?'

'I don't know what to think. Perhaps he's been arrested. I know he was afraid of that.'

'There's nothing you can do about it, Jean. You have to think of yourself. Go out, enjoy yourself a bit, make new friends. All work and no play . . .'

'I said that to Karl once, at the beginning of the year when we went skating on the pit and he was doubtful if we should. It was lovely.' She sighed. 'What a year it has been. All that snow and then the floods, the crops ruined and no harvest to speak of. I think it all contributed to Pa's death. Gordon is really down in the dumps and talking about giving up the farm. He won't, of course, but he misses Pa's advice. I miss him too.'

'We all do.' She paused before going on, 'Think of yourself, Jean. Make a new life for yourself.'

That was easier said than done, she realised as she made her way back to the farm and the milking. Gordon could not manage without her. And she did not know how she was going to manage without Karl.

Karl, standing at the door of his childhood home, was conscious of the stubble on his chin, his uncut hair, his shabby suit and the down-at-heel shoes, nothing like the smart uniform and gleaming boots he had been wearing when he was last at home. He was coming back like a tramp, though he looked no worse than anyone else in the Soviet zone through which he had passed. The state of the countryside had shocked him even more than that of Osnabrück. It was like a strange moonscape, grey and forbidding. Rebuilding was well behind that in the west; rubble still lay about, bridges remained in ruins, especially any connecting east with west. Townspeople lived in the cellars, country people in the remains of their homes. He had seen them using oxen and primitive wooden ploughs to farm.

Johannes had managed to hide him well and the inspection of the barge and its cargo at the Buchhorst–Rühen crossing had been cursory because the Dutchman had bribed the border guards with cigarettes and money and offered them schnapps. Karl was sorry he had doubted him. Since leaving the barge at Potsdam, he had set out to walk, dodging Russian soldiers and German police, until he had been given a lift by a lorry driver he had come across filling up at a petrol station. It was risky because he had no idea if the man could be trusted. Both wary, they had not said much to each other and did not exchange names or personal details.

'I'll set you down here,' the driver said, as they approached the outskirts of Berlin. 'I'm not supposed to take on passengers.'

Karl thanked him and lost no time in disappearing into the city's crowd. It had saddened him to see the once beautiful city in ruins. Women were clearing the rubble, painstakingly separating the whole bricks from the broken ones and chipping off the mortar so that they could be used again. There was little motor traffic, but some of the trams were running. Goods were being delivered by horse-drawn vehicles, and he saw a woman take a packet of cigarettes from her handbag and extract three to pay for a kilo of plums from a market stall. In spite of that, people seemed to be going about their business, shopping, sitting in the cafes, walking with their children. Rebuilding had started, but the devastation was so widespread, he knew it would take years.

He had risked boarding a train from Berlin to Eberswalde, a line that had been repaired, and dodged the guard who came along to examine tickets. As the train slowed to come into the station, he had opened the door, hesitated a second and jumped, rolling down the embankment into the woodland that gave the place its name. He knew it well and was soon marching purposefully for Hartsveld and his father's farm.

He arrived at dusk, when the sun was sinking beyond the trees and the shadows were lengthening, but there was enough light to see the house was a ruin. It was obvious no one was living there. He looked about him, wondering where to go next, a neighbour perhaps, and then he saw a bent figure walking across a field of stubble. At least there had been some sort of harvest, he thought. He walked towards the old man, forming his question in his mind, a simple question, not intended to arouse suspicion, but it flew out of his head as he and the man approached each other.

'*Vater*,' he said.

The bent back straightened and his father looked directly at him. 'Karl! *Mein Sohn. Mein lieber Sohn.*' He stumbled forward and put his arms about him. Karl was surprised how small he seemed; his memory was of a tall upright man who was master of his little kingdom, not to be thwarted or crossed, and certainly not emotional. The man in his arms was openly crying, his thin hands were feeling round his face, touching every curve and contour in the growing darkness. 'I cannot believe it. You are here. We must find *Mutti* quickly and tell her the news. She will be overjoyed.'

He led the way to a small cottage, once occupied by one of his farm workers. 'We live here now,' he said, opening the door. 'It is more convenient.'

'Marthe!' he called. 'Come quickly; I have brought us a visitor.'

His mother came through from a back room wiping her hands on an apron. The years had not dealt kindly with her either. She had once been plump, now she was thin and her hair was pure white. She stood and stared at him for several seconds.

'Well?' her husband queried. 'Are you not going to greet your long-lost son?'

'Karl.' She still did not come forward to embrace him. It was as if she did not believe he was real and would dissolve into nothing if she touched him. He walked forward and took her into his arms.

'*Mutti*, I am so pleased and relieved to see you safe and well.'

She spoke at last. 'Karl. Where have you come from? How did you get here?'

'He can tell us all about it while we eat,' his father said. 'I hope you can find food for him.'

'I have a little,' Karl said, holding up his kitbag. 'I have not come empty-handed.'

'It doesn't matter if you have,' she said. 'All that matters is that you are here. Come into the kitchen, we can talk while I cook. I have soup on the stove.'

While they ate vegetable soup with a little bread, he told them about finding Elise and his journey from Osnabrück. 'Elise is well and working for the military governor as a translator,' he said. 'You were right, *Vati*, to say learning English would benefit us one day. She sends loving greetings and asked me to say not to worry about her.'

They told him about the arrival of the Red Army, the raids and heavy artillery they had used on what had become a defenceless country, the destruction of their house and the ruination of a once-prosperous farm. 'We farm like peasants nowadays,' his father said. 'And what we harvest is nearly all taken in what they call "reparations". They took everything of value from the house, too.'

'It was nothing but looting,' his mother added. 'I am glad Elise was not here. They were raping every woman they could get their hands on.'

'You too?'

'No. I hid.'

Karl was not sure if she was telling the truth, but accepted what she said. 'And now, is it better?'

'Oh, yes. We no longer own the land but we can still farm it. We lost nearly all the livestock but they have allowed us to keep a few milch cows. The milk is collected every morning, but we keep some back for ourselves, just as we keep a little grain and potatoes. We are surviving.'

It was clear while they talked that his parents were uneasy. They kept cocking their heads to one side in a listening gesture and looking towards the door. 'Are you expecting someone?' he asked during a pause in the conversation.

'No, no. It is all right,' his father answered. 'You were not seen arriving in the village, were you?'

'I don't think so, it was nearly dark.'

'Good. Newcomers are viewed with suspicion. We have to be careful.'

'Tell us what happened to you,' his mother put in quickly. 'What is it like in England?'

He told them how he came to be captured. 'The Allies called it D-Day,' he said. 'We resisted as long as we could but everything was in disarray, and then my company was cut off and we were forced to surrender. We were taken to England on the troop carriers which had brought Allied reinforcements.'

'You were treated well?'

'Yes. I was sent to work on a farm. It was a small family farm. The owner had had a stroke and all the work was being done by his daughter. She was friendly from the first and we worked well together. I taught her German songs and she helped to improve my English. Her name is Jean.'

'Ah,' his mother said, looking closely into his face, making him blush, something he had not done since he was a boy and caught out in some mischief. 'She is perhaps more than a friend.'

'Yes,' he admitted. 'I did not want to leave her, but I had to come back to you.' He smiled and changed the subject abruptly. 'And now I am here, I am glad I came. What can I do to help you?'

'Nothing,' his father said.

'Would you come with me to England, if you could?'

They looked at each other but it was his mother that answered. 'No, son. This is our home. One day the Russians will go and we will be left in peace to rebuild our home and our lives. But you must not stay. Sleep here tonight but tomorrow you must leave. We dare not shelter you longer than that. We know for certain that others who have come from the west after being released from captivity have been sent east into forced labour. There are people in the village who inform . . .'

'That is dreadful. You were always respected, they were your workers and your friends.'

'They do it for money and food,' his father said. 'Who can blame them?'

'Tomorrow, before it is light, you must leave,' his mother repeated. 'Go back to the west. Go back to your Jean. Be happy.'

'I have only just arrived. I cannot leave you so soon.'

'You must. Go to *Herr* Beauman. He will help you.'

'Why would Heidi's father help me?'

'He hates the Russians for what they did to Heidi and Gunther. His poor wife died of grief soon afterwards. We know he has helped other people to leave. Go and ask him.'

'What about you?'

'As long as you and Elise are safe and well, we are content. Do not worry about us.'

He tried arguing, but they were adamant and fearful. He did not want to make them any more afraid than they already were; if he could not stay with them there was nothing to keep him. They sat up most of the night talking and at dawn he left them. 'Now I know the new address, I will write,' he said, embracing first his father, then his mother. 'And God willing, I will come back when this insanity ends.'

'God bless you,' his mother said, pushing him away from her. 'Go. Go before the sun comes up.'

Another quick hug and he left them standing at the door of the cottage with their arms about each other. He turned to wave when he reached the bend in the road, but they had gone inside. The door was shut. He stumbled on, his eyes so full of tears he could not see where he was going.

Herr Beauman had once been the mayor of Hartsveld and lived in a substantial house on the square. To visit him, Karl would have to venture into the middle of the village where he might be seen by anyone. If it were true about informers, he had better approach with caution. Already people were rising to begin their day's work. He walked purposefully, as if he were one of them. Looking about him, he realised how much damage there was and how shabby everywhere looked. He had expected to feel elation at being back where he had grown up, and a certain nostalgia for those happy far-off days but all he felt was pity for everyone living here, mixed with a kind of urgency to be gone.

He found the house easily enough. It was hardly damaged at all. A Russian flag hung from a post on the corner of the building. It made him even more cautious. He waited and watched for several minutes, but no one came or went. Guessing there would be a servant preparing breakfast, he walked round the block to the back gate where he knew there was an entrance to the garden. Crossing that stealthily, he knocked on the kitchen door. It was something he had done in his youth when he had been courting Heidi.

The door opened and he found himself looking into a familiar face. '*Frau* Langer, do you remember me?'

'Karl Muller, you have come home.' The housekeeper had not changed and, unlike so many of her compatriots, had not lost her plumpness. Her hair was grey where it had once been brown, but her smile was just as wide.

'I need to speak to *Herr* Beauman urgently. Will he see me?'

'It is not about Heidi, is it, because . . .'

'No, it is not about Heidi. I know what happened to her. I came to visit my parents but they advised me to go back west. They said *Herr* Beauman might help me do so. I have no papers except my discharge.'

'Ah, I see.' She hesitated a moment and he wondered if she was going to send him away. 'You had better come in.'

He stepped into the kitchen. She had obviously been preparing breakfast for several people.

'Sit down there,' she said, indicating a chair in the corner. 'If anyone comes, go into the pantry and, for God's sake, make no noise. There are Russian soldiers billeted here. Thank goodness they are officers who have a little idea how to behave. When I take *Herr* Beauman's breakfast to him, I will tell him you are here.' She busied herself laying out a tray and left the room with it.

He waited. He could hear people moving about in the room above him and sat very still, hardly daring to breathe. When he heard footsteps approaching he dived into the pantry, realising as he shut the door that there was no other way out. To make matters worse, he had left his kitbag in the kitchen.

'You can come out,' the housekeeper said.

Tentatively, he opened the door and peered out. She was accompanied by *Herr* Beauman.

'Come on out, boy, and let me see you,' *Herr* Beauman said.

Karl stepped out, came to attention and bowed. '*Guten Tag, Herr* Beauman. Do you remember me?'

The older man surveyed him from head-to-toe before speaking. 'Of course I remember you, cheeky young devil you were.'

'I was sorry to hear about Heidi.'

'Yes, but we will not speak of her. You want papers to enable you to leave the Russian zone?'

'Yes, *mein Herr*. Can you help? My parents . . .'

'How are your parents?'

'They are well, *Herr* Beauman, but they are fearful and urged me to leave.'

'How did you arrive?'

Karl explained his journey. 'I could perhaps go back on the barge, but I need to get to the other side of Berlin to pick it up.'

'You will need an interzone travel pass. Give me a little time, I might be able to provide one. In the meantime, I suggest you stay in the garden house. You know where that is, I am sure, you did enough hiding in it as a youth . . .'

'I didn't think you knew.'

'Oh, I knew, but it amused me to see the two of you together. Now of course . . .' His voice cracked. 'I am glad to see you well.' He turned on his heel and left the room.

'You must go before anyone sees you in here,' *Frau* Langer said, handing him a thick wedge of bread and butter, covered in honey. 'Take this to the garden house and wait.'

He remembered to pick up his kitbag before doing as he was told. The door of the summer house creaked as he opened it. There was nothing inside but dust and cobwebs. The window was so dirty he couldn't see out of it, but decided against cleaning it and advertising his presence. He sat in the corner behind the door and ate the bread. It was obvious that the presence of the occupying officers meant rations were not short in the house. He was not at all sure that *Herr* Beauman could be trusted and it put him on tenterhooks, ready to bolt.

It seemed like hours before *Frau* Langer came to him. 'Here,' she said, handing him a sheet of paper. 'With luck this will get you over the border into the west.'

'Thank you.' It was an interzone travel permit allowing him to visit relatives in Osnabrück. He was required to return within fourteen days. He smiled at that. 'Is this genuine?'

'The blank form is not a forgery, if that is what you mean, but *Herr* Beauman is taking a risk filling it out for you. He works for the Russians and is required to have everything countersigned and stamped.'

'This is signed and stamped.'

'Yes. Do not ask how. It is not the first time.' She handed him a paper bag. 'This will fill your belly on the way. Do you have money for your train fare?'

'A little.'

'Good. *Herr* Beauman said you should keep to the east–west corridor.'

'I am very grateful.'

'Good luck.'

Thanking his guardian angel for his luck so far, he left the way he had come and made his way to the railway station in Eberswalde. It was quiet, there were few people about and he felt conspicuous. There was nothing for it but assume the confidence he did not feel. The man at the ticket office hardly looked at him as he issued the ticket.

It was a different matter when he boarded the train. The guard examined everything in minute detail. Karl held his breath, hoping the man would not question the signature, which he doubted was genuine.

'Change in Berlin,' he said, handing the documents back.

'Thank you. Can you tell me the time of the connection?'

'Six-fifteen, if we get you there in time.' He passed on to the next traveller and Karl allowed himself to relax.

He had a little time to wait in Berlin for his connection and spent some of the time in a café drinking ersatz coffee, eating a frugal meal and counting his change. He had just enough to get him to Magdeburg with a little left over to pay Johannes if he could find him again.

He would have to stay a little while in Osnabrück to earn enough to take him back to England. His return ticket was already out of date. He wondered what was happening in Little Bushey.

What was Jean doing? How was she managing? Perhaps her brother was helping her more now he must be getting used to his new leg. Was she waiting for him or had she succumbed to Mr Howson's pleas? It would please her parents, he knew.

The potato yield had not been good, much of the crop had rotted in ground and the wheat, which had been sown very late because of the floods, was so poor it was hardly worth harvesting; it was certainly not good enough for bread. Gordon came back from the miller's in a bad mood.

'I don't know why I bother,' he said.

'We've had bad harvests before and weathered them,' Jean said. They were all still living at the farmhouse. Jean had postponed looking for somewhere else until Karl came back, but he had been gone so long, she didn't think that was likely now. Almost all the men had left the camp, either gone home or, allowed to stay, had dispersed into the countryside to find civilian jobs. It would soon be shut, perhaps returned to agriculture or some commercial undertaking. She was as miserable as Gordon, but for a different reason.

'It's all right for you,' Gordon told her. 'You haven't got a wife and child and another on the way to clothe and feed.'

'No, but I do what I can to help.'

'I know you do, so does Ma, but I'll have to think of something to make some money.'

'A proper job,' Rosemary put in. 'Nine to five. I'm fed up with the stink of the farm; you can't get rid of it whatever you do.'

'You knew that when you married me,' he snapped.

'I hadn't lived with it day in, day out, then. I don't want this for my children, working all the hours God sends and for what? No time off. I can't remember the last time we went to the pictures together or went to a dance, and when you come in of an evening you are so tired you fall asleep in your chair. As for shopping, what good is that when we've no money? You should remember you are disabled and shouldn't be doing it. The doctor said to give your new leg time. But have you? No, you haven't. You'll kill yourself, that's what you'll do.' Her anger gave way to tears.

Gordon went to put his arms about her. 'You are tired, love. Come and lie down. You mustn't get worked up, it's not good for the baby and it upsets Stan. Mum and Jean will see to him.' He led her from the room.

'What brought that on?' Doris asked Jean, glancing down at Stan who had fallen asleep face down on the floor.

'I think it's been building up for a while, Mum.' Gordon had confided to her that Rosie had threatened to take Stanley and move back in with her mother if he didn't give up the farm, and he was worried sick about it. She couldn't tell her mother that.

Doris sighed. 'Yes, I suppose it has, but what will we do if he does decide to find a job? What about the farm?'

'I don't know, Mum, I really don't. I suppose you and I could keep it going with a little help. We did it when Pa had his stroke, didn't we? We could keep Joe Bunford on.'

'Perhaps it won't come to that. It's only a tantrum on Rosie's part, after all.'

'Yes, Mum, that's all it is.'

'You had better go and get the milking done. I don't think Gordon's going to help you today.'

After the tense atmosphere in the house it was peaceful in the cowshed with only the sound of the cows munching their hay and swishing their tails. 'Oh, Karl, where are you?' she murmured. 'Why haven't you come back to me? I could endure it all if only you were here.'

* * *

Karl was working on a building site in Osnabrückand living in the cellar with his sister, aunt and cousin. Elise was talking of them finding a place of their own. 'We could manage quite comfortably with both our wages,' she said. They were walking to work a week after he arrived back. 'Maria ought to get a job instead of relying on us. There are plenty going, even if they don't pay much.'

'I'm not stopping,' he said. He had left the train at Magdeburg and made his way on foot to the Buchhorst–Rühen crossing where, not risking the road and the pass Herr Beauman had given him, he had swum across in the dark, kicking out on his back with his kitbag on his chest. A border guard had spotted him climbing out further along and taken a pot shot at him. He had run into the trees, knowing he would not be followed, not from the Russian side, and lay there exhausted until daylight.

With the dawn came optimism. He was once again in the Bizone and his official papers would keep him out of trouble. He had changed his clothes and made for the towpath. There was no sign of Johannes but that was hardly surprising; he had no idea of the Dutchman's schedule. He had walked a few miles when he was overtaken by a barge. He ran after it and begged a lift. It had taken the last of his money and his watch.

'Not stopping?' Elise repeated. 'Where are you going then?'

'Back to England.'

'What on earth for? Your home is here.'

'No, it is not. My home is with the girl I love and she lives in England.'

'*Eine Engländerin!* Karl, how could you?'

'Easy. Jean is very easy to love. *Mutti* and *Vati* told me to go back to her. They gave me their blessing, so as soon as I've earned enough, I am leaving here. One day, perhaps, when I'm old and grey, I'll come back. Or you can visit us.'

342

'You must be mad. No wonder we lost the war when people like you decide to throw in your lot with the enemy.'

'Lisa, we lost the war because we did not deserve to win. We listened to that fanatic, Adolf Hitler, and believed his evil doctrine.'

'How can you say that? He made Germany great again.'

He gave a bark of a laugh. 'Are we great, Lisa? Are these ruins great? Do we have good jobs, good wages? Do we live in comfort?'

'We will again.'

'I hope so, I really do, but that doesn't alter my decision to go back to England. Wherever Jean is, there I must be.'

'You have been gone two months, do you think she will still be waiting for you?'

'I hope so,' he said. 'I really do hope so.'

Chapter Nineteen

'*Liebling.*' It was spoken softly.

Jean, who was milking Gertrude, whirled round and only just managed to save the pail of milk from tipping over. 'Karl!' It was almost a scream. 'You're back.'

He laughed, opening his arms and she ran into them. 'Yes, I am back.'

'I didn't think . . . Oh, Karl, it is so good to see you. I've missed you so.'

'And I you.' There was everything in their kisses: delight, hunger, longing, questions and answers. But they had to draw breath.

She leant back to scan his face. He was sporting an untidy beard, his hair was inches long and curling on his shoulders and he looked as though he had slept in his clothes. 'Was it very bad?'

'Bad enough.'

'Your parents?'

'They are well and still managing the farm, though much reduced.'

'Did you want to stay?'

'I offered. I had to. They would not hear of it. They were convinced I would be arrested.'

'Wait here while I wash and change, then we'll go to Gran's and you can tell me all about it.'

'I have to report to Colonel Williamson.'

'Why? You are not still a prisoner, are you?'

'No, I am a free man, but I need somewhere to stay.'

'We'll talk about that later.'

She rushed into the house, told her mother the news, in too much of a hurry to explain, splashed some water on her face, changed into a skirt and jumper, and returned to Karl in record time. Gordon and Joe were in the yard as they left hand in hand. 'Gordon, Karl is back!' she called out to him.

Her brother came over to stand in front of them. 'How are you, Muller?'

'I am well, thank you.'

'Karl is a free man now,' Jean said. 'We are going to Gran's to talk about the future.'

Gordon looked Karl up and down. 'I'm afraid I've no work for you.'

'I will find something.'

Elizabeth bustled about in the kitchen making an impromptu meal, leaving Jean and Karl to sit side by side on the sofa in her little sitting room to talk.

'Now, tell me all about it,' she commanded him.

He obliged. 'I hated leaving them,' he said of his parents, after he had recounted his lengthy journey to Hartsveld. 'But I knew it was what they wanted and it was for the best, for them as well as me. It meant I could come back to you and I wanted that more than anything. But coming back to the west was even more hazardous than going east. I had to sell my watch and bribe people to help me. I went back to Osnabrück to say goodbye to my sister. She wanted me to stay there, but I said no.'

'Oh, I am so glad you did. Now you are here, you are going to stay, aren't you?'

'Do you still want me?'

'What a question. Of course I do. We will be married, just as you said we would.'

'But I have no job, nowhere to live except the camp . . .'

'That's being closed down as soon as the last prisoners have left. Besides, you can't live there. We must be together.'

'Why did you bring me here, instead of the farm?'

'The place is not what it was since Pa died, Karl.'

'Your father died? Oh, *Liebling*, I am so sorry.'

'He died in his sleep. I think he was just tired of struggling. The dreadful winter and hardly any harvest to speak of was more than he could bear.' She fought back tears. 'It was all so sudden. No one seems able to cope any more. Gordon is finding the farm a struggle and has more than once said he would give it up and find himself a job. He can't, of course, with all of us living there and depending on it.'

'And your mother?'

'It's difficult to tell. On the surface she seems OK, getting on with things as she usually does, but inside . . . I don't know. Mum would be lost without the home she shared with Pa for so long. Rosie doesn't pull her weight. Oh dear, I should not have said that.'

'I understand. I wish I had been here to help you.'

'You are here now and that's all that matters.'

Elizabeth called them from the kitchen to come and have

their dinner and they rose to obey. Over the meal, Jean and Karl continued to talk about what had happened while they had been apart and what they hoped to do in the future. 'My first task must be to find a job and somewhere to live after the camp closes,' Karl told Elizabeth.

'You can come and live here, if you like,' she said. 'I've got a spare room.'

Jean turned to her with eyes alight. 'Gran, you are an angel.'

'It will not be easy for you, Mrs Sanderson,' Karl said. 'I am still the hated Jerry.'

'Don't be silly. The war has been over for two years now, it's time to put it behind us. Besides, who is going to trouble an old lady in her dotage.'

'Oh, Gran,' Jean said, laughing. 'You are a long way from your dotage.'

Jean was determined they would have a proper wedding in church. 'I'm not creeping into a registry office to be married,' she told the family when they gathered to discuss the arrangements. 'I am not ashamed of Karl, nor afraid of black looks. We can survive those. I'm going to have a white wedding and bridesmaids if I can find anyone willing. You will give me away, won't you, Gordon?'

He looked startled to be asked. 'My pleasure,' he said, making them laugh.

'I'll be a bridesmaid, if you like,' Rosemary said, then giggled. 'I suppose I should say matron of honour. And you can borrow my wedding dress.'

'Why, thank you, Rosie. I'll take you up on that.'

'Where will you live?' Doris asked.

'With me for the time being,' Elizabeth said. 'Until they find a home of their own and Karl settles into a job.'

'I've got a better idea,' Gordon said suddenly. 'You can live here, Jean. Rosie and I will move out and you can take over the tenancy. But only if Mum stays as long as she wants to.'

Jean turned to him in astonishment. 'Are you mad?'

'No. I can't make a proper go of it, not the way I'd like, and Rosie isn't happy with the situation . . .'

'I didn't think you meant it when you said you were thinking of giving up,' his mother said.

'I did, but I couldn't see how it could be done until Karl came back and it suddenly came to me. He loves this farm and he obviously loves Jean. Who better to make it work and leave me free to do what I want?'

Jean smiled. 'So he's no longer the hated Jerry?'

'No. Any man who can go through what he went through for you has earned his place in this family.'

'You mean that?'

'Yes. Life's too short to hold grudges. Besides, I did meet some decent Germans while I was a prisoner . . .' He stopped, thinking about that long march and how some of the guards had helped by carrying stretchers and turning a blind eye to Stan's disappearances.

Jean jumped up to hug him. 'Gordon, you are a wonder. But do you think Sir Edward will agree?'

'He already has. I asked him yesterday.'

'I hope you won't regret it.'

'I won't, I promise you.'

'What are you going to do?'

'Alex and Jeremy have set up a business ferrying rich businessmen and celebrities about the country by air. When I told them I was thinking of giving up farming they asked me to join them. We'll be moving to Cambridge.'

'You kept very quiet about this,' Doris said.

'No point in saying anything when it wasn't going to happen, was there?'

'I'm going to find Karl to tell him,' Jean said. 'He will be pleased.'

She ran from the room. Fancy her brother coming up with a solution to the problem that had been worrying them ever since Karl came back. It was ideal. They both loved the farm and her mother would have a home as long as she wanted it. It would be hard work, she knew, but they were not afraid of that.

Karl's reaction was more muted when she found him in the stable, stroking Misty's nose, knowing what was going on in the house and wishing he could be there to support Jean. He had thought there might be arguments. He did not understand this latest development. 'Why?' he queried. 'Why has he decided he doesn't like farming? He hasn't been coerced, has he?'

'If anyone had done any coercing it is Rosie, but I don't think even she could influence him if he didn't want it. He has already asked Sir Edward if we can take over the tenancy and he has agreed. Isn't that wonderful?'

'How much rent does he want?'

'I don't know, I didn't ask, but whatever it is, we'll manage. Karl, my love, we can stay in the place where we've been happy, in the village where everyone knows us, and though they might disapprove to begin with, they will get over it. Say you are pleased.'

'*Natürlich* I am pleased.'

'Let's go to the pub to celebrate.'

'Is that a good idea?'

'It is a very good idea. We'll test the water.'

He laughed. 'I do not think I shall ever learn all these funny sayings you have.'

'But you do understand?'

'Oh, I understand. We will test the water.'

There were several people in the Plough and Harrow. Bill was there with Brenda. He looked up as they came in and frowned. Jean ignored that and went over to him, with a bright smile. 'Hallo, Bill. You know Karl, don't you?'

'I do.'

'We are going to be married.'

'Congratulations!' Brenda cried. 'I hope you will both be very happy.'

'This is Brenda, Bill's wife,' Jean told Karl.

He bowed. 'How do you do, Mrs Howson?'

'Oh, Brenda, please.'

Jean smiled. At least Brenda was friendly. 'Bill, nothing to say?'

'Congratulations.' He stood up. 'A drink to celebrate? Karl, what will it be?'

'Beer, please.'

The ice was broken. While some muttered their disapproval, others came to congratulate them. Little Bushey had become used to the Germans in their midst and many had employed them and accepted them. It did not mean she and Karl were in for an easy time, but they would weather it. As Karl had told her, the future was theirs.

Acknowledgements

I would like to acknowledge the help I received from the British Limbless Ex-servicemen's Association (Blesma) in writing parts of this book. They have been unfailingly polite and enthusiastic in answering my many questions. Nevertheless, any mistakes I have made regarding wartime amputation are mine.